When the World Was Young
A Prehistoric Anthology

When the World Was Young

A Prehistoric Anthology

SakaraFox • Utunu • Huskyteer • J.F.R. Coates • NightEyes DaySpring

Rose LaCroix • Madison Scott-Clary • Kayodé Lycaon • Rob MacWolf

Thomas "Faux" Steele • Haya Baru • J.S. Hawthorne • Pascal Farful

Casimir Laski

ISBN: 978-1-948743-33-4

WHEN THE WORLD WAS YOUNG: A PREHISTORIC ANTHOLOGY
A project from The Furry Historical Fiction Society.

Cover by Heskynn. © 2022 — www.heskynn.co.uk
Title page illustration by The Cheesen One.
Section divider by Maddy's dog Zephyr, who is a very good boy.

This book uses the fonts Gentium Book Plus, **Reggae One**, and Coelacanth.

Stone

Bronze

The Furry Historical Fiction Society

When The World Was Young is a collaborative project by the authors of the stories, with each of us chipping in to help with the process of editing, organizing, and decision-making. Thanks is given to each author in turn for their contributions, and we all hope that you enjoy the fruits of our labor.

Learn more at fhfs.ink

Stone

The Dance of Peruvaan

by SakaraFox

The signs were everywhere, even young Kuveli could read them from beside the low-burning fire. It was much too dark to see the storm clouds forming overhead, but he knew without a doubt that they had come. He knew because they had swallowed the very stars and filled the air with a strange tension that made his fur stand on end.

A great dance was about to take place high over the steppe, and the mighty black reindeer, Peruvaan—spirit of the storm—had graced the young fox with the best spot at his fire.

Yet, Kuveli felt no joy at the prospect. In fact, his hackles were raised and his heart was pounding in his chest, like the thrumming hooves of stampeding elk.

He was so fixated on the sky that his eyes were frantic as he sat in complete stillness. Kuveli didn't even notice how tight his grip had grown, his sharp, vulpine claws tearing holes into the patchwork animal skins that made up his simple skirt.

"Careful now, little bud," said a warm voice from beside Kuveli, a pair of large paws suddenly reaching over and gently holding his own. "A grip like that could break rocks. You haven't hurt yourself, have you?"

The little fox turned toward the voice, seeing the familiar, doting smile of his older brother in the dim light of their fire. His icy-blue eyes, a feature the two shared, seemed to glow in the darkness. Those eyes were as sharp as the stone spear lying between them as they carefully looked over the younger fox for injuries.

"I'm fine!" Kuveli snapped, pulling back his paws and pouting. "I just want to watch the storm, I wasn't doing anything."

But in truth, he was terrified. Kuveli so badly wanted to bury his face in his big brother's scruff. He wanted to feel a gentle arm around his head, and hear his brother tell him that it was all going to be all right, but... what kind of a hunter would he be if he couldn't face his fears?

"Nothing except tearing holes in your clothes so I have to spend all tomorrow sewing patches on them. Making more work for me, right, brother?" Sakara chuckled with a teasing smile, and ruffled Kuveli's head fur.

The young fox returned a timid growl and shook his head, at which point Sakara decided to escalate and wrapped an arm around his brother's shoulders, pulling him into a tight hug. Kuveli resisted for a moment, but quickly succumbed and welcomed the warmth of his brother's body against his cheek, and the beating of his brother's heart in his ear.

Kuveli couldn't deny the comfort he felt in moments like these. It was like being a kit again, swaddled in warm furs and listening to whatever stories Sakara could dream up. No responsibilities, no worries, and no future to think about.

"I'll sew them back together; the shaman says I need the practice," Kuveli replied at length, breathing a sigh as he stared nervously at the shifting mass of black clouds.

"You know Sana means you need practice sewing wounds closed, not leggings, right?" Sakara cocked his head at his brother, but Kuveli did not humour him. His mind was once again focused on the coming dance, dreading its deafening drums.

Letting out a huff of frustration, Kuveli pulled himself from his brother's arms and lazily slumped down in the grass. Sakara would never say it to his face, but he knew it nonetheless. It was the way Sakara spoke down to him, and to the fates their shaman had foreseen. *Coward.* That's how Sakara saw him, forever his little "rabbit-chaser," no matter how many deer he slew, no matter how talented a hunter he became. It annoyed him to no end at times, when he so badly wanted to find his place like the rest of the kids his age.

He didn't even have a horse, unlike the rest of his tribe. They were a tribe of fierce riders after all, and it was nothing short of shameful for a Lentavohi like him to not have a horse of his own, especially when the others had ridden almost as long as they had walked.

"You will be like them in time, little bud," his brother would always say in his usual, soft-spoken voice. "But this is your tenth summer, and you still have so many more to look forward to before you carry that burden. Enjoy what I never got to."

That last part had always lingered in his mind. He knew his brother had lost his boyhood years when their ma and fah had passed away, not long after he had been born. It had to have been hard, but... how was Sakara protecting him by coddling him away from his destiny?

Their shaman had always been good to the little fox. Even though he was only a few summers older than Sakara, the otter seemed to possess an impossible wealth of wisdom, beyond that of even the tribe's few elders.

And within all that wisdom, he had strangely always seen something in Kuveli. Something magical that the fox himself could not yet see.

Honestly, the prospect that he might be more than just an ordinary hunter scared him. The mere thought of it made him hunch over, like a great weight had been placed upon his shoulders, the weight of responsibility that he would carry with him if he walked this path. So much knowledge to memorise by heart, to be called upon at a moment's notice, else someone he cared for might be maimed or... worse.

Sana had taught him some things already, using the wounds that presented themselves as the days went by. Cuts and scrapes mostly, and a few bad gashes, always smeared with honey to stop the bad spirits getting at them, followed by a boiled scrap of leather to wrap around the wound. But such paltry injuries could never have prepared him for the horror of broken bones.

Last winter, a hunter's horse had slipped and crushed his leg. As a hunter himself, Kuveli thought he could stomach it, having gutted animals and extracted their bones for tools and marrow, but it wasn't the same.

When the bone pierces the flesh, and the victim is crying, screaming, begging for his soul to be free of the pain, it takes a whole different kind of nerve. Sana had done all the work himself, and yet the little fox still had to flee the horrific scene while choking back a disgusted gag.

Suddenly, Kuveli was shaken from his thoughts by an almighty boom and his eyes filled with a blinding flash.

By Äituri—their tribe's patron spirit—he had almost leaped out of his skin at the sound of it!

What few nerves he had left unfrayed were at their limit, his hackles raised, and his lips peeled back in an instinctive snarl.

Those wide, arctic blue eyes were utterly fixated on the gnarled finger of lightning that, for a fleeting moment, had come down and struck the steppe with the power of all the stampeding aurochs in the whole world.

The dance had begun.

All across the land would hunters and animals alike hear almighty Peruvaan, as he stomped his hooves to the rhythm of the drums and the chanting of earthbound shamans. No doubt his own tribe's shaman would be joining them, voiceless as he was, divining what he could from the rhythm of the storm god's dance.

It was strange, but deep in his heart Kuveli knew he wanted to join them. He wanted to don the antlers of the reindeer and paint lightning bolts on his calves, just to dance and sing to the rhythm of the storm until his voice was hoarse and his legs could no longer carry him.

"Oh, gods damn it," his brother's voice cut through his thoughts. The words puzzled Kuveli for a moment, looking to Sakara for answers and catching a glimpse of something just beyond the firelight.

"Stay here, bud, I've got to make sure Pekka doesn't break free. I don't want to be chasing her to the ends of the world, again."

Sakara jumped to his footpaws and brushed off his leggings, turning for just a moment to offer Kuveli a reassuring smile and a few pats on the head. He responded with a long, worried stare, but said nothing.

It was at that moment when something strange happened. Another bolt of lightning suddenly ripped the sky in two, but rather than fear Kuveli felt something else...

His heart was still racing as fast as before, and his hackles were still raised in warning, but the primal fear that had eaten away at his heart and resolve was not there anymore. Instead he felt a familiar yet, somehow, completely unknown strength. It was like the rush of the hunt, compelling him to move with haste, only it wasn't coming from within him.

Was it the storm?

Whatever it was, Kuveli felt a pit of dread forming in his stomach. If it was the storm then it was something not of this world, something... magical.

In his brief time with the shaman he had learned just how dangerous the world beyond the veil could be, like the ways demons could poison wounds and slay innocents with invisible claws. How could he possibly face such horrors alone, without even the knowledge to see them?

Only, he wasn't alone. Not truly, anyway.

Prying his gaze away from the gathering storm, Kuveli watched as his brother quickly made towards their horse. The darkness was already swallowing him, the fire growing dimmer as the winds began to pick up and smother the starving flames. Kuveli knew in his gut that he had to follow his brother, it was the right thing to do.

Or was that merely a demon whispering in his ear, like those that had caused him so many night terrors when he was younger?

For a moment he remained still, stewing over the decision. His mind felt as though it were being torn at by the fangs of two hungry wolves: the wolf who wanted to stay, and the wolf who trusted his gut.

Gritting his teeth, Kuveli rose slowly, placing his fate into the paws of something far beyond his understanding.

He drew a shuddering breath and stepped towards the smouldering fire, where the dying embers hissed their final breaths. His leather pouch and a pair of brand new leather leggings lay beside the fire. He took them gingerly, slipping into the leggings and tying the pouch to his belt.

Then, instinctively, he laid a paw on his chest and pressed against something hard. His crude slate knife. It was swaddled in a leather sheath, which his brother had sewn into the shoulder strap that held up his skirt, so he could always keep it close. A good hunter never went anywhere without his knife, and if that's what he wanted to be, he wasn't going to forget about it now.

With that, Kuveli turned his head into the wind and made off in the same direction as his brother, catching a glimpse of his silhouette when another bolt of lightning cracked viciously overhead.

A sign, maybe, like Sana had once explained. But Kuveli refused to believe so.

The dirt and dust crunching beneath his bare pawpads quickly turned soft, as Kuveli entered the grass that towered almost a head above him. With each gust it rustled and swayed, moving like the waves of the great sea he had once visited, many turnings of the Moon ago. It would be easy to get lost here, and end up wandering in circles for spirits only know how long.

For a second he paused, a distant *thoom* making his stomach drop as he glanced about himself. Everything seemed to blur into an identical image, the wall of quivering grass indistinguishable from itself. He couldn't have lost his way already; he had only just begun.

But then, between the rumbles of thunder that shook Kuveli and the howling of the wind that bristled his fur, he heard a sound not of Peruvaan's dance.

A high-pitched scream carried to him on the wind, followed by a deluge of curses. It was Pekka and Sakara, arguing as they often did.

Steeling himself, Kuveli followed the sounds of their voices, brushing aside the brittle blades so parched of rain this summer—some merely crumbling at his touch—before he stumbled into another clearing.

A bolt of white snapped across the sky, illuminating the scene just long enough for Kuveli to make it out. Their horse, Pekka, was reared up on her hind legs and kicking wildly, her dapple-grey coat sparkling with dew. And standing bravely in her way—not even half the reared horse's height—with a length of rawhide rope tied around his waist, was the little fox's brother.

"Easy, girl!" barked Sakara, his voice clearly strained as he clung to the rawhide rope - which Kuveli now realised was tied loosely around Pekka's neck at the other end.

Pekka landed with a thud, her heavy hooves kicking up a cloud of dust that sent Sakara into a hacking cough. But the huge mare wasn't done, as she kept bucking her head against the rope, huffing and snorting. Even grounded, Pekka still stood a head taller than his lanky brother.

"By Äituri, you're as bad as the boy!" Sakara growled as he tugged back on the rope, still not noticing Kuveli. "Since when does a big mare like you get so afraid of a little storm?"

"What did you—?" Kuveli yelled in retort, before throwing a paw over his agape maw. Had his brother really just said that? And behind his back too, when he thought Kuveli couldn't hear him. Did he speak of him like this around the other hunters too?

Kuveli let his paws fall to his side, his heart sinking as he stared across at Sakara, who was staring back with a shocked look in his wide, shining eyes. His brother of ten summers and ten winters, who he had always loved as his only flesh and blood. His brother who had raised him, made toys for him, taught him everything to know about life. The brother who had, and always would be, his entire world. And this was what he thought of Kuveli?

The pain the little fox felt was indescribable, like a knife had plunged into his back and pierced his heart, from which poured a flood of emotions all at once.

Anger. Hatred. Sadness.

And most of all...

Betrayal.

And then it overcame him, all at once. With a snarl, Kuveli marched towards his brother with purpose, spurred by the emotions swelling within him. Raising a clenched fist into the air, he yelled at Sakara with all the force his small frame could muster.

"I knew it! I knew you said things behind my back. I knew you told people I was just a scared little kit. That's why I still don't have a horse, or why they haven't invited me to hunt. You held me back, to 'protect' me, isn't that it?"

"Kuveli..." exhaled the older fox at length, but his brother wasn't done.

"I won't let you hold me down anymore, now that I know," Kuveli said, sniffling as his eyes became heavy. Sakara was heartbroken as he watched his little brother's eyes fill with tears. "I'll walk my own trail, chase the game I am destined to catch. I will listen to every drop of wisdom the shaman has, because he knows better than you."

Stopping an arm's length from Sakara, the little fox stared up at his brother's sullen features. His often perky expression had evaporated, his bright eyes now sunken and dulled, unable to look back at Kuveli, ears pinned back and shoulders slouched. The rope fell by the wayside, hanging slack between the horse and the fox, as Sakara timidly reached out.

"I'm sorry I hurt you, little bud," he mustered in a voice so full of defeat that Kuveli almost struggled to hear him. "Please believe me, I meant nothing by it. I was just-"

A bright flash cut him off, followed by another deafening *ka-boom.* Pekka squealed as if she had been driven feral, and bucked her head violently to the side. With this single motion, the rawhide rope snapped taut and Sakara was ripped off his feet as though he were little more than a leaf on the wind.

"Big brother!" Kuveli sprang forward, reaching out in vain for any part of Sakara, left to watch in horror as he was dashed against the earth with a sickening crack.

A shrill scream sent a chill up the little fox's spine as Sakara curled up and gripped his leg, teeth grit as he writhed in the dirt, as a powerful rear hoof stomped down beside his head. The sight of it banished the inferno of emotion within Kuveli and, as he rushed towards Pekka, replaced it with something born purely of instinct.

"Please calm down, Pekka," the tiny fox pleaded as he threw himself at the colossal beast. Kuveli had never taken to horses like his tribemates, but he had always watched how they soothed their mounts, who often acted like oversized infants throwing a tantrum. "You've hurt Sakara now, are you happy? Please just listen to me, listen to the sound of my voice and relax. It's only a storm. The spirits will not hurt us," he continued to beg through gritted teeth.

In the back of his mind, Kuveli heard a lone, dissenting voice. He could swear he almost heard it snicker as it teased, "Like that ever calmed you, coward."

It was certainly the voice of a demon. Kuveli had always suffered with demons, clawing at his dreams and filling his nights with terror, unless his brother was there to ward them off. They feared the strength of his soul. Clearly they thought Kuveli had a cowardly soul too. And they were fearless this time, whispering into his ears so openly. Something must have emboldened them, most likely the dance and the storm high above, which must have kept Äituri busy with her attendance.

And yet, as Kuveli pressed his cheek to Pekka's breast and listened to the thrumming of her mighty heart, he muttered prayers under his breath. He begged the almighty White Mare to come and drive away the storm, and promised he would leave her a great offering of amber for every day he went on living.

But it was no use.

Even as he kept trying to reassure the horse, stroking his paw gently along her neck and nose, down her chest, all the little fox could feel was tightly woven muscle and sinew.

Horses were beasts of pure strength, after all. As Pekka proved when she suddenly bucked her head to one side and took off like an arrow.

Surprised, Kuveli grabbed her neck, using his momentum to swing over her shoulder, legs kicking helplessly, clinging to her long, black mane for dear life.

Behind them, he heard the rope snap taut and a pained yelp as Sakara was hauled along behind them. The little fox just barely caught a glimpse of his brother with his arms over his face, trying to protect what he could before disappearing into the tall grass.

"STOP!" he cried with all the strength he had left, his arms growing tired and his feet finding no purchase.

Thunder boomed overhead, growing in intensity, while the plains were illuminated under the constant lashing of white-hot bolts. Ahead Kuveli saw a forest lying directly in their path, the birch and pine trees naught but growing silhouettes in the darkness. And it filled him with dread.

A forest meant danger, with low-hanging branches just waiting to snatch him away or, worse, stray rocks and boulders hidden in the undergrowth, eager to split his brother's skull open.

Kuveli kicked his legs again, jamming his foot into Pekka's stomach, crying out for her to stop, pleading, praying, anything that might bring her to a halt. But before he knew it, they had arrived. Trees rushed by, grazing the hairs on his tail, one thorny bush even snagging on his back and tearing his flesh.

He screamed, the pain seizing his body, sapping the last of his strength. It was too much; he couldn't hold on anymore. His right paw slipped first, followed by the other.

He fell, and it felt like the whole world slowed down around him. The wind rushed through his fur and whistled in his ears. The foreboding figures of the trees stood over him, laughing. His heart was full of fear, regret even, as a single thought passed through his mind... by the spirits, would those really be the last words he said to Sakara?

Kuveli didn't have to regret it for long, as the ground quickly rose to meet him. The last thing he remembered was the crunch as his muzzle bit the dirt.

A strange veil of wispy grey encompassed Kuveli, as he stood in the midst of what appeared to be a thick fog, the scent of petrichor filling his nostrils. It was so strong, stronger than after any rain storm he had ever experienced. And he could taste the distinct tang of blood filling his mouth and feel a dull ache throbbing along his muzzle as he looked about.

Something about this place wasn't right.

On a whim he glanced down at his footpaws, expecting to find the soft grass like always. But instead, as he looked down past his skirt, he felt his stomach drop as he stared into a swirling maelstrom of grey clouds, broken up by the odd flash of thunder.

Was he... standing atop the storm?

There was no sight of the world far below, no breaks in the seemingly endless cloud cover. No, he wasn't above the storm at all—it all felt far too wrong—he was *inside* the storm. Inside the very halls of Peruvaan.

At the thought of that name, there came another unsettling feeling, just like the energy of the storm from before. He felt as every strand of fur stood on end, lifting up his arms to see they had puffed up to twice their size, at least. What in the name of Äituri was happening!?

"She cannot answer you here, Kuveli," came a voice from behind that shook like thunder, and yet was strangely comforting.

The little fox felt compelled to turn and meet the voice. And so he did, slowly at first, eyes fixed on his footpaws, uncertain if he wanted to confirm his suspicion, but ultimately even he knew he could not simply hide inside his bedroll. Kuveli had to face this, whether it scared him or not.

Lifting his gaze, Kuveli could hardly have said he was surprised by who was awaiting him. In this realm, at this moment in time, it could only have been one spirit among them all.

The Black Reindeer himself.

Peruvaan.

It was strange, actually. Not that he was witnessing an actual spirit, nor that this spirit had chosen to show itself. It was strange because... Kuveli had never pictured him walking on two legs, like he and his people did. Two-legged prey did not exist after all, else they wouldn't eat them.

Come to think of it, did Peruvaan take offence to the hunting of his mortal kin?

Other than that, he was just as the stories described. His heavy coat of fur was charred-black, like the remnants of a tree that had been struck by lightning, except for his velvety-red antlers. He also wore a simple woven loincloth around his waist. Even the spirits appreciated modesty, it seemed.

And yet, in spite of his foreboding appearance, the spirit wore a broad smile, his features soft and welcoming, shoulders slack, relaxed. This supposed spirit of unknowable power seemed downright jovial.

"You seem afraid, young one. Please, come and sit by my fire," the voice rumbled, almost distant and distracted, making the clouds beneath Kuveli quiver. "We have a lot to talk about."

Gulping, Kuveli hesitantly stepped towards the manifestation as it moved aside—each hoofstep producing a bolt of lightning—revealing a mysterious fire pit that crackled with strange blue flames.

As he approached, he caught the spirit's gaze with his own, and looked right into his eyes. And by all the spirits, Peruvaan's eyes were magnificent, like black opals that sparkled with the light of a thousand, thousand stars. And just like the stars, they inspired in him a sense of awe like nothing he had felt before. A precious feeling only he and his brother shared on cold, clear nights in an open meadow.

His brother...

"But Sakara is still out there, and he's hurt—" Kuveli began, but a thunderous chuckle cut him off.

"How foolish you fleeting mortals can be," the spirit chortled playfully, amused at Kuveli's plight, seemingly ignorant of the offence he might cause. "I cannot merely pick up your brother and breathe life back into him, no—that would upset the balance. And we have worked ever so hard to preserve that."

In that moment, as the laughter rang in his ears, Kuveli felt that familiar rush of strength rise up from within him. It coursed through his veins as he straightened his back and raised his voice to challenge a god.

"Fleeting mortals? So that's what you spirits do. You sit up here, laughing at our struggles, and stepping on us when we don't offer you enough of our precious winter supplies?" the fox hissed, a foul snarl quickly taking the place of innocent curiosity as he hesitated to come any closer.

Only a few moments of silence passed, but it felt like an eternity as Kuveli grew to realise he'd made a mistake. He had rejected the hospitality of a creature that could flick him into the void, or simply torment him for the rest of his days.

What a foolish thing to do! How could he have allowed himself to act so childish at a moment like this?

It seemed his fears were confirmed as Peruvaan's once jovial features soured. The welcoming smile bent into a deep frown, and those all-knowing opal eyes seemed to simmer with an unknowable power.

"If that were so, do you think I would have graced you with the honour of sitting before my fire?" the reindeer responded at length, lifting his nose and staring down at the fox, the clouds rumbling with the fury that surely bubbled within him. "This is no small privilege, boy. Stronger shamans than you have gone mad in the presence of lesser spirits than I."

"I am no shaman!" Kuveli protested, throwing up his arms in frustration. "Why must everyone insist that I am something I'm not?"

"Sana tells me you are, and I trust that otter more than most. Should I have to punish him? What about your Äituri, or the many ravens who squawk on and on about your potential? Am I to tell them they are wrong?"

The fox was stunned into silence. He knew Sana? And by name no less! What business did Sana have knowing the spirit of storms by name, when he was a shaman of Äituri? Oh, but it was obvious. The spirits were like the mortals, in that they bickered and argued like a family, and gossiped like his brother when they ate night meal. The Horse Mother was no different, and Sana probably sought something from Peruvaan on her behalf.

"I was always destined to be a hunter. My brother is a strong hunter, as were my ma and fah before him, so I am destined to be a hunter too. It's the very blood that flows through me!"

"Do not lie to me," the reindeer stated dryly, raising an open palm to silence the fox. "Is it not true that you never knew your parents? The winds tell me that they died long before you can remember. Your mother at your birth and your father-"

"My fah by his own paws," Kuveli muttered bitterly, wrinkling his muzzle and folding his arms. "I don't see how this matters right now, when I might lose my brother too."

Again, silence reigned for a time, interrupted by the odd rumble of distant thunder. It had grown in intensity since the reindeer had arrived, no doubt his anger being its source. Something inside Kuveli, a voice of reason, pleaded for him to cease his childish bickering, but to do so now was surely a sign of cowardice.

And he was done being seen as a coward.

Or so he thought, until he watched the spirit slowly reach behind his back and produce something frighteningly familiar. A carved wooden figure, with scraps of leather wrapped around its waist, and a face...

It was his own visage! Perfectly resembling a toy which Sakara had carved for him many winters ago, to give him something to play with on those long winter nights. He had carved Pekka too, and himself, and even a deer for their little figures to hunt.

"Where...? How did you get that!?" Kuveli asked, his words stuttering. Unless the spirit really had meant what he said, that Kuveli meant more than he believed.

"Do you know why they say my fur is black like charred wood?" the reindeer asked, sounding legitimately curious as he turned to regard the little vulpine doll with a distant gaze.

Kuveli nodded slowly, wrapping his arms around his chest as a tightness seemed to grip his body. Stranger still, the tightness seemed to match exactly where Peruvaan was holding the doll, the hefty muscles beneath his fur contracting as his grip tightened.

Then, there was a flash of red-hot fire in those cosmic eyes, and Kuveli saw... no, he felt the rage rising up inside the spirit. It was like a phantom, a feeling that was there, and yet not quite. The feeling made his hackles rise as butterflies filled his stomach, his every fibre growing more and more anxious. He could feel something bad coming, almost like how he could feel a coming storm.

"Once, the spirit of fire fell in love with my dance. It watched, utterly mesmerised by me, the fire unable to help itself when it embraced me," the spirit explained, each word hesitant as Peruvaan recalled what must have been an unbearable memory. Kuveli saw his features contort as the almighty spirit gripped his arms, the pain clearly still lingering in his bones. "And by thunder, did it burn so terribly. The spirit of fire hurt me, seared my flesh, charred my beautiful fur as black as the night. I cast off the fire with lightning, sending it down unto the mortal realm, but fire never forgives. It follows my dance wherever I go, seeking me and all who know me."

Peruvaan paused and knelt down by the fire, holding the doll over the flames. As he did, the fox felt the heat wash over his own body, burning his bare paws and making him pant.

It was then that the reindeer turned to him, and stared him dead in the eyes with those beautiful, star-filled opals. But rather than awe, they now filled the little fox with dread.

"And now, it will follow you too, little one."

With that, Peruvaan dropped the figure into the fire, the flames erupting to consume the little vulpine figure.

"Wait-" Kuveli barked, but a sudden and intense burning engulfed his body, like the flames were licking at his fur. It felt like his flesh was boiling and dripping off his blackened bones, every nerve screaming with a pain like nothing he had ever felt before. Lifting his maw to let out a scream, he found that he had no voice, the flames having consumed his throat, and now all he could hear was the roaring in his ears.

All around him were flames, burning bright, consuming him like tinder. Fleeting glimpses of the reindeer spirit through the fire became rarer and rarer until, finally, the whole world seemed to twist into a swirling inferno as he writhed upon the floor.

The world of the storm spirit faded away.

He couldn't hold on anymore.

A rich, emerald light filled Kuveli's vision as his eyes flicked open, gasping for air as he floundered for a moment. Like a salmon plucked from the river, he thrashed around as if he had forgotten how to use his body. He grasped enough control to throw a paw over his head as a pounding headache sent spots across his vision.

But this headache quickly faded, leaving the fox to look upon the welcome sight of a rich, leafy canopy hanging overhead. No more lightning, no more Peruvaan, the sky beyond was a gentle blue speckled with soft, white clouds. The reindeer spirit must have moved on and taken its booming dance with it, leaving only sweet birdsong to fill the fox's sensitive ears.

For a while, he simply remained there. The fox's heart was still racing, and his body ached as if he had been trampled by an auroch. Granted, he did fall off a horse, and that wasn't much better. Though, the bed of crushed bracken beneath him was very soft, and he wasn't in much of a rush to get up. Just a few moments longer, to collect his thoughts and let the storm within his own mind calm.

Once he finally decided to rise, Kuveli looked about his surroundings with great care. Pekka might have still been around, just out of sight, but the forest here was too deep to tell. While the numerous birch and pine trees were spaced generously, there grew a wall of thick undergrowth between them. Bracken, buckthorn, and honeysuckle, the latter of which attracted more than a few fluttering moths and lumbering bumblebees, none of which seemed to pay him any mind. Why would they?

There was, however, a very obvious clue as to where Pekka had gotten herself. A great gash had been carved through the undergrowth, the earth beneath torn up and scattered across the flowers and birchbark, no doubt by his helpless brother being raked along the floor.

The gash also revealed a thick blanket of tinder-dry needles and pine cones, the refuse of a hot and dry summer. And although Kuveli saw no blood, he found himself no more at ease than before. He had seen, in his time with Sana, that one does not need to bleed to have their skull crushed or neck snapped.

"Äituri be merciful," he muttered, "please let him be all right."

The fox took a moment to brush the debris from his skirt, the patchwork of furs and leather torn up by the night's events. But his shoulder strap held firm and his knife was still sitting snugly in its sheath, at least as far as he could tell with a quick squeeze.

He also ran a thumb along his lip, lifting it up to his face to check for blood, which he could still taste on his tongue. There were flecks, but nothing substantial. It was probably nothing then, just bit his tongue in the fall.

With that, he practically leaped towards the trail, setting off at a brisk pace. There was no time to lose, especially not as a particular scent was tickling his nostrils. Through the sweet scents of clover and pine, almost overwhelming in their power, there was the distinctive odour of woodsmoke.

Through the forest he ran, as fast as his nimble footpaws would carry him. Although his body ached, he moved with great finesse, ducking beneath prickly branches and skipping over hidden roots that waited to ensnare him. Thankfully the trail was dead straight; Pekka, in her forever-stubborn ways, clearly hadn't stopped to check if she was actually in danger.

Where was she now? Kuveli could not say. Horses always tended to return if they ever escaped, not content to stay far away from their food and a nice, dry bed.

Perhaps that's where she had gone. All the way back to camp, dragging Sakara's broken body along for the ride, so that the tribe might find it. Though, it seemed that he would not be so unlucky this time, as he rounded a sudden corner in the trail and felt something warm beneath his paw pads, followed by a pained yelp.

Kuveli tripped over his own feet as he staggered to a halt, barely catching himself on a tree as he whirled about to make sure his ears weren't deceiving him.

And sure enough, he saw a familiar coat of red, white, and grey fur lying in the grass, writhing weakly as he groaned in pain.

There was no word in the Lentavohi tongue that could describe the sense of relief he felt. It overwhelmed everything, casting the anger and the fear into a growing fire of hope that he sheltered within his heart. Without thinking, Kuveli scrambled to Sakara and threw himself upon the delirious pile of fox he called brother.

"I thought you were gone, big brother. Like I'd never see you again, ever," Kuveli bawled into Sakara's scruff, pressing his face tightly against the bigger fox's warm body as tears streamed from his eyes.

In his ears he could hear Sakara's heartbeat, strong as it ever was, followed by a grunt as the larger fox shifted slightly. Kuveli felt an arm around his back, squeezing him back, if only delicately. But it was enough to make the little fox sob and sniffle, letting out all the stress and worry that had weighed upon him and leaving only a grateful smile.

"You won't... get rid of me that easily," Sakara wheezed, his voice hoarse, as he lifted his head with great difficulty. "Famine, bears, frostbite," he murmured seemingly at random. "I'll be feral if it's my own horse that kills me, after all I've lived through."

Kuveli wrapped an arm under his brother's head, helping him to lift it. Yet he was heavier than the little fox had realised, and Kuveli started to look around for a place his brother could lean against, to regain his bearings.

But the touch of a paw stopped his searching, as his brother gently held the long, white fur on his cheek and began to rub it between his thumb and finger. Sakara's delirious features twisted with worry as he did so.

"You're bleeding," he commented, bringing his paw between them to reveal a bloody finger.

Kuveli felt strange as he looked at his blood on his brother's fingertips, like colour-paste ready to be rubbed across someone's cheek or forehead. The hungry-fanged wolves from last night were back, to tear his mind in half, but they were different now. The one wished to drag him somewhere where he let his brother worry over him as much as he clearly wanted to. Somewhere where finding Pekka and worrying about the smell of smoke were left to Sakara. The other was dragging him into a cloud of dark smoke.

But the second was the one that wore Kuveli's face. Like the toy Peruvaan had burnt.

Kuveli blinked away the confusion. "Let me see, brother," he blurted out.

"But little rabbit chaser, if you're bleeding—"

"If I'm bleeding I can still walk. Can you?" Kuveli snapped.

Sakara recoiled in surprise, but didn't try to stop him. He strangled a yelp into a long whine when Kuveli's paw touched his shin.

"I think," the little fox fought to keep his voice steady, "your leg is broken. I..." What would the shaman do? "I'll go find a splint."

"Stay where I can see you, though!" Sakara pushed himself up on his elbows. But that was stupid, Kuveli thought, as if there would be a usable splint lying in the mossy underbrush within a few paces, just waiting for him to put his hand on.

When he put his hand down in the mossy underbrush he felt something knobby and hard.

Kuveli stood up, holding the reindeer leg bone gingerly, and stared wide eyed at his injured brother.

"That should do," Sakara nodded as Kuveli approached. "There're thongs in my pouch..."

"You don't have your pouch." Kuveli frowned. It was probably somewhere back there in the forest, if not further. And himself with only his knife and his clothes—

Hastily, Kuveli began untying one of his new leggings from his belt before kicking it off. He unsheathed his slate knife as he picked it up, and, carefully but as swiftly as he could, took the sharply-honed stone to the stitches.

Sakara tried to object but Kuveli cut him off. "I'll stitch them back together tomorrow when we're safe. The practice will be good for me."

But he hesitated when it came time to pick up the reindeer leg bone.

"What's wrong?"

"The... it..." Kuveli grimaced at the bone lying beside his brother as if it might bite. "Nothing's wrong!"

"Then what's so scary about a bone?" asked his brother, "Seems lucky to me, it's just what we needed. Here, I'll hold it while you tie it on."

"I..." Kuveli hesitated. Surely it'd be fine if he didn't tell. Just help his brother, remember what he'd learned from Sana, wasn't that enough? "I spoke with someone," he said anyway, "last night. In the storm, after I fell off Pekka."

"Someone looking for shelter?"

"No. IN the storm."

Sakara looked at the younger fox for long enough that Kuveli had time to feel up and down his brother's shin. No crookedness or twisting as far as he could tell, Äituri had given them that much at least. "You mean," the older fox finally said, "you met Peruvaan?"

Kuveli nodded.

"Face to face?"

He nodded again.

There was a peculiar kind of expression he'd noticed, around Sana, around any shaman. The people who had it would have said it was respect. But Kuveli would have said it was more like fear, maybe even disgust, and that malicious voice was whispering that if he looked up now he'd see it in his brother's eyes.

But Sakara was only looking at the leg bone lying beside his own. "Well, that makes this a good omen, then."

"I don't know," Kuveli said, "I think I might have made him angry."

"You made Peruvaan angry?"

"I might have."

Sakara threw back his head and yelped with laughter, until he winced at his leg and stopped. "The spirit of dancing and celebration and drunkenness? The happiest god? The dancer who never stops? You made HIM upset?"

Kuveli's cheeks grew warm. "He's not nothing but dancing! Lightning is dangerous and he can be too!"

"Well, I suppose you would know, little bud," Sakara had found his laughter again, "the mysteries of the spirits! This mere hunter's never met one face to face, himself!"

"Lucky you, then," Kuveli grumbled as he began to lash the bone splint in place with what had until recently been his leggings. "He wanted me to listen to some stories about fire, and it felt like I was being burned... but I think he wanted me to listen more than I did."

"About the fire?" Sakara cocked his weary head.

"It was something about how fire always followed him..."

Some of the details were hard to recall, but he was sure that had been the bulk of the details. The blue fire, the questions about his own past, his worthiness to be called a shaman.

And then the appearance of his own doll, which Peruvaan had burned while warning that—

Oh.

Kuveli's paws made haste to finish the splint and check that it was tight enough. "We need to go! We need to find Pekka! That's why he gave us a splint!"

"What's wrong with you, little brother?" Sakara hauled himself up onto his good leg with Kuveli's shoulder for support. He made to pat his head, but Kuveli ignored him. The young fox's nose was in the air, his eyes were wide, and his ears were up for the faintest whisper, spirit or otherwise.

"Can't you smell it?" he said.

"Smell what?"

"The fire that follows him."

It was growing closer with each moment that passed, a veil of thick smoke clouding the skies overhead, its stench ever-present in the otherwise-calm forest. It was a clear sign that the spirit of fire had found them, and like a pack of hungry wolves it had begun to stalk the pair, its flames eager to nip at their heels.

The foxes pressed on, shuffling through the thick growth with as much haste as their battered and broken bodies could summon, spurred by the oddly warm winds at their back. But already Kuveli knew it wasn't going to be enough, not with his brother's broken leg.

After every few dozen paces they were forced to stop, Sakara grimacing as he rested his back against the nearest tree and huffed with ragged breaths. Even if they had willow bark to dull the pain, it wouldn't have eased the aches in their empty stomachs or the stiffness in their bones. Kuveli found no use denying it, he too was utterly exhausted, but he couldn't allow himself to give in.

It felt like hours had passed, but he could not see the sun to tell, for they had delved so much deeper into the forest, following Pekka's trail, which had brought them to the top of a steep embankment.

Both foxes paused, looking down the relatively short drop into a gurgling stream. A fit hunter would have had no trouble traversing it, but with Sakara in such a state there was a real chance he could fall and do even more harm to himself.

What if he landed wrong and broke the splint? More time wasted making another splint. Time that they didn't have, as the fire spirit was surely gaining on them. His worry was proved when, as he glanced to the sky, Kuveli realised the smoke had descended towards them.

Something nattered frantically in his ear. A gut feeling, a spirit perhaps, was telling Kuveli just to go. Be like a hunter, be brave, and take a step into uncertainty.

Or be foolish, if it had been a demon that seeded the idea.

Either way their time was up and, thinking quickly, Kuveli put a tentative paw forward to begin down the slope. At the same time, he pulled on Sakara's arm, urging his brother to follow, but the bigger and—supposedly—braver fox was none too keen to risk the fall.

"Go on ahead," he gasped between breaths, one arm wrapped around his chest. "I'll find a safer place to climb down and meet you, somewhere near the Salmon River."

"Shut up," Kuveli snapped back, "we won't lose each other again! I swear it upon my soul, may Äituri tear it from my body if we do."

Sakara gulped, his brows knitted with worry as he quickly gave in, following Kuveli to the best of his ability.

"Since when did you get so righteous," he commented after a few moments, giving a forced chuckle. It was hardly convincing, and Kuveli could clearly hear the worry in his voice.

Even as positive as Sakara had always tried to be, the thought that they might very well still die was weighing heavy on him. Neither fox was ignorant of the danger, which, on top of their mounting exhaustion, only worked to fill them with a growing sense of dread as it picked away at their minds like the tapping of a crow's beak.

They traversed the slope at a frustrating pace, one footpaw after the other. Or, in Sakara's case, carefully sliding down the slope on his good paw at the pace of a snail. Though, it wouldn't be careful enough.

About half-way down Kuveli heard a yelp behind him, and in his panic he tried to turn and see only to lose his footing. The crusted mud that covered the ground gave way, seizing what little grip Kuveli had found and causing him to slam down hard on his side. His grip on Sakara was still firm, and as he landed, the little fox was crushed beneath his brother's tumbling form, before they both rolled down the slope and landed in the stream with a splash.

Kuveli gasped as the bitterly cold waters of the stream soaked into his fur and made his body prickle, as if he were being stabbed by dozens of tiny sewing needles.

In that moment he could understand why salmon were so keen to jump out of rivers, and he followed their example and scrambled over his groaning brother, splashing water everywhere as he clambered back onto dry land. He quickly turned and grabbed Sakara by the fur, but froze in place as he laid his eyes upon a terrifying sight.

Smoke was pouring between the trees and swallowing the canopy above, carried overhead by wind, which had begun to pick up rapidly. It wasn't just the overwhelming smell now, but a distant crackling that banished the once-comforting sounds of the forest, and a low, orange glow that seeped through cracks in the thick, choking wall of black.

By all the spirits, it was here. The fire spirit had come for them, at long last, and it wasn't wasting any time, as the menacing smoke rolled over the edge of the embankment and fell towards them. As it did, it seemed to pick up speed, like a predator seeing that its prey was vulnerable, and moving to make the kill.

"Get up," he screamed at his brother, "it's already here, we have to go!"

Sakara looked up groggily, his tired and sunken face turning pale under the fur, his maw falling agape as he watched the smoke descend upon them. When Kuveli yanked on his fur again, he snapped out of his daze and stumbled up onto his good leg.

Pain shot through his features as, in his panic, he scraped and battered his broken leg while hauling himself up by Kuveli's shoulder. And, as soon as he was on his feet, they both began to run.

They could feel the heat at their backs, almost like the comforting embrace of a warm campfire, as if the fire spirit was trying to fool them into a false sense of safety. But foxes were too cunning for such trickery, and they kept running. Over roots and rocks, down slopes and along ditches, the stream shadowing the path they frantically cut through the overwhelming forest.

It should have been impossible, moving at such a pace through a forest that appeared untouched by even good game trails, but wildfire, it seemed, was a strong motivator. Though, as his paws beat the dry and brittle forest floor, Kuveli swore he could feel something else. Something like what he had felt when the thunder was booming overhead.

But it wasn't enough.

Sakara stumbled again, his arm slipping from around Kuveli's shoulders. Before the little fox could even turn and call his name, the smoke overcame them, turning the whole world black.

It burned his every sense, like Peruvaan's fire. His eyes screamed and watered, even as he screwed them shut. His nose and mouth filled with thick, suffocating smoke that caused him to cough violently, dropping to the floor where he found a brief respite.

Down there, all around him, he saw a fiery orange that was only growing brighter with each passing moment. The heart of the fire itself, ravenous for their flesh and souls. The sound was deafening, a rageful roaring like that of a great windstorm, louder than even the thunder.

Though, rather than run, Kuveli merely remained there. His mind was racing like never before, unable to think as the memory of Peruvaan's fire paralysed him. He could feel it, his flesh bubbling and boiling again, his fur charred, his bones rendered unto ash. It made him shudder as he lay there, eyes glazing over.

Terrified.

Until he heard another noise through the roaring smoke. Something animalistic and shrill, and yet... familiar.

It was the whinnying of a horse.

By the mercy of Äituri.

Pekka.

A delirious smile came to Kuveli's muzzle. He rolled onto his stomach and began to crawl towards the sound, but it was hard. Fear still had its claws in his pelt, digging deeper into him the further he tried to run from it.

But he could feel that otherworldly strength growing within him. Like before, it was filling his veins, banishing the poison. Slowly, it brought him to his knees, and face-to-face with a force beyond reckoning: a terrified horse.

Kuveli put forth a paw, and behold, there was a halter for it to grasp. He hauled himself to his feet, leaned against Pekka's shivering flank for balance. "Brother," he tried to yell and only croaked, "can you ride?"

"I don't know," Sakara whispered as he scrambled astride the mare. "I can't properly guide her with this splint on."

"I'll have to do it, then."

"Can you?"

"You just said you can't." Kuveli pulled himself up in front of Sakara. "And actually try to hold on this time!"

Pekka needed little urging to make the best speed she could away from the fire. It wasn't her fastest, tired and frightened as she was, but it was quicker than an exhausted fox could crawl. Kuveli began to hope, as he felt the heat fade behind them and the smoke ahead thin, that they had escaped.

Then Pekka stopped, whickering and grumbling. They were atop a high riverbank, nearly a cliff, and below them churned a wide river, shallower than it should have been, yet still seething with upset. River spirits were malevolent and treacherous at the best of times, and this one would be angry—not only was it parched, but the fire spirits had spent all night blowing ash and cinders into it, just to rub it in.

They would have to go another way. But instead of urging Pekka along the river, Kuveli felt a thought come to him, unbidden, from where he couldn't say.

How had Peruvaan escaped the fire spirit?

He had gone where it couldn't follow.

"Pekka," he growled in a voice it had never before occurred to him to use, "trust me better than my stubborn oaf of a brother does."

He pulled her head toward the cliff, and she responded. He could still feel her panicking beneath them, but she did as bidden.

"For Äituri's sake, jump!" Kuveli yiped.

The flames reached the crest of the hill behind them, exploding between the trees before consuming them all together, gleefully certain their newest lovers were within reach.

Pekka reared, nostrils flared, and her hooves left the ground.

It felt like an eternity as they fell. Kuveli's stomach turned over as he lost his grip on Pekka. And then, his heart stopped as he felt his brother's grip slip from around his waist.

The cool muddy river water caught the three of them a moment later, its embrace surprisingly gentle. Like a reflection of the dull grey sky into which Peruvaan had once lept, leaving the fires, jilted and frustrated, behind.

Pekka was the first to make the opposite shore, as the river had borne them swiftly downstream to where the banks were lower. Its anger, apparently, was all against the fire spirit today, and it was only too happy to aggravate it by rescuing three weary and bedraggled morsels from its jaws. The mare plodded up the sandbank and then flopped to the ground, glaring daggers at the fox brothers as if daring them to try to make her get up again.

Nothing could have been further from their thoughts. Sakara and Kuveli lay on their backs on the sand, toes still in the water, panting grateful lungfuls of clean air.

"Is your splint still in place?" Kuveli finally asked.

"Stubborn oaf of a brother?" Sakara huffed.

"It's only fair," Kuveli retorted, "but is your splint still in place?"

"It is," Sakara answered, "but never mind that. What's Sana going to say when I tell him you reenacted the whole dance of Peruvaan?"

Kuveli the shaman blinked up at the clouds. The ash-smeared fox imagined they were laughing at him.

There they lay upon the bank for a long time, watching the fire consume the forest on the opposite river, raging at its loss. They stayed until dusk began to fall, and the canoes of a friendly otter tribe stopped to help them.

In the end: The forest would regrow. Twice as lush and twice as bountiful, just as it always did after every one of the fire spirit's tantrums, for as long as hunters had huddled in shelters and told stories about it.

And now, he had his own story too—A story brought about by his own tantrum.

Only, unlike the fire, he had learned to be better.

Lids

by Utunu

The cave with no entrance was lit by a light with no source.

It was always the same, every time Sreki dreamt it. He would find himself there in the cave's centre, hyena paws on the soft sand. It was not the sand of the wide river Pindipindi, coarse and spattered with pebbles and sharp rocks, but rather the finer, silky sand of the sea. At least that's what Sreki assumed; he had never been to the sea.

It felt gentle on his paws, and he scuffed his feet in it, reveling in its caress. Yet, as with every time before, his eyes did not linger on the sand, and Sreki lifted his gaze to the cave surrounding him. It was small, with a ceiling and walls of rough grey stone. The walls curved sinuously around, such that some regions of the cave were blocked from view, but Sreki knew it did not extend far, even though he had not traversed the entirety of the cave himself.

Sreki felt safe here. But there was something waiting—a strangeness in the air around him that he could not define.

He assumed it was the pots.

They were where they always were, nestled haphazardly on the sandy floor. All were different—some large, some small, some made of odd materials, some with peculiar designs or emblazoned with unfamiliar glyphs—yet they were all there, all in the same spots. Perhaps two eights of them, all told; he hadn't counted. In the many nights before when Sreki had come to this place, he had walked among them, paws whispering on the sand. In his first visits, when the cave was new to his dreams, he had moved one or two of them, sliding them from their places or toppling them over. But the next time they were always back where they had been. It had felt wrong when he had done so, so he did not try again.

Sreki never bothered with the further recesses of the cave. A few of the pots knelt there in the shadows, but the closer ones called to him. They made his paws itch and his whiskers prickle. And with their summons, the frustration began.

Because each pot was stoppered with an immovable lid.

At first this was a curiosity. But it soon became more, as Sreki realised that no matter how hard he tried, they would not budge. He knew there was something inside, something for him and him alone, but it remained locked away behind unassuming lids. It became infuriating, and as always, his hold on the dreamcave shuddered and wavered and was lost.

"Sreki, wake up!"

He clawed at the shredded tatters of the dreamcave as it drifted away, once again.

The pre-dawn light crept through the entrance of his hut, silhouetting Ruha's distinctive form, hyena ears perked forward with concern. Ruha lightly shook him.

"Sreki?"

"Ruha... I..."

"The dream again?" Ruha's voice was soft, as if it tried to drape itself over the worry beneath, failing to hide it in its entirety. "Your heart is a drum calling to battle."

Sreki struggled to sit up, and the wisps of the dream scattered. Ruha squatted on his haunches next to him, and the touch of his paw on Sreki's face was gentle. It took several moments for the thud of his heart to settle, and he nodded.

"Have you spoken to Old Eye of it yet?" Ruha inquired, tentatively.

"No," stated Sreki firmly. "She thinks I'm a fool, a cub, a screamer at monkeys. Why should I?"

Ruha sighed. "She's a shaman. She says there's something to you. If she felt she were just swinging at the wind she'd not be bothering with you."

"And who would bother with me if she didn't?" Sreki countered.

"You are so angry, Sreki. But please, do not throw your spears at me."

Sreki's muzzle dipped, ashamed. "I am sorry."

Ruha pulled him into an embrace, and Sreki held tight.

"The hunt leaves soon," Ruha said.

Sreki released him, and looked him up and down. Ruha was naked, and there were but a few lines of clay upon his body. "Where's your loincloth?"

"Here," Ruha replied, holding it up, along with a small bowl. "I wanted you to help me prepare."

"Seems Nyota has already drawn some of the reeds by the river. I scent her on you."

"Just a few. Don't pout, Sreki. I love you as well, and I always have. Pindipindi will go dry and the reeds become dust before that changes."

Sreki sighed and got to his feet, taking the bowl of white clay from Ruha's grasp. He began to paint upon Ruha's fur, letting the clay guide his fingers and flow on its own: the reeds to hide amongst the grasses, the waves to slip and evade, and the spears for striking true. Ruha grinned at Sreki as the last spear adorned his sheath. "Thank you," Ruha said, and it was heartfelt.

Sreki smiled shyly, as he always did when Ruha spoke with such intensity, his words shining bright as the sun above the savanna.

"I must go," he added, apologetically, and Sreki nodded. Ruha tied his loincloth around his waist, turning to leave the hut.

"Ruha? Will you be here tonight? Or does Nyota have her claws in you?"

"I'll be here. Nyota knows you'll always be part of me, and I you. She accepts it."

Sreki held those words close. It meant the cough and stutter of the choppy waves in his mind would calm, at least for a while.

"Try again."

Old Eye settled on her haunches, expectantly. The small cooking fire cast stark shadows across her scarred face as she watched the young hyena seated by her side. Sreki ignored her, his muzzle set in concentration.

I'm trying as hard as I can!

Sreki's mind reached for the flames beneath the copper pot, its water bubbling. It felt like trying to grasp dust motes. He had no idea if he was even doing it the right way, and the flames wavered there, mockingly close. For all he strained, the fire might as well have been eights of strides away.

I'd have a better chance flinging a spear at that distance than persuading this flame but a few paws away. But then, that would imply I am invited to the hunts.

He closed his eyes for a moment, trying and failing to calm himself. He knew Old Eye was staring at him. He wondered briefly how Ruha's hunt was going.

Sighing, he switched his attention to the pieces of wood within the fire, as they slowly and stoically gave way to the merry flicker of flames. Silently he spoke to them. They ignored him, as if he weren't there, as if his words weren't meant for them. The wood was as distant as a single stalk of grass on the savanna's expanse, and he needed to whisper to it and it alone.

His gaze flicked briefly to Old Eye. *Of course she's looking at me.*

He moved to the water within the pot. It didn't listen either. *Am I even doing this the way I'm supposed to? I have no idea!*

It bubbled there, but its world did not include him. He glared at the water angrily, his ears flat against his head, mentally groping for it. The bubbles of the water became the bubbles of his anger, and his paws itched with the desire to strike the pot and dash its contents over the earthen floor of the hut.

"!Sreki…"

Gods, I hate how she says my name. I am not a cub any more!

"!Sreki!" Old Eye emphasised the click at the beginning, a warning to a wayward cub, and he turned and glowered at her. She met his scowl calmly and waited.

He studied her face—the left eye a vibrant emerald, alert and intense. The right… well, a horrible scar split it like a chasm, a furless furrow that went from forehead to muzzle, and the eye itself lay there dormant, blind and milky-white. The power behind that gaze unnerved him, and her one eye easily conquered his two as he dipped his muzzle in submission. His flattened ears drooped as he felt the anger dribble away, flowing out of him almost as quickly as it had arisen.

"You push too hard. You're straining with a muscle you haven't yet found, in a limb you have no control over," Old Eye stated quietly, her voice tinged with sympathy.

Sreki nodded, eyes downcast, staring into his lap. He wore nothing but a simple covering of dark brown hide at his waist. *I wish it were a hunter's loincloth. Like Ruha's. Or even Peshu's,* thought Sreki bitterly.

"Why do you think I say your name like that?"

Sreki stayed silent.

"Because in some ways you are still a cub. Yes, you have the height of one grown, the shape, even some of the muscle of the hunt. Even the heft beneath that loincloth, I'm to understand."

Sreki felt his ears grow hot.

"But it is the impulsiveness, the stubbornness, the rawness. You are the chaos of the wind rustling the tall grasses, weaving this way and that way on a whim. Look at you. You throw a spear, and if it does not strike true, you toss the rest aside and storm back home."

"I—" he began.

"How do you think I lost my eye? Shall I tell you?" Old Eye demanded.

He stayed quiet, curiosity and shame sparring for control.

It seemed the flash of that green orb faded somewhat, and Old Eye sighed resignedly. She seated herself on the dirt floor of the hut, arms crossed. Armour of soft hide covered her from breast to thigh, glyphs of her own devising carved and dyed across its surface. The rest of her was covered in tawny fur, spattered with dark spots, like all the tribe—yet hers had begun to grey in places. Much older than Sreki, perhaps, but still strong-jawed, and she held his curious orange eyes with her singular one.

"It was a challenge, simple as that," Old Eye said. "I am not proud of it. Everything was a *now* thing for me then. I did not wish to wait. Young and angry and impulsive and stubborn, much like you. I desired a place above me, a place I did not deserve. I brought my challenge to the village centre, to be seen by all, as is the way these things are done."

Old Eye paused, and Sreki shifted uncomfortably. The silence grew, and Old Eye waited until it became heavy and threatening, like rain-thick clouds.

"Taori defeated me," Old Eye continued, and the tautness in the air broke. Sreki breathed out the breath he hadn't realised he held.

"The wound festered, as if my foolishness would not let it go. I lay as dead for eight and one days, but in the end I lived. Taori's spear took my eye and left wisdom in its place."

She glanced over at the young hyena, who sat there with ears perked forward, attentive to every word.

"That's it. There is nothing more to tell. Taori won, and I lost. And here we sit."

And here we sit. Sreki looked down at the dirt floor between his paws. The silence grew again, needing to be filled. Uncertainty pricked at him, but he tried to ignore it, looking back towards the flames. They ignored him. So did the wood, mostly burned now. The water's boiling bubbles mocked him.

I cannot do this. "I cannot do this," he said, ashamed at the whine that snuck into his voice.

"Tcha!" Old Eye spat, her patience lost. "We'll get no further today. The hunt has likely returned and will need help preparing the kill. Go."

The hut was eights of strides behind him, but Sreki could still feel his hackles bristling, pricked by anger and shame from the bite of Old Eye's words. Pushing it from his mind was hopeless—it was a fly that kept returning no matter how many times he waved it away. As he neared the village centre, he spotted some of the hunting party. By the time he was close enough to determine that Ruha was not among them, it was too late. His hackles rose further.

"!Sreki," said Peshu disdainfully, with the intonation of addressing a cub.

Of course it would have to be Peshu, Sreki thought, and his fury rekindled. He glared over at the hyena who had spoken.

Peshu stood nonchalant, with the lazy posture of arrogant confidence. He was standing perhaps two eight-strides away, his spear leaning against his shoulder. Several others stood by his side with their huntleader, Tal, nearby. Peshu had seen the same seasons as Sreki but had clearly found his place in the hunt—he was tall and muscled, much like Ruha, and Tal herself had praised his youthful exuberance and skill. He'd won his hunter's loincloth several seasons back and used every opportunity to gleefully provide constant reminders of Sreki's lack.

Sreki, ears back and hot with anger, spat the words that bubbled up.

"Peshu. I don't see you carrying any kill. Did you miss?"

Peshu's eyes narrowed. "Fool. The kills are already by the fire, being prepared. Don't want the *cubs* to go hungry," he snarled, the emphasis making his meaning clear. "And miss? I think not. I at least know how to use my spear," he added, then with a grin lifted his loincloth and grasped his genitals, making a show of shaking them in Sreki's direction. "Unlike some. Or did Old Eye take pity on you and show you how it works?"

There were a few appreciative chuckles at the barb.

"Enough," Huntleader Tal admonished him, half-heartedly.

It took all Sreki's control to continue walking; the fury was boiling within him, the lid barely holding it contained. He knew the others could scent both his rage and his embarrassment—it seeped from him, colouring everything, like the blood spreading from a kill and staining the earth below.

Fortunately, Ruha wasn't far, squatting on his haunches as he helped others skin the carcasses. His face brightened when he saw Sreki, then his ears lowered. He set his knife down and walked to meet him.

"Sreki?"

"It is nothing. Just Peshu," Sreki said, failing utterly at hiding his fury. He could read Ruha's face—protectiveness, vicarious anger, sympathy. "Do not worry, Ruha. It's downstream now."

Ruha opened his mouth, then shut it again. He beckoned Sreki over, handed him a knife, and together they carved the kill.

The fire playfully fought the night, and the tribe gathered. The choicest bits, of course, went to the hunters themselves. Peshu had taken it upon himself to portion out pieces, which Sreki dreaded, for he saw it as another obvious opportunity for Peshu to mock him. Sreki sat between Ruha and Nyota; he assumed Ruha had planned it that way. Nyota was affectionate and pressed close, which surprised him. He waited with the two shielding him, walls on either side.

And waited. It was becoming uncomfortable. Nyota and Ruha both had theirs, and Peshu had begun with the cubs. Heat rose unbidden to his face, and he could feel the press of eyes upon him. The scent of Ruha's anger flowered.

"Peshu..." Ruha said, dangerously, a viper coiled.

All innocence and bright eyes, Peshu responded. "More? I shall get you some in but a moment. The cubs are hungry."

Nyota's paw rested on Sreki's leg in silent sympathy and support. It did nothing to cool the flames.

"Peshu. You have forgotten Sreki," Ruha said, each word emphatic and clipped, like the snap of a branch.

"I was getting to him—" Peshu began.

"Now," Ruha declared.

"Peshu, enough," sighed Tal. "This accomplishes nothing."

Meat was tossed dismissively into the dust in front of Sreki. Enough to insult, not enough to challenge. The green of Old Eye's eye flashed at him across the fire. It was too much. Sreki stood, slowly, aware of all eyes upon him. He reached down for his portion, turned, and left.

He had made the walk back to his hut in silence and fury, and had drawn the hide across the entrance. But that didn't stop Ruha. Sreki watched him enter, eyes smouldering in the darkness as he lay on his bed of hides.

"Ruha..." Sreki said, his voice breaking.

"Shhh," whispered Ruha, laying down and holding him tightly.

"Nyota doesn't—" Sreki started.

"Nyota wanted me to come, and so did I. She worries for you too, I wish you would see that."

"Only because you and I are so close."

"I don't think so. I think she sees what I see," Ruha said.

Sreki didn't argue. He kept quiet, and let Ruha's presence calm the chaos in his mind.

Later, as Ruha mounted him, thrusting then arching his back in release, Sreki was finally able to just *be*. For Ruha was here. In that *now*, he savoured it as much as he could, before the chaos returned.

For the first night in many, his sleep was dreamless.

He awoke cradled in Ruha's embrace. Dawn crept nearer, threatening. He wriggled closer, his rear rubbing against Ruha. The gold ring piercing Ruha's sheath, a hunter's reward, rubbed too, a reminder of who was a hunter and who was not. Sreki grew still, and Ruha woke.

Sreki was silent as he painted the lines—the reeds, the waves, the spears. But after the final spear, he pushed aside the glint of gold and beckoned Ruha forth, to be with him once more before he left on the hunt.

"Where is your focus? You are a bird, flitting from branch to branch, thinking each branch is better," Old Eye snapped.

Her emerald gaze held him, and Sreki dipped his muzzle once more. The flames remained unmoved, the wood uninterested, and the water, not yet boiling, yielded not a ripple. She watched as his jaw clenched tightly in concentration and frustration. Muscles corded as Sreki strained, his will palpable. Yet nothing. She remained quiet as his anger kindled, and soon he was panting with the effort.

"It's there, you know."

Sreki stopped, his breathing heavy, and scowled over at her. "What?"

"It's there. Just beneath the surface. A fish about to breach. I can see it, feel it. It's like you're scrabbling for something just out of reach, is it not?"

Sreki's face answered for him.

"I had the same failing," Old Eye continued. "I tried so hard... I pushed and pushed... but there is a subtlety. A caress instead of a strike. For each person, it is different. Most have only one small pocket of it that they can never touch. Others glow brightly, the vessels almost overflowing, begging to be opened."

Sreki's confusion was plain.

"You, like me, have... several vessels. I see fire. I see earth. I see wind. And another perhaps? It is hard to tell, like looking down into deep water. You may even exceed me—there were six for me, but it took me ever so long to open them. Each was difficult, each was a struggle, each was different. Even now they don't come easily. But you have them there. You just need to open them."

Sreki grimaced bitterly, the fury of failure still hot within him, and it burst forth before he could tamp it down.

"I know! You keep telling me this, but it does no good. You push and push, but it does nothing. This is foolish. I should just take my spear and hunt with the rest."

She cuffed him, hard. Her claws slashed across his muzzle and he yelped in surprise, his anger replaced by shock. His eyes were liquid orange hurt, and the words tumbled forth, the barrier lifted.

"Don't you think I know that? Don't you think I see these... vessels?" Sreki cried. "They're *there*, in that cave! Pots upon pots, strangely shaped, strangely coloured, lids tight. Just *sitting* there, but I can see the glow... *feel* the glow. Each one beckons me and I tug and tug at the lids and they just *sit* there and mock me. Night after night! In my dreams... every dream... they're there, waiting. Waiting for me to fail yet again. I *try*, but I don't know how, and you keep telling me things I don't understand and pushing at me and—"

"Pots?" inquired Old Eye, too softly.

Sreki didn't notice and continued on, tears flowing unchecked down the fur of his face, mingling with the blood at his muzzle.

"And I look at that fire," he sobbed, waving his paw in the direction of the small cooking fire nearby. "And I *see* its pot in that cave, and I pull at its lid. But it doesn't come off! I pull at it, and the glow makes my fur stand on end and my claws itch and my paws itch and there's something heavy and strange inside me and I feel it deep behind my sheath and I'm desperate, so desperate to open it, but it refuses! And there... the water?"

He gestured at the contents of the cooking pot, its water still.

"I see its pot too! It's small and dark, almost black, rounded like a river stone, and it has what look like jagged marks on it, they're blue, and *it* won't open either! I claw at the lids, but they're stuck."

Old Eye stared at him with vivid emerald. "A cave?"

"Yes! It's there every night now, in my dreams. There's no opening, it should be dark, but I can see clearly. The floor is covered in sand and pawprints, but I don't know if they're my pawprints, and all sorts of pots sit there, scattered about. Each one looks different, feels different, but they all pull at me, and I pull at them and shake them and try to get my claws beneath the lids, but I cannot. It's maddening! They won't budge."

"How many pots?" Old Eye's query was whispered, unnaturally calm, still water before a storm. Sreki's hackles rose then, and he paused, sobered and wary.

"I don't know, maybe four or five?" he lied, now uncertain. *Two eights, maybe more?* "Some are hidden in the shadows, and I can't quite see them properly. It's hard to walk over to them, but they're there. I can't open *any* of them. I hit them, I pull at the lids, but it is as if I am a newborn cub."

"Why didn't you mention this before?" she asked.

His eyes still wet with tears, Sreki stared sullenly at the shaman. "What for? They're only dreams. It's probably because I'm just angry at... failing every time I try with the fire. Or the wood. Or water. Or anything."

Old Eye was silent, but he could sense her anger there. He opened his muzzle to continue, but she shook her head sharply, causing her bone earrings to rattle.

"You... ah! You young males are all the same. No elegance, no subtlety, just brute force and unchecked rage. You can't just assault every problem you come across."

Sreki looked chastened and embarrassed, and she continued on.

"These vessels are a puzzle to solve. Not something you just beat into submission. These pots of yours have lids, yes, but they are lids with a latch. It could be as simple as that. Just find that latch, and the lid comes off. A gentle push, a slight twist in just the right place, and it could open with ease."

"Then how do I do that?" he asked.

"I do not know," admitted Old Eye. "As I've said, it's different for everyone. All I can do is guide you until you solve those puzzles. Once you have, I can help you direct the powers you uncover, and protect you from them if they prove too much. It can be dangerous when those lids come off; I can help you manage that and master it, once they do."

Then exactly why am I here? Sreki directed his gaze back towards the flames and said nothing, knowing his scent told of his frustration. And more.

The shaman was quiet too, watching him. A rumble of distant thunder interjected itself into the silence that hovered between them, and she shifted slightly, her head cocked, listening.

"A storm comes. It will be a bad one. Go, this day is done."

The cave with no entrance was lit by a light with no source.

He had gone back to his hut, since it was only midday, and laid down on the hides to listen to the rain and wait for the hunt to return. *I must have fallen asleep.* But knowing this changed nothing; the dreamcave remained. With each night, each visit, Sreki had become more aware of it. There was a part of him, always expanding, that realised he was within a place wholly inside the confines of his mind, yet even that knowledge could not touch how real it felt.

Again, he found himself standing in its centre, the sand warm beneath his paws. His ears pricked, and realisation dawned. *There's something different.* He raised his eyes to scan the interior of the cave; the various pots were scattered about, where they always were. *But the sound is different. Ah... the storm.* He could hear it outside the cave—wherever 'outside' might be. It was still distant and faint, with the occasional rumble. It did not matter; inside, Sreki knew he was safe, and he switched his attention to the familiar shapes of the pots upon the sandy floor.

Nearby was the small dark pot, the rounded one with the strange, jagged markings of blue. It stood upright, nestled there between two shallow mounds of sand, and Sreki went and crouched beside it. He gave a tentative tug at the lid, but it was stuck tight. Recalling Old Eye's words, he peered more closely, but there was nothing he could see that might speak to the lid's stubbornness. He tried a gentle push, a twist, a pull in a direction one might not expect—

but it remained unmoved. He glared at the cobalt markings, but they meant nothing.

Keep calm.

Leaving the dark one for the time being, he stood and went over to the next nearest pot—a smooth, tall, burgundy amphora, almost half his height, yet its lid was as small as his paw. There were small divots in the clay, as if it had been struck with a weapon, but it seemed as solid as all the rest. He tried the lid.

Of course it doesn't budge. Why would it?

Sreki could feel the annoyance bubbling deep down inside. He pushed the lid—it was so thin, so small, it should be easy to move! Yet, nothing. Again he lifted, twisted, pulled, and pushed, trying every direction, begging and coaxing the lid to move. He could feel the fury begin—

But no. That was what he did every time, and he was no closer.

Calm. He let the burgeoning anger ebb away, and the choppy waves and gusting winds of his mind settled. He held the calmness there, the quiet, as if he were nestled within Ruha's arms. That outside world, with its fears and its failures, could spin and slash, but it would not reach him here. Not through Ruha.

Slowly he reached for the lid. The placid waters of his mind pushed at it, and it shifted, ever so slightly. His heart leapt, and ripples started to form, so he let the quiet suffuse him until he was calm once more. Nudging the lid, it moved again, enough for a gap.

A brightness shone through, sudden and sharp, like the glint of sunlight reflecting from a speartip.

"Sreki," called a voice.

The light grew brighter, and to his dismay the dreamcave dissipated, flowing away like water through his fingers.

"Sreki?" it called again, and he sat up as the hide curtain on his hut was pushed aside. Huntleader Tal stood there.

Her face told him everything, before she even spoke another word.

Sreki did not remember leaving his hut. But now he was here, accompanied by the entire tribe. The wind and rain swirled, plucking at his fur, but he barely felt it. It made the lighting of the pyre that much more difficult, and Old Eye was forced to step in and coax the flames to honour the fallen.

Detachedly, he felt the press of someone against his side. *Nyota*, he thought, distractedly. He could scent her grief, and that of those gathered. There was immense sorrow within him too, but it was far away. He felt eyes upon him, wondering at him, but they no longer mattered.

Sreki remained still, expressionless, unable to speak. The insistent fire-flicker impinged briefly on his vision, so he raised his head to look upon Ruha one last time, before the flames took him away. He lay peacefully, almost asleep. Someone had placed a piece of hide over the crushed half of his skull; the part of his face still visible was as pristine as Sreki remembered.

It had been an errant hoof from a kudu, Tal had said. Ruha was killed instantly.

Ruha.

He could feel his mind start to struggle, but he couldn't, not now. He tamped it down, he plugged the leaks.

The flames had long since obscured his view of Ruha, when he felt a paw on his arm, pulling him gently away to walk back to the village proper. Numbly he let himself be led.

"What is wrong with him? Has he gone simple?" Peshu's voice.

"Silence, you fool." Old Eye.

Slowly, ever so slowly, Sreki turned to look at Peshu. The bubbling in his mind began to spin. He was at the centre, unmoving, but the sorrow and fury began to trace a path around him, swirling, a whirlpool with him as the nexus, pulling it all in, faster now, gradually focusing.

"Sreki? Come, let's go," Nyota said gently, and he turned blankly to walk with her. She took him to his hut, and obediently he lay upon his hides. She crouched there beside him, her eyes bright with the moonlight that slipped through the half-drawn curtain, but Sreki was silent. When she laid down by his side and held him close, a remote part of him noticed, but that was all.

"Sreki... please speak to me," she whispered, her voice breaking. "I'm alone too."

He heard the words, but they came from far away. A conversation for someone else, not him. The words became tears, and he knew there was a part of him that wished her to stay, wished he could do something, but that part was shut away, buried deep within.

So Sreki neither spoke nor moved, only stared up at the roof of his hut, and eventually Nyota left and pulled the curtain closed.

He was alone. *Ruha.*

The sand was warm beneath his paws.

It was louder now. The storm outside the cave was intense; the chaos of winds, the thunder and lashing of rain, the distant crack of branches as the gale swept over the land. But Sreki barely heard, as the whirl inside him grew.

Gradually the howl of the storm increased, whether the one within him or the one outside, Sreki could not tell, but he could feel his fur start to stand on end. A sharp crack and resounding thud made him jump, bringing him back to his surroundings, and a fine breath of stone dust fell from the cave's ceiling. With it came the familiar pull—a pull against the reality he was experiencing.

No, the dream needs to stay! I know I can open one! I was so close before...

Yet the calmness he had found before was lost, unattainable now. It lay beyond his reach, in Ruha's embrace.

He rushed over to a pot near one of the walls, stumbling briefly in his hurry. It was almost spherical, made of obsidian, with a lid that fit so closely and seamlessly it was almost invisible. Three parallel furrows were carved down it on one side, like the gouging of a huge beast's claws. Its glossy surface was hot to the touch, and he was convinced he could feel it thrum, ever so slightly. But its lid was

as stubborn as the rest, refusing to yield to all of his desperate scrab-
blings.

*Gods, open, curse you! If you had opened before, perhaps I could have
gone on the hunt with Ruha! Perhaps I could have saved him!*

Frantically, he turned his attention to an asymmetrical pot
of rich red ochre, leaning angled against the nearby wall. Ele-
gant stripes of wood engraved with curved glyphs were embedded
around its surface, and Sreki raced over to tug at its lid. It looked to
not fit properly to begin with, it should only take a simple push! But
it resisted, and his anger opened up bright-hot within him. He tore at
the lid and it mocked him. The vortex within him drifted ever closer
to its center, and something shifted inside him and he lost himself
to the rage, hurling his fury at the pot even as the storm hurled its
fury at the earth beneath. There was another sudden crack of fis-
sured stone and a cloud of crumbled rock and dust fell from above,
but he barely noticed. Reality stretched as the cave's ceiling opened
to the sky and the lightning and the rain and the wind, and the whirl
inside him grew brighter and smaller until it was nothing but an im-
possibly intense point. And everything went white.

Sreki awoke.

He was prone, face-down in the dirt just outside the entrance to
his hut. It was dark and noiseless, the night sky brilliant with too
many stars and untouched by clouds. *The storm must have passed.* He
staggered slowly to his feet and wiped the blood from his nose, the
pots still sharp in his mind.

The cave. It opened.

The realisation energised him, and he knew where he must go.

Shakily, he headed towards the hills abutting the village. The
stars above him were wrong, and the hills themselves looked odd
and too close, not the right shape, but the path that led him gradually upslope was familiar. Ahead the hills merged, coming together to form a craggy boundary that bordered his village oppo-

site the river Pindipindi. The simple footing of the hard-packed dirt gave way to more rocky terrain, dotted with jutting stones and storm-broken branches. It looked slightly different, slightly wrong, slightly askew, like the path was not exactly as he remembered, but he was too focused on his destination to notice. The smell of wet air, damp leaves, singed wood, and the underlying smell of iron pushed at his muzzle—yet it was another, different sense that pulled him unerringly upwards. The pull grew irresistibly stronger, and his heart leapt at the unfamiliar silhouette of the stones ahead. Lightning-smell and the spicy scent of scorched rock touched him then, and he slowed to a stop in front of the fresh wound in the earth. It was a narrow fissure, more of a tear than a split, and Sreki quickly dropped to his haunches to peer over its lip.

It was strangely lit, a sourceless light that felt out of place, but he was too enthralled at the discovery to care. For there, in the dimness beneath, were the telltale curves of pots—many pots—*the* pots— and Sreki wasted no time in wriggling his way through the opening. Sharp edges of newly fractured rock caught at his flesh, leaving red furrows in his fur, but he hardly noticed. He dropped down, landing crouched and silent in the soft sand of the cave from his dreams.

They're all here... every last one of them.

His panting breaths and thudding of his heart were loud in his ears as he slowly turned, gazing at all the pots just waiting to be opened.

There it was: that small dark one, the one with the jagged blue markings, exactly as he remembered. He moved towards it, resting a shaking paw on its lid. He held his breath and twisted; he felt it shift, and the lid toppled to the sand. His eyes could not see the blinding brilliance within, but his mind could, and the rush of it was a wind that filled his head, a gust of intense cold that burst open doors that he only just realised were there, blowing down the passageways beyond, and he felt his mind stretch with it.

He staggered back, shuddering, unable to process the new paths, the new way things now were, but exhilarated nonetheless. Gasping, he reached for the second pot, the tall burgundy one, and with a simple flick of a claw its tiny lid slid clear, and windows opened within him in a noiseless roar.

Torrents flooded his mind. It was as if the rains had come and swelled the rivers to bursting, and they overflowed their banks, making new paths. But floodwaters push everything else aside—any small blockade of trees or bushes gets shoved aside and away, and the water strengthens until it makes its own paths unrelentingly.

Of course, the stone—his stone—that was Ruha, that anchor, that safe haven he could cling to as the currents in his head grew wild... Ruha was gone, and the river flowed unchecked.

It was so simple. All of it was. *I must be careful,* some other part of him thought. Yet they were all here, they had been waiting for him all this time, for so long. And he knew how they opened. Even the ones in the darker recesses of the cave—he knew how to open those too. *Just one more...*

He flung the obsidian lid aside, and lightning and thunder broke the cave around him.

Sreki awoke, crumpled by his hut, blood pooled around his muzzle. He was in the same place where he had awoken earlier, just outside its entrance. The storm was full force around him, a violent swirl of rain and wind, and it took him several moments to get his bearings. The storm did not touch him, yet he could see distant trees being torn and broken by it. He had heard of these storms before, strange circular ones, the most dangerous, with the eye of safety within them. *If I just keep within the eye...*

The cave!

Panicked, he looked towards the trail up the hillside... but there was no need. His doors were still open, and the cave was there within him. Each pot was there, and the three he had opened poured their brilliance through him. He stumbled with the force of it. Deftly he slid the obsidian lid back on. It clamped snugly to its pot, and Sreki could think again. The rush of the other two still flowed, but he could handle it now.

Old Eye, I must show Old Eye.

And then: *Oh, Ruha. I wish I could show you too.*

He staggered towards the village centre, following the storm's eye as it roiled about him, absently wiping at the fresh blood that dripped from his muzzle.

Ahead, as the storm's front continued to move, he saw the torches in the village flicker out and the panicked forms of his hyena tribemates desperately making for their huts, only to be dragged sliding across the ground by the intensity of the gale. Sreki yelled at them to take cover, but they were too slow—one by one the storm hurled them aside, breaking them on the trees and rocks, the sickening crunch of each impact cutting short the terrified screams. Briefly he saw Peshu look his way, horror on his face, before he was simply torn in half.

Old Eye, I must get to her!

Her hut was straight ahead, and he could barely make out her form at its entrance. Around her stones and trees and bodies hurtled by, yet she stood untouched, straining against it. She looked at Sreki then, her emerald eye locking onto him, and her face was full of shock and fear.

"What have you done?" She did not shout it, yet he could still hear it above the deafening storm.

"I can open them, Old Eye!" He pulled off the obsidian lid, and as it roared through his mind, he showed her what he could now do.

The bright green fire of her gaze slammed into him then, and he stumbled as the first two pots—the small dark one and the tall slender one—were immediately stoppered, their lids tight. He tore desperately at them, but they would not reopen. A detached part of his mind realised the storm had suddenly ceased, and all was quiet except the plaintive cries of hyenas broken around him—but the lids, they wouldn't budge.

They won't open!

He slowly looked up at Old Eye, and she quailed at the absolute fury in his face.

The others will, though.

He reached, and three other lids came away easily, one by one falling to the sand around him. Old Eye's emerald flame stretched towards him, seeking to silence the beauty of what he now held, and one by one, smothered by green radiance, the lids shut tight. Doors slammed closed in his mind, and he ached with the loss of the barely glimpsed wonders beyond. He cried out and in desperation sought out more—the shadowed pots, there in the far corner. They were barely visible in the dark alcoves of his cave, ancient and covered in dust.

A strange pot, weirdly shaped, greasy and mud-coloured—its lid dislodged, and the world tilted.

One of vivid blue, oddly sharp and sticky to his paws—the lid flew off, and new doors opened even as Old Eye barred others.

And a weatherbeaten wooden pot, simple and unassuming, knotted and burled. It yielded its contents with a satisfying click of its lid. When he saw what was within, he knew that she could not—*must not*—know of it. Its brightness tore through him, twisting, warping, but it was too much, too fast.

Something broke in him then, a soundless snap in his mind.

In silence and utter fury he lashed out, and Old Eye's green fire was quenched, shattered into thousands of shards, its light snuffed. He strained at the many shuttered pots, but they refused him.

Why can't I open them? What did she do?

Finally, he noticed the quiet, punctuated by occasional cries of anguish. Sreki opened his other eyes.

He stood alone, in the centre of the village. Blood drenched the earth at his paws, and unrecognisable lumps of what must once have been Old Eye were scattered far and wide. The village blurred before him, and his wounded tribemates looked upon him aghast, yelling things he didn't comprehend. He struggled to understand what he was seeing, his vision split between the cave—*his* cave—and the world around him.

"Ruha?" Sreki whimpered.

A flung spear grazed him, a hot line across his ribs, and awareness, realisation, and horror all jolted into focus.

Sreki slipped briefly on the crimson stains that were all that was left of Old Eye as he turned and bolted for the river. Those that were able charged after him; he could see each one with blinding detail, and he shut the new eyes in his mind so that he could focus on the river ahead.

He stopped then, at its banks. He reached inside himself and drew the path he desired, and wide Pindipindi let him cross. He paused and opened all his eyes. His tribemates clamoured on the far shore, screaming words that held no meaning. The agony was too much. He closed those eyes, turning away from the river, and the savanna stretched out to embrace him.

Worn-Out Tools

by Huskyteer

The grass rustled.

Bont flicked his ears, and his beady, gentle eyes blinked. Just the wind, blowing across the steppe. He kept walking, aiming for the village below the mountains. His steady three-toed plod had brought him little by little across the vast distance, and he was nearly at his destination.

"Hairy one!"

Bont turned to face the voice, snorting. A young hyena, all legs and teeth, erupted from the grass. Bont snorted again and lowered his head. The forward and greater of his two horns, as long as the hyena's body, sliced his view of the enemy in two. He blew out through his lips.

"Hairy one!" The second attack came from his left flank, but as he wheeled to face it, a third and fourth hyena closed in on his right. The four formed a box around Bont, galloping in to snap at him whenever his ample rear was exposed.

He wheeled and stamped, stamped and wheeled. The hyenas danced around him, and although they backed off when he lowered his head, they were gradually wearing out his strength. Bont tightened his grip on the skin sack he carried. It would have held all four hyenas comfortably, if he could have gathered them into it.

The biggest hyena, growing bold, sprang on his back and clung to his wool. Its teeth gnashed at Bont's hump, but couldn't penetrate the fur and fat. Bont shook it off. It rolled on the ground and jumped back up, thrashing its tail.

Bont broke into a lumbering run. Hyenas bounced off him, scrabbling for purchase. When they grew too close to his front, he swept his horns low, tripping them. In his time he had gored lions with his primary horn; broken skulls with a blow from the shorter secondary. Yelps and hoots accompanied every swing he made. His eyes, made for seeing all around, caught movement everywhere he looked.

They were so fast, moving over the grass like clouds in the sky! The spots and shading of their coats let them hide in clumps of grass or flat against the earth, bamboozling Bont so he could no longer count their number.

The village was close. He aimed his horns at the collection of skin shelters and snorted.

He stumbled as the smallest hyena rushed between his legs, and fell on the trampled pathway with a crash that shook the ground. Dust filled his eyes and his nose. The hyenas, triumphant, bounced on his hump and chased each other up and down his back.

"You cubs stop that!"

The mother hyena spoke in grunts and gestures, but her meaning was clear. The four cubs scattered, but the largest was not quick enough, and she smacked it with the side of her muzzle. Bared teeth clonked against its skull. Bont, who reared a single calf each year with his wife and would have died before he hurt it, winced.

"Welcome, hairy one," the mother hyena smiled.

Bont stood, brushing earth from his knees, and followed her to the largest of the skin shelters. The hyena village was bigger than last year, and it had pushed further north as the steppe receded. It was hard for Bont to see pictures in his mind, but as he looked at the sheets of sunbleached skin, flapping stiffly against branch props, he thought of the deer people, their soft eyes, and the graceful dances they performed.

He lifted the entrance flap and ducked to enter. He sat, and was brought water in a skin bag. The other hyenas entered one by one: the toolmaker, the hunters, and the ones who looked after the cubs.

Bont thought there were more hunters, more cubs than before, but he soon reached the limit of his counting.

"I would like some of the small things that hold small things, and a new grind stick," Bont said when he was refreshed.

"Skin pouches and a pestle, got it, got it." The mother hyena nodded enthusiastically.

Since he started his trading visits as a young woolly rhino, the hyenas had changed leader more times than Bont had toes and horns. Back then, he had understood their speech as well as they understood his. Now, they used noises when they spoke to each other that Bont could not follow. The old, simple words and gestures were for cubs, and for him.

"And what do you have for us?" asked the mother hyena. The cubs had come sneaking in along with the adults. The four that were hers, the ones who had hunted Bont, lolled panting around her.

Bont opened his skin bag. It was hyena-made, and it held many things, more than he could carry even though his hands were large. Inside, smaller pouches held herbs and mosses so they wouldn't get all mixed up.

The hyenas were so smart! They fitted flint to wooden shafts, like teeth that could bite their prey from afar, or chew the branches from trees. They made containers so they could carry and store their food and water. They made shelters for sleep, because their hides weren't thick and woolly like his. But they couldn't seek out plants the way Bont could, and they didn't have his nose for separating the ones that harmed from those that healed.

He showed the contents of his pack, spreading the dried plants out or holding the pouch of seeds up to be sniffed.

"For stomachs," he told them by pointing to his own, "for heads, for bones. This one stops bleeding. This one stops wounds going bad. This one stops pain. And *this* one—" His hand hesitated over the small, dark leaves. "This one...stops. When there is nothing more you can do."

They ate, when the bargaining was done. Bont was brought fruit in a stone bowl. The hyena mother conveyed that it was the four cubs who had gathered them for Bont's arrival, when the wind brought his scent to the village. Bont rumbled his approval and patted heads.

The toolmaker brought him what he wanted, and a new thing, too: like a spear, but with a bigger point and short shaft. The toolmaker showed that it was for digging, instead of Bont's horn. Now he could pull up delicate plants without crushing them.

Bont was fond of the toolmaker, who spoke little and watched everything. Like Bont, he looked for things and he found them, but unlike plants, the things the toolmaker sought did not exist until he found them with his mind and made them real.

The smallest hyena cub crept close to Bont and snuggled up against his side. His fingers worked the soft fur of its neck ruff. The cub stretched, splaying its overlarge paws, and laid its chin in Bont's hand.

When stomachs were full and eyes were closing, the mother leaned close to Bont.

"And the other plant?" she asked. "The danger one?"

Gently, so as not to disturb the cub at his side, Bont reached for his bag and brought out the greyish moss with its strong, bitter smell.

"Not too much," he cautioned, breaking off a tiny piece that would suit a hyena, with its light body and quick heartbeat.

"Or die," the hyena mother confirmed.

"No. Too much and come back without, without..." he tapped his head, where his mind lived.

She took the supply he gave, and left to conceal it in some secret corner.

The hyena cub slept, its head in Bont's palm. Its ears flicked and its closed eyes crinkled as it dreamed. So many thoughts in a little soft head that Bont could break like an egg!

It was warmer here than in Bont's high, far home; warmer than it had been when he first began visiting. Too warm to lie under skins, surrounded by fur and hot breath. He slid his hand out from under the sleeping cub and moved carefully between the sprawled bodies, back through the skin flap into the breeze.

He turned his head so the curved length of his horns caught the setting sun. The forward, longer than his skull, was chipped and worn from a lifetime of uprooting trees, fighting lions, and keeping other men away from his wife.

The horns were heavy, and his wool was heavy too. He lay on the ground and closed his eyes against the orange sun.

He woke to the sound of many paws running, and to yips and yelps of concern. Every hyena was in motion—in and out of the shelters, sniffing and calling. Trying to follow them all with his eyes made Bont dizzy.

When the mother hyena loped by, her eyes wide with worry and her tongue hanging out, Bont stopped her with an outstretched arm and pressed her haunches to the ground. He made her drink from his water bag and he asked what was wrong.

She conveyed that her cub—yes, the smallest, no, not the biggest or the middle-sized ones—was gone. Lost. No scent to follow. The hairy one will help look, yes? He is big and he is good at finding things. The smallest cub likes him.

Bont's eyes and nose were not as good as the hyenas', nor could his legs cover distances quickly. He could travel further than they could, yes, but too slowly to be of use to a lost cub. How long had it been missing? Hyena bodies, warm and small, cooled more quickly than Bont's large frame. And the cub was smaller than small. He wiggled his fingers as if he could still feel the flowerhead weight in his hand.

Bont was not good at seeing pictures in his mind. But he was good with plants.

"I will help," he promised.

He found a quiet spot in the shade, behind the largest shelter. The calls and footfalls of the hunting hyenas were fainter here. He opened his pack and took out the danger moss.

He had warned the mother hyena about it: how it could take you on a journey and return you changed, a shell with the nut gone. Bont had used it as many times as he had fingers and he had always come back, but he could feel that a little of himself was taken away each time, as the pestle that grinds the herbs grinds itself away too.

He broke off a section of the dried moss. Crumbs fell from it to the ground, and he carefully collected them on a damp finger so no cub could lick them up. He placed the moss in his mouth and chewed.

When it was reduced to a wet, dense clump, he tucked it with his tongue between his bottom lip and his teeth. His mouth tingled from the chewing. He settled into a comfortable sit and felt the numbness spread from his lower jaw to his neck and spine. His arms and legs got heavy, and the weight of his horns forced his head down on to his chest.

First he was falling. The ground was above him and he fell into the sky, and it was more frightening than falling the other way because there was nothing there to end the fall.

The world flipped and he was looking down from above. Had a bird of prey taken the cub? Was that the message of the moss? He saw the hyena village below him, and his self, still and calm in the middle of all the activity. With a tug to his stomach, he was lifted higher. Now he could see the whole steppe. There were his wife and this year's calf, tiny as insects but clear in every detail. He reached out to touch them, but they disappeared into the grass.

The steppe shrank. The large people, like Bont's kind and the mammoth, retreated with the grasses, huddling together, dropping in number until none remained. Meanwhile, the hyena village grew, pushing up into the former cold places, and the dancing deer people ran from the hyenas. Soon the hyenas were so many, the deer so few, that the hunters became fighters who killed hyenas from other villages and took their food.

Now the tents in the village lay empty. They fell and disappeared. The hyenas were gone like the mammoth and woolly rhino.

Too far. I need near. I need *now*. He thrashed his limbs, trying to swim back to the hyena village and his body. Instead, the sky over the vanished steppe went from blue to purple to black. Bont was closed in by walls. He stretched his arms and touched rock. At his feet, a small whimper told him he had found the hyena cub.

"I am coming for you," he told it. He tried to pet its ears, but his hand passed through. The cub shivered and tucked itself up even smaller. Its nose was to a crack in the rock, where air and a little light came in.

The cub was alive, but where was it? He pressed himself to the cave wall, trying to push through. Something caught at his throat and he knew he had swallowed some of the moss.

There was light, so much light. He was outside the cave. With the moss fizzing inside him, there were more colours in the world than he could normally see. Everything was bright and clear, as if the noon sun shone on it.

Where was this place? He didn't recognise it. And how had the little one got in? He looked hard at the rocks, thinking. There was no sign that a cave was there.

Look up, the moss told him.

He saw a fresh pale scar on the side of the mountain, where no plants grew. The moss in his mind told him that part of the mountain had fallen to block the cave entrance and trap the littlest cub.

Who knew that rocks could act that way? The hyenas could picture many things, like skin shelters and stone bowls, but none of them had pictured this. And now he had to get that picture from his mind into theirs. He stared at the mountains. He must hold on to the shape of them, to the landscape around, so the hyenas knew where to go. This was their land, not his steppe.

Bont felt that he had left himself a long way behind. He struggled as if something sticky was holding him down. He sat behind his own eyes, unable to move.

Too deep.

Too far.

Too...

High, faint yips found his ears, and he felt himself being nipped and nuzzled. He opened his eyes and saw a blur, which shaped itself into the mother hyena.

"Hairy one!" she said, nudging him anxiously with her nose. She spoke with movements of her head and paws, and with small noises: she'd thought he was dead! Did he take the danger moss? What about her cub? The scent of her, behind her words, told Bond she feared the cub was dead also.

Alive. Trapped. Let me tell you the place and you can find it. He used his arms to make the shapes he had seen. The picture was already fading from his mind as the moss left him, but the mother hyena was nodding.

"Yes. Yes! We know it! We will go!"

The hunters came with them, although Bont tried to explain there was nothing for them to hunt. The toolmaker, too. And the other cubs could not be kept away. Before the journey was halfway done, Bont was carrying two in his arms. How had the smallest come such a way by itself? It must have walked all night.

There was the mountain with the fresh scar, and there was the cave, and the rock that blocked the entrance. The mother called out, and put her head to the rock. From her face, the smallest cub had called back, but it was too faint for Bont's little ears.

The hunters prowled and sniffed, but could find no other way to get inside. It must be the rock. They put their paws on it. It did not move. They looked at Bont.

Hyenas could not do everything, and that made Bont feel happy. He looked at the rock. It was bigger than he was, and when he put his arms around it, he could not shift it either. It didn't even wobble.

He dug the tip of his forward horn into the earth, as if the rock was a plant he could uproot. The strain as he pushed made his jaws go numb and rigid. This way would not work either.

Bont walked backwards from the rock. He lined it up so his forward horn divided it into two equal parts in his view. He lowered his head.

The mountain echo turned the noise of his feet into thunder as he charged. The rock loomed up, and he closed his eyes.

He struck where he had aimed, the base of his forward horn smacking into the rock. The shock shuddered through his head and neck, and his hump trembled as it absorbed the blow.

Bont stepped back, panting. The rock had not moved. He must start from further away, run faster. He scraped the ground with a foot and paced away, counting one step for each of his toes.

The second strike sent pain shooting through his head, and little bright lights. The rock had not moved. He shook himself and tried again.

The third time, he struck wrong, and the rock tricked him so he fell. His lip was cut and bleeding. The rock had not moved.

It was harder to raise himself after he fell again. The rock had not moved. He staggered as he ran. His ears were full of bird noises and the rock wavered into two rocks. When he struck it and fell once more, the hunters leaped upon him to stop him trying again.

They poured water from a skin bag over his face, and squirted it into his mouth. The mother licked the cut on his lip with her tongue and it stopped hurting. But Bont's mind was full of the cub in the cave. Had it been scared by the banging and crashing? Or did it know Bont was trying to rescue it?

The hunters crowded the rock, trying to move it between them. But there was no room for them to push all at once in the same direction. The toolmaker barked at them to stop. When they paid no attention, he came and lay by Bont.

He had the same eyes as the smallest cub, Bont noticed, brown and gentle, and brimming with thoughts. He gazed at the rock, then back to Bont, looking up and down the curved length of the rhino's forward horn. His forehead wrinkled with the strain of all the thoughts behind it.

The mother hyena put her paws on the rock wall of the cave, as if she could touch her cub through it. Bont watched her, his chin on the ground to relieve the weight of his horns and his aching head.

The toolmaker's paw hovered above Bont's forward horn. The gentle brown eyes asked permission, and Bont nodded. He had no feeling there, so he could not sense the rough pads as they traced the dip and rise of the horn. With gestures, the toolmaker asked Bont to root up a tuft of grass from the soil in front of them.

Bont couldn't see why, but he obliged. Why not amuse the toolmaker? He was useless for anything else. He dug the tip of his horn into the earth and pulled the grass up from it with a tearing sound.

The toolmaker seemed delighted. He jumped up and began searching for something.

While his back was turned, Bont replaced the grass and covered the roots over.

The toolmaker returned with a smooth stone that filled both his paws. He placed it under Bont's forward horn, in the middle where the curve was lowest. He pointed to another tuft of grass.

The job was easier with the stone to rock his horn up and down. Bont understood, and he wanted to try the big rock immediately, but the toolmaker made him wait. He tried the stone closer to Bont's head, then closer to the rock, until he found the place where the balance was best.

Then, with the help of the hunters, the toolmaker found a bigger stone. They rolled it in front of Bont. He rested his forward horn on it and dug the tip under the rock that blocked the cave.

So many rocks and stones and people and places to keep track of! But all Bont needed to do was lift and push. The toolmaker had given him what he needed.

He rolled his shoulders, sending strength from his legs and weight from his hump into his head and horn. Resting on the stone instead of the ground gave his horn more room to swing upward, and the weight of the rock felt less.

It was still a great weight, though. Bont pushed until lights floated in his eyes again, bracing his hands and feet against the hard earth. When his feet slipped, the toolmaker scrabbled little holds for them in the ground. He pushed as if he could see the cub on the other side, as if it was his own small family trapped in the dark.

There was a dull crack, and Bont's head jerked. He fell on his side, and in the flashes in his eyes he saw his wife and calf. Something was different and wrong, so different and wrong that he could not tell what it was. He blinked away dust and saw the smallest cub scamper from a black gap in the mountain where the rock had moved.

He was not hurt? In spite of the shock and the noise, his limbs were straight, and he could turn his head.

His head. The white line of his forward horn, like a tree with no branches dividing his world, was gone from his sight. He saw it lying on the ground, a dead thing bloody at the base where it had snapped away from his head.

Bont had never seen the toolmaker so agitated. The hyena indicated with pats and waving paws that perhaps they could stick his horn back on? Or make Bont a spear, such a good spear, longer than his horn and straight instead of curved?

"No," Bont said. He lifted his head. It felt light, and he raised it higher. He stood straight. "I don't need. I will last as long as I last."

The other cubs were already playing with his horn, jumping over it and chewing it. The toolmaker moved to stop them, but Bont reached them first and picked up this piece of himself, the familiar become strange.

He handled it for a few moments, running his fingers along the chips and scratches. Then he held it out to the cubs. They took it in their mouths, fought over it and ran about with it, their tails high.

The mother hyena's voice was full of love and fear and anger. As she held and licked the smallest cub, she was asking it why. What had made it run from the village and cover such a huge distance? The squeaked and snuffled response was not one Bont could understand.

"She says she wants to be a finder and travel with things to trade," the mother told him, her voice gruff with a break in it. "Like you."

Howling to the Moon

by J.F.R. Coates

There was no such thing as silence. Even the quietest movement created a noise for sensitive ears to detect, and the forest was full of hundreds upon thousands of noises. Leaves rustled. Birds chirped. Twigs cracked underpaw. For ears as large as a hare's, those noises should have aroused suspicion, but the three by the stream that flowed through the forest didn't even twitch a nose.

The wolf in the shadows didn't care about the hares spotting him. He knew what their stronger senses were. Slowly, he crept. Keeping to the shadows. Avoiding the fallen leaves and branches. It wasn't long until he was almost at the edge of the trees. Their scent filled his nose, carried by the wind directly towards him.

There were three of them, crouched by the bank of the narrow stream, their backs turned to the wolf in the shadows. One laughed at a joke told by another.

Before they could spot him, the wolf pounced. Arms wrapped around the hare's body, twisting upon impact to drag the prey animal from his feet. Wolf and hare rolled and splashed into the stream, predator on top of prey.

The wolf poked his cold nose to the throat of the hare. "Got you. I could have been any predator hunting you."

White Tuft said nothing, though the other two hares started to giggle. The wolf's ears pinned back at the laughter. Had he gotten something wrong?

"Oh, Found Moon," Grey Ear said, nose twitching in amusement, even as the giggles died off. "We heard you before you even set paw in the woods."

Found Moon hadn't realised his ears could pin back farther. They did, and he slowly leaned back to release White Tuft from beneath him. "You did?" he whimpered softly, a whine coming to his voice in a way only a wolf could manage. "I thought I was being really quiet."

Wandering Star held out her hand to help White Tuft out of the stream. She did not offer Found Moon the same courtesy. "Quiet for a wolf, maybe," she said, cocking a smile to the other hares.

"Then why did you let me jump you?" Found Moon asked. He lowered his eyes, hunching his shoulders to lessen the height difference between himself and his adopted siblings.

"A wolf has to feel like a predator sometimes, or else their teeth start to fall out," Grey Ear said.

"Here, come and see what we've done with the nets," White Tuft said, distracting Found Moon before he could raise his voice in protest.

The wolf tucked his tail between his legs as he allowed White Tuft to lead him towards what the hares had been working on before his interruption. They had been weaving reeds into nets, creating a strong mesh that could be used to toss into the stream or the nearby lake to catch fish.

"We've tried a new way of weaving," White Tuft said. He took the partially completed net in both hands and tugged at a few of the segments. The reeds barely moved. "This way should be a lot stronger, so we're not having to repair them all the time."

"Yeah, but they take so much longer to make," Grey Ear grumbled. He slumped down on the bank, picking up one of the unfinished parts of the net. He started to weave a few strands together, using a fishbone needle to tease the reeds into a regular pattern. He didn't get far before dramatically sighing, his long grey ears draped against his shoulders.

Found Moon resisted the urge to shake the water from his fur as he crouched close to Grey Ear. "Can you show me how? I'd like to learn."

Wandering Star laughed. She pushed both hands against Found Moon's chest, making him topple into the stream again. "A wolf's hands aren't delicate enough to weave a net like this. Just be happy with eating our catch."

The wolf didn't resist the urge this time. He shook the water from his fur, his loincloth almost slipping off from the vigorous movement, with only a quick grab from his hand keeping it in place. His eartips blushed, but the hares either did not notice, or simply did not comment on it. "I'm always thankful you catch fish for me," Found Moon mumbled, hoping to distract from his embarrassment.

"And because of that, we're never short of their bones," White Tuft said, grinning widely on her short muzzle. She tossed an empty basket towards the wolf, who clumsily caught it. "If you're wanting to be useful, go and forage some food for us."

"Make sure you don't get the poisonous berries this time," Wandering Star said.

"But do get those hazelnuts if you can sniff them out," Grey Ear added. He licked his lips.

Found Moon sighed. Not as dramatically as Grey Ear had. A smile touched his muzzle as he did so, tucking the reed basket beneath his arm. The hares, especially his three adopted siblings, helped to keep him fed in a tribe of herbivores. It was only fair that he helped seek out food for them, especially when his nose was able to detect some of their favourite foods hidden amongst the foliage.

Leaving the hares to the net, Found Moon returned to the forest. He hoped his hunt for berries and nuts was more successful than his failed stalking of his siblings. It could hardly go much worse.

Many years of experience had taught Found Moon what to forage for. He knew what hares liked to eat, what was good for them, and what was considered a rare delicacy. He ate little of it himself, with most of their diet disagreeing violently with his stomach and tongue.

The wolf's thoughts wandered as his paws did, meandering through the forest as he slowly filled the basket. His nose led him towards a small grove of hazelnuts, and he made sure to remember just where those trees grew. It wasn't just Grey Ear who adored them.

As he hunted for plants, Found Moon became aware of another scent on the wind. It was an unusual one, something that was both familiar and unknown at the same time, and he soon realised why. The scent on the wind reminded him of his own smell. There had been wolves here, though the scent was old. A few days at least. A concern, but not one that needed him to rush back to his siblings.

Found Moon remained vigilant for the wolves, each sense on alert, but he detected nothing but the stale, old scent. All the same, the presence of wolves disturbed him. There had been none in the area since... well, ever since he had been found sixteen summers ago. He could only hope the wolves were merely passing through the area, because if they had come to stay, then the hares would be in great danger.

The light began to fail, the sky painted vivid orange. Found Moon made his way back to the stream, his arms laden with the heavy basket of food and his mind occupied with thoughts of the wolves. He heard his siblings long before he saw them, laughing and joking noisily with each other, with the occasional loud splash of water. They had not learned of the wolves, then.

Grey Ear was the first to notice Found Moon. The hare crowed in delight and bounded across to the wolf, saying nothing as he rummaged through the basket of food until he found a couple of hazelnuts. His eyes were bright as he quickly crunched his powerful teeth into them, ears aquiver as he closed his eyes.

The other two were slower, taking care to fold up the net and place it on top of a basket of their own, which had a few fresh fish at the bottom. Found Moon's stomach growled at the thought of food, a little weary after a long day foraging for the hares.

Wandering Star grumbled about a missing fishbone needle, lost in the mud and the fading light. Once, that would have been an unfortunate loss for the tribe, but with Found Moon's diet, they had a reason to keep catching fish. There was no shortage of fish bones now.

Grey Ear and Wandering Star bounded ahead, chatting loudly to each other as they picked their way through the well-worn trail that cut through the forest. The shadows grew long and dark around them. Any one of them could have contained a wolf, a danger to them that Found Moon could never truly represent. Even though his nose confirmed there were none around, he still worried.

"You seem distracted," White Tuft said, walking alongside the wolf. He, like all hares, walked with a bouncing gait. Even with his long ears and the way Found Moon hunched, he barely reached the wolf's shoulders.

Found Moon twitched his nose, unsure how much to say. He didn't want to panic the hare, but nor did he want to put them in danger by saying nothing. He kept his voice low, hoping that the two ahead were too distracted by their conversation to listen back. "I thought I smelled some wolves while I was out there. An old scent, a few days at least."

"I've heard nothing," White Tuft replied. His ears were perked, alert to their surroundings. "If they're close, then they're much better than you at walking quietly. And no matter what the others say, you're almost as good as a hare at being silent."

"Almost isn't good enough, though," Found Moon said, sighing.

White Tuft lightly shoved against the wolf. "We're silent so we can survive. You don't have to worry about that. Nothing, thinking animal or not, is going to hunt a wolf."

"Except another wolf. One who knows how to properly hunt," Found Moon muttered. He lowered his eyes and tucked his tail between his legs.

"We'll be careful," White Tuft said, resting his hand against the wolf's elbow. "If we need to leave home again, we'll bring protection, and they're not going to be able to touch us inside the walls."

Found Moon chanced a quick glance up. Through the trees, he could see the walls the hare spoke of. A massive wooden palisade that protected the homes inside, far taller than even the wolf. The thought of a pack of hunting wolves breaching the palisade did seem absurd to Found Moon, but he still worried.

Sanctuary was on top of a low hill, cleared of trees, though the forest continued almost entirely around the settlement. Many of those trees felled to make way for the settlement had then been used to construct the palisade, with the massive trunks bound together and anchored deep in the ground to provide a protective wall around the hill.

Two deep ditches ran around its perimeter, outside the palisade. Further logs were embedded on the inner bank of the ditches, jutting out with the ends whittled to sharp points. Any predator who dared to charge for Sanctuary would end in a bloody and painful way.

There was only one small entrance to Sanctuary, a narrow path that crested the ditches and into a small gateway through the palisade. Found Moon paused at the entrance, turning back to face the sun against the horizon. He held his claw-tipped fingers to his heart and muttered a quiet prayer, asking for the sun to return safely the next morning.

Found Moon followed his siblings into Sanctuary, the gate dragged open for their arrival, and pushed closed again once the wolf stepped inside. The gate was secured by a heavy log rolled into position, with four hares needed to move the fallen tree.

Nearly two dozen roundhouses dotted the summit of the hill, all loosely surrounding an open area at the highest point of the settlement. Around the edge of Sanctuary, just inside the palisade, grew the crops that supplemented the foraging, barley and corn grown throughout the warmer months to provide a surplus of food and other supplies for the hares to use.

Wandering Star embraced another hare who bounded out of one of the roundhouses to greet the returning group. Long Paw was their mother, short even for a hare, but capable of a glare that could quell even the mightiest predator. That glare was nowhere to be seen for the moment. Her nose twitched as she approached Found Moon, her eyes on the basket of food he carried.

"Come to the fire," Long Paw said, taking the basket from Found Moon's hands. "The night will be cold, but the fire is bright and hot, and we have food already prepared for you all."

Found Moon lifted his nose to the cool air. Smoke drifted on the breeze, coming from the massive bonfire lit in the very centre of Sanctuary, at the highest point. Most of the hares were already gathered around its base, preparing food or tending to the flames.

Guided by Long Paw, Found Moon made his way towards the edge of the fire. A few hares looked up at his arrival, ears flicking or noses twitching, but no vocal greeting was given.

Found Moon took a seat a little away from anyone else, a few paces from the edge of the fire. The heat bristled at his fur, keeping away the start of the evening's chill as the sunlight gradually faded from the sky. The first stars twinkled into life, spreading through the inky darkness above. It took all Found Moon's willpower to keep his eyes down, or else he would lose much of the night to stargazing.

Instead, the wolf focused on preparing the fish the hares had caught for him. Not only was it food, but he also needed to extract the delicate but useful bones, which would then be used by the tribe for tools. Wandering Star watched him from a short distance, her nose twitching. She always looked on the verge of saying something, but shut her mouth at the last moment every time.

Found Moon smirked. He knew what she was thinking. Usually she handled the delicate tasks, but like most hares, she didn't like handling meat. That was a task for the wolf, in spite of his big, clumsy hands.

A flint blade made short work of the fish, slicing through its scales and flesh with ease. He began to fill two stone plates; one for the flesh he planned to cook, and another for the bones intact enough to turn into tools. His progress was slow, and all around he could hear the hares feasting on the day's food. Only Wandering Star didn't eat, her eyes fixed on the wolf's work.

"You're getting better at that," Wandering Star said, once Found Moon had finished the entire catch.

Found Moon's smirk grew into a grin. He waggled his fingers at the hare. "More useful than you think, aren't they?"

The hare giggled. "I wouldn't say that. But you're more than just claw and muscle. Usually."

Found Moon stuck out his tongue. His ears flicked back, a poor imitation of the expression and movement the hares possessed. As difficult as Wandering Star could be out in the wild, she was always relaxed and fun to be around in Sanctuary.

Wandering Star held out a hazelnut. "Want to try one?"

Found Moon's tongue retreated into his mouth. "Wh-what?"

The hare grinned. "A hazelnut. Do you want one?" The hint of a giggle came to her voice.

Instinct demanded that he wrinkle his nose and turn away, saying no. But he didn't. He hesitated. Then he shrugged. "Alright. But only if you try some fish."

Wandering Star's giggles stopped. She twitched her nose and stared at the fish Found Moon had prepared. "Alright, I'll try it."

Found Moon carefully picked out a small piece of fish and smoked it in the fire. Wandering Star watched on curiously, leaning over his shoulder with her nose twitching. She already had a couple of hazelnuts grasped tightly in her small hand.

Once the small sliver of meat was ready, Found Moon pulled it away from the flames. He presented it to Wandering Star, who stared at it uncertainly. Her nose wrinkled, and she reached out with one hand, only to withdraw again.

The wolf was aware of a number of eyes watching them. The attention of most of Sanctuary was upon them both. Wandering Star seemed to recognise the audience at the same moment, as her hand lashed out and grabbed the fish from the wolf. Before putting the meat in her mouth, she made sure to press one of the hazelnuts into Found Moon's hand.

"Ready?" the hare asked.

In answer, Found Moon shoved the hazelnut into his mouth and attempted to chew. Instead, his teeth crunched down on the tough nut, splintering it into many jagged pieces that felt like they tore at his tongue and lips. He almost spat out the dry shards, but he looked up to see Wandering Star valiantly chewing, her nose wrinkled in disgust as she worked her jaw. If she could do this, then so could he.

With a great effort, Found Moon crunched and winced his way through the hazelnut, the taste like licking the bark of a tree trunk. He forced himself to swallow, then immediately grimaced and reached for the closest waterskin. He tried to ignore the raucous laughter that surrounded him.

"That was like eating rocks," he gasped, taking a mouthful of water and swilling it around. He couldn't taste any blood, but he couldn't be sure the nut hadn't torn open the soft flesh of his mouth.

"And that was like chewing on wet mud," Wandering Star retorted. She stuck out her tongue, but there was no trace of the fish left. She held one hand over her gut. "How about I stick to my food, and you stick to yours."

Found Moon shuddered. "I think I can manage that."

Wandering Star managed a grin, despite her twitching nose. "I didn't think you'd actually do it. Perhaps we can still make a good hare out of you after all."

White Tuft laughed loudly. He leaned over Wandering Star, his hands on her shoulders. "Come on. We all love Found Moon, but I think it's clear he's a pretty awful hare," he said loudly. The firelight twinkled in his eye as he winked at the wolf.

More laughter rippled around the fire. This time, Found Moon didn't mind joining in. He knew exactly what he was, and never pretended otherwise. He didn't aim to be a hare. He was simply happy being a part of Sanctuary, wolf and all.

The night deepened, but around the fire the cold air of the darkness was kept at bay. No one was short of food, not the hares who shared amongst each other, nor the wolf who had the entire supply of fish to himself. Water was plentiful, from the spring that bubbled out from the ground, inside the walls of the palisade. And far above them, the moon's pale face gazed down upon it all, almost full.

Found Moon's eyes were naturally drawn to her cold light, a smile on his muzzle as he stared as though transfixed. He forgot everything around him, lost to that beautiful sight, ignorant of all other senses. At least, until someone elbowed him in the ribs. His attention snapped back to Sanctuary to hear the giggles of the hares.

"You should do your wolf thing," one of them cried out. Found Moon thought it might have been Grey Ear, but his head was still too full of thoughts of the moon to pay enough attention.

"What?" Found Moon asked, his ears warming as they flicked back, almost flat against the top of his head. "No, I shouldn't. It's..."

Any protests were quickly drowned out. "Go on. Do it," another hare shouted. And then a second, and a third. Soon, what felt like half the community demanded it of him.

Even with his ears growing hotter and his tail tucked against his legs, Found Moon acceded to their calls. He stood up to cheers, which quickly fell silent as he lifted his head and closed his eyes, feeling the moonlight on his face. He breathed in deep, turning his head slightly to avoid the worst of the smoke. Then he opened his eyes and gazed into the moon.

"Ao-ao-aaoooo!"

The rapid barks turned into a powerful howl, ripping itself out of his throat and calling to the untouchable moon. The fur on the back of his neck lifted, hackles rising as a surge of power flowed through his body, a feeling of joy and righteousness.

Half a dozen hares tried to join in, making little yipping noises that were poor imitations of Found Moon's powerful howl. The wolf arched his back and thrust his head up, unleashing another howl that easily drowned out anything the hares could muster.

Another howl responded. Distant. Quiet. Lupine.

A deathly hush fell on Sanctuary.

Suddenly the fire didn't feel quite so warm after all.

Found Moon woke early, beating the first of the sun's light. He rarely slept well at night, preferring instead to sit and stare at the stars, but after the distant howl the previous night, everyone had been keen to get back to the safety and security of the roundhouses, Found Moon included.

Smoke still drifted across the settlement, from the smouldering remains of the fire that had not lasted the night. The scent of charcoal settled on Sanctuary like a lingering bad dream, a reminder of the festivities that had been cut short.

Found Moon crawled out of the roundhouse, moving quietly so he didn't wake his siblings or adopted mother. The dried mud walls of the hut kept much of the night's chill out, but Found Moon still shivered as he shrugged off the nest of woven reeds and leaves that he used as a blanket.

As usual, few hares were awake before the sun. Only two guards stood watch by the gate, their backs turned to the roundhouses. Found Moon knew from experience that they could barely see anything in the darkness, but their ears were usually strong enough to detect any movement.

Found Moon shivered and hugged his arms close to his body. A strong wind blew, coming up from the gatehouse, rustling the grass and reed rooves as it whistled over Sanctuary and the summit of the hill.

The wolf slowly moved towards that summit, where he would get a better view of the first light of day. Already, the sky was beginning to pale pink towards the horizon. From inside the roundhouses, he could hear the hares beginning to stir. Their scents were masked by the haze of smoke, which also stung at Found Moon's eyes. The strong wind was playing havoc with the remnants of the fire. No one must have tended to it after the worries of the previous night.

A catch of sudden pain in his foot startled Found Moon. He yelped and stumbled forward, his eyes torn from the hazy sky to the ground underfoot. Small, dark stains splotched the earth.

Blood. The smoke had obscured the scent, but now he knew it was there, the tang of blood was all he could smell.

While his tired mind tried to reason why there was blood on the grass, Found Moon idly reached to pick at whatever had jabbed into his foot. He expected a sharp stone or broken sherd of pot. Instead, he found a tooth. Not a small, blunt one belonging to a hare. Sharp and curved, like his own.

His hand moved to his mouth, feeling around his jaw. None of his teeth were missing. "Wolves," he whispered. He struggled even to get the word out around the lump in his throat, the fear that gripped his chest and made his body hot in terror. They had been here. Inside Sanctuary. They had spilled blood.

The word came to Found Moon's mouth again. This time, instead of a quiet whisper, it was a howling cry. "Wolves! Wolves were here! Is everyone safe?"

Those hares that had not yet woken were roused by Found Moon's cry. They hurried from the huts, some already carrying flint knives and spears. There was no enemy to find, even as they clustered around Found Moon and the blood spilled on the ground. A nervous clamour grew as the hares demanded to know what had happened.

"Search all of Sanctuary," Long Paw said, speaking loudest of all. "See if anyone is missing."

A search quickly went out, covering the entire hill within the palisade. Found Moon hunted differently. Instead of hare, he sought the wolf who had come into Sanctuary. Using sight as much as nose, he tracked the small patches of blood that created a trail, following the path the wolf and its victim had taken through the settlement. A couple of interested hares mimicked his moves, but their eyes wouldn't be much use here.

The trail led away from the centre of the settlement, but it did not go towards the only entrance at the gate. That had been guarded all night. There would have been no way in or out for any wolves through there. Instead, the trail came to the palisade wall.

"Did they climb in?" one hare asked, her voice a hushed and awed whisper.

Found Moon could see no other way. They must have climbed in, though craning his neck high enough to see the top of the wall made him dizzy. The wolves had not damaged the wall in any way.

The wolf put his hand on the massive wooden logs, once the trunks of towering trees. Any number of the small pockmarks and blemishes in the wood could have been caused by wolf claws as they clambered up the palisade. The small splatters of blood, however, had to be from a wounded hare carried by wolves.

Whispers spread through Sanctuary, all indistinct and merging into each other as Found Moon looked up. It must have been a dedicated wolf to climb so high, especially with a struggling hare. At least, Found Moon hoped the hare struggled. He would feel much better if that was the case, as it would mean no one had died. Not yet, anyway.

Those whispers began to converge, as more and more hares were identified as safe and present. Wandering Star and White Tuft were amongst them, but one name remained absent. One hare missing. Found Moon went cold, his claws digging into the hard wood of the palisade.

Grey Ear was gone.

"How did they get in?" one hare asked.

"Do we build the walls higher?" another added.

Found Moon's claws scratched through the wood. "I need to get him back," he said through gritted teeth.

Silence rippled out through the hares, starting with those close enough to hear him. His words gradually spread back to those furthest away, leaving nervous silence in their wake.

"How?" someone finally asked. Wandering Star, her voice cracked with tears barely held back.

Found Moon slowly turned to face the hares. A few held onto each other. Some hid behind ears flopped forward, with others unable to hold back tears. One of their number was gone, taken by wolves. By a predator like him.

One of the hares spoke before he could. "How can you get him back?" Bright Eye demanded. He was an elder of the village, his fur no longer possessing the lustre of youth, but his eyes remained as bright as his name suggested. "Our precious Grey Ear is probably already dead, killed by a predator like you. What's to stop you from doing the same to us?"

Found Moon lifted his hands and stepped back, bumping against the palisade. "I would never," he protested. He was glad that no other hares joined in with Bright Eye's accusation, but his ears still pinned back. He lowered his eyes, staring at the feet of the closest hares. "I hope none of you feel I am a danger to you, that I might hunt you like these wolves have done. But I am still a wolf. I can use that to bring Grey Ear back."

"How?" Bright Eye challenged.

Found Moon didn't look up. "I can track them, follow their scent. I can find where they're resting. I'm a wolf, they'll let me get close to them. Much closer than any of you could," he said slowly. His eyes lifted slightly, just enough to look to the necks of the nearest hares. "I might even be able to convince them to go away and leave Sanctuary alone."

"But how will you get them to listen to you?" Long Paw asked, her voice gentle and soft, especially compared to the angry demands of Bright Eye.

The wolf's head dropped again. "I don't know yet, but I have to try."

"Then you'll need this," Long Paw said. She held out a spear, tipped with a flint head. The weapon was almost as tall as the hare, the shaft carefully carved from wood to give the vulnerable prey animals a better weapon against predators that might take a fancy to thinking animals.

Found Moon didn't take the offered weapon. "They won't let me get close if I come with a weapon. Especially not a prey weapon," he said slowly. He stared down at his hands, rubbing one finger against a claw of the opposite hand. "These are the only weapons a wolf will respect."

"If it comes to a fight, you won't have a chance," Wandering Star said. She took the spear from her mother and turned it in her hands, prodding the butt of the weapon against Found Moon's chest. "Take it."

This time, Found Moon took it. He ran his hands down the long shaft. Then, with a surge of strength, he took the shaft just beneath the flint head and snapped it in two. A few hares gasped and stepped back as the wolf threw aside the broken shaft. He was left with the flint blade on barely a hand's breadth of wood left.

"Get me some reed," the wolf said gruffly. The shortened spear was light in his hand. He practiced a couple of thrusts into empty air. "I can tie this to my loincloth. Keep it hidden."

No one argued with the wolf. Found Moon didn't know if it was because they didn't dare, or that they had genuine hope that he could come back with Grey Ear. Or that they were glad to be rid of him. None of that mattered. He didn't care what they thought of him. He only cared what he thought of himself, and that meant trying. He had to try to get Grey Ear back.

It didn't take long to get the reed he needed. To the wolf's embarrassment, it was Long Paw who helped him secure the broken flint spear to the inside of his loincloth. His ears flushed hot, and he forced himself to stand still as the hare he considered his mother played around at his crotch. She secured the spear tip with reed, also using a small sheath of thick leaves to cover the sharp flint.

The gathered crowd of onlookers never once moved away, though a few did avert their eyes until his loincloth was put back in position. The extra weight of the spear made his clothing sit uncomfortably, but he knew he would feel better for its presence. He wasn't throwing himself at the wolf pack unarmed.

"You know you don't have to do this," Wandering Star said quietly. She stood back a couple of paces from her mother, with White Tuft by her side.

Found Moon couldn't quite meet her eyes. "I must," he said. "No matter what, I will bring Grey Ear back."

Left unsaid was the fear that Wandering Moon would bring back Grey Ear already dead. Even worse, the thought that he would only bring back devoured remains. That would be better than doing nothing.

"Bring him home. Please," Long Paw said. Her lip trembled. Then she turned away.

Found Moon wanted to say something. Anything. But he didn't know what would make things better. He couldn't make promises he had no guarantee of keeping. He began to walk in silence, with his back straight and head held high. He tried not to think that this might be his last time in Sanctuary.

Finding Grey Ear was all that mattered.

Picking up the scent of the wolves was not difficult. They had made no effort to hide their tracks, running through the forest and leaving behind a trail of broken branches and obvious pawprints. There was no sign of blood, either on the ground or the leaves the wolves had pushed past. If they had Grey Ear, then he was likely not badly injured. Found Moon refused to think about it. He didn't want to give himself too much hope.

Forest eventually gave way to open plains, long grass rustling in the wind and undulating over the low hills stretching to the horizon. The weight of the trees hanging over his shoulders lifted, and the wolf felt a freedom surging through his mind and body that warred with the anxiety in his gut. He couldn't bring himself to be happy, but he did allow his legs to stretch, his strides lengthening as he sprinted in a way he could not do in the forest.

He was born to run in a way hares were not. Sure, they could outpace a wolf over a very short distance, but over more than a hundred strides, a hare could never hope to beat him. Of course, the wolves he hunted had that same freedom, that same strength. He could not hunt down the wolf pack in the wild. He would have to negotiate with them in their camp, wherever that was.

The scent of wolf grew gradually stronger. Each time the wind shifted it drew more of that unfamiliar yet intimate smell to his nose. Found Moon couldn't be sure if he was close to overtaking his quarry, or if their settlement was nearby. The wolves had to live somewhere close. It would be futile hunting too far out from a place where they could rest.

He heard the wolves before he saw them. The pack made no attempt to be quiet, speaking loudly amongst themselves, the exact nature of their words obscured by distance and the wind. They were hidden behind a low rise, so Found Moon cautiously climbed, trying to avoid making any noise himself. At least he was downwind of the wolves, so they would not be able to smell his approach.

Found Moon expected to see a settlement, like Sanctuary. The wolf pack did not live in such a place. They lived at the base of a hill, nestled in a valley, vulnerable to predators. No palisade protected them. Instead, they dwelt in a simple cluster of hideskin tents surrounding a firepit. The closest thing to defences they had were the mammoth tusks and ribs stacked around the largest of the tents.

At first, Found Moon couldn't find the hunting party. Brief worries that he had tracked the wrong wolves flared in his mind, but his pounding heart quickly calmed when he caught sight of them, already around the back of the tents. His blood boiled anew when he saw Grey Ear slung over the shoulder of one wolf. The hare moved, a futile twitch of bound limbs. He was still alive.

Found Moon crouched low as he tried to work out how to approach. He didn't want to recklessly charge forward without a plan in mind. He needed to wait, to be confident of what he needed to do and how to do it.

A hand to his back put all such thoughts from his mind. He froze, barely daring even to breathe. He could smell nothing. Hear nothing. To all his senses, he should have been alone.

If the hand hadn't been enough, the low growl was certainly realisation that he had attracted unwanted company. He struggled not to cower, to shrink lower to the ground. That was what a hare might do. Here, he had to be a wolf. A confident predator. Perhaps he should have swatted the hand away or growled back. He did neither. Frozen in fear, he waited for the other wolf to speak.

"Hunting outside your territory, little pup?"

The other wolf grasped Found Moon by the scruff, hauling him to his feet with unexpected strength. A tight grip held him in place, leaving any struggle futile. His feet dangled off the ground, the loose skin of his neck pulled tight and uncomfortable in the grip of the wolf. Slowly, Found Moon was turned, then thrown back to the ground.

He faced up, his eyes wide. Above him towered the first wolf he had ever seen up close. The predator was massive, covered in thick, shaggy fur plastered in mud and grime. That mud had masked the wolf's scent, hiding it beneath the smell of the land. Admiration briefly warred with fear, but all confidence and courage fled as the predator bared his teeth, exposing yellowed fangs flecked with traces of blood from his last kill.

"A mute, are you?" the hunter asked.

Found Moon managed to shake his head. "No, I can speak." He forced the words out from his muzzle, his voice pitched high in a near squeak.

The hunter sneered. "So you can. Perhaps you can use your tongue to explain why you're in our territory."

"I, uh..." Found Moon's eyes flicked to the side, struggling to focus on the hunter. His throat was dry. His tongue lashed at his lips, running over his sharp teeth. "I need to..."

"Out with it," the hunter snapped.

Found Moon swallowed his fear. He looked up, but he couldn't quite meet the hunter in the eyes. He settled for the dirty white fur of the wolf's throat. "I want to see your chief."

A wide grin broke out across the hunter's muzzle. He held out one hand to Found Moon, muddy claws gripping tightly against the flesh of the smaller wolf. "Well, why didn't you say so before? I can take you to the chief. He just got back from a hunt."

Found Moon immediately regretted the request. He did not like the predatory gleam in the hunter's eyes. Every instinct told him to run, to run fast and far away, back to Sanctuary if he could. But the hunter's grip on his wrist was too strong to break. Feeling like he was almost as much prey to these wolves as Grey Ear, Found Moon reluctantly followed the hunter towards the small village of tents.

They quickly gained attention. Sharp, eager eyes tracked their movement towards the tents. Found Moon had always felt a giant amongst the hares, with even the tallest of them barely coming up to his shoulder. He was just as short to these wolves as the hares were to him. His shoulders hunched, further diminishing his size as he cowered by the hunter's side.

Found Moon quickly lost sight of Grey Ear. He tried not to keep too focused on the hare, not yet. The wolf pack probably wouldn't treat him too kindly if they realised that he was after their prey. His thoughts raced, struggling to work out a way to free himself from the hunter's grip, and also to get away from the camp with Grey Ear alive. His foolish declaration that he would make it safely back to Sanctuary seemed a difficult challenge now.

There were more offerings and talismans around the edge of the largest tent. Strewn amongst the mammoth bones lay the remains of other hunts, as well as small trinkets of carved wood and chipped stone, likely stolen from thinking animals who had been preyed upon. The young wolf could see no evidence that the vicious pack made any tools or weapons of their own.

Found Moon was thrown to the ground in front of the large tent. He scuffed his knees against the coarse, dry dirt, and for a moment he thought his loincloth, weighted with the flint knife inside, was about to dislodge and expose himself in front of the pack. Fortunately, no such embarrassment happened, but before Found Moon could work out whether he was expected to stand or remain prostrate on the ground, another wolf emerged from the tent. Even from the size of his paws, Found Moon knew this wolf was bigger than any of the others he had seen in the camp. His head slowly lifted, higher and higher.

"Who is this?" the massive chief growled. He nudged his foot against Found Moon's shoulder. There was little the smaller wolf could see, his vision dominated by the chief's muscular legs and loincloth.

"I'm not sure, Chief Ripper," the hunter said, from somewhere just behind Found Moon. "I caught him skulking after our raiders."

The chief sneered. "Ah, a thief, then? A wandering outcast left to scrounge off the scraps of superior hunters?"

Found Moon opened his mouth to protest, then snapped it shut again. He would not get any opportunity to rescue Grey Ear by picking fights with the wolves, especially when all the advantages of size and strength lay with them. He bowed his head, ears folding flat. "Yes. I came to learn from better hunters, so that I might provide for myself and my pack."

A ripple of laughter spread through the watching wolves. Found Moon struggled to ignore them, his tail tucked low. He kept his eyes down, not looking any higher than the chief's knees. He was fully aware of the larger wolf's fierce gaze, like heat burning on the back of his neck.

"Why should we share our food with a pup who cannot hunt for himself?" the chief asked, a deep snarl coming into his voice. A few drops of saliva dripped onto Found Moon's muzzle. The smaller wolf kept his hands on the ground, not daring to wipe it away.

"I do not come asking for food," Found Moon said quietly. He swallowed, his tongue feeling twice the size, his throat parched like he had not tasted water in days. "I merely ask that I watch and learn. Please, give me until tomorrow night at least."

The chief did not answer. Not immediately, though the dribbles of saliva continued to fall. His massive feet shuffled closer, the curved claws on each of his toes almost close enough for Found Moon to touch with his muzzle. They each looked a deadly weapon, far more perfect and precise than the jagged piece of flint hidden beneath his loincloth.

"You are fortunate," the chief finally said. A hefty hand closed around Found Moon's shoulder and dragged him back to his feet. The smouldering gaze of the chief's bright yellow eyes met his. "Tonight is one of generosity. The moon will be full, and we must sing our praises to the spirits that guide it through the sky. You may join us for the night, and we shall see what tomorrow brings."

Found Moon could barely stop his tail wagging. He didn't yet know how, but he would have a chance to save Grey Ear. The wolves were giving him that opportunity. He struggled to keep the emotion from his voice as he lowered his eyes. "Thank you, Chief Ripper."

The large wolf snorted in amusement. "What is your name, pup?"

"Found Moon. My name is Found Moon." A ripple of laughter spread through the pack. Found Moon's ears reddened, his head and tail low. The wolves of the pack chuckled to each other, a few even repeating his name in mocking tones.

The chief did not join in the laughter, but a smile twisted at his muzzle. He held up his hand. Silence fell. "Welcome, Found Moon," he said, somehow turning the name into a mocking insult. "We trust you will enjoy our ceremony."

Before Found Moon could question the chief, the massive wolf had turned away, barking orders to the pack. Found Moon backed away, making himself small as the wolves forgot about their mockery. The sun was beginning to sink towards the horizon, with the sky already starting to darken. The moon had not yet risen from beyond the forest, but the wolves seemed to know it was coming with a certainty that had not reached Found Moon.

The wolves prepared a space in the centre of the encampment, clearing away the tents closest to the blackened firepit. Meat came from seemingly nowhere, placed with reverence around the fire once it was lit. None of it seemed to be from thinking animals, though Found Moon couldn't be sure. All meat looked and smelled the same once it was skinned and prepared. A brief panic settled in his gut, fearing he might already be too late for Grey Ear, but as he moved around the camp, trying to keep out of the way, he caught scent of the hare. Fresh and alive. Held captive inside the chief's tent.

The pack ignored Found Moon, but for a few snide glances and avoidable bumps into his shoulder. It was more than a feast that they prepared. Grass was scraped away to bare dirt, with sticks and branches plundered from the forest to partition off a small square in front of the fire pit. Carved bones were deposited around the simple, ankle-high wall.

Then came the drums. Found Moon's eyes widened, his mouth hanging partially open, as three wolves dragged them from one of the tents. The bases of the drums were carved exquisitely from polished wood, with taut animal hide stretched over the top. Found Moon had no doubt they were stolen from elsewhere. He longed to approach the instruments and run his hands over them, but held himself back. He wasn't there to enjoy the ceremony. He needed to find a way to get Grey Ear to safety, but there was always at least one wolf with their eyes on him, or on the entrance to the chief's tent.

The first howl rang out just as the last light of the sun dipped below the horizon. The fur on the back of Found Moon's neck lifted. He looked to the western sky, holding two fingers to his heart. But he was the only one who looked to the dying light of the sun. He quickly turned, ears folded, as he looked to the opposite horizon with the others.

The pack stood in silence, all perfectly still. Darkness swathed the sky, even as the stars burned brighter. A cool wind rippled through Found Moon's fur, coming down from the hills that darkened the far horizon to his left, further away from Sanctuary and the forest.

Pale white light breached the horizon. The moon lifted from below the world, bright and full. And still the wolves waited. They breathed harsh and heavy, chests heaving as though they struggled to contain themselves.

The bottom edge of the moon rose above the tree line. Only then did the wolves unleash. As one, they each drew in a powerful breath, then let it all out in a cacophonous howl, keening towards the heavens with a strength of voice Found Moon could only admire. He longed to join in, but felt the chief's eyes on him, unsure if he was being warned to remain silent, or being judged that he did not add to the howl. He knew he would never match the sheer power the other wolves managed. His own howl was pitiful in comparison.

Three more times, the whole pack howled in unison, a chorus to welcome the moon to the darkened sky. Found Moon was so enraptured in the sound that he didn't even notice any of the wolves moving. Only when they began to beat their hands on the drums did he realise the pack moved anew.

Howls turned to dance and music. With one wolf to a drum, they hammered out a beat in perfect unison, their hands pounding against the taut skin. A fifth wolf kicked to the rhythm, his feet stirring up dust as he scuffed around the cleared space in front of the fire. His limbs and torso twisted with his lithe movement, loincloth swirling and bone talismans clicking against each other.

The pack circled around the firepit and cleared space, cheering on the dancing wolf and drummers. More and more joined in, swaying to the music and clapping their hands in time with the beat pounded out by the drums.

Found Moon lost track of the few faces he recognised. Both the chief and the hunter disappeared amongst the pack, the wolves all little more than darkened silhouettes in front of the bright firelight. Smoke obscured most scents, perfumed by the sap and oils of the burning wood, but the sounds more than made up for the dulled senses.

The rhythm of the drums was a heartbeat, invigorating the blood and fuelling the voice and movement of the pack. Feet scuffed and scraped against the ground. Hands clapped, palms together or against thighs. Wordless voices howled to it all, necks arched so their heads were turned to the spirits in the dark sky.

Found Moon's breath was taken away. He shivered, the cold wind cutting through the heat of the fire. He longed to be amongst the crowd of bodies, closer to the fire, a part of the pack. He wanted to dance with them, to sing and howl to the moon and the spirits, but their attention was all on the dancers. He was ignored, not part of the pack, not a part of the celebrations. Here, he was an outcast among his fellow species, just as much as he was among the hares.

A startled realisation pierced through his mind. It was like the smoke had hazed his thoughts, the pounding beat distracting him.

He was not here to ingratiate himself with the pack. And nobody was paying any attention to him.

He had to take the opportunity. Found Moon tore his eyes away from the smoky celebration and padded around the light, keeping to the shadows and hoping the smoke was enough to mask his scent. He could barely see the chief's tent in the gloom beyond the fire, though the great mammoth tusks outside the entrance did cast dark shadows against the starlit sky.

Found Moon cautiously put his hand out, lightly brushing against one of the tusks. He had never seen one of the massive mammoths alive, though he had seen a corpse once. He could only imagine how majestic such a creature must look when rampaging across the steppe, but with a shake of his head he forced himself to ignore such fantasies.

He glanced back. The pack danced around the fire, clapping to the beat of the drums. Those who looked away from the firepit only did so to gaze at the moon. His tail twitched in excitement as he turned back to slip inside the largest tent, only to bump into something warm, heavy, and full of muscle.

The chief grabbed hold of Found Moon's wrist before the smaller wolf could escape. Claws pinched tight against flesh. Brutal strength dragged Found Moon back, out of the tent and into the firelight. Though the drums continued, the thumping feet of dancing wolves stilled.

To his horror, Found Moon realised he was not the only one in the chief's grip. As his feet dragged against the ground, hauled towards the fire, he caught sight of a shadow in Ripper's other hand. The dark shape of a hare, limp and unresisting.

Both Found Moon and Grey Ear were thrown to the ground, in the centre of the clearing by the firepit. The wolf rolled a couple of times, before coming to rest by the firewood. His heart thundered to the beat of the drums, which seemed louder to his ears now that they surrounded him.

Found Moon looked up at the ring of wolves. Their eyes gleamed. Teeth glistened. Predatory grins were masked onto their muzzles.

His knees and palms pained him as he struggled to his feet. No one approached him, or the hare lying curled like an infant by his side. The wolves all looked down on him, staring with those unblinking eyes and open jaws like he was a morsel of meat.

Standing on trembling legs, Found Moon tried to stare down the massive bulk of the chief. He could not manage it. He looked down as the chief barked in laughter.

"Why would our interloping visitor be sneaking into my tent to claim our prized meat?" Ripper asked, his voice loud enough to drown out even the drums.

"I... I..." Found Moon stammered, no answer coming to mind. Either he was trying to hunt and kill the hare, therefore betraying the hostile welcome he had received from the pack, or he was trying to rescue the hare, in which case he was not a wolf worth protecting. Not according to the pack. He knew there was no answer which would save him, and his throat closed over so he couldn't even speak the truth and suffer the consequences.

"Shall we perhaps show generosity?" the chief asked, turning slowly on the spot to look around at his pack, before shifting his gaze upwards. "After all, is it not the full moon? Why don't we give our friend a choice?"

Found Moon's heart sank, even before the gnashing howls of the pack rose to a terrifying crescendo. He struggled to swallow, his throat so dry. He almost tripped over his own heels.

Chief Ripper stepped forward, moving from the ring of wolves. He gestured down to the cowering hare. "Go on, Found Moon," he said, again twisting the name into an insult. "Take a bite. Kill your prey. You said you wanted help with hunting, so go ahead. You'll never have an easier kill."

Found Moon's eyes darted down to Grey Ear, shivering but otherwise still, halfway between himself and the chief. He looked up again. He chewed on his lip and didn't answer.

The chief sneered. "Perhaps I should make it a little easier for you," he said, taking another step towards Found Moon. "Either you kill the hare, or I kill you. And then the hare."

"I will not kill him," Found Moon said, the words ripped from his throat before he could hold them back. He trembled, feeling so small beneath the cruel smile of the chief.

"Of course you won't," the chief said, his voice quiet despite the howls from his pack, the beat of wolf hands on the drums. The brutish wolf smiled wider, showing his fangs, drooling saliva. "A wolf comes into my territory, stinking of hare, bearing one of their names. And he has the temerity to lie to me, to try to steal my food? You don't even deserve the death I shall give you, mongrel."

"Let us go," Found Moon said, voice shaking almost as much as his body.

The mocking laughter started with Ripper, but soon spread to the rest of the pack.

"Let you go?" the chief asked. He extended one hand, claws glistening in the firelight. "I shall enjoy looking up to your spirit when you take your place amongst the stars. It shall fill me with great amusement. Now, mongrel. Fight me and die like a wolf, however little you deserve that honour."

Found Moon quickly glanced around. The wolf pack had him surrounded. There was no way to run, certainly nothing that allowed him to take Grey Ear with him. His only option was to stand and fight, to defeat the chief and get away then. He almost laughed. Ripper was so much bigger than him, more powerful in every way. His hand shook as he reached for his loincloth.

The chief laughed. "Not that kind of fight, mongrel. I don't know what you do with those hares, but you will not win that way either."

Found Moon struggled to ignore the raucous laughter, his ears low. He tugged free the flint blade and flicked aside the sheath. The sharpened stone felt pitiful and light in his hand, but it silenced some of the laughter.

Ripper sneered. "Of course you would use the weapons of the hares. No matter. Nothing you wield is stronger than the fury of a true wolf," the chief growled. He lowered his head, bracing his feet against the dusty ground. "Now, die."

Found Moon slashed empty air, his knife passing harmlessly over Ripper's head. The chief slammed into the smaller wolf, shoulder against ribs. The impact stole the air from Found Moon's lungs. He fell back, scraping against the ground as the full weight of the chief pinned him down.

Once, twice, three times the closed fists of the chief pummelled against him, each sending a crack of pain through his body. A quick kick to the stomach momentarily dislodged the chief, giving Found Moon the chance to roll to the side. His chest and face ached. The taste of blood filled his mouth. Already, he could barely stand. He was going to die. It was as simple as that. He would die to the howl and laughter of wolves. Grey Ear would be next. The hare would not be able to escape. The hares of Sanctuary would know he failed. There would come a time when they would stop checking every dawn in the hope of seeing the pair return home.

Found Moon's grip almost slackened on his knife. What was the use in fighting? Why delay the inevitable? He stared down Ripper, taking a step back, but he did not raise his arms to defend.

Ripper's fist opened as he struck again. Claws slashed against Found Moon's shoulders and cheek, wetting his fur with crimson blood. A kick to the gut sent him sprawling to the ground again, by the feet of the onlooking wolves.

The chief prowled towards him, a savage gleam in his eye. Someone shrieked, a sound unlike anything a wolf could make. A shadow leaped across the fire. Grey Ear leaped onto Ripper's back, his small hands wrapped around the wolf's throat.

Ripper roared in anger and spun around, his fist grabbing Grey Ear by the shoulder and tearing the hare away. Grey Ear yelped as he was thrown to the ground, quickly gathered up again by another wolf. The hunter growled in triumph as he wrapped both arms around the struggling hare's body. The wolf glared directly at Found Moon as he pressed his muzzle to the hare's shoulder, teeth grazing against flesh.

Found Moon's blood boiled in his veins. His fingers tightened around the knife. It was one thing to know he was going to die; it was another to see the hunter threatening to kill his brother. The diminutive wolf snarled. If he had to die, then he would make something of it.

A smirk flashed across the muzzle of the chief. He bared his teeth and lunged again, claws swiping. They brushed through Found Moon's fur, but just missed his flesh. The smaller wolf slashed back, his adversary narrowly dodging the knife.

Grey Ear whimpered, falling still in the grip of the hunter's arms and jaw. Found Moon struggled to keep his focus on Ripper, his ears twitching to every quiet noise, barely audible over the wolves. Drums beat in time to his heart. Rage bright as the flames burned white hot through his blood, flowing red from his cheek.

Claws raked down Found Moon's side. He shrieked in pain and stumbled back, the agony extinguishing his anger. He panted and stumbled away but was pushed back again by the ring of wolves that surrounded the fighters.

His strength waned. He was in too much pain to think properly. All he could see was the massive bulk of the chief, fur nearly unblemished with blood. Found Moon staggered forward, only to be struck by a powerful punch to the jaw. His vision flashed white as he spun to the ground with a limp crash. Dimly he was aware of the wolves howling, but somehow, over all the noise, over the pounding in his head and the shriek of his thoughts, he heard a hare whispering his name.

"Found Moon, please get up..."

Blinking furiously, Found Moon rolled onto his back. A dark shadow loomed over him.

Ripper lunged for the fallen wolf. Found Moon swung up with his right arm at the same moment. The flint knife sunk into flesh. It scraped against bone as it slid between the ribs. The handle pulsed in time with the beat of Ripper's punctured heart.

The larger, heavier wolf collapsed on top of Found Moon. Ripper breathed in, a death rattle as his hands weakly struggled to find the neck of his foe. "You mongrel..."

Found Moon pushed Ripper off himself once the chief fell still. He yanked his knife out, blood rushing from the incision as the flint pulled free. A deathly silence stilled the pack.

Though he could barely stand, Found Moon forced himself to remain upright. He staggered towards the hunter, his bloody knife lifted. "Let him go," he growled.

The hunter obeyed, shoving Grey Ear away. The hare stumbled into Found Moon's waiting arm, pressing tight to his lupine brother. A couple of wolves hastily stepped away, clearing a route out of the ring. No one else moved. Found Moon wasn't sure if they even breathed, as though their own life had been stolen away with Ripper's.

The young wolf spat out a mouthful of blood. His throat felt dry despite the acrid tang coating his tongue. He struggled to speak. "Sanctuary is my territory," he said, his voice raspy and pained. He had only the crackle of the fire to compete with. He doubted the wolves failed to hear him, even if they did not acknowledge he had spoken. "Sanctuary is mine. As is the forests that surround it. You are not to encroach on my land. I have killed your leader. That means you must obey me. Do you understand?"

At first none answered. Found Moon snapped his jaws and growled. He pointed his bloodstained knife towards the closest wolf, to the hunter who had first captured him. "Do you hear me?" he barked.

The hunter bowed his head, looking to the ground. "We hear you," the wolf said, his muzzle twisted into a bitter grimace.

The ring of wolves parted fully as Found Moon shuffled towards them. He leaned heavily on the hare at his side, blood still leaking from the wounds on his face and chest. His hand ached with how tightly he grasped the flint knife. But no wolf attacked him. None even looked at him, their eyes shifting away whenever he got close.

Turning his back on the pack was the hardest thing. He expected to feel claws any moment, but nothing came. No one approached. No one dared. He had killed their chief. A prey's weapon had done it. Not claws or fangs. A simple stone blade.

"You didn't have to come for me," Grey Ear said quietly.

Found Moon grunted in pain. "You're my brother. I had to." His ears strained, turned back to ensure no one snuck up on them. He could hear nothing but the fire as it burned through the wooden fuel.

The hare fell silent again. Together, they limped slowly away from the pack's shelter, into the darkness of the night. It would be a long walk back to Sanctuary, especially injured as they both were. Starlight would guide the way, but before they reached the forest they would be exposed and vulnerable.

"Do you think it will be enough?" Grey Ear said at last.

Found Moon risked a glance back. No one followed through the gloom. The fire continued to burn, but the celebration to the spirits and the full moon had turned silent. There wasn't even a mourning howl for the fallen chief. He had been slain by a prey's tool. Found Moon doubted there would be any respect left for Ripper. But to the one who had killed him, perhaps.

The hare didn't want doubts and uncertainty. Found Moon gently squeezed his arm around Grey Ear's shoulder. "It will be enough," he said, managing a bloodstained smile to the darkness. "We'll be safe now."

It would be up to him to enforce that safety. He was a wolf, but the hares were his family. He could protect them, with claw or blade. No wolf would threaten his family again.

Sanctuary would be a haven for them all.

The Eyeshine of the Soothsayer

by NightEyes DaySpring

Ahbay awoke in the darkness with a feeling that now was the moment. The cheetah wasn't certain what it was that told him that, but as he lay there thinking, there was the sound of someone at his hut. He knew immediately who it was before he could smell or even see her. The light of the dying village fire outlined Sizan as she pulled the flap over his hut's entrance aside.

"It is time. I knew this moment would come," she said softly, her long thin tail curling up in delight, the only sign of her excitement. In the dark, her spots and markings were hard to make out, but her eyes were clear and bright even though it was a moonless night. They shone with possibilities.

He wanted to protest, to roll over on his mat of grasses and tell her that her teaching and visions were all wrong. The middle of the night, when even the most diehard of the hunters drunk on wine had fallen to the seduction of slumber, was no time for such nonsense, but it would be a lie. He could feel it himself that now was the time for him to complete his training. It was unnerving that he knew that, but something about tonight, something about this moment was right. The vision would be strong. When he had started, he'd only get the faintest inklings of sight, but not anymore. He had begun to feel the currents of fate himself, and all the doubts he had in the beginning had been laid bare.

"Is anyone even still awake?" he asked, rising from his mat, setting the blanket he slept under aside.

"No. I think that is why now the vision awaits."

The soothsayer rarely said something was correct or certain because so much of what she did dealt with the indistinct edges of life. To say something with certainty was to commit in a way that prophecy did not. In the three years he'd trained with Sizan, he'd noticed her way of always leaving the way open to something else. The threads of fate were fickle at best. To tell the weather tomorrow was one thing, to know and set the fate of another was a completely different task. The weather was easy; people were hard. Knowing the will of the gods? Impossible.

He dressed quickly in his loose pants. The night was cool, the wind coming off the distant mountains, but Ahbay did not bother with a shirt. Sizan wore her simple linen robe that fell from her shoulders, tied at the waist with a bit of hemp cloth. She waited for him outside, but her tail lashed back and forth.

"Should we go to the spring to meditate?" he asked, curious.

She shook her head. "No, this is bigger than that." She turned toward her own hut. "Come, we shall gaze into the darkness and from there you shall see."

He nodded. Some visions came best in nature, others in his own bed. He followed her back to the hut and when she pulled the flap open, he entered. Sizan's home had already been prepared, her sleeping mat picked up and set to the back. A single clay oil lamp was already lit in the room, and he took the seat on the far side.

Sizan let go of the flap and entered the hut, sitting down across from him. It was dark except for the lone lamp, and the light barely illuminated her, except for her eyes. They glowed brighter at night than anyone else's in the village, although he could not tell if that was his imagination or a trick she played.

"Tonight, we shall journey. I will guide you on a vision that will take you further than any you have seen before. Are you ready?" she asked.

He could feel his ears flick. "As ready as I can be to answer the call."

She nodded. "The journey ends where it started, but you are no longer a kit in the eyes of the gods. You will be a seer, and the visions will be yours to interpret. Do you understand how much weight I am putting on you?"

"I do," he said.

She chuckled and her eyes sparkled. "What was the first tenet I taught you?"

"Never look for your own fate."

"Why?"

Ahbay cleared his throat. "Because if you see your own fate, you will try and change it. That is the nature of who we are. We always want to fight against it."

"And the second tenet?"

"If the gods show you your fate, accept it. Do not attempt to change it," he replied.

"Look at me, Ahbay, meet my eyes."

He looked at the soothsayer, and in the faintest reflections in the dark, he saw himself, and then he saw himself looking back at her, with her reflection in his eyes, his eyes shining like hers. It had taken weeks to learn this simple technique, to grasp vision, and now it was almost effortless.

"The pull..." she started,

"... is strong," he finished. "This is the moment of my..."

"... of your..." she intoned with him,

"... journey," the cheetahs said together.

Above them the day dawned bright with a few clouds against a blazing blue sky. Around them the village spread out, before it faded from view leaving them in scrubland with the distant mountains standing guard. It was familiar and yet it was different, as if they were wrapped in a dream of where they lived.

"The vision has come," Sizan intoned in a voice that was not spoken yet heard. "Behold!"

"Is this our future or our past?" Ahbay asked, looking around to get his bearings.

"We might never know." She turned to gaze into the distance. They were alone in this wilderness by themselves, until suddenly they weren't. They could see dust rising up and as they watched, a half dozen leopards and tigers equipped for war dressed in brightly colored fabrics hurried toward a fate unknown. The men ran on, there was silence for a bit, and then came a lupine shepherd with her goats, and when she was gone there was a path through the dry scrub toward a place beyond.

"Where does that lead?" he asked.

She hesitated. "I don't know, but it is your path to follow. Go, and tell me what you see," and then he was alone and yet not alone. She was gone, and yet he was still in the room with her. The oil lamp was in front of him, but he could see only the path that lay before him.

"Sizan?" he called out to wilderness and hut alike.

"I am here. This is your path and yours alone," she said, far away and yet right next to him. "Go, the journey is here for you. I have taken mine many seasons back."

He stepped onto the path and felt his paws touch the dirt. The grasses lining the way tickled at his sides as he started walking. "There's a road, and no, wait..." He saw huts, but huts much bigger than theirs, and they were made of stone and could hold two or three families.

"I see stone huts, but they're massive."

"Go on."

He walked toward the structures, and they only seemed to grow. What was a moment ago a few huts became many, and the roofs suddenly reached up toward the trees as the buildings became larger and people came and went about their business.

"The huts are bigger."

"You see the future," she called out.

"And there are so many of them, and people, all sorts of people..." He paused. The road had suddenly become flat and smooth, paved in stone. A wagon went by pulled by a horse on two legs, with people riding by, and then another, and another, and faster and faster and...

"There are wagons, so many wagons," he yelped in surprise. "This is so much bigger than our village."

"What you see is a city. I have never been to one, but down by the banks of the two great rivers you can find them. Keep going. The vision will tell you more."

He wanted to call out. He wanted to scream, but there were things all around him. The stone huts reached to the sky with pillars all around. People were cheering as a chariot passed by, a wolf draped in purple riding in it, leading what appeared to be prisoners. There was so much he didn't understand, so much he couldn't comprehend, as sounds from metal horns echoed in his ears and made them lay back.

"What do you see now?" she called out, obviously aware he was in distress.

"I don't know. There are pillars of stone and deer carrying blades." He paused and what had been a festival turned into a battle as glinting blades clashed and the city burned. People were dying, innocent people, and even in his vision, he could feel the smoke stinking in his eyes. He wandered the streets, but there were flashes of more people and battles.

"I see war, death..." Ahbay whispered, trying to make sense of it all.

"Stay with it. See to the end," she called out, a voice far away and yet right in front of him.

He tried to step down the path, to continue on, but it was overwhelming. Things shifted endlessly around him, and he could feel glimpses of emotions before they were gone. Things came faster and faster, people moving quicker and quicker in things he could only describe as wagons made of metal as the city grew, changed, and died, when suddenly it all froze in a single moment. There was a deafening roar, and a pillar of fire engulfed everyone and everything. The people in his vision vanished instantly, and everything was white hot and burning.

He hit the ground then, not the ground of the road or the path, or the strange world he had just seen, but the ground in Sizan's hut. He blinked, confused. "It's all gone."

She leaned forward, still looking at him, concern on her face. "What did you see?"

"I saw change, and growth, life and death, and then fire. There was a fire that consumed everything and everyone," he sobbed. "That was the end."

She frowned. "Did you see a fire hotter than any you have ever seen that took everything away?"

He looked up at her, blinking back tears. "Yes," he nodded. "What does it mean?"

The soothsayer didn't say anything but sat back and took a deep breath. "I had hoped you would not see that. I have had a vision like this before, with a pillar of flame of unimaginable power consuming all. I've seen it multiple times, actually."

She was silent then, and he shifted, suddenly uneasy. "And?" he asked, still on the ground.

The soothsayer slowly ran a claw through the dirt, watching the way the earth parted. She looked up at him after a moment. "I cannot be sure it is the same one I have seen. I cannot say for sure if that is the past or the future, or even our world. Parts of my visions have been so different than our lives I cannot understand them, but I believe the vision is of a distant future. Not only that, the vision changes. Sometimes there is the fire that consumes everything, and sometimes I float, with the balls of light of our ancestors above us so close that I must be in the heavens above. When I see that, I feel joy. When I see the fire destroy the city, I feel pain."

He picked himself off the ground. "Are these connected?"

"Yes, but it took me a long time to realize they were."

He was silent for a moment. "What can I do with these visions?" he asked.

She laughed bitterly. "What can anyone do with a future or a past they have no connection to, living or dead?"

He was surprised by the intensity of her voice. "I don't know. What can we learn from it?"

She looked back to the marking she made in the dirt. "Perhaps very little, but perhaps that is my lack of understanding of the vision. The path goes on from here, but I am unable to draw this line forever toward the horizon, I am unable to follow it. You might not get much further than I have, but it is important we try."

He felt so confused, so unsure. "Why?"

"Why indeed. Why are our lives like they are? Is this how the gods intended for us to live, or are we destined for more, for something else? Could this all be the temptation of the darkness in war?"

She looked tired then, and he knew what she'd done. "You broke the second tenet," Ahbay said.

Sizan looked up at him. "I have tried to."

"That's forbidden."

"The gods have not shown me so much for me not to know. You saw how far in the future that is, yet you felt it, didn't you? The loss, the pain, that despair?"

He had. Before he'd seen small things or things not too far away, but this, this was beyond his sense of scale. It went beyond the mountains and kept going in a way he could not fathom.

"Why have you never told me about this?"

She looked up at him and her eyes were bright. "I had hoped what I was taught was not wrong, so I taught it to you. I thought you might never see this far. I have spoken to others with the gift of sight, and none see this, and yet I know this vision lies before our descendants when every last one of those of us alive today and our children and their children are looking down upon them. Who should worry about that? How could I say this vision was true without someone else seeing it?"

"But you know it to be true," he said. "If you felt it like I have, you know it's out there."

"Yes, but we control only the now," she responded.

A glimmer of thought came to him. "And by controlling the now, we can control the future?"

She flashed a smile full of fangs as her tail lashed behind her. It wasn't a threat, but in great amusement. "That's correct. You learn quickly, but now you see the dangerous power we have."

Ahbay considered. "I could stop things from happening that shouldn't happen."

"That's true, but you could also stop things happening that should," Sizan responded.

"If I can see the vision again and it changes for the better, would that mean we have done the right thing?"

"One can only hope. Prophecy is a terribly imprecise thing. I have thought you having a vision like this was always a thing that could happen, but I by no means thought this was something that would happen. I was mistaken."

He sat, tail lashing, and looked upon his teacher. "You didn't have to hide this from me."

The cheetah laughed. "What would putting the burden of the future on you do when I don't know how to fix it?"

His eyes shone like the soothsayer's eyes in the dim light. "Because we all must live. We must find a way. The gods ask us to."

She smiled back. "Indeed, they do." She took a deep breath and reached out to take one of his paws in each of her hands, the oil lamp burning between them. "The call is still upon us, so come, let us journey into the dream again, and this time I will accompany you wherever the vision goes. Perhaps together, we can find a clue to aid our present."

He nodded and took a deep breath and locked eyes with Sizan. "Then let us go."

She spoke with the spark of prophecy in her eyes. "Call out to the path..." she intoned.

"... and follow the fates," he replied.

"... together we go," the cheetahs intoned.

Once again the day dawned around them, and the sky opened up above them with a bright blue hue. In the distance the mountains waited, and the road lay before them. Sizan nodded to Ahbay, and together they started down the path to see what fate would show them.

Daughter of Thunder

or

The Land of Many Deer

by Rose LaCroix

Author's note: Between England and France, there once was a lush valley of lakes and rivers, now lost to the rising seas. We will never know many lives were lost or changed forever when that land vanished beneath the waves; only that they were there. Now and then, along Dogger Bank in the North Sea, some diver or fishing boat brings up bits of bone, wood, antler, and stone with the unmistakable marks of having been shaped by careful hands.

I still remember the morning the first wild cherries ripened, all those many years ago.

Half Moon, the seer who lived at the edge of our village, had abandoned her hut and was carrying as much as she could gather into a bag of horse skin. She was following the trees marked with three horizontal bands of white earth pigment, the way westward toward the Chalk Cliffs in the Land of Many Deer.

The old she-wolf's eyes were deep and uncanny, always ablaze like the fire pits we cooked our fish in. But on that day they blazed with a terror that chilled me nose to tail.

Her steps were quick for someone so old. I tried to keep pace with her a while and asked, "Half Moon, where are you going?"

"Away, Starling," she replied, stepping quicker still, nearly breaking into a run as I followed her.

"Away? Where?" I asked.

"The Land of Many Deer! Didn't I tell you?"

She had, in fact, told us. Four moons before, we had killed a deer and saved Half Moon the bones for her broth. But before she boiled them, she cast the bones on the ground and read their signs by the light of our fire.

The bones told her the Great River would flood and sweep our home away forever, some time soon after the first wild cherries had ripened.

None of us had taken her seriously. The little village of horse skin huts our pack lived in had been there since Half Moon's grandmother's grandmother's grandmother's time, and our village was on a rise a fir tree's height higher than the river, high above the highest floodwaters anyone had ever seen.

"Supposing you are right," I whined, my ears back. "What good are you doing us by running away?"

Half Moon stopped in her tracks. "Child, you must understand, the Land of Lakes and Rivers will be swept away. Our home will be lost beneath the sea for all time and if the pack stays there, they'll be gone too. If the pack needs me, come and find me. I'm sure some of you will get your wits about you and when you do, I'll be waiting to help you. I'm of no use to you dead!"

I clung to her waist. "Half Moon! You can't go! We need you!" I begged.

She reached with spindly arms of remarkable strength and pried me off of her. "Then come to the Ancestor Oaks in the Land of Many Deer. That's where I'll be, waiting by the Old One. Go tell your stupid father!"

She flung me away none too gently and carried on, almost running, until she was far out of sight beyond the aspen wood.

I ran back to my village to tell my father, Raven. He was with my younger brother, Bright, knapping flint outside our hut.

"What's the matter?" my father asked, setting his work aside a moment.

"It's Half Moon. She's left in an awful hurry. She says a great flood is coming. The sea will swallow up the Land of Lakes and Rivers," I explained.

Bright sighed and rolled his eyes.

"When has she ever been wrong?" I challenged him, baring my fangs a little.

"Don't you bare your fangs at your brother like that!"

I jumped. My mother, Gentle, spun me around and handed me a wad of grass. "I need you to help me with these fishing nets," she said. "Come on, stop bothering your father and brother!"

"She's not bothering us," Father chuckled.

"Well she's got work to do too. Everyone does their part for the big hunt! Come on," she chided, grabbing me by the wrist and dragging me back to the hut.

We sat cross-legged, on deer skins across from each other, the hearth in the middle of the hut between us burning in warm glowing embers. "Half Moon is leaving," I said as I took a handful of grass from a corner of the room and began splitting the blades into ever finer strands with my claws.

"Why?" Mother asked, picking up a half-made cord and braiding the fine strands one by one.

"She said the Land of Lakes and Rivers will be swallowed up by the sea soon," I told her. "Remember? She said the same thing four moons ago."

My mother stopped braiding. Her eyes went wide. "Starling... last night I dreamed about this! I'd forgotten all about what Half Moon saw in the bones, but last night I saw the river rise and rise until there was no more land, and I saw our village swept away. I saw wolf folk and fox folk and badger folk all running for higher ground. But the waters kept coming and coming... it was such a horrible dream! It felt so real!"

My chest tightened. "We have to leave," I whispered.

Mother's ears splayed, and she gazed down with a long sigh. "We can't. Your father and brother are leaving for the Big Hunt tomorrow."

Every year, near the start of autumn, our pack and the neighboring packs would all go to the east side of the Great River for a Great Hunt, catching fish and hunting horse and deer and gathering together for a feast. Meat-eating folk from all the clans, from the tiniest stoat to the biggest wolf, would all come and share what we'd caught and gathered. And we would give a great gift of nuts and fruits for the deerfolk, and the promise that we would never hunt a deer that walks upon two legs like the wolf folk did long ago, in the wandering times. There'd be gifts and songs and stories, with the hunters acting out the hunt in deer skins and antlered headdresses. And at the end of the feast we would all honor the land together by dancing until we could dance no more.

To interrupt the Great Hunt? No. Never. It meant too much to the clans of this valley.

Mother didn't say another word after that. She put all her attention into braiding, her fingers moving fast, nervous, fumbling at times but never stopping, never lifting her eyes to meet mine. I forced myself to do my part, splitting grasses until the day was done.

We had a supper that night of rabbit flavored with summer raspberries we'd dried and stored in pots some moons before.

"I'm proud of you, going on your first Great Hunt!" Mother said.

Bright grinned. "Father says he's happy to have me along!"

"Well, I'm getting old, son!" he said. "I need someone to help me."

"You're not that old," my mother said. "And you've got my brother to help you. And your friends."

"Starling, you're being awful quiet. What's the matter?" Father said.

What could I say? If they wouldn't listen to Half Moon, why would they listen to a silly young pup like me?

"It's nothing," I said. "I'm tired, that's all."

I devoured the rest of my food and excused myself from the fire. I wandered down to the river, sitting on the wooden planks my father and uncle, Singer, had laid by the riverside to slide their boats in and out. They'd worked hard on this, knapping for days to make great axes from flint and cutting each tree down to size with the help of the whole pack. We'd been here so long and done so much that the land itself had our mark on it, signs of who we were and what we'd done. Would it really all be gone forever, lost beneath the sea?

I cried, my eyes blurring like the moon's reflection on the rippling waters. No. No, it couldn't be. It couldn't be over, my world, everything I knew! I didn't want to leave!

But I knew where to find Half Moon.

I would watch the river, wait for it to rise... and if the water rose one day, I would be ready.

On the day of the Great Hunt, we gathered at the water's edge. Mother held pots of yellow and red ochre dampened with river water and, with a brush made from a boar's bristles, she closed her eyes and waited for the shapes to show themselves. After a moment she opened her eyes and dipped the brush into the ochre and painted those shapes on my father. "A successful hunt and no harm to you," she sang over and over in that ancient plaintive melody I'd heard fifteen autumns in a row.

I smiled, thinking of the day when I would have a husband to bless before the hunt. I was smitten with Kingfisher, the gold-furred hunter one year and a summer older than me; and Kingfisher shared those feelings. Our parents had discussed marriage but never on any serious terms; we were still a year or two too young.

Like me, Kingfisher was a Sky-Child; that is, his heart and soul were different from his body. And two Sky-Children could have children, the same as two Earth-Children like my mother and father.

He held his head high as his mother painted circles of yellow on his chest and arms, proud to be a hunter, but when he saw me his dignity and gravity melted into a silly grin. He ran up to me as his mother finished painting her visions on him, taking my hands in his.

"Kingfisher... listen... I... uh... Look, we're in danger. Half Moon said the river was going to rise and..."

Kingfisher tapped a finger on my nose to silence me. "Oh shush now... that old bone boiler! It's been how many days since the wild cherries ripened? We'll be fine, Starling."

He planted a kiss on my muzzle and my tail betrayed me, wagging all of its own.

Kingfisher smirked. "That's more like it. I'll see you after the hunt, gorgeous."

And for one precious moment I forgot all about the danger bearing down on me. I was young and in love, and that's a powerful herb.

The leader of the hunt, Bright Horns of the Moon, blew a blast on an aurochs horn. Some of the hunters, like Kingfisher, headed into the hills above the village, away from the river; while some of the hunters, like my father and brother, walked to their boats, sliding them into the water as we cheered and beat drums. We watched them all the way to the edge of the wood at the far side of the river, where whole groups of them became tiny dots, and one by one we stepped back from the river.

"Let's go forage," my mother said. "I want to see if we can add something to the feast." Of course. It was my brother's first hunt and if he couldn't provide enough to the feast on his own our family could keep our dignity by foraging the best late fruits, nuts, and mushrooms.

We went back to our hut and fetched our baskets, walking to the higher ground beyond the river valley. A wood, rich with many kinds of trees and bushes, stood at the top of those hills. It took a little while to get there. They looked so close from our bluff by the river but by the time we arrived the sun had already passed the highest point of His journey and He was headed down the hill of the sky into the seas beyond sight.

"Will we have enough daylight left?" I asked as I looked back on our village, now small as my basket.

"Our trip is already worth the bother," Mother said with a smile, shaking a low-lying branch from a hazel tree and watching the nuts pile inside her basket.

A moment later I spotted a large circle of delicious morels and I picked all of the biggest and best. That alone filled half my basket. I even helped myself to one or two.

We were filling our baskets with wild cherries when we felt the earth tremble and heard an unearthly sound, a mighty roar.

"What's that?" I asked, setting down my basket and scrambling up a beech tree for a better look.

Along the Great River there surged a wall of water, spreading out far beyond its banks.

"What is it?" Mother called from the ground below.

The great surge moved so fast. It carried trees and bushes and the destroyed remains of huts from further up the valley as it churned along, horrible and brown. It tore the carefully-laid timbers of our slipway and tossed them aside. It ripped the huts we had built, repaired, and tended for so many generations from the earth as easily as a wind tears the seeds from the black poplar tree. And half our pack, though too small to see, went with the village. I couldn't hear their screams. I couldn't see them swallowed up. But they were there. No one who was in the way of that brown wave of death could possibly escape.

I screamed. The loudest I had ever screamed in my life. The only time I have ever screamed from sheer mortal terror.

I clambered down and threw my arms around my mother. "Half Moon was right!" I sobbed, shaking with dread. "The village! The village is gone!"

Mother grabbed my hand, dragging me away from the river. "Where did you say Half Moon was going?" she asked.

"To the Ancestor Oaks," I said.

Mother stopped in her tracks. "That's a very long way," she said. "And it's getting dark."

I pushed forward, brushing past her. "Then we'll walk in the dark! I know how to find my way by the stars! Let's go!"

The sun was nearly gone for the day when we heard a voice behind us. "Wait! Wait for us!"

It was Kingfisher and his mother, Swan. Their fur was caked in mud and they were panting hard. In the dark, a few yards behind them, I saw the glow from the eyes of about half our pack.

"Are these all the survivors?" My mother asked, scanning for my father and brother.

"I don't know," Swan sobbed.

"We ran, but the river kept rising," said Turtle, a brown wolf who would have been on his third hunt. He was Great Horns of the Moon's nephew, spindly and lean and a bit awkward, but not a terrible hunter.

"Raven? Bright? Are you here!?" my mother called, frantic.

"The last time I saw them they were in their boat," Kingfisher said. "But that was a while ago."

"My uncle didn't make it," Turtle whimpered. "None of my family did. I'm alone."

A wolf so muddy I couldn't recognize him stepped forward. "I'm so sorry, Gentle! I... I lost sight of them. I have no idea where Raven and Bright are."

"Singer! I'm so glad you're safe!" my mother sobbed, throwing her arms around him, not minding the thick, sticky mud all over him.

"Is it safe to stay here?" I asked.

"Go and look," said mother.

I ran to the top of a nearby hill, the highest one with trees on it, and climbed up the tallest tree I could get my claws into.

In the blood-red glow I could see the river that once ran through the middle of our land was now a vast sea, with only a handful of islands. But it didn't seem to be rising. At least, not very fast.

I watched it a moment, my eyes on a stand of trees cast long in shadow and hard to observe. I squinted, trying to make out the movements of the water.

Yes. The water was still rising. It was rising knee-high every minute or so, not nearly as fast as it had been but still alarmingly fast.

I scrambled down the tree and down the hill and ran back to what was left of my pack.

"The water's still rising," I said. "We have to keep walking till we reach the Chalk Cliffs."

There were groans of protest and howls of despair. My heart twisted. What could I possibly do for them all? But we weren't far from the cliffs. And from there we would be another two days from the Ancestor Oaks where our seer would be waiting for us. And so, with night closing over our heads, we forged on, guided by the stars.

By morning we had reached the Chalk Cliffs, but we were too tired to go on. We made camp there, with a clear view of our valley, or what was left of it, and slept together, piled on top of each other to keep warm.

There were other folk escaped from the valley there too. Some fox folk had a camp not far away, and a band of otter folk had a camp further west. They huddled much the same way we did, miserable and hungry and fewer in number. In the glistening morning sun I could see, here and there, bodies floating in the water. But I couldn't tell what sort of bodies they were, let alone whether they were any of our pack. But I begged Moon and Sun that Father and Bright weren't among them.

We woke near sunset a few hours later, still tired, and gathered round a fire to share what little we had with us. Mother and I had some of the berries and nuts we had gathered and the foraging wasn't bad near the white cliffs, but we were too tired to gather too much.

"I think we should wait here, in case anyone else from our pack shows up," Mother said.

"I'm out of ideas," said a voice so hoarse and strained I couldn't recognize them in the gloom of the late evening.

"Fine, fine! As long as we find some food while we're here!" Kingfisher complained.

"Enough whining! I know what we had wasn't much, but we shared it all and it's enough to keep us alive another day. That's all that matters right now," his mother scolded him.

That was when I became aware of a sound I had never heard by the Chalk Cliffs: the sound of waves. I shuddered. I had heard waves only once before, when our family went to the sea in our boat and fished by the shore. To hear that rhythm, to hear the slow rumble of the sea instead of the gentle song of life in the valley, chilled me to the core. I burst into tears, shaking and sobbing.

"Starling! Are you alright?" Kingfisher asked, resting a hand on my shoulder. Not thinking, I threw my arms around him and buried my face in his fur, crying for all we'd lost. He caressed me and I stayed there a while, in his arms, comforted like a newborn pup.

We stayed awake until the fire guttered, then one by one we nodded off, sleeping away the last little while before dawn. My sleep was a dreamless void, full of only feelings. Terrible feelings. Sorrow, longing, and the dread of being keenly aware that one day, I would die.

Nobody from our pack came, from dawn til the time the sun was a little less than a quarter of the way through the sky, and with mutters of agreement we shambled north to the Ancestor Grove to try to find Half Moon.

The way to the Ancestor Grove, marked by trees and rocks painted with three red circles, had once followed cliffs and ridges above our land but now, there was only a series of high cliffs and desolate shores and mud... so much mud! The rising waters had made the ground so sodden in places we were afraid we'd be mired there when the tides came in, but we carried on, helping each other cross.

The sun was three-quarters through His course when we heard panting and footsteps. "Hey! Hey! Wait! Wait!" a voice called.

We turned to see a wolf, about my brother's age, running toward us. His gray-brown fur was matted with mud and he seemed to be favoring his right leg a bit. The pain must have been too much for him, for he broke stride and hobbled the rest of the way toward us.

"Hello, friend," my mother said. "Do we know each other?"

The lone wolf paused and folded his ears back. "No, I don't think so..."

"What's your name?" Mother asked him.

"Dragonfly," the exhausted wolf said. "I lost my pack. I... I don't know if anyone's alive. I'm hungry and scared. Can I come with you? Please?"

Mother looked over the wolves in our diminished pack. "Should we let the newcomer follow us?" she asked.

There were nods and murmurs of approval.

"We're going to the grove where our ancestors live to set up a new camp," my mother said.

"You're going to live in your pack's sacred grove?" The young wolf tilted his head at the thought of it.

"Our ancestors spoke to our seer in a dream and said we must go there," my mother explained. "You can come with us and stay as long as you need to. But once we get there, we will expect you to work hard with us as soon as your leg is healed."

"I'm an excellent fisher. I'm strong and I'm quick with my hands and... it doesn't hurt too bad to stand I guess," the wolf said, flashing a friendly smile, his tail betraying a slow, submissive wag.

"Do you need any help walking?" I volunteered, seeing how much pain the wolf was trying to hide from that leg. Sprained, most likely, or he wouldn't have been able to run on it for any distance.

"Thank you kindly," he said. He was a bit taller than me and his arm rested comfortably on my shoulder. "I'm glad I found you all."

"It's bad times," I said. "We have to take care of each other."

We made camp and foraged by the Ancestors' River. The foraging there was better, and Dragonfly helped us catch a few fish for our meal. We stuffed the fish with some herbs and wrapped them in long grasses from the riverside, placing them by the fire to cook.

It was the first proper meal most of us had eaten in two days, and it did our spirits good to have something to eat again.

Refreshed and our bellies full, we sat warming ourselves, huddled around our fires.

"So, where do you come from?" Mother asked Dragonfly.

"My village wasn't far from here," Dragonfly said, helping himself to another handful of salmon and gobbling it up. "When the waters came I ran up to the top of a nearby down. That down is an island now. I was the only survivor. My pack is gone."

"How did you get here?" Singer asked.

"After a while on that island I decided to take my chances and head west. I found a good, sturdy bough drifting by and I grabbed onto it, and I kicked and I paddled it all the way to the shore."

My heart leapt at his story. "You mean there are still islands above water out there?"

Dragonfly nodded. "Quite a few. Some of them had creatures on them. Some of them were clinging to the tops of trees just above the surface of the water. They begged me for help but... I couldn't. I couldn't save them."

Dragonfly burst into tears and almost out of instinct, I put my arms around him to comfort him. "I don't know where my father is either. Or my brother. I'll probably never see them again. But we'll be your pack. We'll look after you."

"Thank you," Dragonfly sobbed.

I lay on my back in the grass and stared up into the night sky as the fire's last embers glowed dark orange. The night sky is a terrible and mysterious thing. There are so many strange objects out there, fires that burn in the far-away. Gods perhaps. Or put there by gods. Every pack, it seems, has their own story told from generation to generation.

I felt insignificant in that moment, and my heart lurched as if caught in a snare. Did those gods care if I lived or died? Or how? Did those bright points of light even know my name? Or were the gods all dead and gone, and the bright stars above me simply the dust and debris that showed they had once been there, long ago?

I gazed into the black beyond and slept another dreamless night, beneath the indifferent stars.

We walked along the river, westward into the hills from the first red glow of dawn over the horizon until the sun was high in the sky when we came to the Ancestor Oaks. We knew them by the paint of chalk and ochre pigment of red, yellow, and white in bright patterns all over the trees and rocks at the edge of the grove, and the image of the Old One carved into a tall pole that had once been a tree in this grove many years ago that marked the boundary of our space.

And in a clearing at the center, the tallest of the ancestors stood alone. She was called The Old One, the Daughter of Thunder himself and the mother of the Firstborn of our pack.

Those who died easy and with no worries became tall oak trees in this place; but those who died fearful or in despair became the wild sort of wolves who go on four legs and cannot speak, but they can sing. When a wild wolf died, they too could become an oak after one hundred lifetimes; but when an oak died, they were reborn within the pack.

Half Moon was the Firstborn reborn, after the tree she had once been fell sixty winters ago; and when the Old One fell it was said that she too would be reborn among us. But although we came to the edge of the grove every year to honor the ancestors, no one had seen the Old One in seventeen years, and being fifteen summers old I had never seen the Old One with my own eyes.

We stood outside this holiest of places, milling about, all of us trying to think of what to do next.

"Where is Half Moon?" Kingfisher asked.

"She must be camped further in," my mother said. "But we mustn't go in without her."

I sang out a call for her, a long howl to say "I am here." But my howl was lost in the dense trees where no sounds echo. Would she even hear me?

A faint howl in an elderly voice replied a moment later. A short howl to say "I'm coming."

We waited, listening for the sound of her footsteps. They came, advancing slowly. Tired footsteps. Nothing like the footsteps I'd heard falling away from me a few days ago.

Half Moon came into view, haggard and weary. "Child, is that you?" she called.

I ran to her and threw my arms around her. "Half Moon! You're alive!" Tears ran down my face.

Half Moon caressed my head like I was a young pup. "Yes, yes... I'll be with you for... a few more years, I think," she murmured. "I'm so happy to see you, Starling! I thought I had lost all of you!"

"We lost about half the pack," Mother said.

"I lost all of my pack," said Dragonfly.

"Oh, Half Moon, this is Dragonfly," I said. "He's joined our pack."

"The spirits told me about you, Dragonfly," Half Moon said. "They told me a newcomer would cross our path with important news about the flood. Do you know anything, friend?"

"You mean about the islands that are still left?" I asked.

Half Moon's eyes grew wide. "There are still islands out there!?"

"Many," Dragonfly said. "And there are creatures trapped on some of them."

"Child, follow me," said Half Moon, leading us deep into the grove. "Don't be shy! This is important, come on!" she ordered, once more walking like a creature half her age.

We came to the sacred clearing where the Old One stood... or had stood. Her trunk had broken at the base and an ugly burnt scar ran down her side.

"Lightning must have struck her," Half Moon murmured, pointing to the blackened scar. "Probably happened years ago."

"Oh no," my mother sobbed.

"Don't weep for her. The Old One told me in a dream that she has been reborn. She said, 'I will make a boat of this old husk and sail to the island where the son of my pack waits for rescue.' And I did not know the meaning of this. I couldn't see a single island from the shore. Starling, my child, you're sixteen summers old, yes?"

"I am."

Half Moon took my hand. "And the last time our pack came to this grove was seventeen springs ago! My child, I believe you are the Old One reborn! And you will be the one to rescue Raven and Bright."

My heart stopped a moment. "No..."

The Old One? I couldn't be her. I didn't feel old. I didn't look old. I didn't know what anyone would expect of the Old One. I couldn't be her. I didn't want to be her. I wasn't ready!

"I believe you are," Half Moon said. "I may be wrong but... I've always been right before, haven't I?"

There was no sense arguing with Half Moon; the flood had proved her point for her.

"Then what should I do?" I asked.

Half Moon examined the great bough of the fallen oak. "This wood is pretty far gone on the ends, but this bit here in the middle, you see, it's exactly the right size to make a stout boat that will ride the waves, isn't it? So build a boat out of The Old One and find your father and brother!"

"All by myself?" I asked, ears back and tail between my legs.

Half Moon shook her head. "You can have some help building the boat. But when you set out to sea, you must be all alone."

"But I don't know how..."

"You do... and you will," Half Moon said. "Our lost sons need you. Start building!"

For three days we gathered supplies, made tools, and cut and gouged at the wood, shaping it slowly into a boat fit for the open seas, as long as five tall hunters and as wide as my arms spread side to side. Half Moon prayed and burned sweet herbs in a small fire nearby, wafting the smoke with the paddle I would use to propel the boat as we turned my old body into the largest boat that had ever been made.

How could I possibly travel in such a large boat all alone? We kept the hull as light as we could but this boat would be enormous and heavy. I could see the doubt in Kingfisher's eyes too as he eyed the size of the thing.

Uncle Singer did his best to make the boat as light and agile as possible. "If we make the front point just so," he explained, "the water will part before you and you will glide forward."

"You're good at this," Dragonfly said with a smile.

Singer's ears splayed. "So was Raven..."

"*is!*" I growled. "My father *is* alive!"

Singer gazed at me, then at Half Moon. The old seer shook her head in disapproval at him.

"If Half Moon says he's alive, then I believe her," Singer relented.

I gave him a disdainful snort. "She was right about the flood, wasn't she? Really, do none of you believe her, even now?"

"If she's wrong we'll lose you," Kingfisher said.

"And if you're wrong, we'll lose Raven and Bright," Half Moon shot back.

"No more arguing!" Uncle Singer growled. He struck up a working song:

> The sky makes the earth,
> The earth makes the stone,
> The stone makes the blade,
> The blade cuts the wood,
> The wood makes the boat,
> The boat travels far,
> Travels far,
> Travels far!

We joined in the singing, our disagreements set aside for a moment, the pack working as one to save our lost sons.

At the end of the third day, we took a supper of rabbit stew cooked in skins.

I sat with Kingfisher, off a little way from the rest of the pack.

"I just want you to be safe," Kingfisher whimpered. "I may have lost my father out there. We lost so many friends and loved ones. Please, I don't want to lose you too!"

I held his hand. "I promise I will come back to you. I... I trust Half Moon."

"You don't sound so certain," Kingfisher pressed on. "Are you sure you don't want me to come along, just in case?"

I sighed. "Kingfisher, I love you. But I have to trust her."

Kingfisher's eyes went wide. "You... you love me? You really mean it?"

I grinned, rising to my feet. "What do you think, silly?"

That was all. I turned in for the night, letting him sleep on that.

We were up again at the first light of dawn to finish the boat and by the time the sun was halfway down, Half Moon had carved a protective sign into the bow of the boat.

The whole pack admired our work. "The finest boat ever built!" said Bull Roarer, one of the few hunters to make it to the grove with us.

"You've honored your ancestors," Half Moon declared. "This will be big enough to carry you and your father and your brother, and plenty of supplies!"

"I guess this means I'm leaving soon," I said, running my hand along the sides of the boat.

"You must leave at dawn tomorrow," Half Moon said. "We can't wait any longer. You have to save our sons!"

The next day at dawn, eight of us, myself and Kingfisher in front, carried the heavy wooden boat to the river. As we carried we sang the song our pack had sung each time they would leave the Old One at the heart of the grove:

> Goodbye, Old One, mother of our kin.
> Goodbye, Old One, we will remember.
> Goodbye, Old One, we will return.
> Goodbye, Old One, you will be here to greet us.
> Twenty winters come and go,
> Twenty springs come and go,
> Twenty summers come and go,
> Twenty autumns come and go.
> Goodbye Old One, we will return.
> Goodbye Old One, you will be here to greet us.

We came to a shallow inlet of the river with a nice flat shore to slide the boat in. The pack heaped food, tools, and some bone, antler, and hides to work into whatever I needed into the boat, bundled into horse skins and tied in place with sinew strung through holes in the upper sides of the boat.

"Please come back safe, Starling," Kingfisher begged me, his soft brown eyes heavy with sadness and his ears splayed. He took my hand and squeezed it.

"I'll be back," I said with all the confidence I could muster. "Also yes... I did mean it."

Kingfisher tilted his head. "Mean what?"

I kissed him between his splayed ears and held him to me. "I meant it when I said I loved you."

"I love you too," he sobbed. "Please come back. So we can... maybe one day..."

"...Start a family?" I grinned.

"Y... yeah. Start a family," he mumbled, the insides of his ears turning bright pink.

With that I climbed into the boat. Half Moon hobbled up to me, looking very old again, and whispered in my ear:

"Child, listen well... If you don't succeed, it means you were not the Old One reborn. This means nothing bad about you! If anything it means I'm a failed seer. If you die on this quest, don't let your soul be fearful. You will not become a wild beast. You will become a great tree, like the Old One and we will honor you as our hero all the same. But if you succeed, then one day you will become a great seer. I see something amazing in you, Starling. I know you'll make me proud no matter what."

With that she walked round to the back of the boat and pushed with all her might. The heavy wooden hull slid just a little in the soft mud. Then the whole pack gathered round and pushed, and I was adrift, moving out to sea with the current and waving goodbye to my pack, wondering if I would ever see them again.

I paddled along, the current helping me glide fast down the narrow river. I saw wild deer grazing on the riverbank, trees and fields, and the burial grounds of the dead of other packs and their sacred places all along the river. Every clan—the foxes, the wolves, the deerfolk, the otters and stoats—had their own markers and they all seemed to be here, but their markers were a little different than the ones in the valley.

It was a little after noon when I arrived at the sea, at the wide mouth of the river where the current propelled me into treacherous waves that tossed my boat every which way but would not capsize me. Further out there were great swells that I rode, up and down, feeling sick to my stomach after a little while. I wasn't made for this! Why couldn't I have been otterfolk? I struggled to keep my stomach from heaving as I grew used to this sensation, this lack of a clear, straight horizon. I had only a general sense of up and down and it was miserable.

As for paddling, it was of little use. The wind and swells took me wherever they wished, and I was alone, bobbing like a little acorn in a raging river.

But by and by the heavy swells subsided and the sea was calm again. Small swells, maybe as tall as my ankle, now rocked my boat gently in the late afternoon sun.

Then I spied it. The first island I had seen. What had once been the top of a high down was now a small island surrounded by dead trees and debris that still floated around it.

There were bodies. Bloated, discolored, shedding their fur, and stinking hideously. Could I even stay here?

Well, the ground I could see looked dry enough. I turned my boat toward the tiny island.

All at once a mighty swell, maybe as tall as my boat was long, rose up from the sea beneath me and crashed into the island. I was hurled into the treetops where I clung for dear life only to see my boat washed out to sea along with much of the debris around the island.

I was trapped here, no food, no warmth, and no escape. And as the waters subsided from that island I understood who these bodies were. They were the bodies of those who had sought shelter here.

I grew tired as the sun slipped below the horizon, and I wedged myself into a crook in the tree just tight enough to stay put should I fall asleep.

I lay staring into the blackness, my eyes on the shimmering fires of the far, cold heavens. And the tree rocked me in her arms and sang a lullaby like my mother sang when I was young.

I woke refreshed to find no more swells had reached the island. Some of the debris that had been around the island the previous day had returned to the island, once again tangled in the boughs of sub-merged trees, a twisted mass of broken trees and bodies and things I scarcely recognized, things from the depths of the rivers and seas. But my boat was nowhere to be found.

I clambered down from the trees cautiously, watching the waves, careful for any sign of another swell. I reasoned they must not hit this island often, as I scanned through the debris left among the trees and on the ground. Enough wood I could probably build a fire, if there was time for one. But if another wave came? I couldn't risk staying down from the trees past sunset, let alone for very long at all.

One wave, slightly larger than the ones that had lapped the shore most of the night and day, crashed hard into the shore, and I jumped. No... that wouldn't work.

What was I to do? Wait for a boat that might not return when I was surrounded by wood?

But I had no flints with me. They were in the boat, in a sack that might be beneath the waves now.

I climbed back into the trees, waiting for my boat, my throat now horribly dry. I needed water. My waterskin was in the boat too, and the water around me was briny and brown and full of death.

Rain. I needed rain. I was so thirsty. So cold...

From beyond the seas, Thunder stirred and sent his fire down to earth with a mighty crack. The sky grew dark, and the wind, sharp and cold, whipped the waves to white crests as the treetops I clung to swayed perilously.

The frothy white waves became heavy, foamy swells, churning the dense, foul soup of debris around the island, removing some, adding some, macerating bodies and splintering boughs.

The wind cried as Thunder struck his fury across the sky in sharp, jagged bolts of fire.

"Thunder!" I cried in the growing dark as the storm raged on. "What do you want of me!?"

The wind died all of a sudden, and all was deathly silent. Rain fell, sparse and gentle.

Far to the north the sky was too dark to see very far. A distant rumble and a bright flash lit up the horizon and I saw a monstrous wave headed right for my little island.

I held tight to the tree, bracing for the impact.

The wave loomed, slow, unstoppable, and so very high. It picked up speed as it grew nearer, towering almost as tall as the tree I clung to. And no sooner had I judged its true height when it crashed into the island and my tree uprooted with it.

I was thrown from the tree into the water, and struggled a moment before I found a piece of another tree's trunk to cling to. Now in the light of Thunder's fiery bolts I could see my island, far away.

But much closer by was my boat. If I dared swim toward it.

Thunder challenged me with a great fork of fire above me lighting the dome of the sky with a mighty crash. This was it. This was my chance.

I let go of the bough I had clung to and swam as hard as I could across the water. I have never been a strong swimmer and the boat was further away than it seemed, but by and by, my hand rested on its wooden side.

I climbed inside my boat to find my waterskin and my sack of food and tools secured in place just as they had been. I drank from my waterskin, careful to save some for later.

"Thank you," I whispered to Thunder. "Thank you. I will make you proud!"

That was when I noticed there was no paddle. I was all adrift on the cold, indifferent seas.

Two days passed with no land in sight, and my food stores were looking bare. My waterskin had been replenished with a little rain water that had fallen in the boat but even that wouldn't last me long.

For all I knew, I may have been far out to sea, far away from any land that wasn't swallowed up by water long before I was born. Perhaps I would die out here, all alone in horrible pain, and never see my family again.

But I still had a little food, a little water, and a little hope, and I still had my strength. If I was going to die, it wouldn't be for a while yet. And I kept my eyes open for any sign of land, or anything I could use as a paddle.

It was difficult to tell where I was. It felt as if I was heading eastward, or perhaps southward. But there was nothing to tell, only the general direction of the setting and rising sun and even that was difficult to tell when the sky was cloudy, or when mischievous water spirits kept making false suns on the horizon.

At least Thunder had given me back my boat; a reward for my courage. And I knew Thunder was watching me still, that He never abandoned those He favored. And I felt my last reserve of hope grow just a little on those forbidding swells in the middle of nowhere.

And just as the sun was setting on my third day out to sea, my food and water nearly gone, I saw a tree branch floating near my boat that had just the right shape, long and straight with an end that widened into a flat, broad surface.

A paddle made by the hands of the gods.

And with that paddle, I turned my boat eastward, keeping the setting sun to my back and the bright star the elders call the True Light of the North to my left by night until finally, exhaustion from lack of food, water, or rest overcame me and I collapsed in the back of my boat, face up to the pink glow of dawn.

CRASH!

I woke to Thunder's roar and heavy rain on my face. Rain so heavy I filled my waterskin and the boat was still filling with water, riding low, threatening to sink though I scooped it out as much as I could.

But in the gray mist I could see the land. A large amount of land, in fact. And by and by I recognized it. This was one of the ridges on the far side of the Great River from where our pack once lived!

Getting closer, I saw that the high water mark on the plants, trees, and rocks was much higher than the water level now. At least some of the waters had receded.

I bailed and paddled the best I could at one time. But once I got close enough to the island I paddled for all I was worth and felt the boat come to rest on the gentle slope of the ridge. Using a rope of spun grass, I moored it to the snag of a beech tree and waded ashore.

A good portion of land had remained above water here. In fact, I couldn't see the other side. This wouldn't be like the Island of Drowning. This would be an Island of Safety because I knew this land and I knew there would be food and water here. I would live another day.

I set up camp immediately, in a spot that was nice and dry. I built a fire and warmed myself by it. With the tools in my sack, I made a very basic shelter of sticks and leaves and fell blissfully asleep as the day drew to a close.

I woke to a strong hand reaching from behind me and clamping my muzzle shut. "Don't move!" a gruff voice from in front of me said, and I felt the tip of an antler spear point at my throat.

Then a familiar scent hit my nose, and I heard my attackers sniff in disbelief too and I knew it wasn't just my imagination.

"*Starling!?*" said a younger voice behind me, and in an instant he let go of my muzzle.

"*Bright!*" I cried, throwing my arms around my brother.

"Starling! What are you doing here?" asked my father, the one who'd been holding the spear to my throat only a moment earlier.

"I came to save you," I said. "There's a lot I need to tell you."

"And there's a lot we need to tell you," Bright said. "Come on, let's go to our camp. We'll tell you more."

We hid in a cave where, in happier times, our tribe had taken shelter during the hunt. It was near the top of the ridge, but hidden by dense thickets and used as a breeding den from time to time by wild foxes whose pungent scent masked ours. We hunkered down amid the bones of voles and squirrels and piles of orange and white fur, only a dwindling supply of animal fat in a dim stone lamp for light.

"A member of our pack went mad. He killed and ate one of the deerfolk stranded here," Father explained. "The peace between the clans of wolf and deer was broken and they have declared war. They've already killed several of our pack."

"Wait, who else is here?" I asked.

"It's just us now," whispered Father. He sighed. "Gift of the River was here with us, and Carp and Cormorant and Wasp."

"The deerfolk got them, one by one," said Bright. "We couldn't save them."

"How did you get here, Starling?" Father asked. "Were you on one of the islands nearby?"

"No father, we made it to the Land of Many Deer," I said. "About half of us did. And we went to the Ancestor Oaks. Half Moon was there. She told us that the Old One was taken home by Thunder around the time I was born."

Father gasped. "Then you're..."

"...Here to save you," I interrupted. I didn't want him to say it. I didn't want to think about that. I only wanted to get away from here as fast as I could. "I have a boat. It's by the shore."

"Did you hide it?" Father asked, his eyes wide with alarm.

I shook my head. "No, I didn't know..."

"We have to leave tonight," Father said, gathering up his and Bright's few remaining belongings. He and Bright grabbed their spears and hurried out of the cave.

"Show us where it is before the deerfolk get it," Bright whispered, eyes flashing with fear.

Another storm was brewing in the north as we hurried down the hill toward my boat. We were just past the camp I had set up when we heard heavy footsteps and a voice shouting "There they are!" and the horrible screeching, bellowing war cries of maybe six or seven stags.

"We have to hurry!" Father cried. "They've seen us!"

We hurried to the snag where I moored my boat and discovered the water level had gone down a fair bit. Was it the tide? Was the water receding? I couldn't say. But my boat was now slightly out of the water, hung up on the snag on a taut line.

"I'll cut the rope. Starling, take my spear. You're strong as your brother. I believe in you."

Father handed me his spear and Bright and I stood guard, backing toward the water as father hacked through the thick rope with a flint chopper.

"Get in! Get in!" Father cried.

Bright and I half-waded, half swam to the boat. It was teetering side-to-side at the end of its tether and if we climbed in we knew we'd upset it, so we clung to the sides, on our tiptoes to keep our heads above water.

The line gave and the enormous boat splashed into the water, nearly knocking us on our heads. We hoisted ourselves into the boat and Father swam after us, catching hold of the stem of the boat and dragging himself in. I grabbed the gnarled branch that had taken me all this way and paddled for all I was worth, out into the darkening seas.

With a whoop and cry the deerfolk lobbed their spears at us. Most of the spears hit the water but one kept going, headed straight for us. My heart sank. Time moved in slow motion and I was keenly aware of a cold wind at my back like an omen of something unspeakable.

Thunder crashed, far in the distance, and in that instant I reached out my hand, grabbing the spear just as its point came inches from my father's back.

I gave the most feral snarl I could manage, teeth bared, ears pinned back, eyes ablaze, and snapped the shaft of the spear over my knee, throwing it into the sea.

"I'll paddle for a while," said Father. I collapsed into the bottom of the boat, hungry and exhausted.

We hadn't gone far when the seas became choppy and dangerous, and we made shelter from the storm on a nearby island, this one smaller and with no other packs or any creature of two legs. The rain replenished our waterskins, and a lone hazelnut tree filled our bellies enough to live another day. We made the best paddles we could with the tools we had and slept with our upturned boat for a shelter, the best sleep any of us had enjoyed in many a terrible night.

We set off in the morning on calm seas, singing old hunting songs as we rowed together, and by nightfall we could clearly see the white cliffs on the horizon; the seas were not so wide nor the islands so far apart in the south. From there it was only a few days hugging the coast til we reached the river that led to the Ancestor Oaks, and to our new home.

There was no one to greet us when we pulled our boat ashore near the grove. We pulled the boat as far onshore as we could and carried what was left of our provisions with us into the grove.

In the days since I'd left, a village had sprung up around the stump of the Old One. I recognized the faces of a family I thought for sure had been lost in the flood.

"Heron! Cattail! Is Beetle with you?" I asked.

"She's in the tent sleeping," Heron said.

"So glad you made it," Father said, throwing his arms around Heron and slapping his back. "Where were you?"

"We were on a small island about a day's journey from here," said Cattail.

"One with a large hazelnut tree right at the highest point?" Father asked.

"That's the one," said Heron.

"We stopped there on our way back. We were stranded on the highest ridge we could reach west of the Great River," Father explained. "If not for Starling we might not have made it."

"The Daughter of Thunder has returned and brought our sons home!" a voice cried behind me. It was Half Moon, her scruffy old features twisted into a big grin. "Child, you've done it! You are the Old One reborn!"

Mother ran to Father and they threw their arms around each other, sobbing. The young hunters gathered round Bright and cheered for him. Our cousins and uncles and aunts and more distant relations all crushed in, and I was overwhelmed. They were screaming, yelling, reaching to touch me, lifting me up... And my heart sank.

I didn't think I could ever get used to this life, to being the reborn Old One. I wanted to go back to being Starling. The funny, awkward Sky Child nobody expected much from.

The celebrations continued well into the night. Song and dance and prayers sung to the Old One and to Thunder... all for me. It was too much.

But at last everyone had their fill of celebrating, and somehow I kept my composure the whole time. But when the time came to retire to our little horse skin hut, when we had closed the door of woven willow branches that kept the wild animals out, I curled up and sobbed.

"What is it, Starling?" Mother asked.

"I... I can't be the Old One! I'm still young!" I sobbed.

"I think you and Half Moon ought to talk about this tomorrow," said Father. "She'll teach you everything you need to know."

"I just want to... I just want to start a family with Kingfisher! He didn't even get a chance to get near me tonight! No one would let him get close!" I cried my eyes out. I didn't care if they knew how I felt about it. I loved him. I didn't want to have to part ways with him to go live like some hermit.

"You may not have to," Mother reassured me. "Please, try to get some sleep. You can talk to Half Moon tomorrow. I'm sure it will be alright."

Half Moon reassured me that I could start a family; in fact, she insisted I did start a family. The Old One, after all, had to learn the ways of motherhood and Half Moon, with no child of her own, could never teach me that. But first, I had to promise to let her teach me everything she knew.

So it was that for three years, Half Moon taught me the secrets of the seer. Every incantation, every root and mushroom that lets one speak to the gods or heals sicknesses, how to read bones cast on the ground, how to gaze into water by fire light or by moonlight and read the future in the ripples.

She taught me the language of dreams, the tales of the gods, the tales of our pack going back thousands of years.

Then one day, I came to her hut for my lesson, but she wasn't waiting outside for me. I stepped inside her hut and found her lying covered in furs and skins. She looked frail, her eyes were dim, and her breathing was shallow.

A bit of the old light returned to her eyes as she saw me. "Starling," she whispered with a serene smile. "My time has come, child."

I took her hand. "I still have so much to learn from you," I said.

"Nonsense, child," said Half Moon. "I taught you everything you need to know. This is why I've decided it's time for me to rest."

I felt tears burning in my eyes. She'd been so spry just the day before, no sign of illness or distress. She was so old she could let go any time, and she had chosen her own time to go. There was no sense in trying to convince her otherwise.

"I love you, Teacher," I said, stroking her forehead. "I'll miss you."

"One day...." Half Moon paused, her eyes wandered and her breath stopped a moment before she sucked a gasp of air. "One day a child will be born in our pack, and you will see me..." Her eyes became dim. Her feeble grip on my hand relaxed completely. One final gasp, and she moved no more.

We buried the stump of the Old One, her roots now raised to the sky, a little ways from the ocean in the middle of a wood palisade. And in the hole from the roots of the Old One, we buried Half Moon and laid a great stone on her grave to honor Thunder.

Kingfisher and I started a family the very next spring, with gifts of food and tools and skins from the pack as we moved into the new hut we had built for ourselves.

And some months later, when our firstborn's eyes opened to the world, I gazed into them and saw a very familiar light.

Bronze

Unseeing

by Madison Scott-Clary

On the morning of every day, when days are warm and there is no rain, on days when Lyut knows when it is day and when it is night, he will gather his ingredients onto a small board and sit at the entrance to his cave and make his incense for three days hence.

Lyut, blind fisher, blind pekania, works with measured care, for he does not want to injure the pads of his paws nor nick his already-scuffed claws nor shave off any of his fur, nor, Ýng preserve him, damage his carefully honed equipment. He works with measured care and a practiced slowness, with a patience known to one who holds the highest devotion to his labor and to his Lord.

Lyut works with particular care when employing the use of his knife for he has cut himself before. He has cut himself and knows that not only will this spoil his incense for the day, it will also leave his pads aching and sore, will leave his fur matted and sticky, will leave a thin layer of blood upon all he touches until the flow stops and the wound scabs over. Knows that he would have to make his way down to the river to wash. Knows, too, after a particularly bad accident with his knife, that the stick he uses to guide his way down the path gets slippery and would need to be cleaned as well, that to bind a wound with only the use of one paw carries some particular difficulty.

And so he gathers his ingredients and tools onto his board and carries them to the entrance to his cave where he sits and works with measured care.

He works from left to right because he holds the knife and hammer in his right paw, and he builds the scent from bottom to top because that is how he has laid out his ingredients, and because it is the base notes of the scent that are the most forgiving to balance.

Begins, then, with the crushed roots of nardin, which previously he had pounded and which now he lays against the board and measures ten claw-widths thereof and cuts with his knife. To this is mixed ten teardrops of common mastic the width of a claw. On holier days he may find himself using copal in its place, and indeed he may use that later. For now, he attempts to find nodules the size of one of his claws without requiring that it be cut or broken, lest his senses be dazzled and the balance lost.

The middle notes come next and Lyut takes a fingertip's length of sweetgrass and puts it into the bowl with the base notes. The scent of sweetgrass is, yes, sweet, but it provides also the bulk of the material that will burn throughout the day.

To this he adds sweet flag root which has been carefully washed and hung and dried. He grates this first with his knife before adding it to the bowl, scraping the blade almost perpendicular along the root to shave off a fibrous powder.

These are all taken together in a stone mortar and ground with a stone pestle to pulverize them into a uniform powder, which he checks with gentle touches of the last fingertip on his left hand, which is the most sensitive.

Judges with his nose and, deeming it correct, finishes, now, with the lone top note of a precious dried pod of cardamom and what he judges to be one third again in weight of makko powder to bind the incense.

To build a scent from the bottom up is to tell the first of three prayers of creation to Ýng, and Lyut works with devotion in his heart as he grinds. He does not speak his prayer; the sound of stone against stone are his words. He does not look up to the heavens where he knows Ýng to reside for sight is not a sense he possesses; allows, instead, his Lord's presence to pierce his heart and travel down his limbs and guide the motions of his paws.

The powder of the incense, thus created, is sifted into a small bowl, the finest silt brushed from the mortar with the very tip of his tail.

To mature incense in the quiet and the dry and the cool is to tell the second of three prayers of creation to Ýng, and Lyut again works with devotion in his heart as he unlimbers himself from where he had been kneeling and carries the bowl to the back of the cave where it will always be driest. He does not speak his prayer; the sound of his paws padding in dirt and fingertips dragging along stone wall are his words. He does not look for the shelf containing the other two incense bowls for sight is not a sense he possesses; allows, instead, his Lord's presence to pierce his heart and travel down his limbs to place the bowl beside the other two.

Lyut then cleans his board, bringing it back into his cave and replacing unused ingredients in their bowls, jars, or baskets by touch and by scent.

At last, he picks up the rightmost bowl in the line and scoots the other two up into its place and carries it to the mouth of his cave. Along the way, he bends down and lifts a dish filled with ash, and carries it with him as well.

To lay the incense trail is to tell the third and final prayer of creation to Ýng, and Lyut works still with the devotion in his heart as he tamps down the ash in the dish into a smooth plane with the tip of his finger, then draws a careful furrow in the fine powder, sowing incense in its wake. He does not speak his prayer; the rhythm of the tamping and the quiet hush of incense and ash are his words. He does not look at the boxy spiral he draws for sight is not a sense he possesses; allows, instead, his Lord's presence to pierce his heart and travel down his limbs guide his left foreclaw while the right hand follows by touch, dropping the powdered incense in its wake.

The presence of his Lord burns bright within him. Lyut does not know light from darkness, but were he pressed to answer, he would say that Ýng's presence is that of light, Their absence that of dark, and by this point in the day, Lyut is filled with light.

The prayers of destruction follow the prayers of creation.

Against a crease in the rock at the entrance of his cave is his fire pit. The night before, he brought in sticks and bark from the near-woods and laid them at the feet of the fire. In the mornings after preparing his incense, he begins the first prayer of destruction, of breaking down the sticks and shredding the bark into tinder and kindling. The sound of the crack of dry wood and the tear of fibrous bark his words, the spirit of his Lord guiding his every movement.

The second prayer of destruction is the forging or rekindling of fire. If there are embers left, then the words of this prayer are the sound of Lyut's breath against them and the slow crackle of kindling catching alight. If the coals are out, then the words of this prayer are the singing of the bow drill between his feet, thermoception stretched taut as he strains to feel the warmth of the new flame starting in the tinder.

The third and final prayer of destruction that Lyut offers to Ýng is that of the lighting of the incense. He works with the same measured care as he lights a punk from the fire, the spirit of his Lord singing along his limbs, and touches it to the small mound of incense at the center of the trail he has built. The words of this prayer are silence.

Only now does he speak his prayers aloud, and by now, he is overflowing with light. It seeps out through his fur, falls from his mouth in honeyed drops, shines from darkened eyes.

Ýng is with him now as he chants, as the smoke wreathes him, as the scent of his labors fills his cave and the clearing and rises up past the tree-tops.

Ýng is with Lyut, and I am as well.

After prayer, Lyut feeds his fire and sits for a while before it to ensure that the sound of the wood burning is just as it should be and no louder and that the heat of the fire is neither too hot nor too cool, for he knows that a hot-burning fire that roared and rushed with the voice of Ýng's anger was one that would at best burn out too soon and he had been taught that at worst it would claim souls as easily as wood.

With the smoke of the fire mingling with that of his incense, with the scent of his devotion lingering in his nose and clinging to his fur and stinging sightless eyes, he takes up his walking stick and pads slowly down the path from his cave to the section of river he calls his own. His feet guide him with soft shuffling. His stick guides him with gentle tapping. His ears guide him with the sounds of the river. Ýng guides him with Their hand on his shoulder.

At the river by his cave, there is a pool where the water flows out from between two rocks, and it is across that gap that he has strung a net.

Lyut sets his stick aside and crawls on hands and knees to one of the rocks and with a long-practiced swish of his fingers through the water, he catches up the cords of the far end of the net from where they lay on the bank and sweeps his arm around to draw the net around and back toward him.

I have smiled on him today, and in the net he feels the dancing of a fish and, upon dragging the net ashore, feels in its knots also the hard-shelled bodies of the crawfish that live their silent lives on the bottom of the silt-bedded river.

The net entire is laid flat upon the shore to let the fish and crustaceans drown in air while Lyut cleans his paws and knife in the water of the stream.

To wash in cold water is to speak a prayer of cleanliness to Ýng, but also to me, to me who knows the meaning of light dancing on clear water in a way the god of the sun cannot, in a way that blind Lyut cannot, and so I sustain myself with those prayers even as the ascetic guts the fish with measured care, washes once more in the stream, and then with practiced slowness strings his net once more, letting the constant stream of water flow brightly through the pounded and knotted reeds to catch fish, to catch food.

Dripping and naked, Lyut crawls upstream along the shore, fingers crawling among the grass until he comes across the fronds of a fiddle-head fern of which he plucks two. Washes these, then wraps in them his daily catch of fish and sluggish crustaceans, and packs around the bundle clay from the riverbank.

Takes then his stick in hand and taps his way back to his cave, where, after banking a portion of the fire, he nestles his bundle among the hot coals until it is dry and parched on the outside.

In the meantime, Lyut walks carefully into the woods perpendicular to the hill on which his cave rests, brushing aside further fronds to the place where his nose tells him he may have his toilet. After finishing, another trip to the river is made, this time carrying a jug slung over his shoulder to be filled with water for his camp.

By then, the smell of steamed fish is beginning to escape from the clay baker that he has formed, and the time to break his fast is upon him.

His walking stick, hard and long-cured, is used to drag the baked clay from the embers and the jug of water put in its place to bring to a boil. He says a short prayer to Ýng for his bounty, for his food, and for the taking of three lives in order to fill his belly, and by the time the last word is finished, the clay is cool enough to tap and crack apart to exposed his steamed food. I sup from that prayer as well, for I provided him with his meal.

He sets the spent clay aside and unfurls the ferns from around his food. His first bite is of the curled heads of the fronds, seasoned with the fat of the fish and the heady scent of crawfish. His second and third bites are the flesh of the fish scraped away from soft bones with sharp teeth. The rest of his meal is a silent contemplation of what wonderful complexities the silty life of a crustacean must hold, as he pulls the tails from the crawfish, eats the meat within, and sucks the butter from the heads.

Fish head and skeleton and crawfish shells are placed in the jug of water now boiling, the makings of a thin broth which will be his sustenance for the rest of the day.

For the third and final time, Lyut washes that day, and I revel in the act of his careful attention to his postprandial grooming. This is the time when he ensures that his pelt is clean and free of ticks and fleas. This is the time when he massages the dirt out of his pawpads.

This is the time when he brushes his whiskers. This is the time when he lays his fur in order. This is the time when he makes himself pure in body before Ýng, having already made himself pure in spirit.

Too, this is the time when he makes himself pure before me, though he knows it not. This is the time when he gives thought to the direction his fur is facing. This is the time when he gives thought to any dirt which may cover him. This is the time when he, blind pekania, blind fisher, puts thought, however abstract, into what a watcher may see.

Lyut lives his life in prayer and devotion. It is a life that is lived ascending in a steady spiral of years, for time moves upward and yet is echoed below by the change of days, the change of weeks, the change of seasons. This year, this day, this soft spring is an echo of last soft spring beneath it. It is antipodal to the autumn that will come

Cycles within cycles, spirals within spirals. This morning, too, is an echo of the day beneath it, behind it, in the past. His days are defined by the cycle of incense, prayer, fishing, foraging, meditating. He knows that it is day when he wakes when he feels the warmth from the sun. He knows when it is night when he feels the warmth fade. He knows when it is morning because he hears the birds sing. He knows that it is night when the birdsong of the day settles into the chorus of insects.

Clean now, he meditates on this. He meditates on cycles. He meditates on warmth and coolness. He meditates on his relation to it, and on his relationship to Ýng.

He has surmised, for instance, that his fur is of a particular quality that the sun is drawn to, and he has surmised that this is as worthy of prayer as the incense he makes, for was not the sun with Ýng? The sun is drawn to him as it is drawn to the rocks and the dirt and the bark of the trees. It is drawn to them and it dwells within them, for the sun powers him as warmth, and the sun fills the trees with a captive warmth that is released by fire.

And are there not things that the sun shies away from? The sun shies away from night, from water, from the cool fresh leaves that interrupt it, for one need not sight to understand directionality, to understand shade as a consequence of sun's arrow.

Lyut lays on his back to let sun's arrow dry him, to let that warmth pull the water from his fur and the chill from his bones, and then he lays on his front and lets Ýng's light bathe his back as well.

Not all prayer, Lyut knows, is in ritual.

In ritual lies comfort. In ritual lies service. In ritual lies the active participation of worship, that portion of devotion that is a conversation with his Lord. The time of ritual is the time when Lyut may speak up and say to Ýng: I am here, I am yours, I am your vessel of light and all that I do is in service to you and by my very existence, my every action, I serve your glory.

Not all prayer is in service to Ýng, either, for some of it is to Their servant, to himself.

In service of Their servant, he keeps himself clean and free of sin and distraction. In service of Their servant and to Their servants, he prepares the incense that wreathes himself and the village below. In service of Their servant and servants, he subsists only off a single meal drawn from the river and whatever alms the village cares to provide him along with the ingredients for the incense that he makes in turn.

But in meditation lies the comfortable companionship. In meditation lies love. In meditation lies reassurance and trust. The time of meditation is the time when Lyut may sit next to Ýng in silence and appreciate the wonder of Them and the world that They have made.

So this morning, he lays in the sun next to Ýng, beside Ýng, and revels in all that Ýng has created rather than singing praises to Them, because it is important even for the ascetic to understand the beauty of the world, the wonder and delight in it. It is as important for Lyut to feel the way his fur tugs at the sun, collects the warmth, and the way the sun pulls the water from him. It is important for Lyut to feel the ground beneath him and hear in its silence the praises to his Lord. It is important for Lyut to marvel in the way Ýng's sun shuns the underside of leaves and follows the bark of the trees on the side it faces. It is important for Lyut to bake until he's panting and gulping in breaths of air, and then it is important for him to crawl back into his cave, stricken from the sun by the laws of directionality that he understands on a visceral level in lieu of a visual one, for sight is not a sense he possesses.

And then it is time for him to remove his simmering broth from the fire and to sip it from the cool shade of his cave, straining it through sharp teeth to prevent fine carapaces and finer bones from getting caught in his throat, unsalted but nonetheless savory, until, despite the heat of the broth, his thirst is quenched.

This, Lyut knows, Lyut relishes, is the cycle of the day, the cycle of the year, and, his Lord promises him, the cycle of his life, for he will surely be reborn when the hours of his life slow to a stop.

In this, Ýng is a liar, but it is a kind lie, a lie of omission, for when Lyut dies, *I* will take him unto me. I will take him and his acts in life together into my bowl and crush and knead and he will rejoice with me and I will rejoice with him and then whatever rest he has now, whatever glory he knows now, whatever elation he may feel shall be pale in comparison to what comes after.

Lyut prays and works for the rest of the day, for today is the day that he makes incense for the town below.

This week is the week of fasting and next week is the week of rejoicing, and so this week he must prepare for them three times the normal amount of incense, as this is the week they subsist on smoke until they cannot tell, Zita promises him, the white thread from the black after the sun sets and the cool night comes. This is the week they live on prayer and next is the week they live on celebration, when they bake small cakes in the heat of their fires, in the heat of their ovens, and five of which Zita will leave for him.

Zita may or may not be her name, or perhaps only her title. He does not know, because beyond a few kind words, she will only pray with him and pick up the incense from the edge of the clearing before his cave and leave in its place the alms that the village provides, of flatbreads and berries, of the ingredients for the incense which they grow or perhaps purchase from other villages, who may purchase in turn from villages going south, going south and east.

So today he retrieves his board once more from his cave and on it stacks all of the ingredients for the incense of the week of fasting that will feed the village and the two amphorae that will hold it. He sings wordless hymns to himself as he works with measured care to cut the sweetgrass, to shave the calamus root, to count the cardamom pods. He sings to Ýng as he pounds and grinds batch after batch of incense until his hands are humming, until his pads are singing along with him.

And then he takes his board back into the cave and returns with the stack of ingredients for the incense of the week of feasting, with the base notes of cassia and vanilla, the middle notes of ginger and turmeric, and the top note of star anise, the spices that season the cakes that they bake in celebration, and these he pounds with laughter and with tears, for with celebration comes mourning and with devotion comes the sudden feeling of loneliness brought on by laughing by oneself.

It is evening and he can feel the sun's arrow striking horizontal by the time he finishes, and when he steps out of his cave, cradling his three amphorae to his chest, he can smell even above the incense Zita sitting at the entrance to the clearing. He walks carefully until he can hear her breathing and then sits cross-legged before her and sets the vases down between them, and they pray together:

> They who make the world,
> They who end it,
> They who bring the thunder,
> In Tsuari which fell,
> In Tsuari which rose from the ashes,

We offer up the words of our forefathers,
We offer up the smoke of our forefathers,
We offer up our hearts to you.
In Ýng's name we pray, In Ýng's world we pray,
In Ýng's own voice we pray,
By the light of the sun we pray,
By the heat of the fire we pray.

And on until the sun's arrow has wandered off course and into the night sky.

This week, this week of fasting, Zita has not brought him alms. There are no soft leaves of flatbread or ingredients for incense, just as one year ago there were no leaves of bread, and one year before that, there were no leaves of bread.

This week, Lyut does not smile kindly to Zita as she collects the amphorae and walks the path down the slope to the village, because the fasting of prayer is also a fasting from emotions and worldly attachments.

And the next day, it is truly a fast, for there are no fish in his net, and if there are no fish in his net, he knows that he must not collect the fiddlehead ferns, and instead of savory broth, Lyut drinks only boiled water, hot and cleansed by fire, and he spends the rest of the day in meditation, and he goes to bed hungry.

I watch as he sleeps, fitful, and leave for him two fish in his net for his unknowing devotion to me.

It is the last night of the week of fasting and it is the thirtieth year that Lyut has served Ýng and myself that I have decided to change him and by changing him, change the world, for while I am the god of the water and the god of watching and the god of death, am I not also a trickster god?

I am the trickster god who confounded Ýng in Their creation of the smooth plains of the world by carving the land with my rivers. I am the trickster god who confounded the Lord by setting the moon in the sky to tug at the waters of Their oceans in tides, even when the moon is not seen. I am the trickster god who brought death to Ýng's ever-living world.

I am the trickster god and my trouble will come back on me thirtyfold, I am sure, but Lyut is the thirtieth ascetic who has served me and I am ready.

Lyut has once more gone to sleep hungry, belly filled with prayer and contrition and boiled water. No fish in the net, no ferns to be had, no stale leaves of flatbread or sun-dried berries. I come to him then. I come to him and I touch the back of his neck, then the crown of his head, then the lids of his eyes and the scars around them, and then I sit in the clearing and wait for him to waken. I sit and watch, for that is my jurisdiction.

When the pekania stirs at the slow warming of day, his eyes drift open as usual to the slit of relaxed muscles that is his habit, and then he shouts.

He shouts because I am a trickster god and after forty years of life, after thirty times thirty years of blind ascetics serving Ýng and myself, I am ready for change and I have given him sight.

I know his thoughts: I know that when he perceives the light of the sun for the first time in his forty years, blurry and bright, that he is struck with a mighty pain and a fear far greater than any accident with a knife could cause. I know his terror, his confusion, and his instinctual need to escape, and so I watch him scramble back into his cave and press his face to the back wall for minutes on end, barely breathing, eyes clenched shut.

"Ýng!" he cries at last. "My Lord, my Lord, what is happening?"

I answer in Ýng's stead: "You see."

He pants into the silence that follows. I know his thoughts: I know that he hears Ýng within his heart and within his bones and within his breath. I know that I have spoken to him in the language of sound, and that this brings with it its own fear.

"You see," I say again.

"You are not Ýng."

"I am Týw. I am the god of the moon and the water and of watching and of death."

"Týw?"

"Týw," I repeat, and smile at his confusion.

"But Ýng is the god of all things. How are you the god of those things?"

"Ýng is the god of all things, and They are the god of me, but of those things not under Their direct dominion, some are under mine, and I am the god of watching, of looking, of seeing. I am the god of water, and I am with you when you fish and bathe. I am the god of the moon, and when it shines down on you, I am with you. When Ýng is with you, I am as well. When you serve Ýng in these ways, you also serve me."

Tears course freely down his cheeks, and he says: "It hurts to see."

"You have never seen before. Come out of your cave."

He does not move, and so I wait. I know that he will need to attend to his day soon, and I know that he is praying to Ýng and feels the compulsion to perform his acts of service, his rituals, and I know that the village below is waking up to ready itself for a day and night and week of celebration. So I wait.

Too, Ýng waits, because although I sense Their wrath on the horizon, I think that it will not come yet, because this is also new for Them, and They also watch.

Eventually, Lyut crawls, eyes clenched shut, on hands and knees, crawls out into the sun, and sits cross-legged in the center of his clearing.

"Open your eyes."

He does not. I know that he can see the warmth of the sun behind closed eyelids, showing dusky orange through them. I know that he can sense the shadows cast in the sun's arrow by the leaves above and around him. I know that even this seeing is too much for him.

"Open your eyes, Lyut, faithful."

"You are not Ýng, you cannot command me."

"No," I say. "I cannot command you, but you are as faithful to me as you are to Them in the ways that I have described, and so I ask for this small obeyance."

Lyut ponders this for a long while, his tail flitting agitatedly behind him, drawing praises to me in the packed earth. Finally, he opens his eyes, a crack, a squint. He opens his eyes and looks at the ground before him. He looks at his naked body. He looks at the clearing and at the trees around him. Looks in wonder. Looks in awe. Looks in terror and in panic. Looks at the ground and the trees and the sky. Tries, even, to look at the sun, and learns that the sun's arrows are keenest above all to the eyes.

"It hurts! It hurts!"

"Do not look directly at the sun, faithful," I laugh. "Ýng has decreed that the sun provides your life, and so it is too dear for you to behold."

He grinds his palms against his eyes and smears his fur with tears and with dirt. Even as he cries, he is marveling at the flashes and swirls of light that come to him now, and each phosphene that blooms in pink and white and green is a prayer to me, so I allow him this moment of non-darkness until the moment passes and he can open his eyes once more without pain.

"Where are you, Týw?"

"I am with you."

"Can I see you?"

"We are also too dear for you to see with your eyes, Ýng and I, but do you not feel the way we pierce your heart and burn along your arms as you prepare the incense for our offering?"

Lyut is silent once more, still once more. He prays. He prays to Ýng with a fervor he has not yet shown in his forty years. Tears stain tracks down his cheeks as he struggles with the sudden, overwhelming sight. Sight, a sense he now possesses.

"Go and prepare for your day, faithful. I am with you."

Lyut is slow to begin moving, and when he does, he walks as though a great dream has come upon him. He lets Ýng guide his movements and I stand apart from the Lord and Their servant.

Lyut moves as though a great dream has come upon him and lets Ýng guide him, and even so his morning task of making incense is far slower than usual, for his eyes water constantly and he marvels at just how drab the ingredients, so bright and colorful in the nostrils and so familiar to the touch, are to behold. He has not known the comparison of color before, but even to one for whom sight is a new sense, he is surprised to find that the crushed root of nardin and the shaved root of sweet flag look so similar despite the vast difference in aromas and purposes, that the mastic, that steadfast base of a scent, nearly glitters in the sun while the jewel-bright scent of cardamom is belied by so dun a color.

He moves as though a great dream has come upon him until it is time to lay the powdered incense in the bowl of ash, that third prayer of creation, and he realizes that he can see the furrow he digs in ash with his claw, can see the tan powder that he packs in its place, and can see the spiral he builds, and then tears come upon him once more, and all of his prayers of destruction are completed through sight blurred by shock, and he relies on his habits and Ýng's guidance to make it through to the end without burning himself.

I stand apart from the Lord and Their servant and watch, and drink in what prayers I may along the way.

At last, the time for ritual passes and Lyut stumbles into the woods to tend to his toilet and lingers a while in wonder at the sight of his own body, the sight of the woods and the leaves and humus on the forest floor, before returning to his cave and, out of the habit of so many years, grabbing his stick to guide him down to the river.

"Do you need that, faithful?"

After a moment's confusion, the fisher laughs. "I suppose I do not, Týw."

"Will you leave it behind?"

His answer is a long time in coming. "It is comforting in my paw. I will take it with me."

Guided still by habit—and perhaps by Ýng, for I do not know the Lord's every thought—Lyut taps his way down the path to the water, and perhaps it is for the best that he has brought the stick, for his eyes are drawn constantly to every detail along the way, from the way the suns arrow strikes the leaves to the way their shadows dance across the ground when the wind moves across them. His eyes water still, for he is overflowing with sensation. A life lived without a sense is still a full life, and to one born without that sense, raised without that sense, he did not think of himself as blind except in comparison to Zita who picked up the amphorae of incense with such ease that he had never known.

Stops, at last, at the edge of the stream and stares at my domain, mouth open as though to speak, though no words come forth.

I wait a while, and then ask: "Faithful, do you see the wonder of my creation? My friend the water?"

"I had never imagined that it looked like this." His voice is barely above a whisper, and his eyes drink deep of the sight of the stream. "I did not know that something could be as beautiful."

This fills me more than any prayer yet that day. "I am the god of the water and the god of watching and the god of the moon and death. When you come here to fish, when you come here to bathe, when you come here to drink, those are praises that you sing to me."

Lyut tilts his head. "Is Ýng not the god of all things? I am sorry for asking again, but I must know."

"They are the god of many things, and They are the god of me. To sing praises to me is to sing praises to Them in turn." At this, I feel the Lord's anger at me soften, though it does not wholly retreat.

"I do not know the words to any prayers to you, Týw."

"That is alright, faithful. You may pray all the same by fishing and bathing and drinking, by rejoicing in those things that are under my jurisdiction."

Lyut nods and steps into the water. This is not the usual order of his mornings, but as the wonder on his face at the sight of the water moving around his legs fills me to overflowing, I do not complain. He stands in the middle of the section of the stream that is his own, in the pool held up by the narrow gap across which he strings his net, in the cool water where the sun's arrow pierces the canopy of the trees. He stands there and he watches the way that the light reflects off the surface of the water. Watches, too, the way the water eddies around rocks, around his legs, explores the funnels of whirlpools with his fingers, peers through clear water to the silt and rocks and algae below the surface.

"What am I now, Týw?"

"What do you mean, faithful?"

"Before this morning, before today, when I did not see, I was complete."

I remain silent.

"I am sorry, god of water and of watching. I do not doubt you, for your gift has spoken for you. I do not turn away your gift, and I offer my praise to you. But if I was complete before and a servant to Ýng, then what am I now?"

I watch him curiously, this servant of mine and of my Lord's, standing in the middle of a pool in a stream where his thighs are steeped in the cool water. "You are Lyut, faithful of Ýng, faithful of Týw. Has that changed with your sight?"

He runs his hand above the water, feeling the boundary between water and air with his pawpads. He feels the surface tension of the pool, and through him I feel his wonder. He tests and plays as might a kit of his people even as he begins bathing. Each time he comes up for air, he sings a line of praise to Ýng, and every time he is beneath the water, I know that he is thinking about what he is now. Each time he dives, he is singing his praises to me as well, and now he is cognizant of this as well.

After he has said his prayer and cleaned himself he wades to his net in which he finds three small fish. He gives thanks to Ýng and, after a moment, to me as well.

With the fish on the shore, wrapped in net and stunned, gasping and drowning in air, Lyut watches. He watches them glitter and wiggle. He watches them die their slow deaths. He traces sun-struck scales with a claw and asks: "Do the fish see beneath the water, Týw?"

"Yes, faithful. They see my domain and all its beauties."

"Do they smell beneath the water?"

"After a fashion, yes."

"Do they smell my incense?"

"No, faithful. The boundary between the domain of air and the domain of water is too firm for the smoke of your incense to pass. After all, do you smell your incense beneath water?"

"No, I do not breathe under the water." Lyut looks angry, then laughs. "Only, I wonder."

"Yes, Lyut?"

"I wonder if the fish upon the shore here has the chance to smell the incense and hear the prayers to Ýng before it dies."

I do not answer directly, saying instead: "You are not going to die, faithful."

He looks satisfied at this answer and I realize that I have said what he needed to hear. I know that Lyut holds terror in his breast even still, that he will hold it there until the end of his days, for I have taken his innocence from him. I am pleased to see his satisfaction, and I sense Ýng's bemusement at my anxiety over pleasing a servant.

I am pleased all the same, and I remain with my servant.

I am with Lyut as he gathers his fiddlehead ferns and pawfuls of clay. I am with him as he sets his net once more. I am with him as he cleans his fish and heads back to his cave to prepare his daily meal.

Three times, he closes his eyes and his whiskers droop as he attempts to settle back into his unseeing routine. He is testing himself, I know, and I do not stop him. I do not stop him because I know that when his eyes are open, he is closer to me, to Týw the watchful, and when his eyes are closed, he is closer to our Lord, Ýng, the god of all things, and it is good for him to understand this.

He closes his eyes to shut out the sight of preparing his meal, too confused by the twisting of the ferns around his fish. The leaves which make so much sense to his long-practiced fingers do not behave to his eyes the ways in which he expects.

He closes his eyes to eat his food after cracking open the clay baker, for the sight of the fish changed by fire is unnerving. The change in texture he had always known had changed, as too with the taste, for Lyut was no stranger to the flavor of raw fish. Now, sight-ridden, he finds the taste of the fish reduced when his eyes are opened, as though too much of him, of his mind, his being, is taken up processing that which he sees.

And he closes his eyes, last, when he lays on the ground to dry and meditate.

He closes his eyes as he lays on his front, and then when he rolls onto his back, he keeps them closed, and I see his cheeks wet with tears.

"Speak to me, faithful. Why are you troubled?"

"You say that you are the god of watching, yes?"

"I am."

"Must watching always be with sight?"

Again, I do not answer directly. "Do you wish now that you had not regained your sight?"

"It is too much, Týw."

"You are strong, faithful."

"It is too much." He shakes his head. "I feel less holy. I feel less pure when distracted by seeing. How can I serve Ýng as faithfully now that my time spent watching is time spent serving you?"

I feel Ýng's anger rising against me once more, and I answer carefully. "To live is to be holy, to live and rejoice in life, to be pure and clean in your actions and words. Ýng is the Lord of all things, and to Their servants They gave life as a way for the universe to recognize its own beauty and wonder."

Lyut's face twists in anger. "And yet I cannot hear Ýng as well today as I did yesterday. He is with me, I know, but..."

"The only mind that can hear as purely as it sees when both eyes and ears are open is that of Ýng, true, and yet in seeing, do you not also praise Them? It was They who made seeing as well as hearing. It was They who made me."

At this his features soften. His words are slow, and he processes his thoughts and feelings aloud. "I, as a servant, do not understand the hierarchy of the gods, but, yes, if Ýng made the light and the sun and colors and also you, then I suppose I pray to him as easily by rejoicing in sight as I do in sound and touch."

The sun is overhead and tipping down its long path through the afternoon. The colors of the trees are bright and I am with Lyut. "Rejoice, then, in your sight, faithful, for in doing so, you offer prayer to Ýng and to myself."

A slow minute passes as the fisher meditates. At last, he opens his eyes and looks up to the trees and cloudless sky.

"I will try, Týw."

"That is all we ever ask of our servants, Lyut."

When Zita comes up from the village, bearing an armload of flatbread and a small basket full of spice cakes for Lyut, he had since ceased his conversation with me and had ceased meditating by laying on the ground, and had instead settled for sitting cross-legged in the entrance to his cave looking out. Zita sang as she walked, as she had for the last ten festival weeks that this had been her duty, and so Lyut hears her before he saw her.

He debates for thirty heartbeats whether or not he is willing to keep his eyes open for her arrival. He debates whether or not he is willing to see, to perceive someone with senses other than those he had been born with.

Lyut makes up his mind and closes his eyes when he hears Zita rounding the curve of the path toward the clearing before his cave. He sees her shadow move in the trees, he sees a hint of her between the trunks, and all courage fails him in that moment.

"Faithful, why do you close your eyes?"

Lyut stays silent.

"As you wish, faithful, but know this: while some miracles are private and must be held close to the heart, not all of them must, and to hide this one would be to live a lie before me and before the village."

"I am not brave enough."

Zita's singing crescendos as she enters the clearing, then abruptly stops. Lyut supposes that because he is not sitting in the customary place with the customary smile on his face, that she must sense in him some change beyond her ken, and at this, his fear only grows.

He turns over what I had said within his head. He turns it over ten times and considers the ramifications of it. Were he to keep his newfound sense a secret, then yes, he would in some way be living a lie. He would have sight at his disposal and yet the village would know not of the incredible power of the gods that had granted it to him. And yet there was terror to be had at the thought of anyone finding out. He was holy in part because of his unseeing, was he not? He was pure before Ýng at all times, and he was pure in the ways that the village could not be, for that was his role as the ascetic, as the incense-maker, as blind Lyut.

And yet to lie is to sully oneself. To lie before the village was to betray his role as ascetic and to make himself less holy in the eyes of Ýng. To tell the truth was to test the village and change tradition, but to lie was to destroy it for the sake of the village.

To live a lie until Ýng took him and decided at what point in the endless cycle should be placed his death was too terrible a thought, and the need to tell truth, to remain as pure as he could be, won over in his mind.

"Lyut?" Zita speaks, tentative.

And so he opens his eyes. He opens his eyes. He opens his seeing eyes and looks across the clearing and sees Zita there, shorter than him, softer and rounder than him. Too, she is better fed than him—though that is not his place in the world—but she is different on a level more fundamental than any he could have imagined. She is, he thinks, unlike anything he had expected her to be.

He smiles. "Zita."

That he had opened his eyes and looked upon her seems to startle Zita, and she takes a half-pace back away from the cave.

He speaks as calmly as he is able, but he does so quickly as to preempt her leaving. "Zita, Ýng has blessed me this day. Ýng and Their servant have blessed me, and when I awoke and opened my eyes, I saw. I saw for the first time."

She frowns and walks toward him. She moves slowly, and then steps a few paces to the side when she is halfway across the clearing to approach him from a diagonal. It is a test, I know, and when his eyes track her movements, she rushes to him and sets down the bread and cakes beside him.

"Ýng has done this?" she says quickly and quietly. "Ýng has worked a wonder! Such a wonder!"

"Yes," Lyut says. It is a small lie, but one easily fixed when first the topic of me, of the god of sight and of watching comes up. "Ýng has granted me sight. I have been praying and meditating, and I do not yet wholly know the reason why."

Zita's eyes dart this way and that as though to take in all of his face, to look at his eyes and to check for the scars that Lyut had sometimes felt beneath his fur while washing, though he knew not where they came from. At last, she looks into his eyes for a long while.

This makes Lyut uncomfortable, and he does not rightly know why. Was there something to behold there? He can see her eyes, and is seeing them for the first time, and to do so fills him with anxiety. They are round and dark, and seem to be made of a ring of brown surrounding a circle of black, and as her eyes move, he sees that the circle of black sometimes grows larger or smaller, though perhaps it is some trick of the light.

But those were simply the mechanics of sight. He can see her eyes, yet he feels that to look directly into the eyes of someone else is to *truly* see them, and he worries that, on some level, Zita will be able to read his thoughts and fears, that she will know deeper secrets about him than he could possibly ever know about her. Was this some knowledge of the sighted that he must someday learn himself?

As well, this close to her and he can smell her better than he ever had before, and she is in no way, in no sense unpleasant.

The feeling of being sullied and unholy hangs around him like a cloud.

He asks, then, quietly: "What do you see, Zita?"

"I see you as I always see you, but I see you with your eyes open and clear, where they used to be cloudy and dim, and I see your fur brown and thick without the scars that my mother says have lined your eyes since a year you were born."

"Yes, but what do you *see*?"

Zita finally averts her eyes, though only to pick up a cake from the basket and split it in two, holding out one half for Lyut and keeping the other for herself. The cake is the color of the sun and bespecked with the cassia and cardamom which had gone into the incense. "I see that Ýng has wrought a miracle and that our time of fasting and keeping holy has led to something truly wondrous."

Lyut lets his shoulders relax from a tenseness he had not known he was holding, and he accepts the spiced cake from her. "I see. Thank you, Zita. I have been praying and meditating on this all day, and though I know I must not, I doubted this miracle and felt unholy."

She bites into her cake and chews, her eyes focusing seemingly on nothing. Lyut can hardly read her expression, so new is his sight, so he remains silent. She swallows her cake and says: "I think that you are as holy now as you were at the beginning of the time of fasting. You have kept holy as have those who came before you, and the village has kept holy, and perhaps the whole world has kept holy, and now Ýng has provided for us a new thing."

Lyut eats his spice cake and thinks on this. He thinks about what I had told him. He thinks about the shock of sight, still so new to him that the brightness and colors in the world sting his eyes and bring him to tears. He thinks of the newness in things that have always been there. He thinks of how overwhelmed he is by this mere fact, and he thinks about how small he is before me and smaller still before his Lord.

He thinks about how small he is and realizes that his devotion burns more strongly within him than it had ever before. And, though he does not know or understand my motives, he knows that any servant, that *every* servant of Ýng's is master of him, for the most holy are truly the servants of servants.

He thinks about this and then he smiles to Zita once more and nods. "Yes. Yes, this is a new thing that Ýng and his servant Týw have done, and in their presence I will continue to be holy."

Zita tilts her head to one side, and Lyut wonders if perhaps she had not heard well. "Who is Týw?"

I break my long silence and say, "I am."

Lyut stiffens and Zita startles to her feet.

"I am Týw, and I am the god of the water and of the moon and of watching and of death, and I am servant to Ýng, and I have given sight to Lyut."

When Zita understands, she falls to her knees and prostrates herself before Lyut, seeing no one else to bow before. "A spirit! A spirit!"

Lyut laughs at this, though not unkindly. "I believe Týw, that They are the god of the water and of watching, though I know not what the moon is. I have prayed to Ýng about this and I believe that Týw is Their servant."

"I am. I have given Lyut sight and Ýng is watching all of us."

"I cannot see you, though," Zita says.

"As the sun is too dear to look at, so are the gods, faithful."

"How can I be your faithful?" There is an edge of frustration to her voice, and her tail dances about behind her. I accept her agitation just as I accepted that of Lyut.

"Every time you bathe or drink pure water, every time you keep watch on the world, every time you behold the beauty of the moon, and every time you mourn the dead, you give praise to me, for not all prayers are in words, as Lyut well knows."

He nods in agreement.

"These things are my dominion and Ýng is my Lord in turn."

Zita sits up slowly. Still frowning, she considers this. "Why have you given Lyut sight?"

"That is not for you to know, faithful, not yet. There will be a time when you may, however."

She relaxes at my words, for she knows the workings of the gods and the mystery therein almost as well as Lyut does.

"Now, it is almost evening," I say. "Put away the bread and the cakes lest the night animals take them."

Zita nods and moves to help Lyut gather his food before remembering that he can see the basket and the flat loaves of bread as well as she, and they laugh together.

After the food is put away, both fishers kneel together and begin to pray aloud to Ýng.

> They who make the world,
> They who end it,
> They who bring the thunder,
> In Tsuari which fell...

I let them finish their prayer and bask in the jubilant way that Zita's voice rings out to her Lord.

When they finish, Zita smiles to Lyut and stands once more. "I must go down to the village and tell them of this miracle. Tonight you will see the moon, holy one, and know its beauty and that will be your praise to Týw."

The thought fills me with joy, for the moon is indeed beautiful, and I watch Zita put her arms around Lyut in an embrace—his first in many years—before departing down to the village once more.

Lyut stays up late into the night at the promise of the moon. Night is not day, this he knew, and the subconscious understanding that the sun brought light would mean that the absence of the sun would bring darkness does not surprise him.

He remains curious about all things. He marvels at the red and pulsing glow of the embers of his fire. He wonders at the way the sun's arrow disappearing colors the sky pink, purple, navy, black. He drinks in the way in which the color drains from the world.

The first night of the week of feasting is the night of the full moon, which Lyut had known but had not understood, but now he does. He understands the moon and its importance when first it creeps into view of his clearing. He understands its beauty, and he weeps. He weeps for my creation, and I am filled with praise unclouded by words. Filled to overflowing as I have never been since Ýng created me at the beginning of all things.

And that night is the night when Ýng comes to me and makes his decision.

The next morning, a second strange occurrence greets Lyut when he opens his eyes. Sitting at the entrance to his cave is a creature very much like him in many ways, but in many ways different. Long and lithe, yes, strong and slender, yes, but shorter, and with fur of the purest white as opposed to the dark brown of his own. A face more slender and ears larger, and on the tip of his tail, the fur is dark black.

"Who are you?"

I smile to him. "It is I, faithful. It is Týw."

A look of confusion comes over his face, and I must hold back amusement as the fisher sits up and rubs his eyes, looking around as though the answers were to be found in the air itself.

"Týw?"

"Yes, faithful."

"I thought that the gods were too dear to be seen?"

I close my eyes. I revel in the blackness this brings. I revel in the feeling of terror and the exaltation that come with being embodied. I revel in the power of our Lord. "Yes, this is true. This has always been true through the long years and longer millennia. However, I was not completely honest with you yesterday, Lyut."

He frowns, staring intently at me in my new form. "If you are a god and you are holy, how can you lie?"

"It was a lie by omission, for I am the god of water and of watching and of the moon and of death, but I am also a trickster god. I am the god who sows chaos while Ýng brings order. Forever we work together or strive against each other. Forever we move in a cycle. This is our very nature. This is the way of things, for Ýng must have something to strive against that time move forward and his creations grow and change with it."

Lyut sits cross-legged and bows his head as he thinks on this. He knows that, on some level, it must be true, for there are times when the weather is bad for days on end and he cannot—or could not—tell the difference between day and night, and there are times when he will go a week without food from the river, and once there was even a time when something happened to the water of his section of the stream that caused it to taste bitter and plant-like, and no amount of boiling could remove the flavor and he was sick with fever.

"You sow chaos and Ýng fixes it?"

"There is no fixing chaos, faithful. I sow chaos because that is who and what I am. Ýng brings order because that is what They are. There is no moral ground on which to judge the chaos that I sow, just as there is no judgment to be made on the order of our Lord. Both are holy in their own way, because they are the chaos and order of gods."

"Is the chaos of your servants not holy, then?"

"It is not. It is my role in the world to sow chaos so that you may learn and become better for it, but when you sow chaos for each other, you lower yourselves in our eyes." I see confusion on his face and sense questions in his mind, but he does not speak, so I continue. "The chaos sown by living beings is an exchange of power. Inevitable, perhaps, but it bespeaks a lack of devotion."

Lyut frowns as he considers this.

I give my servant time, for he has learned more in the past day than any of his predecessors have in their spans.

"So then," he says at last. "How can I see you now? What are you?"

"I am the god of watching and of water, of the moon and of death, and I am a trickster god, but all of these things are a part of the world separate from you. I am, this body is, the concrete manifestation of myself and I will take this form for a time. I am this concrete manifestation because I committed a concrete act by giving you sight, and the ramifications to me are also concrete."

"You made it so that I can see you?"

"No, faithful. Ýng has made it so that you can see me, for They are my Lord and I am Their servant, and I sowed chaos and They have in turn brought order to *me*. At least, for a while."

Lyut looks startled at this. "Is it a wicked thing that you have given me sight? Have you made us both unholy?"

"No, faithful, dear Lyut." I smile and hold up my hands. "It is good and holy that you may see, and Ýng agrees. However, They control the balance, and so they have decided that the balance, the exchange, for you seeing is for me to be seen. I will live for thirty years among the world in this embodied form, and you will find that the chaos that I bring is vastly reduced while I am here, for in this form, I cannot work my usual methods."

"Is that not a punishment, for a god to have their power lessened?"

I laugh. "No, I do not think so. Ýng was at first angry with me and perhaps They wished at one point to punish me. But They understand now, and this is instead a matter of me experiencing what you experience in the way that only a god can, for gods must learn and change along with their servants."

He thinks for a long while on this, and I know that he is praying to Ýng throughout, that he is closing his eyes so that his hearing is sharper and his smell is more keen and perhaps his sense of the holy is as well. I do not interrupt his prayer, for Ýng is with both of us. I pray with him. We sit in silence in the cave and hear the wind and the stream and the birds, and we smell the cassia and cardamom and copal, and we share our prayers.

"Týw," he says at last. "I have faith in Ýng and I have faith in you that I will remain pure and that the world will remain pure with us. I do not understand, but I have faith."

"Good. Now, I will teach you to see, faithful, and you will teach me to be seen, for everything—*everything*—will be different now."

Priest of Lilies

by Kayodé Lycaon

The wind rustled through dry savannah grass under a hazy morning sun. Akachi's ears swiveled forward and stiffened with determination as he saw a lion in the distance. A younger lion—the painted wolf guessed—probably a hunter from the large bow she carried.

His paw tightened around his atlatl and he crouched low in the tall grass. Another hunter who had stepped too far. He turned and slowly made his way towards the shade of a broad acacia tree.

The Great War between their peoples was over, but his atlatl was carved out of a lion's thigh bone. He wasn't done fighting. The lion clans, safe behind the walls of their sprawling cities, were ever reaching out their claws to steal more territory. Everything they saw they claimed as theirs. No tribe, no people could stand alone against them, but he had to try. As long as he lived, there would be hope.

Akachi exhaled, reminding himself to focus. He kept his eyes on the lion while his ears turned to either side, listening to make sure she was alone. Then his foot slipped into a hole and he stumbled. The lion's ears twitched towards him and she pulled out an arrow from the quiver on her hip.

The painted wolf froze. He wasn't ready. Nocking one of his long darts to his atlatl would give away his position. He bit back a curse. She was sniffing. He was downwind, but the wind could change at any moment.

This was not something he could solve with skill, but he was reluctant to ask the spirits for their help. The pouch on his belt only held three lily petals. They were precious and he had no way to harvest more. For a moment, his heart despaired; they may be the last he'd ever have.

Even so, his life was worth more than any petal. He pulled one out and crushed it between his paw pads, whispering a gentle song as his offering.

For a moment, nothing happened. Then blue dragonfly-shaped lily spirits came to flutter around him, hiding him. Where his ears had been, there was nothing more than grass blowing in the wind. It wasn't much, but it was enough.

If he had been blessed, they would have done more. During the war, a single flower held in the paws by a priest of lilies would have summoned cold, malicious mists that rose from the earth as far as he could see. He had done it once, long ago, but those days had passed and Monsoon was not so giving to her priests.

He reached the tree and nocked a long dart—one of three his brother had prepared—to the spur of his atlatl. The flint head, two arm-lengths in front of him, was covered in a sticky black paste. The dart's white feather fletching rippled in the wind.

The painted wolf took a deep breath and placed his feet. The atlatl was almost cold in his paw as he held it up. A sudden gust swirled around him and a strand of wind brushed his ear, whispering— seventy-three paces.

Then the winds stopped, as if holding their breath.

Akachi felt pity. The lion stood there in front of him. She was not a warrior. She had never fought one of the Avoniya—nor a priest of Monsoon. The demons from the mists were nothing but stories to frighten children. If she heeded them, she would have dropped prone at the first sight of a black ear or the sudden stilling of the wind.

Now, she would know; then she would die.

Akachi stepped forward, turning his body and swinging his arm—driving the dart forward. Then he snapped his wrist to complete the throw.

The dart flew true and buried its flint head low and deep into her belly, just inside the joint of her hip.

She screamed and dropped to the ground.

The painted wolf knelt beside the tree, waiting. It didn't take long for the lion to stand up, highlighting her form against the clouds. He huffed out through his nose. Pity gave way to contempt. She was as foolish as she was young. Contempt turned to hate in his heart; not at her, but what she stood for—the ignorance and arrogance of her kind.

Then he felt shame.

He knew better. Nature was harsh and unforgiving, but not vengeful. All life was sacred and his duties as a priest came before those of a warrior. He closed his eyes and took a deep breath, then he pulled out his dagger.

Akachi stood up and left the shade of the tree. He waded through the grass, trusting the spirits to hide him. When she fell, he would be there.

The lion broke off the haft of the dart and staggered towards a cluster of trees. Akachi walked forward as her cries for help became weaker. Slowly, the poison seeped through her. Her left leg was the first limb to become rigid. She fell, but could no longer draw breath to scream.

When he reached her, she was writhing on the ground, back arched as every muscle pulled tight—no longer able to fight. If he did nothing, the poison would take hours.

He knelt beside her and grasped her ear, turning her head so she could see his face. In her eyes, he could see the terror and the pain. He hoped she could see there was no longer any malice in his.

Gently, in her own tongue, he whispered, "May we find peace when we meet again."

With a single cut, the lily spirits flew away, abhorring the taking of a life.

The painted wolf closed her empty eyes and said the prayers that would guide her soul to the world beyond the veil, but he could not bring himself to continue. He stayed beside her, repeating the prayers under his breath, her blood staining his fur and loincloth.

Eventually a vulture croaked overhead and he looked up. Three of the sacred birds waited, impatient. The painted wolf picked up his knife. He would fulfill his duties to Monsoon and then let her winged servants take care of the rest.

Hours later, with the sun high in the sky, Akachi returned to the valley with a pelt over his shoulder and his darts in a paw. Each step felt heavier than the last. He reached the stone path and walked past three jackals standing guard on the wall protecting the entrance to the valley. They looked up from whatever game they had been playing to thump their clenched fists against their chests in respect. He thumped his chest in return but didn't wag his tail like he usually did.

Where the well-trodden path came down beside the river, the welcoming scent of clean water and wildflowers surrounded him. Despite the heaviness of his heart, it sang when a lily spirit brushed against his muzzle. Even stained with death, lilies had welcomed him; he was home.

He dropped off the lion's pelt at the tanner's hut and continued down the road, where trees gave way to broad fields with round mud houses. A few jackals looked up from their work to thump their chests in respect as the guards had, and he returned the gesture.

It was good to be back. Thousands of jackals lived in the valley and everywhere he looked, they prospered. Even the poorest family had a field they called their own.

On the far side of the valley, at the end of the stone road, was a towering red mesa with a village carved into it; but it wasn't just a village and a home, it was a fortress. Each of the four tiers were carved deep into the rock, with only narrow steps connecting the increasingly higher and smaller levels. On the third tier, deep caves held enough grain for three years and sheltered a spring with cold, clear water. It would be an extravagance, if not for the grasping claws of the lion clans. These walls were all that stood against the further enslavement of their kind.

After he reached the first set of narrow steps, he was greeted with a chorus of yips from the six jackals standing behind a wooden palisade. When he got to the top, they set their large wicker shields and short spears aside and ran over, tails wagging.

The painted wolf knelt to avoid leaning over them and nuzzled their jaws in the traditional greeting of his own people. Jackals were less effusive towards their packmates than the Avoniya, but for him, they returned his affection with equal enthusiasm.

After exchanging licks and wags with everyone, he lingered over Okori. The jackal tilted his head so they could kiss muzzle to muzzle. Their tongues intertwined for one slow exhaled breath before they separated.

"See you tonight?" Akachi asked.

"Ye-" The jackal's tail froze before he could finish speaking, then he ran back to his post.

Akachi turned around to see an elderly jackal wearing a heavy necklace of clacking lapis stones striding angrily towards him. The guards had turned their attention back to the valley and kept their ears forward. The painted wolf stood up to his full height, towering above the jackal. Someone must have told Tahir about the pelt he dropped off. His hackles rose.

"What are you doing!?" Tahir whispered harshly. "You'll bring the clans down on us. Is it not enough for you that we already deliver tribute, so they do not come into the mountains?"

"We've had this argument," Akachi growled—not caring who could hear him. "You paid twice this year what you did last. How long until you can no longer pay? Besides, this one—" he pointed towards the far end of the valley, "—was not three hours walk away."

They stared at each other until the jackal snapped his jaw shut, huffed out his nose, and pointedly walked away towards the large house carved into the stone beneath the second level.

Beating the elder with his own gaudy necklace would be counter-productive, but that didn't stop the painted wolf from imagining it. The jackal's arrogant naïveté was infuriating.

After Tahir was out of sight, Akachi turned towards the stairs to the second level.

As he slowly climbed and stepped around the smaller jackals, he reflected on the past. Tahir was one of the few elders left who had reservations about him, but it hadn't always been that way.

All of the elders had been hesitant to accept him and his brother at first. He couldn't blame them. The ways of the Avoniya were not theirs, but the village had been desperate to find a shaman; they had no one who could train others in the way of the spirits. His brother—Chima—freely offered all he had despite his lame leg.

Over the years, suspicion lessened and friendship grew. Friendship had become family—even for Tahir, who would vehemently deny it. Akachi smiled in memory of the week before when the jackal had done just that.

One end of the fourth level, the furthest point from the stairs, the painted wolves had been given a generously proportioned three-room dwelling carved into the mesa. It was a long, distant walk from where all of the elders lived on the first level. Akachi smiled as he heard the mournful drone of his brother's flute. The breeze and shade made the highest levels of the village almost comfortable in the afternoon heat of a late dry-season day.

Chima sat on a golden pelt laid over a pillow stuffed with straw. His left knee didn't bend completely, so his foot rested on a low wooden stool. He set his flute down as Akachi approached.

"The lilies don't like when you do that," Chima commented, wiping his paws on his loincloth.

"I know," Akachi said quietly. "I'm a priest of Monsoon. They understand."

"Understanding or not–" His brother looked down and folded his ears back. "That's a lot of blood."

"Yes it is," Akachi said tiredly, and walked into their house.

The painted wolf leaned his darts up against the corner of the wall and set his belt and loincloth next to them before stepping into his brother's workroom to wash. The other painted wolf limped in behind him and leaned against the whitewashed stone.

"You didn't bathe before coming back?"

Akachi didn't reply as he dipped a cloth into a large bowl of water and started scrubbing his head with it. His ears hung off his head. Finally he spoke. "Why are you up here so early?"

"I never went down," his brother said evenly.

"Why? Is your leg bothering you?"

"No more than usual." Chima turned to look out past the balcony. The blue sky was nearly cloudless. "Begu came up and we did some reading. He left a couple of scrolls if you want to practice." The painted wolf grinned and pointed at the shelf above the work table.

"I have too many things to do to spend my time learning to read and you're not going to get me anywhere near a stylus unless you add some fletching to it." Akachi remarked, grasping for something to talk about—anything except the blood. "Did you eat?"

"Naqua brought me some of the fruit bread she made yesterday." Chima folded his ears back. "You ready to talk?"

Akachi's ears sagged and almost a minute passed in silence before he spoke. "I'm losing it."

His brother's ears turned attentively forward.

"She was strong enough to use a hunter's bow but too young to pay attention. Caught a glimpse of me." Akachi inhaled deeply. "And just stood there. Stood there like startled prey."

"Well, that makes for an easy kill," Chima frowned.

"I hated her, Chima." Akachi choked on his words. "Hated what she stood for. Wanted revenge for all the clans have done."

Chima's eyes widened and his ears pinned back. "Please tell me you didn't…"

"I didn't. It was a long throw and I missed her heart. I only waited for the poison to work before giving her a quick death." Akachi picked up the cloth to start cleaning his legs. "Looked her in the eye, said the prayers, took her pelt; all the things I'm supposed to do." He sniffed. "I waited for Monsoon to claim her before offering the flesh and bone."

"Waiting… was not wise," Chima said softly. Then he flicked his ears. "Sorry. You know that."

"It's just too much. So much death. I know I'm supposed to kill people, but the balance is slipping away from me." Akachi set the cloth aside. "I need the lilies."

Chima nodded and frowned. "There isn't much I can do as a shaman, they need a priest."

"I know," Akachi replied, waving his paw towards the broad valley. "But there is only us. There's no way to get anyone from Lavotabar to live here." He stepped out onto the balcony and stared out. "They still blame us for the lions killing our family."

His brother said nothing. There was nothing more to say.

The rains were coming. If all had gone well, they would flood the valley and the lilies they worked so hard to plant would bloom. For a time, the swollen river would have become a sea of blue flowers. With a faithful priest of lilies, no person with ill-intent could find the valley through the mists protecting it.

But now, the seeds would rot without a gentle priest of lilies to coax them to life. In a few years, the clans would stake their claim on the valley and any jackals who remained would become their slaves. What happened to him afterwards would be of no consequence.

"I don't have any lily petals left," Chima said. "But I do have some lavender."

"If that's all you have." Akachi sighed. "At least the rest of the spirits haven't forsaken us."

"Yet," the other painted wolf replied with a slight smile. "We can call some spirits at twilight. Maybe a blessing will help."

"I asked Okori to come tonight."

"We can include him. Jackals and lavender have some under-standing." Chima grinned. "Less stuck up than lilies."

The sun was low in the sky when Okori arrived with a clay pot. The young jackal's tail wagged as he walked in without announcing himself.

The painted wolves were still on the balcony but had moved to sitting on a soft, yellow pelt, an empty pot of stew and a frame drum between them.

"Brought some embers like you asked," Okori said and sat across from them.

Akachi gave the jackal a tired smile and nuzzled him. "Glad to have you here."

Chima ruffled the fur on the jackal's head. "Hope you don't mind having me around tonight."

"Uh...sure. You haven't invited me up for a ritual before." The jackal's ears folded back. "Is there going to be a lot of blood?"

"Not all Avoniya rituals involve blood," Chima said dryly.

Akachi coughed and looked away.

"Okay, most of *mine* don't." Chima looked pointedly at his brother before turning back to Okori. "Hand me the embers and we can get started."

The painted wolf slid himself to the edge of the pelt and settled the pot in front of him. He removed the lid and stirred up the embers. Akachi stood up to retrieve a copper pot of water and a small bundle from the workshop.

Soon, the water was boiling, filling the air with the scent of lavender. Chima divided the tea between three small cups before picking up his drum.

"Mind if I sing?" Akachi asked.

"That would be best," Chima said as he started a simple repeating beat. "You're the one asking for their blessing."

"What do you want me to do?" Okori asked.

"Watch and drink the tea," Akachi said quietly. "If you can meditate, it would help."

"I'll try."

"Try closing your eyes and listening," Chima added.

Akachi cleared his throat and took a sip of tea. Then he started singing. His voice was an octave higher in his native tongue and the words of his childhood flowed smoothly from his muzzle; the Avoniya language lacked the harsher tones and stops of the jackal's language. Okori sat, mesmerized.

The sun slid below the mountains, leaving a cloudless purple sky. The brightest stars were becoming visible.

A single ghostly moth appeared. Chima stopped drumming to sip tea. Another moth appeared. Then a swirling cloud of them descended on the balcony.

Akachi let his song fade and started reciting an ancient poem. Translucent wings fluttered. Chima tapped the edge of his drum.

The moths vibrated and then vanished in a cloud of petals. Akachi whispered his thanks, with tears sliding down his muzzle.

Okori was the first one to break the somber silence. "That was amazing."

"It was," Akachi agreed as he rubbed his eyes. His voice was stronger and steadier than it had been.

"How do you feel?" Chima asked the jackal.

"Like I just woke up."

"Then it worked." Chima smiled and drank the last of his tea. "You two have fun; I'm going upstairs."

Akachi nuzzled his brother before the other painted wolf got up. "Thank you."

"Any time."

Late the next morning, Akachi sat on the stone edge of the balcony, watching the jackals tending the fields. On the first level, there were shouts and grunts as the town guard trained. The sounds were too distant for him to pick out Okori's voice among them.

The painted wolf looked over as his brother walked out to sit next to him.

"How do you feel?" Chima asked.

"Amazing. We should have asked the lavender spirits a long time ago," Akachi said.

"That would have been a bad idea."

Akachi folded his ears back. "Why?"

"It would have upset the lilies." Chima tilted his head. "How could you forget that?"

The painted wolf scratched behind an ear. "The lily rituals seem like a lifetime ago."

"Five rains—or was it six?"

"Weren't you just past your rite of passage?" Akachi said.

"Yeah," Chima said, staring off into the distance. Then his ears flicked. "Speaking of that, you're a priest of Monsoon."

Akachi blinked and stared at his brother. "How did *you* forget *that*?"

The other painted wolf ignored the comment.

"When you became a priest of lilies, Weyrn took you as her consort."

"Yes?" Akachi replied hesitantly. "That didn't exactly go well."

"That happened later. Do you remember the coronation ritual? Enough to do it?"

Akachi tilted his head, remembering. When a priest of Monsoon took a consort, they usually would become the tribe's priest of lilies. Usually male and female respectively, though reversed or same gender pairings weren't unknown. The ritual of rebirth at the end of the rains had no requirement for the coupling to produce pups.

"Is there any reason you can't take a jackal as a consort?" Chima asked, interrupting his brother's thoughts.

"And you're talking about *me upsetting* the *lilies*? The consequences of Monsoon's fury..." Akachi pinned his ears back and smacked his tail against the stone. "Well, that would solve most of our problems."

Chima ignored the jab. "Does the coronation ritual do anything transformative?"

Akachi's ears relaxed as he considered the question. "It's a minor summoning that merges a lily spirit and part of the priest's soul into the consort. Why?"

"That probably counts." Chima tapped his flute against his muzzle and looked at his brother. "Any reason we can't change a jackal into an Avoniya?"

Akachi felt the blood drain from his ears. That was something no one had ever done before and there was only one way he could think of. He curled his tail around his waist. "You want me to summon Monsoon herself, out of season?" Akachi swallowed. "Even if I had a coven to work with, and the appropriate sacrifices, we'd risk destroying the entire valley and the mountains around us! We have rituals for a reason. Monsoon is not forgiving."

"So it's possible?" Chima pressed.

"Did I mention destroying the entire valley in the process?"

"Would you rather the lion clans do that in a year or two?"

Akachi buried his head in his paws. "No."

"Just think about how much Tahir is going to be screaming." Chima grinned.

"This idea is insane and the rest of the elders are going to throw us out of the village."

"Good." Chima brought the flute to his lips again. "I'll start making paints. And you should practice your sophistry."

"My what?"

"Absolutely not!" Tahir shouted, lapis necklace rattling.

There was only the faint red light from the stones glowing in the brass bowl in the center of the circular room. Akachi's white markings stood out from his nearly invisible markings of orange and black. He hoped no one could see his ears pinned back.

"I would like to hear him speak," Awiti said calmly.

Awiti was one of the newest members of the council but, as a spearmaster, she had considerable influence among many of the younger jackals. In addition, she was also one of the few in the village who could commune with spirits as Chima did.

A general rumble of agreement rose from the other elders. No one else supported the eldest jackal's objection.

"Continue," Awiti prompted.

Akachi laid out his plan to find a suitable jackal in the tribe who was willing to take the risk. He downplayed the possible consequences of a failed summoning. The floods would prevent a second harvest this season. Everyone should be safe enough in their homes for the few hours he needed. The risk was manageable for the possible benefit of hiding the valley from would-be invaders.

The arguments continued deep into the night. In the end, Tahir was outvoted by the other elders and Akachi breathed a sigh of relief. But when he left the council chamber, Awiti came out to stand beside him.

"Would you walk with me?" she asked. "I would like to see where the flooding will be worst."

With the moonless, overcast sky, it was far too dark to see much in the valley. The painted wolf agreed and followed her down the steps and onto the stone-paved road. When no one else could overhear them, the jackal clasped her paws behind her back.

"You haven't been fully honest with us."

Akachi didn't reply.

"And furthermore, not everyone will approve of you taking a man as a consort," Awiti said evenly.

"Oh?"

"Everyone knows of your dalliances with the younger men," Awiti snorted. "It is inappropriate. Boys fucking boys is a thing puppies do when they are still exploring the world and themselves. Not a proper thing for a man to do when he grows up and knows who he is."

"Then why hasn't anyone objected?" Akachi asked.

"You're a warrior and a priest, which is rare in these lands." Awiti turned towards him. "And I have seen the spirits that surround you. You wield great magics. For that alone, even Tahir is willing to forgive many of the flaws you might have."

"I see."

"I don't think you do," she said reasonably. "People are swayed by power. Your power is such that people ignore that you murder lions and attract men to yourself. And tonight, you used your influence to ends that we don't fully understand, for promises we trust are not empty. I see this but I fear the others don't."

Akachi rested a paw on the jackal's shoulder and looked into her eyes. His voice was barely above a whisper. "If you don't approve of me, why did you back me in the council?"

"I trust you, and they trust me," Awiti replied, "but I want honest answers before you do this thing."

"What would you like to know?"

"I want to know which one of our men you are going to take. Then you're going to tell me the truth about this ritual."

"Okori," Akachi said quietly. "We are close and he is one of many warriors. The village can afford to lose him."

The jackal crossed her arms. "He is young and will do anything you ask, simply because you ask it of him."

"I know," Akachi agreed, his ears pinned back. "Chima and I will make sure he knows the risks. Say what you will about other people overlooking my flaws, I am not a monster who sacrifices his family for a spirit's blessing."

"And what about the lion pelts you collect?" The jackal's tone was sour.

"The Avoniya have always done so. We take those who stray into the mists and offer their bodies to Monsoon, she leaves us their pelts in return. Our shamans and priests have many uses for them."

Awiti huffed out her nose and furrowed her brow. "That's not much of an answer."

"Did you want me to explain the rituals? They aren't secret."

She frowned for a moment. "I think I'm happier not knowing."

Akachi shrugged.

Awiti turned to continue walking down the road. "So tell me the true risks of this ritual."

Again, Akachi followed the drone of his brother's flute across the village's highest level. His ears relaxed at the sight of a small flame flickering from the oil lamp in the workshop.

"How did it go?" Chima asked.

"They agreed."

"That easily?"

"Not quite." Akachi sat on the bench beside his brother. "Awiti twisted Tahir's arm and no one else knows what to do about the lion clans."

"Literally twisted his arm?"

"I wish," Akachi said with a shake of his head. "After the meeting, she followed me out." He sighed. "I told her how bad it could go."

"And?"

"She trusts me." The painted wolf's tail flicked. "And she's worried for Okori."

"I figured you would choose him."

"He wasn't my first choice."

Chima looked down and folded his ears back. "I know. He's young." Chima looked up. "But so were you."

"I was." Akachi scratched behind an ear. "Any ideas how we're going to do this? I know too much and keep worrying I'll get it wrong."

Chima leaned back against the wall. "As a shaman, I know most of the stories. In some of them Monsoon is pleased by a warrior's audacity to stand against her."

"There's a very thin and deadly line between audacity and disrespect." Akachi's ears folded back and he stared at his brother. "Just how many of those stories don't end badly?"

"Two or three." Chima rubbed his chin. "No, it's definitely three."

"Not exactly a promising solution."

"More than you think. We are Avoniya—the 'People of the Lily'. Lilies don't grovel. Furthermore, if we want her greatest magics, we should demand it. Monsoon isn't going to respect anyone who whines like a hungry pup."

Akachi's tail flicked. "You make it sound simple."

"It is." Chima placed his fingers on his flute. "Besides, I already made war paint and I'd hate for that to go to waste."

Three days later, the sun rose and painted the sky a bright, ominous red. Even though the rains were months away, dark blue clouds grew to the south. Furious lightning strikes flashed a blinding white. Distant thunder rumbled and Akachi's tail flicked nervously back and forth as he watched from the balcony. The scent of rain was heavy in the air and the hot, wet wind washed over his unclothed body.

"Weather looks promising," Chima said, coming over with two necklaces of lion teeth.

Akachi nodded and took one of the necklaces. He looked over the valley. There was not a spirit in sight and most of the jackals in the valley had taken shelter in their huts.

Okori came up to rest on the low stone wall of the balcony, undressed like Akachi. His ears were folded back and he frowned. "I've never seen a storm like this out of season."

"Definitely eerie," Chima said and held out the other necklace.

Okori took it tentatively. "Are these lion teeth?"

"Of course."

Akachi ignored the discussion. He turned his ears forward, hoping to hear a voice in the winds. Instead of a voice, a light drizzle—almost a mist—started to fall. He swallowed and stepped back under the relative shelter of the overhanging stone.

In the sitting room open to the balcony Chima had laid out a straw mat on the floor and covered it with a white pelt edged with tassels of small bone beads. Okori was sprinkling lily water from a wooden cup.

His brother looked up. "Ready?"

"We have her attention."

"Oh good. That was kind of important."

Akachi huffed but didn't reply as his brother picked up a small clay pot. Chima held the pot out to Okori and both of them dipped their fingers in the turquoise paint it contained.

Chima started drawing forked lines of lightning on his brother's chest while instructing Okori on how to draw small rain drops. It was a pattern neither painted wolf had used before.

As they were painting Akachi's arms, Okori paused. The jackal pressed his fingers together with curiosity. The paint was drying into a sticky film that was stubbornly clinging to paw pads and fur.

"What is this?"

"Huki," Chima said. "It's a plant resin mixed with crushed rock. It dries pretty fast once you take the lid off."

Okori's tail flicked and he looked out towards the growing storm. "Um–" He cleared his throat. "What's it used for?"

"We paint ourselves with it before going out to make war," Akachi said, allowing himself a smile as the jackal started painting his legs.

"Wouldn't you use blood for that?"

"Well, like my brother said, not every ritual uses blood. We mostly use blood for rituals of offering. Huki is used for blessings."

"Right."

Chima clapped Okori on the shoulder. "Don't worry, we'll teach you all about this later."

Akachi's ear swiveled. His brother's tone was almost jovial, but he could hear the strain under it. He hoped Chima would remember to show proper respect or at least stay out of the way when Monsoon arrived.

When his markings were finished, he and Chima started painting Okori. Instead of war paint, they covered him in black, white, and orange. If this ritual worked, they should become the jackal's new colors.

The rain started to fall harder and Akachi looked into Okori's eyes. The jackal had difficulty returning the gaze.

"Are you ready?" Akachi asked.

"Yes. I'm not afraid," the jackal stated firmly.

"Yes you are," he countered. "And you should be." He softened his voice. "There is no shame in fear. You are a warrior. Fear should be your companion. Embrace it, because without it, there is no courage, only ignorance."

"Okay," Okori swallowed. "I'm terrified."

"Good." Akachi nosed Okori's muzzle. "Remember you are brave and you are strong." Then he looked into the jackal's eyes. "Stand beside me and everything will turn out well."

Okroi folded his ears back. "Do you really believe that?"

Akachi nodded as he finished painting. Then he shrugged. "What's my other option?"

"Death," Chima said flatly.

Akachi looked up to glare at his brother.

"Ready when you are." Chima said with a forced smile.

Akachi shook his head before looking around. On the floor, the beads of lily water seemed to glow against the white fur of the pelt.

There was nothing left to prepare.

He took a deep breath and turned towards the balcony with Okori trailing behind. "Let's do this."

The rain was falling harder now and the clouds were almost black. He couldn't see the valley.

His fur started to prickle and then a resounding crack shattered the air as lightning struck the mesa above. Through the afterimages, he could see the full fury of the storm standing before him.

"She's here," he whispered, as much to himself as to Okori standing beside him.

He didn't wait for the jackal to reply. It was time.

"*Monsoon!*" he yelled with all his might.

Lightning flashed, making his fur prickle again.

"Every rain, my knees quaked in awe of your power. Every rain, I've done my part in remaking your world. I have hunted my enemies in your name. I have given your servants their share while I have taken my due. There is not one kill I haven't given you respect."

The wind swirled around him. He felt small and insignificant. He imagined himself as a lily in a storm—petal fluttering—but not breaking. He looked up into the torrent, refusing to blink.

"As you remade this world, I demand you remake this jackal."

The crashing drops stung his eyes. He felt the paint burning hot against his fur.

"He will be my consort as I am yours," Akachi screamed. "If you find me worthy, I deserve no less!"

The world shattered with a crack and then the thunder died away to become distant rumbles.

Akachi gasped as his sight returned and his paws burned with blinding light. He looked down to see his fur crackling with static. The house was still standing, its stone unmarked. "I'm worthy," he whispered. "I'm worthy."

Okori shook his head, trying to clear the ringing in his ears.

There was only one thing left to do.

Akachi grabbed the jackal by the shoulders and shouted. "Will you be the Lily's priest?"

"Yes!" Okori yelled.

The painted wolf pulled the jackal close. He grabbed the jackal's head and turned it to fiercely kiss him muzzle to muzzle.

Lightning cracked and they stumbled onto the now soaked pelt on the floor. Okori was still a jackal, but the white and orange paint on his fur glowed.

Akachi rolled Okori face down on the pelt and whispered in the jackal's ear. "And you will be my consort."

Thunder roared.

Akachi woke to the soft patter of gentle rain. Soft, wet leaves brushed his muzzle and he inhaled the sweet, sacred scent of blue lilies. Everything around him felt young and vital as if the world was new, unspoiled by other's paws. The world as it was meant to be.

A lily spirit gently fluttered past his ears and Akachi opened his eyes to see a ghostly blue dragonfly. The spirit dipped its head in respect before it flew on.

The painted wolf smiled and stared up at the overcast sky, only blinking when raindrops fell into his eyes.

Eventually, his restless heart forced him to sit up and look around. He was in a field planted high on the valley's southern wall. The red mesa stood tall and proud to his right. Smoke rose from cooking fires. Joy blossomed in his heart as he saw the village intact. Tears blurred his vision.

Only then did he notice the rest of the valley. The lowest fields had completely flooded up to the carved stone banks that protected the road. Everywhere the river had touched, lilies bloomed; the entire valley was covered with their sacred blue.

Then his ears flicked as he heard the rustle of someone approaching in the grass. He turned to look and saw Chima, and another painted wolf.

"Okori?" he asked tentatively despite recognizing the former jackal's colors.

"Yes!" The painted wolf ran to embrace Akachi.

They held each other closely and Akachi wept and wagged his tail. "You're more beautiful than I ever could have imagined."

Chima limped over and wrapped his arms around the other two and nuzzled them. "We did it. The lilies agreed to raise the mists around the valley."

"Already?" Akachi asked.

Okori smiled. "Chima helped me."

Akachi looked at his brother and sighed. "You two couldn't wait to do it properly?"

"Of course not." Chima nuzzled his brother. "Our family is safe. Isn't that what's really important?"

Akachi looked around the valley and sniffed against sudden tears. For a second time, he could let go of tradition and simply agree. "Yes. Yes it is."

Let Him that Speaketh Fate to Man Have No Fate of His Own

by Rob MacWolf

The Isle of Ocrit was not a mighty power. No great battles had been fought there. No tales were told of it. No riches were to be found there. It would be a half-century or so yet, ere the cultivation of grapes would make its slow migration from the mountains beyond the east horizon, so it had no vineyards. It would be nigh onto a dozen centuries before the great empires rose and matured enough to crave silphium, so it remained only a pale yellow flower in the woods and a savory tang in meat broth. Anyway, Ocrit did not have so very much silphium, either.

What Ocrit had was a true and genuine Oracle. And a true and genuine Oracle, even if it were not so famous or prestigious as the Cybeles of Delphi or Iliun or Cumae would one day be, was worth a journey.

Let us imagine some tyrant, brooding on next season's harvest of conquest. Or perhaps an heiress, seeking an interpretation of a troubling dream. Or an oratorical nobleman, seeking an advantageous marriage for his favorite nephew. They would come to the small harbor, make their way up the winding path through the sighing cedars. They would begin to question, more than once, if they had lost their path, only to soon see, ahead in the dim forest, an oil lamp guttering in the constant cool sea wind. They would hear ahead in the darkness of night—for the Oracle would speak to none unless the moon were overhead—something wild and dark played on a haunting pipe, invisible beyond the trees. And just when they would consider going back—surely a seasoned war leader can make do without prophecies, surely a village wise woman can interpret a dream, surely one's dear nephew can find his own way into a marriage bed—the trees would open up, and the sky would reappear.

On the left hand would be goat-grazed cliffs down to the lights of town and harbor, where the sailors who had brought them here sat in the taverns in the company of that most enviable of lovers: a full belly, plenty of beer, and a warm fireside. But on the right hand would be the sanctuary.

I have heard it claimed it was a lightless palace of obsidian columns, where chthonic vapors from the underworld took the shapes of shades of the dead and vengeful spirits. But I would not believe such things. Obsidian makes poor columns. And what vapors there were would have come from the braziers, not the underworld. Such things are for oracles as they are imagined, not as they are—or were, rather, I know of none today. More likely it was like any other shrine to a little god among the little islands in those little days, magnified to terrifying and august by the darkness of the hour and the loneliness of the journey.

Now follow our hypothetical pilgrims in. See them startle as a masked acolyte steps forth from the shadows. The warrior blusters, perhaps, and the heiress pouts, but they are told to enter of their own free will, to speak only once, and that only to ask the question they have brought.

Then in through black curtains, to an inner chamber. The only light, the moon through a single high window and the smoldering of something sharp-smelling and smothering in the braziers all about the room. Perhaps the orator is curious, steps near to examine one of them, and staggers back at a sharp word from a masked acolyte. The same one who led him in? Ah, impossible to say! They are all about the room he now can see, and all hooded and cloaked the same. And something in the braziers made him lightheaded.

Best to be done with this unworldly business and away. So they speak. They ask,

"Shall I see victory when I lay siege to the clan of the northwest?" says the eagle.

"I dreamed that my grandmother, dead these thirteen years now, pierced me through the heart with a spindle, and left me hanging in the fig tree. What does it mean?" says the goat.

"Young Tammuz is of a marrying age, will he make an advantageous match?" says the stag.

And then they wait, nervous, while their question rolls away into the close heavy darkness. They cannot even see who it is they are asking. Until they can.

Across the room, hunched over one of the smoldering braziers, smoke and darkness wreathed about their head—and a fearsome head it was indeed—Behold! The oracle would turn toward them ominously just after they were noticed—and how it was the oracle knew when to turn, when to stay statue still, who can say—then rise to an impossible height and stand in the shaft of moonlight. A great mask, some primeval and forgotten monster of a bird, cruel bulwark of a beak and imperious eyes, like a vulture god risen from the underworld. It would stare, yet how could it stare, with eyes of blank stone? Yet not a one, of all the years of pilgrims, had not felt the weight of the oracle's regard as surely as they felt their own breathing.

And when the tension was just a hair from becoming unbearable, the oracle would speak:

Thou would be conqueror, thy snows fall red.
The oldest mountains turn their backs on thee.
The serpent shall lie burning in thy bed
Ere you return to set it laughing free.

Or,

> Go ask the spindle what the fig tree means.
> Go ask the beehives what the spindle spake.
> Go seek for thirteen months of sleep and find
> The spindle cracks, and all the skeins unwind.
> Thy grandmother has left her shawl behind
> And somebody must wear it to the wake.

Or perhaps,

> The golden apple, lovely to behold.
> But green is sweeter on the tongue than gold.

And that would be that. And then an acolyte—did it matter if it was the same one?—would usher them out again, to ponder on what it could have meant—the eagle sullenly over a now-less-likely campaign, the goat pensive as if picturing herself in her grandmother's place at the table, the stag uneasy and now less sure if that favorite nephew really is his favorite after all. Perhaps, for some additional alms, beyond what they had given to be admitted? Ah, but of course, the acolyte would confess, the deep meaning of the oracle's wisdom could be explained, by one who had initiation and familiarity, perhaps on the way down the path to the village, for it is dark now indeed...

And that was how the art of an Oracle was practiced, in those days.

Historians today, I suppose, would shrug, would say it was some drug, to induce trance in a practitioner who would then believe themselves possessed by Apollo—or at least something close enough it might as well be called 'Apollo' in the history books—and deliver whatever pronouncements bubbled up in their brain.

And they would not be wrong about this, in the way a man who calls a fresco only plaster and paint, who says a mosaic is only a great many fragments of broken glass, who says a sacrificial cake is only corn and honey and fat, much as one eats every day, so what is the difference really, is not strictly speaking wrong.

But what the historians do not, could not know, is that after our pilgrims left, and the doors were locked for the night, the oracle would fumble his way out the back. Would slip off the trailing androgenous robes, pull off the top-heavy bird mask, and take deep breaths of clean clear air until there was no oracle there at all. Only a young dog called Talzu—brindle coat, darkened to an ash-brown mask around his face—naked and shivering till he staggered exhausted into the bed in his little hut, hidden behind the oracle's sanctuary.

Talzu remembered very little before his life on Ocrit Isle. And that which he did remember, he held of no consequence.

His mother—perhaps as oracle he could have said where she was now if he cared to, but he did not—had seen some signs in him. Perhaps she had a touch of foresight herself, perhaps there was some omen or augury, perhaps she saw he showed no fondness for girls at the age it was to be looked for, and any oldwife will tell you that means a man's path in life leads to the mysteries of the half-world.

Perhaps she merely needed to rid her house of another mouth to feed.

Whyever it was done, Talzu had been sent to the nearest oracle— for 'nearest' was the oracle of Ocrit Isle's most notable quality—in the midst of his tenth summer. He had served as an acolyte. He had lit the lanterns in the woods, he had played the haunting pipe in a hidden alcove, and had never thought to go farther. Most did not.

But he did. And when he did, his life truly began.

"You are dwelling on the past again," Histuman would have said, had he been there.

Talzu walked among the cedars on the upper slopes, down the path the orator, the heiress, the general would have trod last night. It was late morning, and in the light of the sun the woods were less aweful and numinous. Working at night meant he could sleep as late as he liked, do whatever he liked in the day. Some of the acolytes, he supposed, expected him to remain in his room. Perhaps he would have stayed in his room were he a grander oracle, if anyone cared to pry after his secrets, if there were luxuries for him to send acolytes to fetch. But on Ocrit Isle the only luxury to be had was freedom, so it was what he took, when he could.

"You could have more," Histuman would have said. "Those who come for what we do, they pay well."

"You're chatty today," Talzu muttered and picked up the pace toward the market.

"You could send an acolyte to the market for you," Histuman would have maintained, "as you used to go for me. You could send a ship to fetch you fine linens and rich spices."

"There is none," Talzu navigated the stepping stones across the gully where, during the spring rains, there would flow a busy creek. "Who could bring aught I want."

To that, Histuman would have had no answer.

If Talzu gets to dwell on the past, tis only fair we do as well. So let us look back at Talzu the acolyte, when he has been tending the pomegranates in the side garden, where pilgrims were led if they were too overcome with fear or sorrow on hearing their prophecy. It did not see much use, and the pomegranate bushes never set fruit for they did not grow well on this side of the mountain, but there was little else to do to keep busy until the next pilgrim arrived.

But when the step of a bare foot sounded on the wind-worn stone behind him, Talzu straightened and froze.

"Somehow," the voice of a wolf, dried to gravel with irony, had said, "you knew I was no pilgrim, eh lad?" Had Talzu not already straightened and froze, he would have done so again. Histuman the Oracle sat himself on the stone bench just beside one of his sworn-silent acolytes, the only ones to know his identity, and looked Talzu up and down like a farmer considering whether to buy a prize bull at market.

"What would you have of me?" Talzu had said. It was forbidden for him to kneel, or use any titles of reverence, for that might reveal who it was to whom he spoke. But he could not wholly keep a tremble of fear from his voice.

"Much, boy, I fear very much indeed," the old wolf chuckled. "How many years do you wear?"

"This coming harvest will be my nineteenth."

"And in all that time," Histuman's eyes strayed to the sunset over the edge of the sea, "have you yearned to leave this island? Forsake my service and secrets? Go out, see the world, and win glory in it, eh?"

The dog shrugged. "I know of nowhere I would go."

If Histuman were disappointed at that, he showed it not. "And there is no woman whose favors you seek?"

"I... no, I don't..." Talzu blurted.

"No ruddy maiden at the market? No plump matron? No prosperous widow?"

Talzu had felt a growl rise in his throat. "I have never lain with a woman, if that's what you mean."

"But you have," Histuman glanced at the young dog slyly, "disported between Kuruhdu's knees of a night, when the two of you were on vigil together. Aye, and warmed his bed of a morning after long sleepless watch."

Talzu's breath had caught in his throat. But then... this old wolf tormenting him was Oracle, was he not? What man could have secrets from him?

"You will not have long to love him. Within a moon, a trading ship will come by, unexpectedly, bearing a hired blade who hails from the far Cimmerians. A great sabrecat of a woman, and Kuruhdu will be so enamored of her, though she will be twice his height, that he will seek release from his vows and my service. Which I will give him, of course, why not? He will sail away with her, and that will be the last we ever see of him. Now, when you went to the market, a morning ere last," Histuamn had been suddenly done with that line of discourse, "You brought back chickpeas, leek, beets, and a good bit of lamb."

Talzu had nodded, confused. The wolf had tossed all of these into a stew—and Histuman almost never cooked himself—with a good helping of barley to make it go round, and it had been a very fine meal indeed for the oracle and his four acolytes.

"How did you know," Histuman had pressed him, "to bring back the makings of the equinox stew my mother used to make, when I was yet a boy among the cities of the plain? Which I have not tasted since?"

"I..." Talzu had had no idea what Histuman was talking about. "I did not."

"Oh, was there nothing else to be had in the market that day?"

"No, there was..." the dog had wracked his mind to remember, "there were pears and salt cheese and tunny fish..."

"And why is it, boy," the wolf had interrupted, had risen to his feet, had suddenly and softly stroked Talzu's cheek with the back of his hand, "that I have never once heard you speak a lie?"

The memory of that still put cold fingers between Talzu's shoulderblades.

"You know the answer to your own questions," Talzu had said. Had been unsure if he were begging an answer, or making an accusation.

"An oracle who knows his business," Histuman had answered, "rarely asks a question to which he does not know the answer."

And that had been the day Talzu had been no more acolyte, but apprentice. Every moment, waking and sleeping, he had spent with the old wolf. Learning not just signs and omens, in the stars, in the clouds, in the patterns the curls of smoke from the sanctuary braziers wrote on the air, but how to stand amid them and see the whole story they told as a woodwise hunter may stand amid trees and understand the whole forest. Learning not just the rites, but the multitude of meanings behind the rites, how they meant the moon journeying to the underworld and returning with its secrets, but also meant the man hung living on a sacred tree as sacrifice from whose heart's blood all harvests sprang, but also meant the unnamable watchers who stand motionless and stern at the gates of death in the uttermost west keeping secrets no mortal mind could know and live.

Learning, aye, but also practicing. Tasting with his breath the bitter secret mix of incense and oily seeds and sacred herbs burned in the braziers and fighting to keep his head steady amid the warm and weightless rapids that would then swell within his ears as he held that fume-filled breath, a little longer each time. Memorizing whatever verse the sanctuary could remember, much of it nonsense, and then changing it, a word at a time, so that nothing remained but the rhythm and rhyme, that whatever visions might come, his tongue would have the agility to tessellate into verse on the spot. Balancing the heavy mask, until he could sit with it, stand with it, turn with it as if it were his true face.

By the time the ship had come, just as Histuman had said it would, and Kuruhdu had disappeared to sea with his saber-mawed warrior, just as Histuman had said he would, Talzu had begun to see. Or rather, had begun to realize he had been seeing, all along. How the present burned down the future like the wick of a lamp, fixing it into the past even as it consumed it. He understood, though he couldn't have put it into words, how the old wolf did what he did, and therefore, he supposed, how the young dog did also what they did. He began to know the answers to questions before he asked them, once he had learned to ask them the right way round.

And when he awoke just before dawn, with Histuman's arms around him, with the old wolf's taste on his breath, with the oracle's kiss on his forehead, Talzu would feel the future rolling towards him, clearer every day, like a great island-swallowing tide.

But now, of course, that future had dwindled to mere present. Histuman had been among the things its tide had swept away, and Talzu had taken his place as oracle, just as foreseen. And who was to know the difference? The other acolytes were just as sworn to secrecy as ever, and anyway by now they had been all replaced. Arikimra, now keeper of the island's smaller tavern, was the only one still to dwell on Ocrit Isle, and he had been released from his vows while Histuman yet lived. As far as he, or anyone else on the isle could say, Talzu was just another of the acolytes.

"You miss me," Histuman would have said, as Talzu approached the buildings clustered about the harbor, "more than usual."

"So what if I do?" Talzu returned an idle salute from a sow driving a herd of goats toward the upper pastures. She had no idea to whom it was she offered an upraised hoof in casual greeting. Two moons ago he had told her that either her next child would be stillborn, or the birthing of it would cost her life, and now rumor said she had put off her husband, he had gone, with great bitterness, to be a fisherman with his brother on the next island southward.

"You know very well," the old wolf's voice would have been peevish, but he would have nuzzled the young dog's ears as he spoke, "what. Find yourself a distraction. A cheese dumpling or a bowl of beer or a handsome fellow, well, handsome enough, here."

"All the same distractions," Talzu shook his head, "as have distracted me less and less with each passing of winter. You know what it is to grow old, old man."

"I am glad I did not live," Histuman would have said, "to hear a mere lad of single score and seven winters call himself 'old.' "

Talzu stopped at the pile of stones at the crossroad—the only crossroad on the island, in truth, worth piling stones at—to add a pious-enough pebble to the windward side. He paused a while there, and before continuing spoke.

> "A lifetime is a road before us each.
> The man who sees his road laid plain unto
> The gates of death, though yet so far away,
> May call himself an old man, and speak truth."

Talzu stood in silence a while before his feet found the will to walk again.

"How long have you been brooding on that one?" Even in death, the former oracle would not have asked a question to which he did not already know the answer.

"Long enough," Talzu whispered.

And it may be the old wolf would have taken pity on Talzu, had he been there. It may be his teacher would have appreciated the passive despair he had not meant to teach. It may be that is why he would not have said anything as the dog he'd loved in life walked to the harbor, for it may be he would have known that even an Oracle needs to be surprised from time to time.

It may be that is why Talzu had no warning, either natural or unworldly, of the proud ship with the saffron colored sails and the burnished copper prow beached comfortably in the harbor, nor of what twist of destiny it had delivered to the Oracle of Ocrit Isle.

You will not have heard, I daresay, of Ouanaxes, whom some called Pirate King. The kingdom of which he was both prince and exile has no name in the remembrances of mortals. He lived too soon for the invention of history. And though epics indeed were sung of him, and tales told, the only one to make its way, limping and exhausted, to these cold latter days is this.

Ouanaxes was not such a man as to have any care for whether you and I had heard of him.

Imagine him, then, as Talzu first saw him. Begin with a lion, give him all the strength and royalty a lion ought to have, but take from him all concern, and all dignity, for he is free. His silt-brown fur knows well the touch of sunlight, the indistinct pebble-grey stripes are acquainted with the storm-streaked clouds they resemble, the dun mane smells of salt spray.

Rather than princely finery, give him a kilt of toughened leather, the kind divided for easy movement, a sash of brightly woven cloth across his chest, and a trusty sword in a worn scabbard, with the hilt of which, just as you catch sight of him, he has gestured some of his men up toward the woods. In his other hand put a bowl of ale, brought out by the tavernkeeper, whom he pays by tugging free one of the dangling golden beads sewn to his sash. It is the most wealth she has ever seen at once, in her life. Then around him picture a whirl of activity, sailors and pirates, fighting beasts all. The ram barters for provisions, the cormorant fills jars of fresh water, the ibex seeks carpenters to repair those bits of the ship, the hoopoe seeks smiths to sharpen these spears, or the rats and foxes and seals merely look for a comfortable bed and a willing wench. A chaos of seaborn manhood, at least by the standards of Ocrit Isle, and at its epicenter is Ouanaxes, as if it emanates from him as the philosophers claim the true natures of things emanate from the gods, with heavy sandals undone and bare paws at ease, as if he had no more cares than an innocent shepherd in the golden age of lost Arcadia.

It may be he did not.

It took Talzu some time to make his way through the storm of activity to the lion that was its eye. This was good. It gave him time to consider what to say.

But he would consider in vain, for the pirate spoke first. "Well met, honored sir. I presume you king of this fair island?"

"We have no king here," Talzu said, cautiously, "in all honesty, we have not folk enough even for a chieftain."

"Why, it's a thousand pardons I must beg!" Ouanaxes' eyes sparkled, Talzu would come to know, whenever he grinned like that. "I took you for a king at least, for it's myself and you alone who take a breath of leisure amid this bustle. Come then, take that breath with me? If your fair isle has offered my poor band hospitality, why, it's only fair I offer it back!"

And that was a better opening than Talzu guessed he would have been able to plan. "If you but saw us when no pirates had made harbor," the dog took a seat beside the lion, "you would find little else but leisure here."

"Pirate, you say?" Ouanaxes affected great innocence and drained his bowl of beer.

"An islander," Talzu shrugged, "knows a pirate when they see one. You would not see a hubbub like this for a fisherman!"

"I daresay not!" Ouanaxes laughed.

"Nay, for a fisherman brings no wealth from the treasure barges. As never a one of them thinks to stop here themselves, we islanders are not like to see any of it save what a pirate comes to spend."

"Ah." The lion seemed, for the first time, less than perfectly at ease. "You have trade with pirates often, then?"

"Here? Never." Talzu accepted a bowl of ale from the tavernkeeper, who then gave another to Ouanaxes and bustled away before the dog could pay her. "Other islands, to be sure, but Ocrit is overlooked by all save those who seek the Oracle."

"Oracle?" The lion perked his ears, and oh the sound of his voice was stirring like promise of a journey begun just at dawn.

"If you come not seeking the Oracle, you are the first," Talzu huffed.

"In good faith, I heard not there was such a thing until now." Ouanaxes ran claws through his windblown mane, and oh the roll of dusky fur over the muscles of his bare shoulder was a perilous thing to see. "I saw only an island where an honest captain might rest his crew, patch his hull, and fill his belly."

The dog glanced down the shore at the slender ship beached there. Several oars were broken, and more than a few arrows, hafts snapped off, heads buried, studded the starboard side like the stubble of an old boar's chin. "How long it will be safe to do that," Talzu said, very carefully, as he finished his bowl of ale, "may take an

Oracle to say. If you will excuse me, captain, I must be about my business."

"Perhaps we two can share drink and speech again?" Ouanaxes stretched to his feet as Talzu rose to go, and oh the possibility of laying upon that fur seemed more comforting than any bed. "If I might ask to know you better, of course."

"They call me Talzu," the dog said. "Any of the islanders, I trust, can tell you where to find me."

"Then find you I shall," smiled the lion.

And oh, that smile was more intoxicating than the fumes of a dozen oracular braziers.

Talzu strode away from the harbor, back toward the heights and his sanctuary.

"Are you then in love so quickly as that?" Histuman would have asked, greatly amused.

Talzu saw no purpose in replying. An oracle rarely asks a question to which he does not already know the answer.

It was a few days yet, ere Ouanaxes visited the oracle.

Betimes Talzu met him every day in the market, or the tavern, or the shore. Every day the lion had another task in hand—his men were scouting the coast for a cove where a ship might anchor out of sight, or seeking a woodcutter to see about felling a cedar for a new mast, or trading necklaces strung with amber and lazuli beads for flatbread and dried fish, or merely all heaving stores into the hold, naked and sweating and unashamed as primordial gods at their world-shaping labor, before he charged with them, laughing, splashing, into the surf to bathe. And every day he would set whatever task aside long enough to smile at the dog whom he knew as nothing more than a fellow man, and talk, and share a bowl of beer.

Every day Talzu felt his heart become a little less his own, and foresaw that tomorrow it would be even less so.

When finally Ouanaxes took him by the paw, pulled him without a word onto the ship, and led him to the stern where cushions were laid under the canopy, Talzu accepted that his heart was lost entirely.

"How did you know?" Talzu asked, when their muzzles had parted. The taste of the pirate's lips clung to his.

"I am not a fool, my friend," Ouanaxes gently unfastened the dog's tunic, pulled him free of it and down into his arms. "I know enough to know when a man wants me." The same motion of the lion's paw somehow contrived to run up the dog's side, explore the shape of his flank and underarm, then take him by the wrist and lead Talzu's paw down Ouanxes's chest to rest between his bare thighs. "And I know," it took only the smallest motion of his hand to touch the other man fully, but the lion had left that motion to Talzu to make, "that I want someone who wants me."

No man had touched Talzu, had held him, had loved him thus since Histuman had died.

"Tonight," the lion whispered, after, to the dog who lay in his arms, head on his breast, clutching him tightly. "I must at last go and seek your Oracle after all." Ouanaxes gently stroked Talzu's ears, and if the lion felt the dog freeze, for just a moment, he acknowledged it not.

"What is it you seek to know? I may be able to answer it myself."

"Alas, I ask not after your heart, my friend. That," the pirate kissed him, slowly, gently, "I mean to win wholly myself. I'll not suffer fate's interference there. No, someone advised me, when I first arrived, that the oracle might tell me how long it were safe to remain here. I needed to be ready, if it's an unfriendly answer I'm given, to go at once."

"And you lay with me now." Talzu's brow furrowed, "knowing you might be about to leave?"

"It was the last thing," Ouanaxes smiled, "I had need to see completed, ere I could bear to depart."

Talzu had but barely enough time to make it back to the sanctuary, don his robes and mask, and calm himself before Ouanaxes came to seek the Oracle.

"If you falsify prophecy, boy, because you wish to keep him..." Histuman would have whispered ominously in his ear, had the former oracle been there, "then may your spirit never again know peace."

"I know!" hissed Talzu, without moving. "Distracting me will not help!"

The two nearest acolytes shared a worried look, behind their masks. But there was no time for concern, so the one went to the entrance, to meet the pirate, to command him to speak but once, and that to ask the question he had brought.

It twisted Talzu's heart within him to see the lion, so near, yet be unseen, be unknown. But Talzu's heart was not what was wanted here, was it? Talzu was not who this man had come to seek. He sought the Oracle, did he not? And Ouanaxes needed the Oracle, no matter what the Oracle had to say, not Talzu.

That thought proved enough to stiffen his will and empty his mind. He breathed in the fumes, steadily and silently, and felt fate fill him like a rising sap in spring fills the unfurling leaves. Just in time.

"If I make harbor here, if I return here, from my raiding, when my ship and men have need—" The lion wore a cloak across his shoulders, drab and rough. Perhaps he meant to be disguised, seem less the warrior, more the peasant? Or perhaps he meant to seem humble before whatever divinity moved in the darkness before him? "—will it remain for us a safe refuge?" But in fact it only made him seem the larger and more solid, like a wall hung with tapestries, "Or will we be discovered here?"

He was not the only one in this room, was he, whose concealing garments made him into something larger than he was? But of the two of them, the dog could see through the embellishing disguise to the man beneath, tense and uncertain, and the lion could not. That was, perhaps, the burden of being an oracle.

This was the last thought in Talzu's head before prophecy chased it out, to rattle about the inside of the mask, while the oracle declaimed,

> "Thy throne upon the sunset's pillars calls
> In vain. From these obscure haunts you shall flee
> No more. Forsake you all that you could be,
> And frail old age you may yet live to see
> Beneath the hand of these oracular halls."

Surprised relief flashed across the pirate's face. Whatever he had expected to hear, it was not that. Talzu's head swam, his senses returned, and he first credited them not, for he thought he saw Ouanaxes on his knees, arms spread and palms raised in supplication. And only when the lion raised his face again, opened his mouth, eyes shining, for effusive thanks that never came because he remembered, just in time, he was not to speak again, did the Oracle understand that somehow his soothsaying had indeed been in both their favors.

There had been no need to adulterate or bend it to keep his beloved. Fate, at least the piece of it Ouanaxes had asked, the piece Talzu had spoken, had been on their side.

The lion left the sanctuary the one way, his step lightened, his eyes lifted up. The dog, after a time, left it the other way, shaken and scarce able to believe what his own mouth had said.

Talzu found himself collapsed beneath the fruitless pomegranates he had once tended. One of his acolytes pressed his shoulder, gently, relieved to see he yet drew breath.

"You spoke true, lad?" Histuman would have helped him to his feet by now, if he had been here. "That was prophesy indeed?"

"I did," Talzu croaked, and the acolyte startled, for he knew not to whom Talzu spoke, "It came on me so strong that I couldn't have resisted if I'd tried."

"Why then, rejoice," Histuman would have said.

"Please, can you stand?" whispered the acolyte.

"I will try." Talzu answered both of them.

"Some good fortune even we do not foresee, so it may as well fall to you, eh?" Histuman would have shook his head, baffled, as he was left behind in the tiny side garden to think on how strange the ways of fate had become.

And as Talzu let himself collapse into bed, into sleep, he was grateful Histuman was not there to ask what else he had seen, of which he had spoken not a word.

Now step forward, in your imaginings, a month or so. The season had turned, and Ouanaxes announced the winds had turned with them. Those ships which went north and east, he said, bearing gold and incense from the God-Kings in the south, have weathered the summer becalming and now mean to bear back cargos of rare metals and jewels, from the unknown shores of the north and whatever nomad warlords they could find to trade with there. So the season was come for piracy.

"I will bring you back," Ouanaxes bid farewell to his dog, on the shore, with a great abundance of kisses, "a gold ring for your tail. Set with amethysts, maybe."

"I would rather," Talzu returned every kiss his lion gave him, "you bring me back your self, safe and unhurt." But there was little fear in him. Three among his crew had visited the Oracle, the night before, and all had asked if any among the pirates would be slain. Each time the answer had been no.

"Still, amethysts would look most striking against your fur!" Ouanaxes laughed, and his eyes glinted, and he went aboard.

Once the boat took the surf, and passed the breakers, Talzu went to the high bluff, to watch it drive west on a score and six oars until the sail caught the wind to carry them toward the sunset.

"You said yourself," Histuman would have reassured him, "he will not be harmed."

"Aye," said Talzu. "But it will be wearisome, waiting for him to return."

Over the next fortnight, an architect came to ask if the hill on which he planned a fortified place for a local despot were firm and stable, a rich matriarch came asking to which gods she should make sacrifice so that her yet-to-be-born grandchildren would live healthy and prosperous, and a lovesick young fool came wanting to know if a woman to whom he had never spoken loved him.

Each night, after he had answered them, Talzu's dreams were a torment.

The first, he dreamed of Ouanaxes, robed and crowned, seated in a high place to deliver verdicts both just and merciful.

In the next, he dreamed of Ouanaxes bearing a sacred torch, on a quest through haunted mountains, to relight the altar fires at an abandoned temple and appease the curse of an angry god on a whole people.

On the last, he dreamed of a city fully in celebration, dancing and singing in the marketplace and on all the rooftops, as their prince, long promised, returned from exile to take the throne and restore peace and plenty. And below, Ouanaxes's ship drew into the harbor, stately, on sea as smooth as beaten metal and clear as glass, under showers of silver apple petals cast upon the breeze.

"Sleep has failed you, lad," Histuman would have said, if he could have sat beside Talzu, "and this is a poor place for breaking your fast."

"True," the dog clutched his breakfast cup in the sanctuary garden as the stewed grains and sweet herbs in it grew cold, "but it faces west."

"When other men are troubled by dreams of ill portent," Histuman would have sighed, "they consult an oracle."

Talzu scowled at where the old wolf would have been sitting.

"Break your fast first, lad." Histuman would have said. "What will your pirate think if you waste away to nothing before he returns?"

Talzu's scowl deepened, but he gulped down his gruel and curds. "Did you ever," he said, "know more than what you were asked?"

"Aye," Histuman's voice would have grown cautious and grave. "Rare it was, but from time to time there would come one on whom the fates had laid a finger. Those with great and noble destinies, or monstrous and horrific ones. And whatsoever they actually asked, some part of the deeds they would someday do would bear down upon me like a deluge."

Talzu bit his lip.

"I have heard, indeed, I have seen, what may happen if it be too much." Histuman would have relaxed easily into lecture, "I was not apprenticed here, you know. I learned at a temple on the mainland, and that land is thick with heroes. When they would come, my teacher, an old and august woman, a leopard, she would sometime snap, deliver them prophesies unasked for, that she had not the strength to hold back. Many was the time they could not even speak their question entire. It became, I think, a part of her fame—that you might be told not what you wanted to hear, but what you needed to know—but it broke her in the end. Her soul could bear the weight no more. And that is why, when I came to the mastery of my foresight, I sought out an obscure sanctuary, to unknown gods, where few would think to bring anything so pestilent as a hero's destiny."

Histuaman would have fallen silent, then, on first noticing how tight Talzu gripped the cup, how wide the dog's eyes were, and how fixed on the horizon toward which Ouanaxes had gone. And the old wolf, who would have known better than to ask what his student had seen, would have only put an arm around the dog's shoulders and held him close.

The day the ship returned, Talzu was awake before the sunrise, and down waiting at the harbor hours before he sighted it.

Ouanaxes was standing on the prow, leaning forward. He was too distant for what he shouted when he saw Talzu waiting to be heard, but he dove off and swam ashore without waiting for the ship to make land, so his feelings were not difficult to infer.

It would perhaps be thought very shocking, in these days, for man to kiss one he loved in full view of all the island and a shipful of his sailors, but those were simpler times.

When they at last lay, peacefully, blissfully, in one another's arms, all appetites sated—which had taken no little doing to accomplish—Ouanaxes kissed Talzu again, on the side of the neck, and said "I suspect it's as sorely as I missed you, that you have missed me."

"That may be," Talzu said. "But it's also that you are a man whom it is a joy to welcome."

"Oh, I am welcome, then?"

"Must I welcome you still further, to make you understand?"

"Let it never be said," the lion nuzzled him, "that I rejected offered hospitality."

The raid, indeed, had been a brilliant success. They had come upon a barge heavy-laden with tribute, bound for a warrior queen—who purposed to build a palace that outshone her father's in splendor—in an attempt to win the allyship of her armies. Because these armies were so desperately needed, no warriors had been spared for the ship, and they had taken the whole cargo with but little bloodshed. They unloaded all manner of rich and comfortable furniture—as well as the to-be-expected gold, silver, fine patterned linens, incense and spices, and all manner of jewels—and the homes of Ocrit Isle were suddenly all more gracious than they had ever before dreamed of being.

And there was indeed a tailring of amethysts set in gold for Talzu, as promised.

But for all the time the pirate and the oracle spent in eachother's arms, rather than seeing to the treasure, you would have thought neither of them cared a bean for any of it.

The next three years passed much as has been described. There was plunder and victory on the sea, and there was love and comfort on the return.

For the dog's part, when Ouanaxes was gone the dreams of his beloved's glory and heroism, if he but left him and his isle, would haunt him. Then when the lion was in his arms again, they would recede like the tide, always threatening a return.

"So, when I am away," Ouanaxes said, "you are some manner of priest at the sanctuary of the Oracle?" His head lay in Talzu's lap, in the whitewashed brick cottage the pirate had taken, a half hour's walk from the harbor, to be his dwelling on Ocrit Isle.

"If I were," Talzu stroked the lion's ears, "I would be bound by sacred oaths not to reveal it."

Here discourse was obliged to wait for a time, while Ouanaxes's tongue attended to more important matters.

"I do recall," the lion nuzzled the belly that cradled his face, "a number of mysterious fellows, their faces all hidden, who attended my audience when I went. If I were to ask if you had been one among them, what then might you say?"

"I suppose," Talzu laughed, "I would ask you to tell me about your country. Where did the journey that brought you to my bed begin?"

So Ouanaxes, who was no fool and could see plainly what was plain enough, moved up beside Talzu on the bed, and told the dog of an entire city that was a palace, of the topless towers, and the temples on the high places. Of eating melons cooled in springwater and meat skewers hot from the grill in the market square, of the warm and steaming public baths, and the festival parades on the holy days dedicated to the queen of the night sky, and the lady of the underworld, and the sacred king of the harvest between them. And if his voice grew low and wistful, heavy with nostalgia, and if he slowed to a halt, and shied away from any mention of why he was not there now, or how when folk spoke of the absent prince they oft used the words 'banished' or 'exile,' then Talzu mentioned it not.

They each understood what it was for the other to have secrets.

"I understand what you are doing, lad," Histuman would have said, "but do you?"

Talzu turned not away from Ouanaxes's ship, departing on what the pirate said was likely the last sortie before winter storms came to shut all the merchants in their ports.

"You have not said you saw more of his fate," the old wolf would have followed Talzu as he strode up the path, past the cottage where he meant to spend the winter with his lion, and into the forest toward the heights and the sanctuary. "But neither have you made it hard to guess. Will you tell me, at least, what grim future you fear in your dreams? What keeps you from restful sleep every night you are not with him? What does my shade linger with you for, if not to give you counsel?"

Talzu strode faster.

"If some danger awaits him, or even death inescapable," Histuman would have been snarling by now, "what good does it do, to keep this from him?"

"I saw he was going to leave!" Talzu turned on his heel in the sanctuary gates to howl back at the empty forest. "I saw the grand and glorious destiny—throne, triumph, and a hero's renown—that awaits him if he leaves this place and never returns! Fate means him to be much more than mine, and by the gods, if any man knows he can indeed be much more, it is I!"

Histuman would have been too shaken to reply.

"Yet as long as I do not tell him, as long as the oracle stays silent," Talzu shot a disgusted look at the hall where he had stood, masked and robed, to tell Ouanaxes it would be safe to dwell here, "he has no wish to leave! He is happy with me, I am happy with him, and I'd be glad to count whatsoever glory might have been as worth nothing, as a thing that will never exist and therefore matters not, if it were not that I cannot unsee what I saw!" The dog could not keep a whine out of his voice, "Every dream grows clearer. In each of them he is more glorious. And in none of them am I anywhere to be found."

"Is that not his choice to make?" Histuman would have drawn near, tentatively, as if trying not to startle away a frightened animal, "If you lay the two futures before him, and let him decide?"

"He will decide to stay, because he will decide not to hurt me."

"You have foreseen this?"

"I do not need to."

"Then," Histuman would have said, "all will be well. Why this woe?"

"Because he should go! It is an unjust thing to deprive a rightful king of his kingdom, is it not? Is that not what I am doing, old man?" Talzu retreated into the sanctuary proper, hushed the concerned acolyte with a gesture, and strode into the hall. The braziers were unlit, the mask set aside in an alcove shrine. "And what of the fates? What plagues will they send on my head, or on his, if I continue to defy them?"

"If you wish," Histuman would have stood by the mask he had worn in life, one paw on it, wistfully, "I will play the oracle for you, lad. You journeyed to the sanctuary, you came within, you asked your question."

Talzu could hear his own heartbeat in his ears as he nodded.

Then, without ceremony—perhaps the dead need not the things, to see fate, that do the living—Histuman would have recited,

> "Trade crown for heart for crown, and be forevermore
>   alone.
> Lose all thy self within the masks you did not ask to bear,
> But none but those outside of them can read what masks
>   fate wears.
> Let him that speaketh fate to men have no fate of his
>   own."

If there had been an acolyte who had the gift to hear what Histuman would have prophesied, then perhaps for some additional alms, beyond that he had paid to be admitted to this place—and Talzu indeed felt he had paid much, by now—someone could have offered an interpretation.

But there was none but himself.

"What did that mean?" he asked, quietly.

"I suppose," Histuman would have sighed, as he gestured for Talzu to follow him into the garden, "you have not foreseen wrongly. If he leaves, if he returns wherever it was he came from, he finds glory there. And aye, that may be what the fates intended for him."

"But if he does," mulled Talzu, "he loses himself in kingship, in the mask of it? The same as I was becoming nothing but the oracle, ere he arrived."

"A likely reading, lad," Histuman would have nodded, "what make you of 'those outside' who 'read the masks fate wears'?"

"I suppose that means us." Talzu said. "Means me. In order to foretell fate, I had to shake loose of it, to be without it. That is why all that can be interpreted of what you said is about him, not me."

"If all I can do is foresee of him, then I shall tell you what I foresee." Histuman would have taken a good breath, gathered his thoughts. "On the one path, he leaves you, and all is as you have foretold. Glory and a throne, the kind of destiny all men dream of and few attain to. On the other, he remains with you all his days, and those are unremarkable. Eventually the petty kingdoms know better than to send their ships past here, they will have learned to fear the peoples they meet on the sea. By then he will scarce care. He will have brought wealth enough to make Ocrit Isle a comfortable place for himself, for the one he loves, to live out the rest of their days."

Talzu wore the face of a man who expects a trap.

"The dreams, on this path, either fade, taking much of your foresight with them, or they grow until your mind snaps under the strain. And one day," Histuman would have growled, "some strange and foolish people may discover your forgotten tomb, look on your bones and his, lying paw in paw and arm in arm, and say 'they must have been brothers.'" He would have pointed a finger at Talzu without looking at the young dog, "And it is you, lad, that must choose, not he. He came to you, the oracle though he knew it not. And aye, he had a glorious destiny before him, but if keeping him is what you choose, and all that comes with it, why, is that not a destiny too? Is that not a path the fates have set before the man, just as much as is the glory you saw?"

"And perhaps," Talzu whispered quietly, "I would rather be broken in his arms, than whole and alone?"

Histuman would have had nothing to say to that. Which is hardly to be wondered at, since he was not there. He was dead.

The dog squeezed his eyes shut against his tears, managed to contain them. "I would you had not died. That I were still only your apprentice. That I could know, if I let Ouanaxes go, I would still have your bed, and your arms, to take comfort in." And Talzu hoped Histuman would have said something like, 'But then you would not be Oracle. And you are a greater Oracle than I.' But there was nobody there, save himself, to say it.

Thus did Talzu set his shoulders, and dry his tears, and turn to do as a great oracle would do: To choose the future, by choosing which prophecy to say, and which to leave unspoken.

So it was, alas, that I must tell you: when Ouanaxes returned—empty handed, as he had said, the season of storms when none could safely set sail was all but upon them—it was to see Talzu waiting, as ever, at a high place above the harbor. But this time it was without eagerness.

"The oracle has summoned you," he told the lion, his face all concern, "they say there is something they must say."

"You cannot warn me what it is?"

The dog shook his head.

"It is uncommon, is it not," Ouanaxes ran a paw through his mane, and oh the way the fur rolled over the muscles was a precious and bittersweet sight, "for the Oracle to call for a man? Usually tis pilgrims who seek them out."

"I have never known it to happen before," agreed Talzu.

"When?"

"As soon as can be."

"Very well," Ouanaxes breathed in his courage, like the hero Talzu had foreseen him into, "lead the way."

When they reached the sanctuary, Talzu stopped him. "You must wait here. An acolyte will come to fetch you, in the Oracle's own time."

"Will that acolyte be you?" Ouanaxes asked, very earnestly.

"I..." Talzu shook his head, "...cannot say."

The oracle was lighting one of the braziers when the lion was admitted. He had not had to wait very long. The room was lighter than usual, for rarely was a pilgrim permitted to see it during the day.

"Hail. I was told," Ouanaxes went to one knee, "you would have words with me?"

The oracle nodded, slowly, for they had to be careful with the enormous mask. No moon was overhead, no sacred herbs burned in the braziers, no rites had been performed. But it seemed, today, such things were not needed. The oracle spoke, quietly, casually, as would two citizens who met in the street:

> "Why do you tarry, King Ouanaxes, here?
> Thy house sits empty, and thy crown unclaimed.
> Thy uncle is unseated and undone
> And, jeered out of the orphan's gate, is fled.
> His treachery can no more threaten thee.
> The goddess waits, upon her lantern hill,
> To crown again her sacred king, and cries:
> "Why do you tarry, King Ouanaxes, there?"

The lion flinched back, as if he had been struck. He opened his mouth, thought better of it, closed it again.

Someone observing very close might have seen the oracle's mask tremble.

Finally, Ouanaxes gathered himself again, bowed graciously, and made for the door. But when he reached it, he stopped. "I know it's forbidden to speak more than once, but it would not be the first time I dared do what I must, for I knew it was banishment for me already, and nothing had I to lose. So I will say: may I know if Talzu is here among you?"

The oracle turned their back.

"Well, whether or not he is, I would say this: I will never forget him. I swear it."

The acolytes all looked to the oracle, who whispered "It will be made known to him."

If any noticed the tail, visible beneath the oracle's robes, with a ring of amethysts set in gold, none dared remark on it.

Talzu walked the path down through the cedars utterly alone.

It would be well, he supposed, to retrieve all his worldly possessions from the whitewashed cottage in which he had meant to spend the winter, return them to the hut behind the sanctuary. Without his beloved, what use had he for the place?

The dog froze as he stepped through the doorway. "You are yet here?"

"You thought I would go," replied the lion sitting on the bed, awake with a lamp though it was after midnight, "before I saw you at least once more?"

"I feared-" was all the dog managed to say before the lion was upon him, clutching him tight, kissing him with a desperate hunger.

"Nay," sobbed the lion, between kisses, "never. To be with you is the last thing I must see completed, before I may leave."

In the morning, the Pirate King gathered his men on the shore.

He spoke to them of his homeland, which many of them shared, and told them the tale of his banishment, as a youth, by his mother's brother. He warned them they might face dangers—for it was nigh to winter, and the season of storms where only fools and desperate men set sail was upon them—and battle at journey's end, for who could say how many of his uncle's party might yet remain? But any man who sailed with him, he would regard forever as a hero, and if the gods were with them and he did reclaim his throne, their names would be etched in stone to be remembered for as long as his house endured.

Alas, no, I can tell you none of those names now.

He would not command any of them go. "Let any man speak," said Ouanaxes, "and then I will lead those who will follow, and I shall think no less of any who choose to remain, for aye," and he could not keep his eyes from straying to the high bluff above the harbor, where Talzu watched, "Ocrit has been a home to us indeed."

In the end, some stayed, and some of the islanders of Ocrit left. For such is the way of the lives woven for mortals by the fates: they intersect, they tangle with eachother, and never do they meet but some go their separate ways. And yes, it was a hard voyage. The storms were dire, but some god of the winds must have been with them. For yes, they arrived safely. The lookouts on the lantern hill spotted the burnished copper prow and saffron sails. And yes indeed, Ouanaxes entered into his city, amid rejoicing, under showers of silver apple petals, and he relit the altar fires, and was crowned, and ruled both justly and with mercy. Just as the oracle of a distant island had once foreseen.

And some have said that when the time and signs were right, the dog left the island. Left behind the oracle's mask. Another acolyte took it up but had not the gift, and the Oracle of Ocrit Isle was no more renowned, faded into curiosity and mere fortune-telling, until it was forgotten. But Talzu, they say, journeyed across the seas and found his hero once again, found the city he ruled, and there they lived as many years of destiny and noble deeds, in eachother's arms, as mortals might dare to have.

But others have said not. Have said that is all lies of poets, a drop of honey at the end, to make the tale more palatable. They say Talzu remained at his duty, passed the rest of his days as Oracle, though from that day on when he took off the mask he went not to the market or the tavern, but to the high bluffs to watch the sun set over the western seas. And he slept no more in the hut behind the sanctuary. Though it were a longer walk, each night, he made his dwelling instead in a whitewashed cottage, about half an hour's walk from the harbor.

And still others say they both wander the earth to this day, seeking one another. For being reunited is the last task they must see complete, ere they depart this life together.

But I cannot tell you which of these, if any, is the truth.

I am no oracle.

The Shrine of T-am-ădad

by Thomas "Faux" Steele

"Hey, Amalu! Wait up!" Naoum darted out from behind a retaining wall, huffing and puffing under the weight of the cloth sack slung over his shoulder. His tufted caracal ears swiveled left and right to check for eavesdroppers before he continued. "Where are you going in such a rush? You're not hiding a girlfriend from me, are you?"

"Ha, I wish. I'm just trying to find a place to hide from my shame." The trim fennec fox braced his paws against a retaining wall and stretched until an air bubble popped beneath the bands of hard-earned muscle in his shoulders. "Do you... happen to know of any?"

"It's a happy coincidence you've found one." Naoum wiped his blood-stained paws off on his apron, making sure they were clean before giving the fennec a pat on the back. His fingers were sheathed in a healthy layer of fat from constantly snacking in the communal kitchen. "This storeroom has been abandoned since the Two Banks raided our village."

"Oh." Amalu's heart skipped a beat as he noticed signs of charring on the acacia wood door. He nervously fiddled with a band of silver set with a triangular piece of polished coral that adorned the middle finger of his right paw. "That was many moons ago indeed."

"It's where I escaped from my sisters growing up." Naoum shook his head and tapped a small doodle beneath a window of what looked like a steaming bowl of something tasty. "Making pigments from animal fat and burnt charcoal was the hardest part. Leftover drippings in the summer heat are..."

"So that's why you've never complained about supervising the nursery." Amalu slid down against the mud-brick structure and buried his muzzle in his paws. The full sleeves of his dark brown *djellaba* robe slid across his wrists, giving him the appearance of a large bundle of un-milled grain. "Since I know you're going to ask—"

"Did you uh—"

"Yeah, I failed to face the red deer again." Having uttered the dreaded words, Amalu lifted his head up as a gust of wind carried Naoum's scent to his muzzle. The caracal's musc—earthy and a little sweet—recalled the comforting odor of a household kitchen with warm bread baking in the oven. "I was *right* there, my spear was in the perfect position, and... I... I couldn't do it. My father had to salvage the hunt for me."

"Maybe you're just not cut out to be a hunter." Naoum shrugged as he retrieved a small mortar and pestle from his rucksack and flopped down next to the fennec fox. Humming softly, he began grinding a few stalks of dried sweet marjoram. "I like to have my meat pre-slaughtered. I can carve up a carcass no problem, it's the killing part that turns my stomach. It really spoils my appetite."

"But everyone expects me to be brave. I'm the only son of the Imazighen." Amalu sighed, cuffing himself on the side of the muzzle in frustration. "It's *fucking* hard when everyone expects me to face danger without flinching and... I just *can't*. I freeze up like a dim-witted animal when fear strikes me."

"Well, if you're dead set on filling your father's hunting boots... I bet your courage will come to you when you most need it." While Naoum had not yet proven his manhood, the occasional dispensing of sage advice gave him the gravitas of an elder brother the fennec had never been blessed with. "Trust in yourself... and in the First Gods. Oh! Speaking of which—"

"Hrm?" Amalu cocked an eyebrow as Naoum's face lit up.

"Haziz needs to see you. That's why I came looking for you in the first place."

"Don't you have cooking to do?" Amalu replied, playfully punching the caracal on the shoulder. "I didn't take you for Haziz's errand boy."

"My sisters want to prepare tonight's feast... but I always have a spare moment to help the old man," he said with a smirk. Throwing his pack on the ground, he offered the fennec a clay pot decorated with crudely illustrated pictograms of what Amalu assumed were fruits. "Hopefully they don't burn the meat too badly. Take this to Haziz for me—you know it's his favorite."

Tugging the lid free, Amalu was delighted to see his favorite—preserved dates. Harvested a few weeks earlier, they'd been left to ferment in the village's preserving hut before being sprinkled with salt, blended with mint leaves, and garnished with a few delicate threads of wild saffron. "And mine as well. Did you pack any—"

"Extra? Of course," Naoum said, dropping a small oilskin on top of the jar.

"Maahnoor is coming along well in her learning, isn't she? She should know how to prepare red deer by now." Amalu pursed his lips in thought. "Let me guess... Maahnoor preserved the lemons and Layla decorated the jar?"

"Layla is quite the artist... for a toddler." With a grateful smile, Amalu plucked a quartered date from the bag and popped it into his muzzle. Sweet with a pleasantly salty aftertaste, the fennec held it in his muzzle for a good minute before finally allowing himself to swallow. "Delicious, as always."

"Don't eat the entire bag on your way. You'll ruin your appetite," the caracal admonished. After neatly packing his thoroughly crushed herbs away, Naoum waved as he set off toward the central kitchen of the village. It was readily marked by the pillar of dark woodsmoke its enormous oven produced. Amalu's stomach growled at the thought of dipping a hunk of *khobz* into a rich bowl of cumin-seasoned red deer stew. "And you better *actually* get it to Haziz this time!"

"Have some faith in me!" Rolling his eyes, Amalu made sure the jar's lid was tightly sealed by softening the beeswax lining around the rim with his paw pads. Plucking a few lingering thorns from his side—the unfortunate result of dodging into a spiny bush—the fennec stood up and stretched before setting off toward Haziz's dwelling at the outskirts of the village.

Known as Henchir-Aïn-Dourat, Amalu's village was half-encircled by the Mueti Alhayaa river flowing downward from the mountains. The snowmelt water was crisp, almost transparent, and refreshingly cool, a boon to the women doing the washing as the heat of the day faded. They kept their bodies comfortable with towels soaked in river water while draping colorful blankets and robes along drying lines formed from braided lengths of reed.

Haziz lived alone in a traditional tent, a short distance from the village and close to the foothills of the awe-inspiring mountains that had long guarded Henchir-Aïn-Dourat against invaders from the east. Their ink-black slopes were dusted with snow, which occasionally drifted down to the village during the height of the cool season. "Magnificent," Amalu muttered, pausing to admire the work of the First Gods.

It was said that the peaks were formed from the scales of the great demon-snake, Thueban Shaytan, who had battled the First Gods to a standstill in his quest to consume all that ever was and would be. Unable to defeat him through strength alone, T-amădad, the hyena god, had offered him tea to spare just one village—Henchir-Aïn-Dourat. Thinking the hyena foolish, Thueban Shaytan consumed the poisonous oleander flowers hidden amongst the tea leaves and was thus felled by trickery. Ever since, his village had honored the hyena god as their patron.

Amalu turned his claws toward his heart in a gesture of reverence before crossing a wooden footbridge over the river. A few red-belly tilapia darted among the reeds, wriggling their streamlined bodies against the powerful current. The color of their undersides matched that of Haziz's humble dwelling, a triangular structure with a sharp and distinctive peak dyed brilliant vermillion.

"You asked for me, Haziz?" Amalu brushed aside the flaps of the hartebeest-hide tent and stepped onto a lightweight *kilim* rug.

Though the Caspian culture had abandoned their nomadic lifestyle many years ago, some elders still had a longing for the old ways running in their blood. "Naoum caught me just as I returned from the hunt."

"Yes, yes, come in." A paw covered with close-cropped sandy fur waved him inside. Haziz was seated on an intricately woven *kilim* dyed a yellowish shade of ochre. The remainder of his tent's floor was covered with rugs of varying quality—most given by the women of the village in exchange for his skills as a healer—which kept the dwelling pleasantly warm. "Please, have some water; you must be thirsty. How was the hunt?"

"The red deer are moving higher into the mountains, where there is more water. Tanamart is bringing the meat back now." Amalu glanced at the silver hyena idol resting on a small sandstone platform behind Haziz's cot to avoid making eye contact with the shaman. "Though it will be a long walk... even longer than the last hunt."

"And did you find your courage?" Haziz stroked his chin as he seemed to magically draw Amalu's gaze. Not that there was much else to distract him; aside from rugs and pillows, Haziz's tent was sparsely decorated.

"No, I failed at my task." Amalu's shoulders slumped as he met the fennec's milky eyes. He was the oldest member of their village, considered ancient even when Amalu's grandfather was Imazighen, the leader of their tribe. "The First Gods, they—"

"The First Gods provided for the village with a successful hunt. There is still something to celebrate, is there not?" Gazing out at the distant sea, Haziz took a deep breath and curled his paws. "I see great danger on the road you travel, young one."

"What is the danger? My own cowardice?" Amalu sighed as he rested against a semicircular pillow decorated with colorful seashells. "I let everyone down. They were depending on me."

"The danger comes from seeing your own struggles as unique. You forget that all members of Henchir-Aïn-Dourat are equal before the First Gods." Haziz sighed. "Do you think that your father never lost his courage?"

"I..." Amalu awkwardly bit his tongue.

"Your father's first hunt was a disaster. When it came time for him to spear the red deer, he acted with too much vigor and hit another youth instead." Haziz's expression briefly softened. "That young fennec was my grandson. After that, your father never wanted to hunt again."

"What changed?" Amalu leaned forward, heart pounding in his chest.

"I forgave him for the good of Henchir-Aïn-Dourat." Haziz reached out and grasped Amalu's paws in a trembling embrace. "When he realized that even the accidental taking of a life would not be his end, your father found his courage. Courage is the willingness to pick up the pieces of yourself and carry on after even the worst failure. Now, let us speak no more of this."

"Yes, Haziz." Amalu respectfully bowed. He then retrieved the jar of preserved figs from his knapsack and placed it in front of Haziz. The fennec fiddled with his ring as his stomach growled. Anticipating a productive hunt, he had only eaten only a pawful of pistachios that morning. "Naoum sends his warmest greetings."

"I know the Kitchen-Maester keeps too busy to deliver, so it is fortunate he has a reliable friend to arrange for such things. Now, let us discuss why I called for you... and it wasn't simply to bring me a jar of preserved figs." Haziz set the jar aside as he stroked his tongue across his bottom lip. "Though your small kindnesses are always appreciated."

"I can tell by your tone that you haven't brought me here just to dispense some sage advice." Amalu sighed. "Why am I really here, Haziz?"

"What I would give to sit you on my knee and allow a dollop of sage advice to be the end of this." Haziz stroked a paw through his ragged headfur and closed his eyes. "There is a disturbance in the heavens. Surely you have seen the signs, yes?"

"The fishermen's catch is not what it once was... I remember when the Mueti Alhayaa was so teeming with life a toddler could bring home a meal by tugging open their catch-cloth and letting the fish leap inside." Amalu reached for a hollowed-out ostrich egg perched upon a stand made from aromatic thuja wood. He jiggled the top free and poured himself a cupful of cool mineral water. "Is that because the First Gods are displeased with us?"

"I don't fully understand what I've seen in my visions... but I feel that something has happened to bring discord to our lands." Haziz's gaze remained fixed towards the distance, where an ominous cloud of sand had begun to gather near the Northern Sea. The thrashing sandstorms had increasingly blocked Henchir-Aïn-Dourat from the village's traditional fishing grounds. "The sands roll in a little further every day. Soon, they will be blanketing my tent in a layer thick as mountain snow."

"Are you sure of that?" Amalu gazed toward the shimmering water just before it vanished from his sight.

"Are preserved figs delicious?" Haziz asked rhetorically as he popped the jar's seal. He set a whole fig on a carved olivewood bowl in front of the idol of T-am-ădad before pouring the remainder onto a mat equidistant between them. "Please let Naoum know that I will make an offering for young Layla. I know she has been troubled by nosebleeds."

Amalu waited for him to finish murmuring a prayer over the food before interjecting. "My father says—"

"Your father is a wise Imazighen." Filling his own tin cup with a trembling paw, Haziz took only a small sip. He looked like a sunbird drinking from a bead of freshly gathered dew. "But he has never been the most attuned to spiritual matters."

"He certainly has never taken it upon himself to dust the household shrine. Is that why the First Gods are displeased with our people?" Amalu's brow furrowed with concern as a list of potential sins raced through his mind like a scimitar oryx across the veldt. "Is my cowardice—"

"No, this is not of your creation." Haziz looked like a gnarled desert tree as he used a flint to send a cascade of sparks into a small nest of tinder beneath a bronze teapot. "But it falls to you to restore balance to our village... much as I wish the burden would not be yours."

"How can I help?" Amalu took a preserved fig and added it to the bowl in front of the idol. "I may not be courageous but..."

"Don't sell yourself short. The First Gods have ordained this task for you."

"What would you have me do?" Amalu tilted his head as an ember began to glow in the depths of the densely packed straw. Like a tiny cherry, it took on a beautiful shade of red before finally transforming into a dancing pillar of flame that climbed until it licked the teapot's blackened bottom. "This isn't the kind of task where you die, right?"

"I would hope not. I'd miss your red deer jerky." Haziz poured the remainder of the water into the teapot along with a smattering of brightly colored desert herbs. Leaning in to watch the petals swirl in the gentle heat currents of the water, Amalu caught an intense whiff of musk rising with the steam. "You must go to Lalla Khedidja."

"The Weeping Mountain?" Amalu asked. "But such journeys were forbidden after..."

"Bachar's ill-timed disappearance was most unfortunate." Haziz shot him a soft frown of acknowledgement, showing off his missing inner incisors—the mark of manhood among the Caspian culture. "But we must do as T-am-ădad wills. Now, drink the brew I've prepared. You will need to augment your strength... it is a long night's walk."

Haziz poured Amalu a full cup without spilling a drop. The younger fennec tried not to gag as he dumped the noxious concoction down his throat. It left a lingering tingle on his lips, core muscles almost immediately lighting up with a pleasant buzz of energy.

"What's in this drink, anyway?" Amalu sighed and gratefully accepted a small clay bowl filled with dried green olives in date vinegar.

"A nut from a distant land. Very rare and hard to acquire... especially since the traders haven't come in many moons. I was saving the last of it for an occasion of sufficient significance." Solemnizing the proceedings, Haziz presented him with a papyrus scroll upon which the elder fennec had scrawled a prayer in his inscrutable handwriting. "Take it to the Weeping Mountain and lay it upon the Cracked Altar. This is your task."

"But Haziz!" Amalu started to object as the older fennec brusquely ushered him out of the tent. "How will I know the way? That's further than I've ever gone on a hunt."

"How should I know?" The fennec shot him a sly smile as he gazed upward toward the last rays of the evening sun. Gently turning the scroll over in his paws, Amalu was surprised to find a crudely drawn map. "I'm blind."

Amalu drew his cloak up against his body as he followed one of the precarious hunting trails upward toward the Shrine of T-am-ădad. Taking a glance back at his house—a circular structure at the center of the village with the luxury of two mud-brick chimneys to fend off the chill of night—he sighed and finished the last of Haziz's invigorating tea.

"I can't believe I agreed to this," Naoum muttered, rock crunching beneath his rawhide sandals. Pudgy belly visible beneath his light yellow *djellaba* robe, he kept his muzzle busy by chewing on a rod coated with crystallized sugar. "Your red deer jerky is good... but not worth dying for. We're probably going to end up just like Bachar. I still miss that old fennec."

"Don't be so pessimistic." Amalu kept one paw resting on the hand-me-down sword belted next to his right hip, trying to avoid accidentally cutting his knee on the noticeable bend near the tip. "Maybe Bachar opened a *sahlab* stand just up the road and will give us a free sample."

"At least we didn't miss the feast." Naoum changed the subject to something less morbid before pausing to nibble on a crusty bread roll. He fell a few steps behind the fennec while searching for a small pot in his rucksack. A few drops of fragrant sauce spilled onto the dirt as he thoroughly drizzled the leading edge of his *khobz* with left-over mint sauce. "Why the long face?"

"The mountains aren't what they used to be." Amalu saw better in moonlight than in the afternoon sun, easily dodging the ruts and gashes in the trail where a lack of maintenance had allowed signif-icant erosion. He tried to ignore the sheer drop-off along the edge, no barrier separating him from the unforgiving rocks below. "My father says they're infested with bandits now… people displaced by the Sea-Raiders."

"Maybe we can bribe them for safe passage?" Rummaging around in the canvas bag strapped around his chest, Naoum's ears perked up as he tugged two jars of preserved figs free. "I packed plenty of provisions."

"First, I'm not much of a haggler," the fennec said with a soft sigh. "Second, I'm not sure they're too interested in arranging a par-ley. Showing off any valuables might be treated as an open invitation for them to cut our throats."

"Point taken." Paws trembling with nervous energy, Naoum traded the jars for a weathered dagger, handle wrapped in fraying rawhide. "Do you think this is enough protection? I'm not much of a fighter."

"Here… you've taught me how to preserve my hunting spoils, and I think it's about time I return the favor." Amalu gestured for the caracal to pass the dagger. "First, we need to make sure your weapon is in good repair. It'll be of no use if you can't cut through leather armor."

"Right." Naoum's eyes lit up with interest as Amalu made a quick test cut against a flat stone plucked from along the trail's edge. "So how do you sharpen one of these things?"

"You didn't bring a whetstone, did you?" Amalu cocked an eye-brow as the dagger left a barely visible scratch on the argillite. He repeated the test on his forearm and found it barely penetrated the dense fur of his undercoat, let alone breaking skin.

"Would you be mad if I said that I don't even have one?" Naoum apologetically rubbed the back of his head. "I know I'm older and should be better prepared but—"

"Good thing I always have one handy. You'd be lucky to slay a carrot with this edge." The fennec frowned, holding the dagger's surface up so that it caught one of the twinkling moonbeams. Beneath the pitted surface, Amalu noted the metal was of surprisingly high quality. "Did you never learn proper knife sharpening in the kitchens? I'd imagine a cook would take care of all his cutting tools."

"My mother usually handles that. You know how she is," Naoum replied.

"Overprotective, I know." An oddity among the young males in the village, Naoum was more likely to be seen gathering desert herbs or overseeing the preserving hut than honing his fighting skills. Amalu chalked some of that up to his upbringing—Naoum's mother still breast-feeding him and changing his catch-cloths at the age where Amalu was beating other cubs in mock combat—a fact he had only learned recently. "You will eventually need to stand up to her."

"I'm not an adult yet. Maybe she'll finally take me seriously then." Naoum shrugged. "At least then she might back off a little, you know?"

"Is that why you've always tried to act so mature around me?" Pulling a compact whetstone about the size of his palm from a pocket on his scabbard, Amalu gave it a splash from his waterskin before putting it to use. Amalu meditatively dragged the dagger's edge across the quartz, ears swiveling back and forth at the sharp noise. He found the process soothing, intermittently pausing to check the sharpness against the softer test stone.

"That and taking care of my sisters." Naoum shrugged, picking his teeth with a small length of whittled antler. "You're a natural fighter... and I've been blessed by Em-ăsăww. One must accept such gifts as they come, even if we sometimes might wish things were different."

"Would you ever trade places with me?" Em-ăsăww was the lioness god, the protector of the hearth, and it was said that she bestowed the gift of fire upon his people in the form of a burning branch taken from the Ancestral Hunting Grounds. Though many men in the village derided her as weak, Haziz had once told him that she was the fiercest warrior among the First Gods.

"I don't know about that... but I'll start keeping my dagger sharp." Leaving a deep scar in the rock, Amalu gave Naoum a satisfied nod before passing the weapon hilt-first. The caracal inspected it approvingly before tucking it into his rough canvas belt. "For you, at least."

"Hopefully you'll never have to use it for anything other than slicing through sinew." Amalu briefly tensed as Naoum hugged him from behind, the caracal resting the base of his chin on the close-cropped fur on his neck. "H-hey—"

"Thank you." Naoum held him close for a moment before stepping back to pick up a discarded glass jar which might have once held a traveler's supply of honey. "For an *akhi alsaghir*, you have a lot to teach me. Speaking of which... what exactly does Haziz think is causing this mess?"

"He claims it's something to do with the First Gods, but I'm not sure how much I believe that." Amalu sated his thirst with a long draw from his wineskin before continuing. "My father believes the drought is worsening the storms... all the vegetation that holds the sand back is drying up. At the fishing outpost it's all you can see. It's nothing but dead grass in every direction."

"Perhaps the heavens are causing the drought," Naoum replied as Amalu held up a closed fist. In the distance, far beyond any of the village's outlying homesteads, the flicker of a campfire was visible against the pinkish rock. "What do you think that is? Other travelers?"

"Whoever they are, I don't think they're friends to us. Keep your head low." Dropping down into a crouch, Amalu tried to minimize the crunching of stones beneath his foot paws as he cautiously advanced to a position behind a boulder shaped like a thumb. "Oh, shit."

A small camp had been set up next to the trail, beside an ancient fountain constructed over a natural spring to offer relief to thirsty pilgrims. Several bedraggled tents were circled round a dim campfire like a herd of gazelle facing down a leopard. Standing directly on the trail, a lone figure blocked their path as he kept watch. "What do we do, Amalu?"

"They look like Two Banks," Amalu muttered, squinting to get a better view. The watchman turned, revealing himself to be a ram with a prominent *ankh* in high relief on his bronze chest plate. "This is not good. Should we turn back?"

"You got a task from Haziz, right?" Naoum placed a reassuring paw on his shoulder. "I think this is your chance to prove yourself. I won't stop you if you turn tail and run but... I'm not going to abandon you while my dagger is still sharp."

"You're a good *akhi*." Amalu gingerly drew his sword and flicked his head toward the ram. Fear turned his blood to ice as he stared down the guard and imagined facing him. "Do you think you can draw the watchman's attention without getting yourself killed?"

"I've gotten pretty good at drawing attention." Naoum smirked, pulling a small glass phial from his bag. "But I assume your plan calls for something with a little more subtlety than a *cla-chiss*," he said with a wink.

"Yeah... something that won't wake the rest of the camp. There's no way we can take all of them. Frankly, even facing one in a straight fight will brush up against the limit of my capabilities." Amalu nervously scraped his claws against the sand-smoothed trail stones.

"Give me your wineskin, if you would." As soon as Amalu handed it over, the caracal poured about half of its iridescent red contents into a marble pestle. After adding a small measure of the thickening agent in the phial, Naoum blended the contents into a fine slurry that—on first impression—replicated the hue of freshly-spilled blood. "Convincing, isn't it?"

"Under the moonlight, I can barely tell... other than the smell." Fire burned in his nostrils, the intoxicant swirling around deep in his skull. Naoum began staining his nut-brown fur while Amalu judiciously cut swatches from the caracal's coat, trying to make them appear as haphazard as possible. By the time they were done, it looked as though a bandit had done an extremely poor job of attempting to slash Naoum's throat. "Okay. Do you think you can act the part? I just need you to buy me enough time to get him off-balance."

"Pfft... do you know how I get out of doing the difficult chores? Acting like I've caught a stomach bug does the trick every time." Sliding his fingers down across his muzzle, Naoum instantly transformed his countenance into an agonized snarl. "Just don't let me down... and don't die."

"I've got you," Amalu said, gripping the caracal tight. "We do this *together*."

"Then here we go. Spear the red deer this time... for me, okay?" Naoum cracked his shoulders before stepping out of cover and into moonlight that glittered like fish scales.

Steeling himself, Amalu gripped his sword tight as Naoum staggered forward, moaningly just loudly enough to catch the guard's attention. Paws trembling with fear, the guard held his sword out like a protective amulet as he moved forward and gradually out of earshot of the rest of the soldiers. "W-who goes there! Name yourself, stranger!"

"I... I-I've been stabbed!" Tottering forward like a newborn calf, the caracal spurted the remainder of the viscous liquid down his robes for dramatic effect. Stretching a paw out, he groaned before collapsing with a soft *crunch*. "H-help me... bandits!"

Raising his khopesh—a sickle-shaped sword that reminded Amalu of a skinny ax—the ram rushed over to the fallen caracal while sweeping his blade from side-to-side to fend off any threats that might strike from the darkness.

Heart pounding in his chest, Amalu's mind flashed back to the red deer charging at him, horns leveled at his throat. Claws digging into the fish skin leather that bound his blade's handle, he crept forward as the watchman hesitated, unsure of how to respond to the situation.

"Sometime this moon," Naoum mouthed, as the watchman seemed to make up his mind. Taking a few furtive steps toward where the caracal's collapsed body lay still, the ram twisted his *khopesh* vertically as if preparing to plunge it through Naoum's chest.

It looked like their plan to catch the ram entirely off-guard had gone awry.

Amalu was a few seconds too slow to intercept the blade outside the zone of danger. Speeding downward, the pointed tip came within inches of touching Naoum's robe before Amalu's blade connected with a muted *clang*. It threw the ram off-balance, and he stumbled a few feet off to the fennec's side. "Sorry! I could have planned that better!"

"Well, don't stop now!" Naoum unsheathed his dagger and wildly slashed at the ram, driving him back toward Amalu. "I'm passing him to you!"

"I've got him!" Spinning his *khopesh* like a sharp-edged windmill, the ram kicked Naoum's leg out from under him before pivoting to go on the offensive. Grimacing, Amalu was pushed back nearly a foot as their blades met again. Spittle collected on the ram's lips, powerful shoulders supporting strikes that landed like blows from a blacksmith's hammer despite his weapon's dainty appearance.

"Is that the best you can do, whimpering cub?" Snarling, the ram nearly battered the blade out of Amalu's paw with a vicious two-handed blow. "After I'm done with you, I'm going to turn your plump little companion into cooking fat!"

"I won't let you hurt him!" Amalu bared his fangs as he hacked and slashed at the ram, all-consuming rage compensating for poor technique. Fueled by tempestuous prayers to T-am-ădad, the fennec managed to push his opponent back with the might of the First Gods briefly on his side. "Naoum and I will lay eyes upon the Cracked Altar... together!"

"Ah, so it is your people who worship the false gods," the ram said, delivering a brutal kick to Amalu's knee that threw him off-kilter. "Time to end your blasphemy."

Employing relentless overhead strikes, the ram slowly battered the sword out of Amalu's paws, leaving the blade bent at a nearly thirty-degree angle by the time it finally slumped into the hard-packed dirt. Too weak to put up further resistance, Amalu shot the ram a defiant glare. By happy accident, the fight had taken them well beyond earshot of the camp, the lonely campfire still flicking in the distance. "Are you going to strike me down?" Amalu asked, panting and exhausted.

"Admit defeat and renounce your god and I will spare you... though you will forfeit your right paw for attacking a servant of Aten." The ram sunk his *khopesh* into the ground and fumbled about for the ram's horn slung over his shoulder.

"It is better to die whole in service of T-am-ădad than to die a scarred unbeliever." Drawing his tongue up against his teeth, Amalu hawked a glob of spit straight into the ram's eyes. "May the hyenas feast on your heart."

"Why you—" Stumbling backwards, the ram's claws grasped around the horn just as Naoum's dagger plunged through his sternum. Gasping, the ram touched the razor-sharp tip before dropping to his knees. "You're nothing but a cub... you're—"

"We are the servants of T-am-ădad." Without hesitating, Amalu drove his sword through the watchman's chest exactly like he would a red deer. Eyes shooting open, the ram registered an expression of intense surprise before he expired. "And we are your end."

"Were you... waiting for a moment to use that line?" Naoum started to lose his balance as Amalu wrapped an arm beneath his shoulder. He gently lowered the caracal to the ground, bracing him against a rock before handing him a leather bag packed with healing supplies. "Because you couldn't have just come up with that, right?"

"I mean... I didn't think my first kill would be like this." Amalu dragged the ram's body out of sight as Naoum applied some medicinal herbs to his swollen ankle. "I figured it would be more... triumphant."

"We're alive, aren't we?" Climbing to his feet with a grunt of effort, Naoum took Amalu's paw with a weary grin. "Come on. Let's get out of here before they wake up. Servants of T-am-ădad should not linger around unfriendly spirits..."

"You were brilliant back there, you know that?" Amalu brushed his wrist through the sweat-drenched fur on his forehead as he excavated the last few shovelfuls of dirt from a hastily dug grave. With a thick layer of mountain frost still coating the ground, it was effortful work. "Thank you for doing what I couldn't."

"I just got a lucky shot. You were the one who really fought him." Dressed only in a loincloth, Naoum tipped the last of the wine into his muzzle. His robe had been donated as an improvised burial shroud for Bachar's body. They had found the wizened fennec at the base of the shrine, bow in paw, surrounded by three Two Banks warriors studded with arrows. "Your father would be proud."

"You really think so?" Amalu rolled his eyes, turning away to hide the hotness beneath his cheeks. "You don't have to flatter me."

"I'm only speaking the truth." Naoum stretched his arms wide as clouds drifted low above the Shrine of T-am-ădad. A massive and ancient statue far beyond anything Amalu had seen in his village, it covered most of the western face of the Weeping Mountain. Water flowed downward from the hyena's eyes to his cupped paws, which then spilled into a midnight blue waterfall feeding the Reflecting Pool that stretched as far as the eye could see. "You were the one who had to be brave."

"More foolish than brave... but I'll take the compliment." Amalu chuckled, refilling the empty wineskin with water from the sacred pool. Crisp and sweet, it tasted as though it were expertly blended with the finest honey. "Have you sated your thirst?"

"Yes... but let's make sure we drink again before we leave. It's a long walk back to the village." Amalu sighed, filling the wineskin to the brim before tucking it next to Bachar's shrouded form. Naoum had already used the last of their supplies to provision the grave with a jar of preserved figs, a clay amphora of olive oil, and a few strips of aurochs jerky. "Is there anything I'm forgetting?"

"You've forgotten the prayer-dust." Naoum hummed as he dusted the shroud with a thick layer of ochre pigment. "Let us bid our old friend a safe journey. Hopefully he will cook *sahlab* for the First Gods in the afterlife."

"T-am-ădad will show him to the Ancestral Hunting Grounds. I am sure of it." Amalu sighed as the first pearls of dawn peeked over the eastern horizon. Walking over to the Cracked Altar, the fennec tucked the prayer scroll in the largest fissure. Sighing as he held back tears, the fennec lit a small beeswax candle in the alcove above the altar, which contained a smaller figure of Em-ăsăww—placed by Naoum—beside the main carving of T-am-ădad. "And Em-ăsăww will give him a bottomless canister of the Divine Spice for cooking."

"Do you think we've proved our manhood?" With their task complete, Amalu rejoined Naoum, the caracal staring into the mirror-like surface of the Reflecting Pool. Two hopeful reflections stared back at them from the depths, both missing their inner incisors. "Facing another life-or-death challenge this year might be a bit too much for me."

"I'd certainly hope so." Naoum's belly jiggled as he anointed Bachar's body with water from the sacred pool, allowing the dye to saturate the wizened fennec's light tan *djellaba*. "I think we both earned our manhood today... in the eyes of the First Gods, if not the Elders."

"I'll ask Haziz to put in a good word for us." Driving the shovel into the earth to serve as an ersatz headstone, Amalu padded over and helped the caracal cover the body with fresh sandy dirt. "Now let us lay old Bachar to rest."

Chanting in unison, the pair sang a wavering melody as they returned the shrouded figure to the earth, their voices echoing off the

Weeping Mountain's contours until they replicated the agony of a thousand mourners. Though the meaning of the words had been lost to time, each syllable burned their throats with the melancholy of a soul leaving the mortal plane. They kept singing until their voices were hoarse and the grave's surface was smooth as the Reflecting Pool opposite it.

"And it's done." Flopping down against one of the Shrine's crackled marble pillars, Amalu sighed as he gazed back toward his village with heavy eyes. "I just realized we haven't gotten a wink of sleep."

"Rest then, little fennec. These should provide plenty of shade until at least midday," Naoum said, giving the pillar a gentle tap. Sitting down beside him, the caracal allowed Amalu to rest against his well-padded shoulder. Taking a deep whiff of his feline scent, Amalu sighed with contentment as he began to drift off to sleep. "I'll keep watch, just in case the Two Banks camp sends a scout to investigate."

"Thank you. Hopefully the First Gods hear Haziz's prayer... and ours." Amalu yawned and snuggled up against the caracal with a contented sigh. Off in the distance, where the village sat at the edge of the horizon, silver-tinged rain clouds began to gather.

"Rest well, *akhi alsaghir*." As Amalu drifted off to sleep, Naoum watched with hopeful eyes as, for the first time in many moons, rain began to fall on the dusty village of Henchir-Aïn-Dourat.

Unmourned

by Haya Baru

You must undertake a pilgrimage of seven days, because seven is a number of ill omen. Of all the things the gods gave us, none can be broken apart evenly into seven: the twelve knuckles and five fingers that we use to count, and the thirty days in a month. It is under ill omens that you must live out your days with grace.

Tehq felt the muscles in her shoulders burn as she carried the boy's body out of the nameless, rain-soaked vassal canton. The winter rain had soaked through the thin burial wrap, and the leopardess could smell the mint leaves that she had placed over the young boy's chest. Under normal circumstances the boy's father would carry him—he was undoubtedly stronger than Tehq herself, whose years had been spent hunched over manuscripts and clay tablets. His ankle still swollen from the very avalanche that had taken his son's life, he merely hobbled beside her, mute, his head lowered as the rain battered his neck.

They reached the family's burial land after a few short minutes, the plot marked only by the traditional red strips of fabric, tied to low-hanging branches in the surrounding trees. She set the boy's body down while a young girl, now an only child, opened a sack of fern seeds Tehq had asked her to bring. The father took a shovel from his wife, who held it back from him for a moment, as if to protest on account of his condition, but she soon relented. Tehq, stiff and awkward with inexperience, watched as he shakily fought with the black mud that covered the forest floor. Tehq noticed only a few burial mounds around her, covered with the lush green ferns that hastened the dead's return to the soil: two less than a decade old she guessed, and one mere months old, but much smaller. The rhythm of a shovel piercing mud carried Tehq away like a morbid lullaby, the lyrics known to her since childhood. By the time the father was done, the sun had turned her head and left them for the horizon. She reluctantly steeled herself for the prayers that were to follow.

After the burial was complete, Tehq returned to the family's cabin, where the family patriarch practically strong-armed her into accepting an offer of salal wine. It was tradition to offer a funerary priest such trifles, even if she could not stomach the company of a grieving family. The boy's mother, scarcely older than Tehq herself, but whose figure and unkempt fur testified to the hardships of motherhood, fell into a cushion opposite the fireplace and began to quietly sob.

Tehq was too cold, and too sore, to make eye contact with anyone. She had never done this before—not on her own, at least. She had never seen any of these people before yesterday, and this was about as awful a way to meet anyone as she could imagine. The boy's sister, just a few years younger than Tehq, sat down beside her, and put a hand on her mother's shoulder before she turned to Tehq.

"I feel a bit guilty, asking a funeral of you when you haven't even finished your pilgrimage yet," she said to Tehq.

Tehq shook her head. "Death herself is unconcerned with such formalities, so neither am I." The remaining formality would be satisfied in two days' time, she thought.

"This is not our first death this year," the girl said.

"I'm sorry," Tehq said stiffly.

"I had my first son last spring, but the goddess turned her head at him, and she did not breathe air into his lungs once he was born." The girl paused. "When a priest came to bury him, I asked him why the goddess would do such a thing. He said that the gods make all things so that they may one day die, for without death nothing would live. But why would the goddess not let something live before it dies?"

Tehq recalled the freshest mound she had seen in the burial plot. "By the time I was your age, I had spent years of my life trying to make sense of what had happened to me during the war. As a young girl I couldn't fathom why the gods would permit such an excess of suffering. After so much philosophizing and thinking and praying, after enlightenment eluded me, I realized the truth: neither reason nor faith would ever provide me with answers."

"Then where does the answer come from?"

Tehq forced herself to finish up the last of her wine in one swig. "The fault lies with the question. Just as reason and faith allow us to conjure the phantasms of greed, pride, and loyalty that drive us to war, it carries us towards that question of yours that is no less illusory. Truthfully, there is no *why*."

> *There will be hardships across your seven days. Some your in-experience may create for you, some the gods will select. How you overcome them is not important: as in life you may suc-ceed in many things and fail in others, but the grace of death levels all equally.*

By the time Tehq had returned to the tavern where she was staying, she felt about as wretched as she had ever felt in her life. The rain-water had soaked her clothing along with every inch of her fur, and every muscle above her chest ached.

She had stripped herself down to a loin-cloth and a chest wrap-ping and collapsed in front of the tavern's fire pit, along with a dozen other merchants and traders who were in similar states of undress. Liquor flowed freely, drunken conversation mingling with the scent of burning peat-moss and cider. Tehq seemed disinterested in all of it, at least until her fur dried. Her first unaided ceremony was about as unpleasant as she had imagined it would be. She felt as though she had somehow failed, although she wasn't sure why. She always looked up to the older priests who had raised her, shown her grace, wisdom, and dignity in the wake of tragedy. Why did she feel so far beneath them?

"You look like you've had a harder night than most." The voice came from a tigress who sat down beside her. She was beautiful, with flowing elbow-length black hair and bright red robes that wrapped tightly across her generous figure.

"I think the merchants can offer you more for the night than I can," Tehq said, her eyes unfocused as she watched flames lap up the sides of the wooden logs.

"What they have in coin they lack in conversation," the tigress said with a smirk.

"What makes you think I'm any different?"

The tigress paused, and Tehq could feel the woman's large brown eyes sinking into her fur like the rainwater.

"Priestess in training, probably a war refugee. Hardly the dull type."

Tehq's brow furrowed and she turned to stare at the tigress. "How did you—"

"You have a southern accent, but you're not a trader or a nomad. Only people like that who end up this far north are here because they have no home to return to. As for the under-priestess part, one of you passes through here every few months. You're easy to spot."

Tehq gave the woman a glance that said all it needed to. The pair sat in silence for a number of seconds, the pain in Tehq's shoulders drowning out the din of the drinking traders who surrounded the rest of the fire.

"I lost my father during the siege," the courtesan continued. "He was a merchant, selling weapons to the provinces in the south. A week into the battle, the king tracked him down, and killed him."

"I'm sorry," Tehq said, for the second time that day. The phrase felt just as useless this time.

"Sometimes I take comfort in the fact that all the men responsible for his death were either killed or had their hands marked after the siege failed. Do you think it's right to find solace in such violence, priestess-to-be?"

Tehq couldn't tell if the woman was making professional small-talk or genuinely asking, although the delicate way she rested her muzzle on the back of her hand suggested a bit of both.

"We shouldn't guilt ourselves for the emotions our hearts drive us to feel. At the same time—feelings that are born from pain will only beget pain, if we're not careful."

"Spoken like a true priestess," the tigress said, beginning to look just as lost in thought as Tehq was. "I have a habit of checking the hands of any older male clients before I take their money, but I feel much less compunction about that."

Tehq laughed mirthlessly. When she was young, she remembered hearing stories of captured warriors who chose to fall on their swords rather than be branded with the usurper's mark. The thought still sent chills down her spine.

"I suppose I would do that if I was in your position."

"What about you?" she said, her voice soft like a caribou foal's coat, despite the subject matter.

"What about me?" Tehq said coolly.

"Has the priesthood tempered all that bitterness?"

Tehq thought, unsure if she felt like answering. "One time when I was fifteen, I saw a man with the mark in the middle of town. I had this thought—so immediate and all-consuming it nearly swept me off my feet—that I wanted to kill him. The only reason I didn't was because I knew I would never get away with it. Later that day I told one of the priestesses about what had happened. She said that great men go their whole lives without letting go of that anger, even if it ravages them."

"Perhaps that anger will be what you confront in the woods, then." The tigress said.

"Confront?"

"The locals think under-priests go into the woods to fight a monster at the end of your pilgrimage," the woman said. "I know it's just children's stories, and the fight is metaphorical, but the priests I've met always talk about the end of their journey in such a way. Like it's a battle."

"I'm surprised you pay such close attention to your patrons' pillow talk."

"It's my job, but I'd be lying if I said I didn't find it interesting."

"A less cynical person might think you're taking a shine to me," Tehq said. She couldn't help but let the corners of her muzzle curl upwards in a smile.

The tigress laughed. "No need to temper your cynicism. Like I said, your types come through here every so often. To the surprise of no one, a dreary funeral priest tips better than a drunk merchant."

Tehq couldn't help but chuckle. The tigress's attention felt like a summer breeze across bare fur, and she couldn't help but notice the fluttering in her heart. "You're right—about the battle, that is. However, no one tells us what we'll be fighting."

The tigress stood up and offered her hand to Tehq. "How about some tea, perhaps somewhere more peaceful where you can tell me more? You look just as cold as you do lonely."

Tehq took the courtesan's hand, and lifted herself out of her seat.

There is no removing oneself from the flow of the cycle, that which changes all things, brings the living closer to death and the dead closer to life. However, you may find moments of reprieve on your pilgrimage; they will humble you, as like all things they are temporary.

When Tehq woke, dim slivers of moonbeams pierced the clouds and poured in through the window in one of the tavern's private rooms. She instinctively reached a hand across the bed, but the tigress had left. She felt her heart drop into her stomach—nothing good came from late nights where she had nothing to distract her from the pull of her wandering mind. Through the murk and moonlight, Tehq saw a silhouette by the door.

She bolted up and stumbled out of bed; without the moose skin sheets, the cold ate through her bare fur and chilled her skin. The silhouette was gone, leaving nothing but a cold spear of fear lodged between her ribs. She stumbled towards the door, hand outstretched, as though her claws might make contact with the ethereal shadow she had seen seconds ago. Her knuckles brushed the door, at which point she gave up her search and turned around.

The shadow stood between her and the bed.

Its head was down, unkempt black hair glistening in the moonlight. Tehq felt her breath catch in her throat, her feet nailed in place as it hobbled forward, into the light.

For a moment, Tehq thought it was the boy she had buried hours before. The shadow was the right height, with the same hair. The clouds shifted, bathing the room in pale light. It was not the boy.

"Ikarih?" Tehq asked.

The young girl did not respond. She was wearing a moose skin jacket, little more than a cut-down section of pelt with a button at the top and a hood roughly stitched on. Tehq had one just like it as a child. The girl looked up at her, face dirty, her eyes bloodshot and wet with tears.

"Ik—"

Ikarih's lips did not move, but Tehq heard her voice.

You haven't grieved at all. Why?

The girl's face contorted in agony. Blood poured down from her hairline as she stumbled forward, her bloody hands grasping at Tehq's bare fur. Ikarih started to fall, and Tehq could see the arrows sticking out from her back, the tanned leather of her coat drenched in blood. Tehq tried to scream, but the air froze in her lungs.

She awoke to an unpleasant tingling radiating throughout her body, her heart beating with such speed it felt like it might burst. The cold air stung her lungs as she pulled the blanket over her face, her claws digging holes in the fabric.

By the time Tehq crawled out of the tavern in the morning and hobbled to the stables, fog was rolling over the canopy of the black-green forest that surrounded the little canton, as though the uniformly gray sky was falling to earth to wash the town away.

"I hope you slept better than I did, Tik," Tehq said. Her caribou did not respond.

She threw her pack over the animal's haunches and hauled herself onto his back. Tehq had convinced herself to eat an elk sausage for breakfast; she was hungry, but couldn't summon the motivation to eat. It was already late in the morning, and Tehq thanked her god that most of the merchants had disembarked long ago; she was hardly in the mood for conversation.

"On your way?" a voice said from across the stables. It was the tigress from last night. She was wearing an expensive seal fur coat over her robes and leaning against the wall of the stables with her arms crossed.

"I have two days of travel ahead of me. Places to be," Tehq said tersely. She couldn't remember the tigress's name, and although the consort was probably used to such things, Tehq couldn't help but feel slightly ashamed.

"One of the girls I work with said she heard a scream coming from your room last night. I said it wasn't my doing."

Tehq pushed on the caribou's antlers, egging him forward. "Rough night."

"Hey Tehq!" the woman shouted as the caribou canted out of the stables and towards the muddy cobblestone road out of town.

"What?"

"Do you know where the word *trauma* comes from?"

Tehq felt thrown by the question, even if she should know the answer. She rolled the root over on her tongue, the way one might taste wine. *Hʷaušuš.* It took her a second, her skull still foggy from lack of sleep. *Hʷaušuš.* From *ihʷišauš.*

"That which ravages itself," Tehq answered.

The woman said nothing, just nodded and bade her farewell. By the time Tehq realized she should be courteous and say farewell herself, Tik had turned a corner, and they were nearly out of town. Her heart sank as she realized it would be the better part of a week before she slept in a proper bed again.

> *The battle you shall undertake on the seventh day is unique to you, and thus the high priest sends everyone on a different journey. No matter where you are sent to, the sixth day remains the same for everyone. Your revelations at the steles of the old temples will be your last chance to anticipate what*

awaits you the seventh night. The meditation of the previous five days will moor you to the earth. The terrorflower of the sixth night will unmoor you.

The forests were as vast and as dark as the seas that surrounded all four corners of the gods' lands. Roots roiled the mossy, wet earth, tripping Tik's experienced hooves. His antlers scraped against the tree trunks that appeared to squeeze them in from the sides of the dirt path. Before they had entered the woods proper, Tehq had allowed the sun to guide her, but the canopy of the gods' conifers choked all but the faintest slivers of sunlight. To the degree that her path was predetermined, it was with the graces of the gods.

"You've gone this route before, haven't you?" she said to Tik. She had never spoken to a caribou like it was a person, although she could understand where the term *mount-mumbler* came from; they merely listened, without judgment.

"I've only seen the old steles once before, not long after I was taken in by the temple as a young girl. A priest took me up the hills to one not far from the temple. He said that one day I would understand them."

The beast snorted.

The dirt road became even narrower, and they soon turned a corner to meet a series of rocks jutting out of the dirt, improvised stairs leading upwards to the top of a hill. She dismounted the caribou and let him traverse the steps on his own weight, the leopardess walking just ahead as the cervine awkwardly climbed up the rocky stairs, errant tree branches scraping his thick winter coat. The air was heavy with the scent of camphor and rain.

They reached the top of the hill, where she tied his reins to a tree and stepped forward, mossy soil sinking under her feet. The clearing reminded her of the stele she saw as a young girl—not from location but from feeling, the way her breath caught in her throat, the way her heart strained against her chest.

The petroglyph set into the stones was only a head shorter than her, spanning a smooth section of the rock face that was only an arm's length wide. Swirls and jagged symbols lined the edges of the carving, where they framed a human figure, its arms hanging down from narrow shoulders, its head set with two sharply-carved eyes, countless antlers protruding from its skull and mingling with a series of six-pointed stars. Above the figure, a circle with six marks was drawn in the center. If she squinted, it looked like an outline of the very statue that rested in the center of the temple where she lived: Irṛhaukt, goddess of death, her arms outstretched, with the body of a leopardess and the head of a caribou.

Tehq recalled something she read on a tablet as a child, when she was still learning the scribal arts: there were ten such steles of the goddess known, their age a mystery, but in the dawn of writing, when the god of wisdom gave Tehq's ancestors the knowledge of words drawn into clay, the first scribes wrote of the steles. They said the carvings depicted the goddess as she showed herself in countless sleep visitations to those who did not know of cities nor kings, in the shards of the nightmares of the guilty and the soothing dreams of the martyred, before the rivers split all lands, and before the ice sloughed to the south.

It was a full minute before Tehq could summon the confidence to move her feet from the ground. She returned to the caribou, his snout digging into the soil as he foraged for food. She reached into her pack and pulled out a coiled length of goat hair twine, crow feathers tied into the string at regular intervals. She tied one end around a tree, walked across the clearing until she wrapped it around five other trees, then finally tied it off where she began, forming a lopsided hexagon in front of the stones. She untied the caribou's reins and moved him outside the circle, pulling the twine upwards to make way for his antlers.

"Sorry, friend. I don't know if anything rests in the soul of a farm caribou besides dreams of salmonberry and lichen, but I don't think you'd want to find out."

She lifted up her robes and sat down on her knees in front of the petroglyph, her hands shaking as she pulled a goatskin flask of salal berry wine from her bag and uncorked it with her teeth. She libated it onto the earth, the dark red liquid swallowed up by the soil.

"I suppose one doesn't ask for niceties from the goddess of death," she said as she returned the empty flask to her bag, "so I won't deign to do such a thing. If you have seen fit not to bring me to submission yet, perhaps you will grant me something more."

If the goddess heard her, or cared, she did not know. After all, a man does not justify himself to a caterpillar. She pulled a little leather pouch from her bag and dumped the contents, a coarse green and black powder, onto her fingers. She tried desperately to steady herself as she opened her mouth and rubbed the powder on the underside of her tongue. It tasted earthy and bitter, like seeds of the thorny-bulbed flower from which it was extracted. She closed her eyes, lowered her head, and started to chant.

aküśunån asšåqåk aqᵂitülåk	*I survive, I pass into darkness, I fall silent*
ikśånån sšaquk äqᵂitüluk	*The Shadow traverses the silenced...*

The words stuck to her soft palate until they became a mumble, and before she noticed, she had stopped speaking. Her mouth felt like it was full of dirt. When she opened her eyes again, the forest was darker, broken apart, as though she was viewing it through the reflection in a murky lake. She tried to pull herself to her feet, but her limbs forced her to the ground, muscles leaden and inflexible. Shadows flexed and flickered in the corners of her vision, the shapes pulling into a dozen crawling monstrosities the moment her eyes did not focus upon them. Terror thrummed in her veins as the monstrosities moved around her, but she could not bring herself to run.

With great effort, she lifted her head, and met the shadow.

She was not sure if it was god, or man. Thoughts passed through her head like rainwater through woven cloth. It was a child.

"Ikarih?"

The edges of the shadow sharpened. It was not Ikarih, the hair was wrong, she was too old. Tehq understood.

"Why am I seeing you?" Tehq said to the blurry image of her younger self.

"Do you not always see me? Sometimes in a dream, sometimes in your reflection in the water?" The shadow's lips did not move as she spoke, the words instead rising up from the earth.

"Why now?" Tehq could not force her throat to pull language from the mire of her mind for more than a second at a time.

"You ask the wrong questions, as always."

Her heart felt as though it was trying to punch its way out of her ribs. "You're... you're..." she tripped over her own tongue, "...supposed to have a clue for me."

"Clues cannot save you from yourself."

"You're supposed—" Tehq repeated herself.

"Tomorrow you will face what you have yet to mourn."

Something sour turned over in Tehq's stomach. She swayed on her knees, the world tilting around her.

"You're wrong," Tehq spat.

"You speak from anger, not wisdom."

Against her better judgment, Tehq pulled herself to her feet. She towered over the shadow of her younger self, but she did not feel like it.

"Of course I do." She could not tell if she was raising her voice, her head was a rock sinking to the bottom of a lake. "Ikarih died in my arms. I saw my parents put to arrows." She stumbled backwards, her legs beginning to fail her. The monstrosities writhing around her moved in, like spiders crawling towards their prey. "I still have nightmares. I cried for weeks. I felt nothing for years. I had no choice but to mourn them!"

"Your sister and your parents were the first to fall under the soil of the earth, but you have not mourned all."

"Then tell me what I have forgotten! My sister, my parents, my innocence—"

The shadow of herself pulled towards her, as though the ground between them had disappeared. It grew, surrounding her from all sides, it did not speak, it did not open its lips, but she heard it screaming, the sound of a hundred avalanches. It no longer looked like she did, it was a monster, a nightmare, with pale eyes like moonlight beaming through a blizzard.

She fell to the ground.

"The day the war arrived dozens of futures did not come to pass, some died, others walk as shadows. You must meet the eyes of the one you have forgotten, and you will see judgment in its gaze—be it judgment of forgiveness, anger, or capitulation," it said.

Tehq tried to scream, but she could not; her tongue remained frozen, and she felt her lips babble like an infant's.

"You must look into the eyes of the unmourned, and with grace you must make peace," it roared.

The monstrosities in the corners of her vision moved in, and forced her into darkness.

> *The gods have decreed that all things must suffer. Therefore, there can be no enlightenment without suffering. On the sixth night you will acknowledge your suffering, on the seventh you will not be victorious unless you know how it has shaped you.*

Tehq was awoken by Tik's rough tongue licking the morning dew from her cheeks. The sunlight, even dulled through the clouds, burned her eyes as she opened them. She did not know for how many minutes she lay on the ground, the veins in her head throbbing.

Eventually she summoned the power to grab Tik's reins and pull herself shakily to her feet. She wrapped her arms around his neck, unable to stand on her own as the earth wobbled beneath her.

"Time. What time?" Tehq mumbled. Tik snorted in response, lowering his head to pick at the mossy earth.

Tehq squinted up at the sun, the dim overcast morning making her eyes water. It was mid-morning. She let her arms fall to her side, and immediately stumbled backwards onto the ground, where she decided to remain until her body told her otherwise.

After she regained control over her legs, she stumbled over to where her bag rested by the stele, and rummaged around for a folded cloth of rations. She took a few nibbles from the corner of a slice of acorn bread, testing to see if her stomach would allow her to keep food down. After a few more minutes of waiting, the acorn bread was joined by elk sausage and dried salal berries, washed down with more wine. After the world no longer tilted every time she stood on her legs, she pulled herself gingerly onto Tik and consulted the guide that the high priest had written for her.

Written with ashy ink on finely-pressed cattail paper, the final set of instructions were no more than a sentence:

Leave the clearing of the stele via the path to the northeast; half a day's travel on the main road will bring you to a western trail, where your journey will end at a lake.

Typical high priest behavior; extracting meaning from vagueness is left as an exercise to the reader.

As Tik canted down the pathway down to wherever the high priest was leading her, shadows of last night flickered in Tehq's memory. Part of her knew she should prepare for what awaited her at the lake, but she couldn't bear the thought of uprooting whatever memories the shadow was directing her to; it seemed to her that her memories did not need further examination. Whenever she closed her eyes, she could still see her sister's body in her arms.

The pathway down the hill led to a main road that was part of a trade network, as indicated by the heavy wheel tracks carved into the hardened dirt. The hours passed in bitter, exhausted silence, the cold air biting at Tehq's hands as she relentlessly gripped Tik's leather reins. She stopped on the roadside once for lunch, although it was mostly to give poor Tik a rest, after he had spent the better part of two days carrying her. Trade caravans creaked by them as Tehq listlessly nibbled her elk sausage while Tik rummaged through the moss and mud with his snout, foraging for mushrooms.

By late afternoon, a light drizzle of sleet had set in, blanketing the dirt road in glittering white ice. Tehq unconsciously clenched her jaw, wishing for her journey to end. The shadow still murmured to her, words creeping across her thoughts. She had done enough mourning to last a lifetime, what wound could be left that she had forgotten to heal?

Tik stopped in the middle of the road. He lowered his head, bearing his antlers at the road ahead, just as the two were about to turn a corner.

"Tik?" She put a hand on his head, petting his sleet-covered fur.

She heard a commotion, followed by a scream, then a hoarse, piercing roar. Bears.

Tik snorted angrily, threatening to buck her off. A war-mount he was not.

She dismounted and pulled a bow and quiver from her saddle bag, stringing the bow as Tik backed away. Another scream. She nocked an arrow, readying another in her mouth. The priests had taught her archery once when she was sixteen—and she was not particularly good.

She ran forward, paws slipping on the ice as she turned a corner.

She didn't even see the source of the screams at first, just a dead caribou, and a massive brown bear wrestling with *something* on the ground. The bear shifted, and Tehq caught a glimpse of a bloody red hand between folds of fur, clutching a knife buried in the animal's side. The knife was too small to make a difference, but just large enough to make an angry bear even angrier.

Tehq yelled and stomped her foot in vain, the bear disinterested in her as the man—an older tiger—pulled out the knife and weakly slashed it across the bear's face, angering it further. The two briefly made eye contact before Tehq raised her bow and let the arrow fly, bronze tip striking the bear firmly in the shoulder.

The bear roared furiously, lashing around to charge at her, great paws slipping on the blood and ice. Her hands shaking, Tehq nocked another arrow, the bear closing over half the twenty paces of distance between them by the time the second arrow flew, grazing the bear's back. Left with no other choice, Tehq hit the ground, rolling off the road and colliding with the mossy tree trunks that separated the trail from the forest. Pain bloomed in her back as she hit the trees, numb fingers grasping for another arrow before she had even registered where the bear had come to a halt.

Disoriented and bleeding, the wild animal spun around to face her, its limp slowing it just enough to spare Tehq from the claws as she had dived. She pulled the arrow back as the animal charged, the bow's string scraping her cheek just as she let go.

The arrow embedded itself in the bear's neck with a *thud,* its feet giving out from under it as it slid across the mud, massive body thrashing uselessly in a growing pool of dark blood.

Tehq pulled herself weakly to her feet before nocking another arrow. She still remembered a prayer her father had taught her when he took her seal-hunting with the nomads, before the war. It was the same phrase said by the corvée warriors who hunted the men who killed her sister:

I am sorry. To the soil you must return.

She aimed for the animal's skull, and released the arrow. The bear became still.

For a brief moment, she felt an inner peace she rarely felt, as though the bear's death had loosened something inside her.

The tiger behind her groaned. Ears perking up, she spun around and ran towards him just as he was wrapping a torn fragment of his coat around his bleeding leg. His eyes were unfocused, and most of his lower torso was smeared in blood, although she was unsure if it was his or the bear's.

"You know, my dad always told me it was a good omen to see bears this time of year. It means winter is over," he said shakily as he tightened the scrap of fabric around his leg. Blood oozed from a gash just visible under his riding trousers.

He was a good head taller than Tehq, approaching middle age, with a wiry black-and-white beard. His muzzle was dotted with scars and scratches, and a tip was missing from his ear.

"You should get that taken care of," Tehq said awkwardly, kneeling down to examine his leg.

"And the sky is gray," the man said. "The name is Šōhen, by the way."

"Tehq," she responded, hoping her caribou hadn't run too far.

"You saved my life."

"And the ground is wet," she responded, smiling weakly.

Tehq stuck her fingers in her mouth and whistled, summoning a very nervous Tik from the woods. He trotted towards her reluctantly.

"And if you had arrived late, I would have had a funerary priestess to bury me anyway," he said.

"Do you have anything to boil water? A bear's claws are heavy with sickness, you must wash it with boiling water," she said, ignoring his earlier comment.

"Trust me, this isn't my first scrape," he said as he pulled himself up with his hands and pushed himself to the side of the road, bloodied leg dragging across the dirt. He pulled a flint from one of the pockets of his oversized jacket and stuck it in his mouth while he reached for any dry tinder on low-hanging branches. "I come prepared these days."

Within a few minutes, Šōhen had testified to his survival skills by starting a fire while Tehq gathered sleet in a small copper pot. The fire crackled warmly as the sun kissed the horizon, and Tehq couldn't help but rest her hands in front of it as she waited for the water to boil.

"I'm sorry about your caribou," she said.

Šōhen grimaced, the shadows in his haggard face dancing by the fire. "If the gods spare my leg from rot, I can mourn my mount."

Tehq's ears perked up. Between the bear and Šōhen, she had completely forgot why she was here. "Do you know if there's a lake here?"

He nodded. "Big one, just off the main road. Not long by caribou."

Tehq breathed a sigh of relief. The water started to boil, and Šōhen removed the bowl from the fire, bracing himself as he poured the steaming water over his leg.

Tehq could see the muscles in his jaw clench as the water poured over raw flesh.

"That won't be enough to stop the bleeding," she said.

He grimaced. "I was hoping you wouldn't say as such. My family has a small cabin nearby—I keep a supply of chokeberries there. A simple salve should staunch the flow of blood."

Tehq got up and adjusted Tik's saddles. "Do you think you can make it?"

"I'm afraid I don't have a choice."

Tehq wordlessly bent down and let him wrap his arms around her shoulder, muscles in her legs straining as she laboriously crawled onto Tik's back with Šōhen holding onto her. Her thoughts returned to her pilgrimage, and she wondered if the gods would put such an incident before her if they did not intend her to intervene. Šōhen's next words, however, answered her question.

"There's a trail leading west around the next bend. It'll take you to that lake; my cabin is there."

Tik slowly canted forward, unaccustomed to a doubling of his passengers. A chill ran down her spine as she realized that Šōhen's life had not collided with her own on accident.

Sure enough, only a few minutes later, the road split in two, with a smaller path heading downwards into the woods.

"That one," Šōhen said, motioning weakly, his other hand firmly gripping Tik's saddle. The path leading down to the lake was almost as narrow as the path she had taken to the stones, the two enveloped in darkness as the woods swallowed them again, errant branches tugging at Tik's antlers. Tehq could smell her passenger's blood mixing with the scent of conifer sap and wet earth.

Šōhen adjusted his grip on Tik's saddle as he tried to steady himself, the sleeves of his jacket catching on Tik's saddlebags and riding up his arms. Out of the corner of her eye, Tehq saw the mark on his forearm. An *X* carved deep into the flesh, rippling scars visible through the striped orange and black fur.

A priest's voice came to her through the twisting inky-black woods like a crack of lightning.

"Our enemy is not our teacher. If we turn our swords to unarmed men, by what measure are we better than them? Still—something must be done with them."

Tehq, wearing robes that were at least two sizes too big, watched in horror from the window of the temple along with a half-dozen other orphans and the priest. The warrior was as naked as the day he was born, ribs stretched against thin and patchy fur, his lanky frame dragged through the snow by two men who held him by his arms. A crowd gathered, watching silently as the men pulled him into the center of the town, where a blacksmith's forge waited. One of the men wrapped his hand in leather and pulled a knife from the forge, the bronze hot and glowing like the sun. A few of the children gasped. The warrior screamed as the other man held him to the ground, forcing the warrior's arm out into the snow. With two quick cuts, they drew the X into his arm with the glowing blade, the naked warrior screaming with a ferocity that made Tehq's blood run cold. She pulled her robes up to her eyes as the man thrashed helplessly on the ground just as another was dragged out, the condemned warrior thrashing fruitlessly against his captors.

Tehq buried her head in her robes as she felt bile rise to the back of her throat.

"Are you alright?" Šōhen asked weakly.

Tehq pulled herself from the riptides of memory, her mind's eye burning like an open wound splashed with sea water. For a few seconds she did not respond.

"Yah."

"You sound almost as bad off as me. Traveled long, I assume?"

The currents pulled her under. Her stupid, weak little hands tugging uselessly at the arrows embedded in Ikarih's back. The splattering of blood on snow as swords cut through flesh.

The tide came out, the dark forest around her seeming nothing more than shapes, as unreal as a child's ink brush drawing.

"Seven days." Tehq felt her lips move, but the words seemed to come from across a great distance.

Šōhen mumbled something in acknowledgement, but the words were lost on her. As reality seeped back into the clamor of shapes and sensations around her, she felt as though she might crawl out of her fur. Every muscle in her body rippled as her soul thrashed against her flesh like an animal caught in a trap. He was one of them.

The tides swallowed her again, and Tehq tried to moor herself with the distant voice of a high priest. *You must live out your days with grace. Death will hang over you always, demanding inner peace as the earthen world rages around you, as the nights become deep, as the soil of time is watered with both rain and blood.*

A pristine lake stood before them, still surface glimmering with the orange-red haze of the sunset.

"Here," he said. "There's a few hunting lodges halfway down the lake, one belongs to my father-in-law"

"It's a beautiful lake."

"As good a place to bleed to death as any," he said sarcastically.

She pulled on Tik's antlers, bringing him to a stop before she dismounted, awkwardly stumbling onto the ground.

The cabin was more a small hunting lodge, the inside populated with little beyond a bed of animal furs, a fireplace, and a table. Tehq sat on the ground, staring at the patterns in the rough hewn wood. She didn't notice that she had her hand clenched around one of the arrows in her quiver until Šōhen said something.

"Don't worry, I'm not going to attack you, even if I was in a state to do so," he said between clenched teeth, holding a dripping cloth sack of chokeberries over the gash in his bleeding leg, the astringent purple liquid dripping down onto exposed flesh.

"What?"

"Your hand. On the arrowtip," he said.

"Oh." She loosened her grip, palm drenched in sweat.

"Don't blame you. Young priestess traveling the woods with a strange old man. I'd have a hand on a sharp object too," he said, his tone suggesting humor, but his words became a jumble of sounds in Tehq's ears.

"No, it's just—your arm." She spoke before she could decide if she even wanted to say it.

Šōhen was tying a fresh strip of linen around his arm. He stopped, his jowls turning downwards to a grimace. "I was hoping you wouldn't notice," he said before tying off the fabric. "That was a long time ago."

"It was six years ago," she said, her voice barely a whisper.

He leaned against the bed, nursing his leg, his eyes focused on some distant object behind her. "Sometimes it feels like a lifetime ago, sometimes it feels like yesterday. Particularly the nightmares. Those—those don't feel like ancient history." He briefly made eye contact with her, before his eyes darted back towards the floor.

Tehq opened her mouth, a small instinctive part of her wanting to mention the nightmares, but she couldn't bring herself to say such a thing, to bring voice to the unconscionable idea that something might connect the two of them.

"I saw my sister die." The feeling of words in her throat told Tehq she was speaking.

"And I my nephew. Sometimes I'm not sure if I'm being haunted by ghosts or by memories. Even in the moments when you forget, the memories are still there, not as images or sound but as pain. Aren't memories strange like that? What happened has passed, the beast has been slain, but still it ravages; but then I wonder, is the beast still ravaging me, or is it myself?"

"She was ten."

"He was seventeen." Šhōhen gazed at something beyond the walls of the cabin. "The last time I saw him, a sword had opened him like a butchered goat. I remember standing there, wondering if I was dreaming, because none of it seemed real. I spent so much time mourning him I forgot that a part of me died as well."

A part of Tehq wished he would stop talking—the more he talked the harder it became to be mad at him, and she preferred to be mad at him; if her anger was just, there was nothing to her experiences beyond good and evil. They were victim and victimizer, caribou and bear, black and white. The thought of a world beyond that duality gripped her with sudden and unexpected terror.

"Do you expect me to feel sorry for you? Did you not choose to pick up a blade?" she said.

Šōhen looked grimly at the floor. After a moment, he shook his head. "I was a debt laborer. I didn't choose anything. I killed a farmer's caribou. They dragged me into court, I didn't have the silver to pay."

"I lost my parents. My whole family. A temple took me in when I was thirteen. And you—you went to war for a caribou?" She didn't realize she was speaking through clenched teeth until she felt the pain in her jaw. "Why should I believe you? Why should I feel the same sorrow for you I feel for my family?"

"I'm not asking for sympathy. I've had to forgo such wants years ago. As for the belief, they said I didn't have a choice. I was released two months before the war ended. The court gave me a copper seal to prove I paid my debt—"

He moved his hand to reach behind him. Like the rush of an avalanche, Tehq's mind flung itself back into the present. She thought back to the road, with the bear, to Šōhen sheathing his knife just behind his right hip.

Her hand squeezed the arrow again, arm swinging around to point the glistening bronze tip at his throat. The motion was violent enough to undo the leather strap holding her hair in place. He stopped. She looked at him through the unkempt locks of black hair that had scattered across her face, her pupils wide like a cornered animal. Her hand shook, the dull metal less than a thumb's length from his skin. He looked at her, but his expression was not one of fear. For a brief second, as the moonbeams pouring in from the window rippled across his face, Tehq thought she saw a look of understanding, sympathy even.

"I'm not going to *hurt* you," he said, his bloodshot eyes locked on hers. "I told you, I have a coin..."

His hand reached under his robes, he shifted his weight, and Tehq saw a glint of metal, pale and red like the bronze body of a dagger. The world around her turned to shapes, the way images dissolve right as one is falling asleep, sense disappearing in the murky waters of unreality. She felt her arm swing around, muscles flexing and then stabbing forward just as he reached his hand behind him. She felt her hand connect with fur, the knuckles holding the arrow connecting with sinew and muscle. She felt warmth on her hand, saw the river of red, scented blood in the air, just like when she was a little girl, when she held Ikarih in her arms.

She pulled the arrow away. More red, more than she had seen in years.

She scrambled to her feet, backing herself into a corner. She heard a clattering sound. The arrow had fallen from her bloody hand onto the floor. Šōhen was covered in blood, one hand reaching up at her weakly, the other clenched into a fist. Tears rolled down his cheeks as his hand weakly grasped for his neck.

The hand fell to the ground. His eyes rolled back, lifeless gaze settling on the ceiling, mouth agape, cheeks sinking into his mouth dotted with missing teeth. As his muscles loosened, Tehq heard a clattering sound, and looked down just as a large bronze coin came to rest by her feet.

Outside the cabin, the moon shone brightly in the cloudless night sky, the first she had seen since last summer. Pale light blanketed the lake as she stumbled outside and fell to her knees at the water's edge. She forced her hands into the water, letting the blood wash away into the clear, sparkling water. Tears fell down her face and into her mouth, where she tasted the warm brine, a distant sensation among many. Tik trotted up beside her, snorting and resting his head beside hers. Tehq envied the ignorance of animals.

Her whole body was jittering and alive with fear, her heart frenzied as it beat within her, the furious rush of blood in service of nothing as she stared blankly at her hands in the water. As her body steadied itself, she could only think that the chaos of her childhood had slipped a yoke over her. The war was over, the blood it had spilled had long since sunk into the soil, but still it controlled her, sometimes in dreams, sometimes in feelings, and now in violence.

She leaned forward and squeezed her hands together under the water, forcing the blood out from the white and yellow fur on her hands and wrists, little streaks of crimson spreading out across the lake. She pulled her hands from the water and dried them with the front of her robes, watching as the droplets of water sent ripples along the surface. The water calmed, and Tehq stared down at her reflection, her own gaunt and tired eyes staring back up at her in quiet, resigned disappointment.

Iron

The Last Giant

by J.S. Hawthorne

The golden torc, covered in feathered designs, felt heavy around Prince Ennachu's neck and across his shoulders. He had to resist the temptation to scratch at the lime encrusting his hair, turning his usually brown fur white and forcing it into spikes. He was surrounded by the hushed murmurs of the sailors and soldiers his mother had handpicked for this raid. Their susurrus could not quite drown out the soft slap of the waves beneath the gentle creaking of the boat they rode and the two that followed in their wake. They were mostly wolves, the derbfine of Ennachu and his mother, a few others trusted enough to accompany them, and the druid. Ennachu found himself watching the cloaked skua where they stood, impassive, at the stern of their ship. Their hood was up and all Ennachu could see of the druid was their black, hooked beak. It clicked impatiently from time to time.

"My son." Queen Katodirean laid a hand on his shoulder, startling him out of his reverie. She and he looked very much alike, though she had the wisdom of many long years of experience, reflected in her eyes, golden like his, and the streaks of white along her muzzle. Her hair, a little longer than his, was also spiked with lime, but it had long ago gone white of its own accord.

"Mother," he said, his tone low. "Has the druid sent you?" He could not entirely conceal the suspicion in his voice.

She tsked at him. "Soita wants only the best for you. One day, you will have to take up the throne and..."

"And defend our land from our enemies. You have said, Mother."

"And you have not listened, my son," she said, her voice as sharp as the biting winds over the dark and temperamental sea. Ennachu tugged his blue and white cloak a little tighter against the chill of both. "Soita says that only a tusk from one of the giants of Albiyu can protect us from the southern invaders."

Ennachu scowled, his ears twitching back before he could summon the wherewithal to hide that betrayal of his unease from his mother. The giants of the island to the south of their home on Iweru were renowned for their fierce prowess in battle and their territorial natures. They had woolly hides capable of turning back even an iron sword, and long, curved tusks that could disembowel a band of warriors as easily as a turn of their head. Ennachu looked over the company rowing across the sea that separated his home from Albiyu. It had seemed a mighty force, twenty strong, when they had left the tribe's lands on the cliffs of Mena. In the face of even a single giant, it seemed paltry.

"And how are we to defeat such a foe?" Ennachu asked. "Will the druid offer some of their hidden magics for once?"

He jumped as a soft voice hissed in his ear, "Do not make light of that you do not understand, child." Ennachu whirled to find Soita, the druid, standing just to his left. This close, Ennachu could see the druid's red-gold eyes, gleaming like fire under their dark hood. A faint, almost cruel smile graced their short, hooked beak.

"I'm not a child," said Ennachu, full aware of how childish it sounded. It was true that he had passed his majority some seasons before, but, in truth, it had not been that many seasons. It was very likely he was the youngest person on the boat, save for one or two others.

Soita snorted. "You will take the giant's tusk. I have seen it."

Ennachu stared.

"You have trained for this, Enni," said the queen. "You are ready. I have faith that you will carry out this most important task."

"Mother," Ennachu turned, hoping to impress on her how foolhardy the druid's task was. If he had had any belief that Soita was capable of such simplistic plots, he would have assumed that they were trying to get him killed. "This is madness. I cannot kill a giant."

"It is foreseen, in smoke and ash and entrail, child," whispered the druid. They swept to the bow of their ship and Ennachu, in spite of himself, followed, straining his ears to hear the skua's soft words against the wind and slapping waves. "Again and again, I have cast the bones and spoke with the sídsat. The wind whispers that you will, you must, do this."

"Madness," Ennachu repeated.

"Silence, child," Soita was bent low, their beaked face and burning eyes were inches from Ennachu's muzzle. "Silence and listen. The giant awaits in a camp in the forests overlooking the coast. It does not know why it waits, but it will wait for you. You must strike a tusk from its head. With that, we can save our home, save all of Iweru from the invaders from the south. The ocean we cross will be forever closed to them."

"Can you guarantee it, Soita?" asked the queen.

"They will slaughter my siblings, there," the druid pointed towards the sandy shore, "and their governor will stand at that spot and stare with jealousy at your home. You will live to see it, Ennachu. But they will never cross this ocean. Their empire will crumble and wither and die, and Iweru will stay safe for more than a thousand years. *If*, princeling, you recover that tusk."

The shore, for most of their journey just a distant green line capped with grey-white mountains, loomed large now. Before them lay a soft, sandy beach and rocky hills covered in thick green forests and then the distant mountains beyond.

"Why me?" Ennachu asked, running a hand through his spiked hair. It just made the lime more uncomfortable.

Soita answered his rhetorical question. "Child, great forces are in motion. They move in all of us at times, and at this time, they move in you. The choice you make over the next few hours will have great consequences across these isles. Now, there, you see? The giant lights its fire." Once again the old skua pointed towards the distant shore.

The faint, flickering light grew so slowly that at first Ennachu thought he was imagining it. But as the flames grew, and the boats neared the shore, it became impossible to deny. Unconsciously, he checked the beautiful bronze sword he had inherited from his father, which hung at his waist. He brushed his fingers against the iron axe his mother had given him, a gift for the raid, tucked safely into his belt.

"It is your command, my son," Queen Katodirean told him, as they reached the shore. Several of their clansfolk hopped into the shallow water to pull the boats onto the sandy bank. When they had beached, and one of the warriors had handed Ennachu a wicker shield painted with the blue and gold sigil of their clan, Ennachu leapt down. The sand felt cool and soft under his paws, but as shifting and treacherous as the sea it abutted.

He turned to face his warriors. They stood, silhouetted by the setting sun, against the salt-scented waters. Ennachu could just see, half-shrouded in mist, the distant cliffs of Iweru. He thought of his home, conquered by the southerners who had already landed on Albiyu, who had demanded tribute in the name of an emperor who had come and conquered and left, as uninterested in the wild lands of these northern isles as he was of their people. Ennachu thought of life under the heel of a foreign lord who knew nothing of custom, of duty, of what the land demanded of its people.

He drew his sword and raised it above his head, so that it flashed red-gold in the light of the dying sun. Every eye turned to him.

"We seek the tusk of a giant!" he announced. The warriors fell silent, a mixture of eagerness and fear flashing across the faces before him. "Our druid says that only with the giant's tusk can we protect Menu and Iweru from the invaders of Rhow. That makes our mission here a sacred duty, in the eyes of the gods and our ancestors. The creature awaits us there," he swung the sword around to point at the glimmering distant fire, "and by all of the gods, in the names of our forebears, we will take that tusk!" He thrust the sword into the air once again, and the warriors cheered and shouted oaths that they would do whatever it took to save their home.

"You did not mention that it is you that needs to slay the beast," the queen murmured as Ennachu turned and began to lead the warriors into the forested hills.

"The druid says I must take the giant's tusk. They said nothing about me striking the final blow." Ennachu caught Soita giving him an appraising look, and he stiffened. "I will recover the tusk, but this is not an honor fight between clans, Mother. I will not risk the safety of our home in vanity." The druid tugged their hood down a little closer, but Ennachu thought he caught a smile on the skua's beak.

Ennachu stared at the druid, but they merely turned and stalked towards the distant flickering firelight. Ennachu glared at the back of the druid's cloak as he followed, the muffled sounds of his small army marching behind them.

The land was wild, the ground overgrown with grass amidst rough, rocky hills. Nonetheless, the hike up the mountain was not too difficult, though the sun had fully set by the time they reached the scrubby woods. Even there, the trees were spread apart and the undergrowth sparse. The comfortable smell of pine filled their nostrils, blocking out other scents, and the soft needles of the trees quieted their steps. By the time they had ventured deep enough that they could no longer see the coast, Ennachu had begun to forget that a world existed outside of the forest. Everything seemed muted, faint, a lifetime away from the tiny existence he found himself in. He focused on Soita's back, because every time he tried to look around, a wave of vertigo washed over him while tiny will-o-wisps flickered in the far distance. The druid's steps were sure and unwavering, and Ennachu, against his better judgment, followed them.

From the size of the fire they had seen from the beach, Ennachu had estimated an hour, perhaps two, before they reached the giant's camp. It was closer to three before they found the clearing. Ennachu realized immediately that his sense of scale was entirely off—this was no puny campfire, but a roaring inferno that stretched almost to the tops of the trees.

And there, sitting on a log nearly as large as the ships upon which they had sailed to this island, her back to a cliff down the other side of the low, hilly mountains, was the giant. She was bigger than Ennachu had been expecting. He doubted that, had she been standing, his head would have reached her midriff. Thick legs ended in heavy, round feet, and equally dense arms with beefy hands that Ennachu thought could have grabbed him around the torso as easily as he could pick up timber. Her head was unlike any creature he had ever seen before, with a long, blunt face terminating in an even longer, prehensile trunk. Two ivory tusks jutted from her upper jaw, curved like scythes and bound in burnished metal, perhaps copper, though it was hard to tell in the firelight. The giant was covered in a dense layer of shaggy brown fur, enough that she didn't require even the hide tunic and kilt she wore to protect her from the elements.

In her trunk, she held a branch thicker than Ennachu's leg, and she was whittling at it with two bronze knives, one in each hand, shaping a tool that Ennachu did not recognize. She had not yet seen them, hunched as they were in the darkness at the forest's edge.

Ennachu pulled his sword free, slow and gentle, and it slid from its scabbard with no more than a whisper. It was enough, though. The giant's large, flap-like ears twitched and she lifted her head to stare into the darkness. Across the flames, Ennachu couldn't see what color they were, only the burning red of the reflected fire.

He raised his hand and, with a gesture, ordered the attack.

Ennachu saw instantly that it was a mistake. They were too slow and too far away. Not by much, but by enough that it would matter.

The giant was on her feet, roaring in rage tinged with something else, something Ennachu didn't quite recognize. Dropping a knife, she pulled a long spear of ash from a cache he had not seen behind her. In one smooth motion, she launched it. The spear, copper head reflecting dull red, passed within a whisker's breadth of Ennachu's head to impale one of the derbfine—Aidi, a close cousin, some still-rational part of his mind thought. A second spear followed, another of Ennachu's kin killed, pinned to a tree, before the band reached the giant.

The giant struck out, one spear held in her hand, another in her trunk, and the gleaming bronze knife in her other hand, and Ennachu's warriors fell back, frightened or wounded or both. The giant tossed her head and Ennachu saw another cousin thrown aside by the metal-bound tusks as though they were a grass doll.

Ennachu shouted, bronze sword raised high, and the giant turned towards him, hatred and death in her eyes. She roared and raised one of her spears as Ennachu brought his blade down, aiming not for the giant but for one of the gleaming tusks. Sword met ivory with a bone jarring shock that numbed Ennachu's arm. His sword fell from nerveless fingers, clattering to the ground as the giant's spear drove towards his heart. He met her glare with his own, prepared for his end.

A rough shove knocked him sideways and, as he fell, he saw the druid Soita standing where he had been moments before. Soita flung a hand towards the giant and there was a bright flash of light. The giant's spear caught Ennachu in the shoulder instead of the chest, and he spun as he fell, twisting around. He put a hand out to brace his fall, but the cliff's edge was looming, the faraway coast swimming past wild mountain forest. His hand touched soft soil and for the length of a breath, he thought he had been saved.

Then the ground crumbled away and he fell into space. He shouted, his voice lost to the roar of the giant and the ringing clash of bronze and iron and wood and flesh. He thought he saw the druid's eyes watching him fall, thought he heard his mother shout his name as he pinwheeled through open air. Something hard, a branch perhaps, caught him just behind one of his ears, and then the entire world narrowed to a point. He felt his shield catch on the canopy of a tree, thought as he slowed that it might be enough to stop him, before the shield was roughly whipped away and he was crashing through branches.

He had no memory of hitting the ground, nor any real sense of the passage of time. He simply went from spiraling into space to laying on his back on the loamy forest floor, surrounded by broken tree limbs and foliage. He ached from head to claw, there was a sharp pain halfway down his tail and another behind his ear. When he touched the back of his head, his fingers came back wet with blood.

Conscious that there might be more injuries he couldn't see, Ennachu stood up gingerly. None of his bones appeared broken, at least, though his cloak and shield were lost somewhere to the grasping branches above him. The axe his mother had given him was mercifully still secure behind his belt, but his bronze sword was still in the giant's camp where he had dropped it. His head hurt a little, but he didn't feel sick or dizzy when moving, which he took as a good sign.

Ennachu squinted up the way he had come. Aside from the occasional broken bit of foliage, there was nothing to mark his rapid descent. He caught a flicker of light from the clifftop, but without tools he had no hope of climbing back the way he came. He strained his ears but couldn't hear any sounds of battle. Sniffing at the air didn't reveal any information, either. As far as any of his senses could tell, nothing alive thing had passed through this part of the forest in living memory.

He stood alone beneath the trees, the ground soft and damp with a recent rain. No paths gave him a clue as to which direction to go.

"Which way, then?" he asked himself, speaking aloud simply to break the silence. Addressing his band, he had felt confident, or at least had been able to hide his fears. Alone, in the dark, in a foreign land of giants and monsters, he felt like a boy again, not yet old enough to sit at his father's table. He pulled his iron axe free, the comforting weight of the balanced applewood shaft a welcome feeling in his paw. He dug his claws into the wood, its solidity bringing him a sense of security.

"Left or right, Enni," he prodded himself. He looked to the left, something vague tugging at his memory, then turned right.

Ennachu crashed through the sparse underbrush for twenty minutes before he remembered that he was deep within foreign territory and that dangers, potentially including more giants, lurked around every corner. Taking more care, he chose his path, slinking through the shadows, keeping close to trees where he could keep his footing on thick roots. He tried to keep the cliff to his left, never straying far from it, hoping to find a path leading back to the summit, the giant, and his people. The hills rolled underfoot, though, and soon he was crossing through rocky terrain and merely guessing at where the giant's camp was.

A half hour's walking and a gust of wind brought the scent of smoke and campfire to his nose. He waited for a moment, hand on a gnarled old oak, sniffing curiously at the air. He had not seen any other fires from the beach, he was sure of that, and he certainly hadn't smelled any others. The scent wasn't coming from his left, though, and he was fairly certain that was the direction the giant's camp had been.

Indecision gripped Ennachu. He wondered if he had been wandering, lost, in the wrong direction this whole time. How long had he lain on the forest floor? Even if he found the camp, what would await him there? Ennachu had a vision of his family and friends, his mother, dead at the hands of the giant they had challenged, his home conquered by the legions of Rhow.

Strangely, it was his lost sword that most affected him. It was all he had left of his father. Old-fashioned, out-of-date in this age of iron, he nevertheless felt its absence most keenly. The thought of it becoming a trophy for the giant filled him with resolve. Trusting to his nose, and not a little to luck, he followed the scent of the fire.

It was definitely the wrong way. Ennachu recognized that within minutes of setting out. The fire was coming from downhill, not up, away from the cliffs and into a softer, less wild forest. He thought about turning back, but the woody scent of fire was the only clue he had to anything, and he preferred something, even the wrong something, to endless wandering in the dark. He kept his axe gripped tight, though.

Soon he found himself haunting the edge of a clearing. A large fire, though not nearly as large as the giant's, pushed back the darkness, illuminating the camp's lone occupant. He was a hare, certainly no older than Ennachu, with a long, lanky frame and piebald black and white fur. He wore brightly colored clothes in blues and greens, not very different from Ennachu's own, except for woolen breeches instead of a more fashionable kilt, tucked into a sturdy set of leather boots. The hare was whittling a long length of bone with a thin knife. Next to him was a rucksack, and leaning against the boulder was a longbow. Even strung as it was, it was nearly as tall as Ennachu.

The hare brushed the bone idly, then lifted one end to his lips. Ennachu recognized it as a flute before the stranger had played the first faint, ethereal notes. The music was beautiful, haunting as mists and moor, and it tugged at Ennachu's loneliness, but the hare seemed unsatisfied. He tapped the instrument against his paw, then took the knife to the end, shaving a sliver of the pale white end away.

Ennachu watched, taking in more details. The hare was slim but broad-shouldered, and moved with a kind of restless, nervous energy. He shifted and readjusted his seat almost constantly, sometimes sitting up, sometimes slouching almost to the point he was laying down. Ennachu had never met anyone who seemed so incapable of sitting still. He was mesmerized.

He was clearly a native, Ennachu decided, and that meant he might know the best path back to the giant's camp and, hopefully, his kin. He steadied himself, then stepped into the firelight.

In a flash, the hare was up and reaching for his bow. Without thinking, Ennachu flung his axe, which whipped through the air and sliced neatly through the bowstring before embedding itself in the tree, the hare's paw still a breath away. It left Ennachu weaponless, but all the hare appeared to have was the thin knife.

Ennachu, grinning, straightened and approached. The hare held the now-useless bow in his hands, his gaze travelling back and forth between the snapped string and the axe.

"I'm sorry," Ennachu said, and the hare looked up at him. This close, Ennachu could see that the hare was a handsbreadth shorter than him, and rather frail in comparison. He didn't appear weak, in fact Ennachu found his physique rather appealing, but he didn't have the burly body of a warrior, at least in Ennachu's opinion. "But I need your help."

The hare said something, his speech fast and accent thick, so that Ennachu understood little beyond the accusatory tone, and something that might have been an insult.

"There's no call for that sort of language," Ennachu said, adopting his most royal demeanor and the cool, detached mien that his mother had taught him to affect when sitting as a prince of the tribe.

The hare pointed a finger at Ennachu's chest and told him, in barely understandable language but unmistakable meaning, that he had best clear off.

Ennachu laughed. "Or you'll do what, fling an arrow at me?"

The hare looked down at the bow, gritting his teeth, then glared up at Ennachu. Ennachu put his hands on his hips and couldn't resist a smug smile. The hare snorted, then swung the bow as hard as he could. Ennachu attempted to duck out of the way, but he was too slow and the last thing he remembered was the loud cracking noise as the ash bow slammed into his temple, a bright, blinding light, and then darkness.

There were no dreams in the darkness that Ennachu found himself in. At first it was just a vague sense of discorporeality, but then a sharp, throbbing ache made itself known. Once Ennachu acknowledged the pain, he found that it had a place to exist, just behind his left ear. That realization forced Ennachu painfully back to reality, with all of the hurts that he had picked up in his short time in Albiyu. He blinked a few times until his eyes focused again, and found himself stretched out in front of the hare's campfire, the hare himself kneeling anxiously by Ennachu's side, a rag in one paw and a small bowl of some liquid in the other. This close, Ennachu could see the hare's eyes were sea green, burnished gold in the firelight and looking like sunrise over the ocean.

"You're beautiful," Ennachu said, before he realized what he was saying.

The hare blushed and shook his head. He told Ennachu that he was having trouble understanding the wolf's accent as he washed the cloth in the liquid and then began to dab at the side of Ennachu's head.

Ennachu winced and pulled away. He started to sit up, but the hare put a restraining paw on his shoulder.

"What?" Ennachu asked.

"Don't move," the hare told him, then explained that he was worried that Ennachu had more serious damage than just a broad cut. It did, the hare noted, look like he had taken more than one nasty hit to the head.

"I'm fine," Ennachu growled. "And I don't have time to be nursed. I need to find my people." He tried to push the hare's hand away.

"Stay," the hare said, speaking slowly and firmly to ensure that Ennachu understood him. "Let me clean you, at least." He added something in an undertone that sounded a great deal like stubborn fool.

With a sigh, Ennachu stopped struggling, and let the hare clean the side of his head. "What's your name?"

"Weithli," the hare responded. He tsked as he examined the cloth, sodden with what Ennachu recognized as blood. "You?"

"Ennachu. And you shouldn't worry, head wounds always bleed like crazy."

Weithli raised an eyebrow at Ennachu and asked him if he got injured in the head often.

"Very funny," said Ennachu dryly. He lapsed into silence while the hare finished cleaning his wounds. When Weithli was done, Ennachu asked, "May I sit up now?"

Looking sour, Weithli granted him permission, then scooted back a few paces while Ennachu propped himself up on his elbows, then into a full sitting position. He felt sorely abused, and he wondered if his head would ever stop aching, but none of the symptoms of internal injury that Soita had warned him about—sickness, dizziness, confusion—manifested, which he took as a good sign.

"Why care for me?" Ennachu asked. The hare shrugged and looked discomfited, then muttered something about acting rashly. Ennachu wasn't sure if Weithli meant himself or Ennachu. "Well, thank you."

"You're welcome," Weithli said in his peculiar accent. "You said you needed help? Before?"

Ennachu nodded. "I have to find my people." Briefly, he explained about the druid's prophecy, and needing the tusk of a giant to protect his land. By the end of his tale, Weithli was looking as stormy as ever.

"What?" asked Ennachu.

Weithli sniffed, and asked Ennachu a question the wolf did not quite understand. He seemed to be asking who mattered more, but Ennachu couldn't figure out whom Weithli was talking about.

Ennachu shook his head in response. "Will you help me find my people or not?"

Weithli was silent for a long time before he finally said, "No."

Ennachu gritted his teeth. He should have known better than to even ask the hare. With a grunt, he stood, then went to retrieve his axe, still buried in the tree.

"Where are you going?" Weithli asked, still sitting.

"To find my mother and my kin," said Ennachu. "With or without you." The axe was buried deep and it took a bit of effort, in silence filled only by his soft growls and the crack of the fire, to pull it free. He tucked the weapon back into his belt, then whirled on Weithli. "My people need me. I won't abandon them."

Weithli watched Ennachu cross the campsite, aiming for the tallest peak he could see over the trees. Before Ennachu got more than three paces into the forest, the hare called him back. Ennachu turned to see Weithli dousing the flames with dirt.

The hare didn't meet Ennachu's eyes, but spoke as if to the dying fire. He asked if Ennachu would come with him to see something. If Ennachu did, the hare promised, he would take Ennachu to where his tribe most likely was.

Ennachu glanced towards the mountains. He was, he had to admit, thoroughly lost. But he also had to find his people as quickly as possible. It was, however, an easy decision. As much as he hated the idea of a detour, he couldn't promise himself that it would be quicker to retrace his steps by himself than it would with Weithli as a guide.

"Fine," Ennachu said. "Lead on."

The hare offered Ennachu a smile which seemed, to the wolf, strangely melancholy. Picking up his useless bow, Weithli gestured for Ennachu to follow him into the darkness.

There were no paths, at least that Ennachu could see, but Weithli moved with the surefooted confidence of a native who had spent his whole life combing these lands. They were almost immediately out of the deep forest and into rocky scrub hills, their way lit only by the shining silver light of the moon. Weithli didn't march so much as bounce from spot to spot, careful not to get too far away from Ennachu, but unable to stand still. In the few moments when he did stop, it was only to point out pitfalls or hidden sinkholes, before bounding away.

In ten minutes, they were on the mountain proper again, and ten minutes after that, Weithli veered them off onto the first path Ennachu had seen since the battle with the giant. They rounded a cliff and passed into a copse, revealing the landscape all the way to the sea. Here, Weithli stopped, actually turning as still as the mountain stone behind him, to stare out over the distant waves.

"Is this what you wanted to show me?" Ennachu asked. The sight was beautiful, certainly, but he had grown up on the hills of Mena and seen such vistas all his life. There was a kind of magic to it—a different country, connected by the same ocean, a reminder of what he had left behind—but if this was the trade for Weithli's aid, it hardly seemed worth the price.

"No," said Weithli, shaking his head as if clearing away an enchantment. "It's just..." He trailed off with a sigh.

There was that inexplicable sadness again. Against his better judgment, Ennachu felt an urge to hug the hare, to comfort him. He settled for placing a paw on Weithli's shoulder.

"Are you alright?" he asked.

Weithli startled, looking up at Ennachu in confusion. "I'm fine," he said hastily, then dropped his gaze, adding something about how he could see his home.

Ennachu frowned, then turned back to the view. "Where?" There were no lights, no fires, to mark a settlement, no sign of movement amongst the dark hills. He supposed a roundhouse might blend into the rolling land, particularly at night, but to his eyes the whole country, from the mountains to the sea, was devoid of habitation.

Weithli, his eyes still downcast, pointed. There was nothing there, not as far as Ennachu could see.

"Do you not light fires at night?" he asked.

"There's no one left to light them," said Weithli. Ennachu froze, then turned to face the hare. With a sigh, Weithli explained how his tribe had been caught between a band of invaders, what he called Sassonu, and a derbfine of giants who had lived by the ocean's edge. There had been few survivors, none from Weithli's immediate family, and their little village had been razed to the ground.

"None of the Sassonu survived, either," Weithli told Ennachu with bitter satisfaction. He took the wolf's hand off his shoulder but didn't release it immediately. "And only a few of the giants, but it didn't matter much." He gave Ennachu's hand a squeeze and then released it. "I forgot that you could see it from here, that's all. It surprised me."

Ennachu didn't know what to say, even less so when Weithli raised his eyes and Ennachu could see they were filled with tears. Under the light of the moon, they were large and liquid, wild and sorrowful as the sea.

"It's been two years," Weithli told him. "But I miss them all." He took a deep, shuddering breath, then nodded up the path. "This way." Without another word, nor a glance towards the sea, he pressed on. Ennachu lingered a moment longer, staring out over the hills. With Weithli's story ringing in his mind, he thought he could see the dark shapes of broken houses, hidden in two years of verdant growth.

When Ennachu caught up with Weithli, he asked, "You don't hate the giants? For their part in this?"

Weithli shrugged and said that his people had gotten on well with the giants, or at least that particular group of them. Closer inland, giants quarreled with the villages and kingdoms, and the Sassonu, whoever they were, hunted them like animals. Here, along this wild coastline, where the Sassonu and Rhowanu were only distant threats, and the sea provided more than enough food for all, there was little to fight over.

"It's the Sassonu I hate," Weithli told him, and his voice was cold with that hate. "The giants lived peacefully until they came, thinking of sport and treasure." He fixed Ennachu with an icy stare.

"It's not like that," Ennachu said. Weithli snorted. "No, listen." He grabbed the hare's wrist to pull him to a stop. "I'm here, my people are here, to protect our home. The druid told us what we have to do. Weithli, I promise, I'm not here for a trophy."

"How do you know?" Weithli asked. "Do you trust this druid?"

Ennachu hesitated for a moment. "I…" He sighed. "Yes, I think I do. I don't like them, but I've no reason to doubt them."

"But do you have reason to trust them?"

Ennachu opened his mouth to say yes, but he found himself unable. Weithli gave him a self-satisfied smile, then nodded to a path half-hidden amongst wild ivy.

"This is what I want to show you," he said, then held a finger to his lips to caution the wolf to silence. They crept through the ivy to a small ledge overlooking a deep chasm. There, below, was the unmistakable sign of habitation: a well-worn firepit, surrounded by benches the size of a canoe, a lean-to with a pallet, big enough for all of Ennachu's derbfine, even a trough filled with half-made beer.

"Is this… a giant's home?" Ennachu whispered into Weithli's long ears. The hare nodded, and pointed to the far end of the chasm. There were three cairns, tumbled rocks not yet worn smooth by the wind and rain. Two were barely bigger than Ennachu and they flanked one bigger than any creature he had ever encountered. Sitting atop the biggest mound, gleaming like fire in the moonlight, was a glittering bronze sword. Ennachu had the wild thought it was his lost weapon, before scale reasserted itself. The sword was as long as he was tall.

"The last," Weithli whispered back. They were crowded close, the ledge not truly large enough for them to put any significant distance between each other, and Ennachu was aware of Weithli's warmth.

There was no fire here, and when the hare turned to look at him, his eyes were the deep sea color of midnight from the cliffs of Mena. Ennachu thought he might get lost in them.

The wolf forced himself to look over the empty camp. Wordlessly, he pointed at the cairns.

"Her mate and their children," Weithli said. He was still staring at Ennachu. "They survived the Sassonu, but then the children fell ill. She came to me for herbs and medicines, there wasn't anyone else, but I don't... I mean, I've learned a great deal since then." His voice failed. Ennachu reached out and squeezed his hand. Weithli looked startled, but didn't pull his paw away.

"I'm sure you did what you could," Ennachu said, not unkindly. "What about her mate?"

Weithli sighed. "There was a storm, a terrible storm, while they were out hunting. I don't know the full story, I can't speak her language well, but she said there was an accident. Her mate, they fell and were hurt." Again, his voice quivered and died, but Ennachu didn't need to hear any more. Wordlessly, he pulled the hare away from the ledge and back along the path.

They paused on the main path. Ennachu stared up at the moon, wishing it could offer him some guidance.

Something tugged at his hand and he jumped before he realized that Weithli was simply pulling his paw free. He had forgotten he was still holding it. He grabbed the shaft of his axe simply to have something to do with his paw, which felt strangely empty without Weithli's own in it.

"You can't hurt her," the hare told him.

Ennachu sighed. "I don't want to," he confessed. "But I can't abandon my people. I can't let them face what the druid has foreseen."

Weithli scowled and turned away from the wolf. Ennachu found that hurt as much as any of the blows he had suffered that night. Weithli asked him how he could be sure that the druid was telling the truth, and Ennachu had no answer.

"What about us?" Weithli added, after Ennachu's silence stretched on. He asked if taking the giant's tusk would leave Albiyu unprotected, to become another territory in Rhow, another jewel on the emperor's crown. He added a lot of what Ennachu thought was unnecessarily flowery language which the wolf found hard to follow.

"I don't know," Ennachu said, plainly and plaintively. "Gods help me, Weithli, I do not know. My mother trusts the druid, and that has to be enough for me." He took a step towards Weithli, who stiffened but did not move away. "If I could save the world, I would. But I have to do what I can for my people."

"Even if it means adding pain to someone already so hurt?"

"I don't have answers," Ennachu said. He realized his voice was shaking. "Maybe no one can have answers to questions like this."

Weithli sighed. "I don't like to hurt you."

Ennachu couldn't help but laugh. "Says the hare who cracked my skull with a bow."

Weithli grinned reluctantly over his shoulder. "Your accent was so thick, I wasn't sure you weren't Sassonu."

"*My* accent?" Ennachu said in incredulous tones, and Weithli's grin widened. He had a beautiful smile, Ennachu realized, at the same time he realized how full of pain Weithli was. It melted away from his face when the hare smiled, and it was only then that Ennachu could see the weight he carried. He offered the hare his paw again.

"If you ask it of me," Ennachu told him, "I will leave the giant alone."

The smile slid away, replaced with wonder and a hint of confusion. All the same, Weithli accepted the proffered hand. "I want..." he started, then stopped. "Gods above and below, Enni," he said more to himself than to Ennachu, "I've known you all of two hours."

"What does that matter?"

The hare shook his head with a laugh, or maybe it was a sob, Ennachu couldn't tell. "I can't ask it," he said, his voice soft. He let Ennachu pull him close, almost to the point their bodies were touching.

Ennachu found himself wanting to be closer. "I know what it means to lose a home. I can't ask it."

They stood, not quite touching except for their hands, and let the silence wash over them. Neither seemed to have anything more to say, but neither did they want to step apart. They existed alone together, a world of their own under the watchful eye of the moon.

Eventually, Weithli pulled away, his ears folding back. He pointed up the mountain path.

"The camp you fell from, it has to be that way," he said. He waited the length of a heartbeat, then started up the path, not looking to see if Ennachu was following. Confused, unsure, Ennachu trudged after Weithli, his thoughts torn between home and the sad cairns of the fallen giants.

They walked in the comfortable silence of a living forest. In the lengthening quiet, Ennachu noticed how alive the silence was, with the sound of insects and night creeping lizards, the soft whisper of the ocean winds rustling leaves and tugging at branches. Weithli was quieter than the forest, his booted feet making no sound that even Ennachu's keen ears could make out. For his own part, Ennachu moved softly enough that he was unlikely to draw attention, but in this foreign wood, he couldn't help but make a thousand tiny missteps, cracking twigs and kicking up pebbles.

They did not talk, both lost in their own thoughts, cloaked in the forest. Near the peak, Weithli led Ennachu off the path and into untouched woods. The moon reached its zenith before the landscape started to seem familiar to Ennachu, and it was noticeably moving towards the horizon when they found the giant's camp.

The bonfire had burned itself down to embers, and there was no sign of the giant. Four of the Ennachu's warriors were still present. Someone had rearranged them, moving them from where they had fallen and laying them respectfully on the edge of the cliff, their eyes closed and their hands crossed over their chests. He recognized three: Kentu and Aidi, wolves like him, were siblings a few years his senior. Aidi still had part of the giant's spear protruding from their chest. Beside them was Sentichin, a rat barely old enough to sit at her father's table. The fourth was a stag that Ennachu didn't recognize, an old and scarred warrior with a complicated tattoo along his neck. He had to be from a different tribe—Ennachu's didn't tattoo, at least not frequently. He wondered at the veteran's story.

"Were you close?" Weithli asked. He remained at the edge of the small clearing, reluctant to get closer to the dead.

"To her," Ennachu said, nodding at Sentichin's still form. "Him, I didn't know at all. Those were cousins."

"I'm sorry."

Ennachu shook his head. "They came willingly. They knew what the risk was." A small voice asked him if that was true. He had not known their mission when they had sailed out from their home. Had they known they might never return again? He knelt down and took Sentichen's paw. It seemed so small, so frail. It was cool but not cold. The muscles were rigid, and he dared not attempt to rearrange her. Better to let her, to let them all, be in peace. "I will see you again, my friends," he told them, "In the utter west, in the Silver Fortress. Wait for me."

They did not respond, but he hadn't expected them to. He stood suddenly, no longer wanting to be near them, and had to force himself to walk, not run, back to Weithli. He scrubbed his hand against his kilt without realizing it.

"Tracks," Weithli told him, pointing at the ground. The hare's eyes were evidently better, at least in the dark, but now that they were pointed out to him, Ennachu could follow the churned dirt easily. He knelt down, careful not to disturb the marks.

The giant's tracks were the easiest to follow. They were large, heavy ovals, almost circular, much deeper than the boot and paw prints of his kinspeople. Overlaying the giant's were the raiding party's. She had fled, he guessed, and several of the warriors had followed. Others must have stayed to check on the wounded and tend the dying and dead.

Ennachu skirted the edge of the clearing, especially careful around the trail the giant and her pursuers had taken. He found another set of warriors' tracks, heading back down the way they had come. They were heavy, too. Clearly they had been carrying something, or someone. Injured, he supposed. Unless his mother or the druid had been among those killed. They would have to be carried back to Mena to receive a full funeral.

Ennachu frowned. Soita had never, in his experience, worn shoes, and the skua's strangely shaped feet should have left clear sign of their passing. He saw no sign of the druid at all in the tossed earth.

"Enni?" Weithli asked.

"Some of my people went back to the boats. They might still be there, or they might have set sail again. Others followed the giant."

"Which way will you go?" Ennachu had expected some hint in the hare's words to urge him to go back to his boats, to sail back to Iweru and leave this land, to let the giant live out her life in peace and then join her mate and children in the west. But the hare's tone was carefully neutral.

Ennachu took a deep breath. He found that he did not want to disappoint Weithli.

"I will follow the giant," he said, unable to meet the hare's eyes. "My people are counting on me." His gaze fell on the four warriors. "We have sacrificed so much already."

Weithli nodded. "If I asked you, would you leave the giant be?"

Ennachu hesitated. "I... I would."

"Please look at me." Reluctantly, Ennachu lifted his eyes to meet Weithli's. They were sea-bright again. "I won't ask. But I will ask you, before you kill her, to consider what her death would mean."

"I will."

Weithli nodded again. "I think I know where she's gone. There's a faster way we can go, if you don't mind a little climbing."

They took off into the woods once again, moving at a brisk pace. They followed the tracks for a time, before Weithli led Ennachu off the path. Soon, they found themselves skirting a ledge that arced around the side of the mountain, ending in a rough wall twice Ennachu's height. Weithli bounded up the wall as easily as a ladder, turning and perching on the edge. He touched his finger to his lips, and then tapped one of his long ears.

Ennachu, taking Weithli's meaning, pricked his ears and listened. After a moment, he heard the shouts of fighting, the sound of bronze and iron and wood clashing. Then, the unmistakable roar of the giant challenging his warriors. They were close enough that the giant's voice caused the leaves to tremble on the branches above his head.

Ennachu leapt for the wall. He was not as sure as Weithli, nor as practiced in climbing, but determination drove him on. His claws dug into the rocky face of the cliff and he pulled himself, inch by inch, up the wall. Weithli reached down and, when Ennachu was close enough, grabbed the wolf's arms and helped him the last few feet up. Ennachu had half a mind to stop and catch his breath, but another roar echoed through the forest, seeming much closer than it had when he was boxed in by the mountain's wall.

"This way," Weithli whispered, before pressing his finger to his lips again. He turned and slipped into the undergrowth, nearly vanishing before Ennachu's eyes.

There was no path here, and wild mountain heather and bilberry clogged the space between the holly and elm that grew close together. Weithli moved with practiced grace and the experience of his young life spent wandering these mountains. Ennachu crashed through brush, one hand over his axe to prevent it from being tugged out of his belt, the other held in front of his muzzle to protect his face and eyes from scratching, clawing branches. He would have blundered straight into the middle of battle had Weithli not grabbed him and pulled him to the side.

He lowered his paw to see another clearing, thinner and covered in the dead leaves of many past seasons. Several of his warriors, led by his mother, had trapped the giant. Queen Katodirean held Ennachu's bronze sword in her left hand, her right hanging uselessly by her side, the fur matted flat with blood. Two of the derbfine were huddled at the far end of the clearing, both clearly too injured to fight. The remainder, eight in total, were spread out in a ring around the giant, preventing her from running. There didn't seem to be a one who did not have some injury. The giant herself was bleeding from a hundred tiny cuts. None seemed life threatening on their own, but her thick, wooly fur was matted and tangled with her own blood. She held a spear in two hands, her wicked knife in her trunk.

The giant roared a challenge, then rushed towards Katodirean. The queen, her teeth gritted, raised Ennachu's sword. He could see the sluggishness of her movement, a tiredness born of exertion and injury both. She parried the spearpoint awkwardly, the bronze blade visibly deforming under the giant's strike.

"Mother!" Ennachu screamed. He pulled his axe free and ran to her as the giant swung the spear down. Katodirean caught it again, but the sword slipped free, swinging end over end and landing somewhere in the dark woods. The giant raised the knife in triumph, then brought it down, aiming for Katodirean's chest.

Ennachu collided with his mother, sending her sprawling to the ground. The giant's knife took him in the shoulder, biting deep. For the second time that night, he lost feeling in his arm. He would have dropped his axe, if not for the deep gouges in its haft which caught on his claws. Switching the weapon to his left hand, he faced the giant. She snorted and glowered down at him, brandishing spear and knife and the cruel ivory tusks.

"I don't want to hurt you," he told her. She snarled something at him, then stabbed at his stomach with her spear. He batted it away with the axe, then ducked another swing of her knife. His axe lashed out, forcing her back a step, then he had to dance out of the way of her swinging tusks.

Out of the corner of his eye, Ennachu saw Weithli rushing to Queen Katodirean. The hare helped her into a sitting position, then began to examine her wound. They were speaking to each other, but Ennachu couldn't risk turning his attention from the giant to focus on them. She swung spear and knife, her hot, strangely sweet breath washing over him as she growled out a challenge or a threat. Maybe it was both, or neither. Ennachu darted forward, axe lashing out, coming within a hairsbreadth of her throat.

The image, unbidden, of those lonely cairns flashed into his mind's eye. He froze for just an instant, but it was an instant too long. She caught him with her tusks, driving the breath from his lungs and sending him sprawling onto his back. He rolled away just in time to avoid being stomped on. She stabbed down with her spear, and he hacked it away with the axe, sending the head skittering away into the darkness. She jabbed down into his ribs, hard enough that he heard them crack, but his thick shirt stopped her from skewering him. He swung up at her, gaining a precious handsbreadth of breathing room as she dodged out of his way. Her knife bit into his thigh as he scrambled to his feet, and he nearly collapsed back to the ground.

Instead, Ennachu swung the axe downward, leaving a long, dark wound in the giant's trunk. Surprised, she jerked backward, leaving the knife buried in his leg.

"Enni!" Weithli shouted. Ennachu waved him away, his gaze locked with the giant's. She snorted, pawing at the ground like a bull. He knew what she intended even before she lowered her head and rushed him, the ground rumbling under her feet, tusks swinging scythe-like to mow him down. His injured leg barely held him upright, there was no chance he could dodge out of the way.

Instead, praying to each god individually, he held his ground and waited. He swung at the last minute, aiming for the tusk. His axe hit almost exactly the same place his sword had an eternity before. Between the force of his swing and her momentum, the blade cut deep into the ivory. With a crack, the tusk broke along the damaged point, shearing off and skittering across the ground. The giant roared in anger, and her other tusk caught him in the stomach, sending him flying again. He hit a tree with a bone-jarring finality. His strength fled completely, and he crumbled to the ground. He half wished he had struck his head again, if only because he wouldn't then be conscious to watch the giant charging him.

And then Weithli was between Ennachu and the giant, cracked bow held in both hands. Ennachu had the surreal experience of watching the hare swinging the bow, just as he had when he had cracked the wolf's skull, into the giant's face. She was stronger and denser than he, though, and Weithli didn't knock her unconscious. She recoiled, though, shouting in pain and, unless Ennachu's imagination was running away with him, confusion.

He struggled to his feet, letting his axe drop to the ground, and limped to Weithli's side. He yanked the knife from his thigh and tossed it to the giant, who snatched it out of the air, looking suspicious.

"Can you translate?" he asked Weithli. His leg buckled and he would have fallen if Weithli hadn't caught him. Leaning hard on the hare, he looked up at the giant. "We were wrong."

Weithli stared at Ennachu for a moment, but translated dutifully into the giant's language. The giant hesitated, and Ennachu waved his warriors to lay down their weapons and step back.

She spoke, her voice, when she wasn't roaring battle cries and challenges, deep as mountain roots but gentle as a stream. She still held her knife, but dropped the broken spear and took a step back. Progress, Ennachu supposed.

"She asks what you mean," Weithli said.

"We came here and attacked you, without provocation. We had our reasons, but that did not give us the right to treat you as we did. And for that, I apologize on behalf of my people." Weithli translated, and the giant responded.

"She wants to know if you think that makes what you did acceptable."

Ennachu shook his head. "No. But if it will assuage you, in exchange for the life of my people, I offer you mine." He heard his mother, now being supported by two of their warriors, hiss. The rest of the band stiffened, then turned to watch the giant.

Weithli hesitated. "Tell her," Ennachu said. Weithli searched his eyes for a moment, then turned back to the giant to translate.

She was quiet for a long time, weighing his words. Finally, she said something curt, then turned and strode off into the darkness, away from Ennachu and his people.

The assembled band let out a collective breath. One stooped to grab the shorn tusk, as tall as Ennachu was.

The world was starting to spin, and Ennachu worried for a moment that he had, in fact, hit his head, but it was just Weithli lowering him to the ground to tend to his wounds.

"These are deep cuts," he said, as Ennachu's mother was helped to the hare's side. "But I don't think they're life threatening, so long as they don't catch an infection."

"Can you tend him?" Queen Katodirean asked. Weithli nodded. "Then do so, please." While Weithli worked, she turned on Ennachu. He was surprised to see she was smiling. "That was foolish, perhaps, but it was very brave, Enni."

"Yes, well," said Ennachu, feeling embarrassed. He was uncomfortably aware of the band watching the hare. "I had good advice."

"I see. And how did you happen to meet your friend?"

While Weithli worked, Ennachu told Katodirean what had happened since he had fallen from the camp, leaving out only the part where Weithli had cracked the bow over his head. He caught the hare's smile as Weithli tended his wounds.

"It seems we owe you a debt, Weithli," the Queen said as the hare helped Ennachu up. "You have saved the prince's life at least twice over tonight, I think, and mine as well." She touched her bandaged arm. "You have the gratitude of our tribe."

"It was my pleasure," Weithli said, bowing as best as he could with Ennachu leaning on him. The Queen graced him with a faint smile, then waved for the band to return the way they came. As he helped Ennachu follow, he mouthed, "Prince?" at the wolf.

Ennachu shrugged. "What did you think the torc was for?"

The journey back to the beach took much longer than the trek up the mountain had, owing to the slow pace of the injured and the need for the weak and weary to take frequent rests. By the time they reached the shore, the first grey-pink light of dawn was creeping up over the mountain.

The rest of the band, except for the druid and the four whose bodies still lay on the mountaintop, were waiting for them by the boats, most dozing or resting around low, smokeless fires. The sentry gave a great shout when she recognized them, and a second when someone raised the tusk up high enough for her to see. The rest jumped to their feet and rushed forward to greet them. Ennachu was deluged with questions about what had happened, where he had been, and how he had managed to defeat the giant. Queen Katodirean waved them all back.

"There will be time enough for stories on the trip back to Mena," she said in her most imperious tone. "Where has Soita gotten themself to?"

But everyone seemed to have lost track of the druid in the chaos of the first battle. Her muzzle set in a grim expression at her missing advisor, the queen began ordering the boats readied to leave while the injured were given a moment to rest.

Ennachu found himself seated on a log next to Weithli, his head on the hare's shoulder while they watched the least hurt prepare sails and push the boats off of the beach.

"Thank you," Weithli told him, his voice pitched low.

Ennachu smiled. "It was the right thing to do."

"Will I see you again?"

With an effort, Ennachu sat up to look the hare in the eyes. "Come with me."

"Leave my home?" Weithli asked, his eyes wide. But Ennachu saw the faint twitch of a smile play on the hare's muzzle.

"You could build a new home. If you want."

"With you?"

Ennachu blushed. "Would you if I asked you to?"

It was Weithli's turn to blush. "I... Let's not get too ahead of ourselves." He squeezed Ennachu's paw. "But you've seen my home, it seems fair, perhaps, for me to see yours?"

Ennachu squeezed back as he leaned against Weithli. They sat together in silence and watched the sun rise fully above the mountains. And, when the boats were ready, Weithli climbed aboard with Ennachu.

Requiem

by Pascal Farful

"Come in."

Bodarn, a badger amidst his twenty-fourth summer, stepped into the temple.

In the centre sat Zohan, a fox clad in a loincloth and covered from eartip to toe in intricate bodypaint and tattoos. They were a Dreamweaver, a religious leader and spiritual interpreter for the community. Much of their role emphasised music and dancing and the bright, colourful use of body decoration. They were devoted to the celebration of the Gods' will, and particularly to the most significant part of that will: Love.

On the walls behind them was a statue of a canine, bearing three eyes. This motif was continued all around the room in the artwork, drawings, and in small statuettes placed about the temple.

The fox turned and smiled at the badger, but this smile faded as Bodarn's discomfort was apparent.

"I have questions," Bodarn began, his throat catching, then releasing. "About the spirits of the dead."

Zohan nodded and gestured the badger forward to sit with them. "It's about your father, isn't it?" they whispered. "May you have reprieve from grieving."

"It's not that simple," Bodarn said, sitting down on one of the benches, trying to keep his paws still and to his side, but failing.

"Nothing ever is," Zohan assured him. "But your father loved you, and you loved him."

Bodarn stared abruptly up into the fox's eyes. "No. That's precisely the problem."

The temple was a sprawling pyramid, located in a jungle clearing. It was surrounded on all but one side with thick trees and dense bogs. The steps up the pyramid gave way to large, open floors, then sprouted more steps from the centre to climb higher, thus producing external walkways around the diameter of the structure.

For now it was bright and the sky was clear, so Zohan invited Bodarn outside with them to make the most of it. Rainstorms were common and divine, but were ideal for singing, dancing, and celebrating, not for the kind of guidance Bodarn needed.

"Please," Zohan said softly. "Speak freely."

Bodarn nodded, still struggling to look Zohan in the eye. "My father and I... couldn't decide what I was to be," he explained. "He wanted me to be close, to be protected from the wilds of the world. And I was perhaps less than keen to adhere. I wanted to be like the others, out in the jungles, learning, exploring, adventuring. In the garden of the Gods." Finally, Bodarn's wandering gaze came to rest, looking into the trees where a trap had been set. "You remember when Father had the accident with the snare?"

"How could I forget," Zohan nodded, reaching out and taking one of Bodarn's paws in theirs. "I performed the incantations while the botanists did what they could to heal. And heal well he did." The fox sighed wistfully. "But you were there too. The son was beside the father in his time of need. As was he with you in yours. He gave you that jade necklace, do you remember?"

Bodarn nodded. "The necklace, yes. He'd crafted it just prior to the accident. He was going to wear it on the hunt, but after the accident he gave it to me so I can remember him when I hunt in his stead." The badger took a long breath. "The pain he was in after that. It drove him mad," he explained, able to bring his eyes back to Zohan, meeting the tattooed fox's soft gaze at last. "Few people outside myself and my mother knew of how the pain was affecting him. Few saw him, and those that did only saw him when we had enough herbs to numb the demons." Bodarn's gaze wandered again, staring towards the village they called home. "I just remember the pain," he muttered.

Zohan nodded, easing Bodarn into an embrace, guiding his head to their chest. "You did what you could."

"No," Bodarn sniffed. "I didn't."

"May you rest from grieving."

"Thank you," Bodarn replied, looking at the jar that contained his father's remains, loaded with care upon a pallet, such that it could be transported to the burial site. Bodarn stared at the jar. Normally he'd have someone else to defer to at a time like this. Not so anymore. The weight of his kin; past, present and future, was his alone to carry.

"Have you decided where they are to be buried?" the morgue-keeper asked.

Bodarn nodded. "In the grove by the brook. It's where we used to sit when I was young," the badger said. "Back when we talked."

The last comment puzzled the vulture, but the bird nodded and tilted her bill, and the badger bowed in return.

Bodarn led the vulture outside, helping to wheel the large ceramic jar out of the morgue. Outside, they met Zohan again, and the three made their way with the jar through the village, across the muddy holy bogs to the north and towards the burial site.

Within an hour, the jar had been moved to the grove. The badger thanked the vulture, who retired back to the town, leaving Zohan and Bodarn alone.

In the silence, Zohan broached the question.

"Do you feel his death was your fault?"

"No, I…" the badger stammered, a firm shake of the head. "I don't pretend to understand life and death. I know only of myself and of how my father and I were. And I know when he died we were father and son in name alone."

Bodarn stared off towards the river, holding himself firm and letting anger rise, bubble, then fall and decay. The whisper of the wind wafted through the evening air.

He could hear the voices ringing in it.

The shouting.

The fighting.

A memory cast into the sky.

"As the pain grew worse, so did my father's temper. He was never violent, nor did he threaten it. But he had high expectations of me, and was very controlling. I couldn't always give him what he wanted and he would grow angry and I would hide away," Bodarn explained.

He began to dig into the ground where he would lay the jar, with Zohan helping. The terrain here was soft soil. Wet from the rainfall, reasonably fertile, but too close to the river to be useful as farmland. It was easy for the badger's paws to scoop through it, but it remained fairly solid and able to be piled up, unlike the thick, comfortable mud of the bogs or the strong, hard ground onto which the town was built.

When Bodarn's arms became tired, he sat back and spoke again.

"I didn't want to anger him, or to hurt him. I just… couldn't give him what he wanted. And as he grew more angry and we fought, I grew to resent his control and his temper. I wasn't as helpful, as kind and considerate as perhaps I could have been. He'd do things that would hurt me, probably not on purpose but… I could never tell him that he'd hurt me and have him understand. When I went to see a healer, he demanded to know what was wrong. When I didn't want to tell him why, he grew so terribly cross. Eventually, he deceived me into telling him and I couldn't handle the shame." The badger grunted. "I must believe that I had done things in kind, but by the time he passed, we were so incapable of talking, I don't think we'd ever be able to apologise for our transgressions."

"These are the questions I have," Bodarn said at last, looking Zohan in the eye. "Will my father, in death, know what I feel inside? Will he see that I don't love him anymore? And if he knows... can he hurt me?"

Zohan nodded. They looked out to the sea and the sunset, then took a deep breath. "Have you ever read the parable of Three-Eye?" they asked. "The wolf who was given the gift of a third eye by the Gods? Capable of seeing the past and the present in one perfect image?"

Bodarn shook his head. "Not particularly closely. Only what you've said of them at ceremonies."

The fox nodded, standing up and stepping around to the water. "When Three-Eye saw the past, they could see their mistakes and their failures. But what is forgotten is that Three-Eye also saw their achievements and their sacrifices." Zohan reached into the river water, lifting it up in their cupped hands, then bringing it to the grave, pouring it slowly over the jar. "Thus it is important to remember that sometimes, in family and in friends, we will have failed. But sometimes, we will have succeeded in great ways too."

The pair moved to lift the jar, slowly easing it down into the dirt, manoeuvring it to lie flat. The ceramic lay only a foot or two under the top of the grass.

"We are not expected by the Gods to be perfect, and this is true of both you and your father. Not even the Gods can achieve perfection, and they have powers beyond our wildest dreams." They took a deep sigh, looking into Bodarn's eyes again. "But what you describe, transgressions which divide both you and your father to the point where your love is severed, that is not..." The fox paused and considered. "That is not a sin. It is a disappointment, a pity, a shame. But not a sin."

With the jar lowered into the grave, Zohan sat down to rest. "To find but a lack of love in your heart in the face of such adversity is... understandable. It is simply, as I'm sure you feel, a shame that it is this way." Zohan looked back towards the jar, Bodarn sitting down with them. "The Gods give love and they can take it away, but they can also let it fade. Love is the most powerful force in the land, and if the Gods saw fit not to preserve it between you... it is the Gods' will, not yours, nor mine, nor your father's."

"But will he still be angry?" the badger replied. "Will he have hate for me for not being able to love him anymore?" Bodarn deflated. "He was so affected by the way I stopped saying that I loved him. When he feared it was true. Now he knows his fear is correct."

Zohan and Bodarn sat in silence. They stared into the distance, the intangible far, hoping that something from the Gods might hand them the words, the actions, the divine wisdom.

None was forthcoming.

"We should collect the adornments for the jar," Zohan said at last.

Bodarn nodded and got to his feet. With heavy hearts, the pair began to walk back towards the village.

"It is a great disappointment that it fell apart that way," the fox continued. "Fault is wrong, but fault is not the right word. It is a shame. A miserable shame," they muttered. "The Gods may judge you for your failures, and for his, but they will judge you both for your sacrifices, your attempts, your willingness to try. They will not judge for the dimming of the love. It... is beyond your control. If your father is angry and hateful for that failure, then the Gods will judge him too. Some situations are unfortunate, like his injury, and what befell your kinship." Zohan paused abruptly at the temple of Three-Eye. "But if what you say is true, then... it is just that. A tragedy of mutual transgression and entropy." They put their paw on the badger's shoulder, looking deeply into his eyes again. "I wish you peace from your sorrow."

Bodarn nodded, looking quietly up at the fox, before wrapping his arms around the wise Dreamweaver, pressing his head to their shoulder and beginning to weep.

Inside the family home, now quiet but for himself, Bodarn reached into a small box and pulled out the jade necklace.

The stone was cold. Just like his father.

He put the box back, but kept the necklace in his paw. He began the walk to the burial site, as other mourners slowly began to congregate.

It was a small crowd, maybe twenty at most. But each had a story to tell. One of their experiences with Bodarn and his father. How much they resembled each other. How well they got on in a public capacity. That special bond of father and son.

What once was.

What might have once become.

What now lay in ruin.

The throng of people parted such that Bodarn could walk to the grave.

Night had fallen. Lit torches were placed around the grave site. The inky black of night swirled, as if the creatures of the night had gathered to pay their respects too.

The jar lay still, dirt ready to cover it, while Zohan stood between it and the river. They had been freshly adorned with intricate body paint, giving the fox an ethereal look, breaking up their outline in a series of dazzling patterns.

People took their places.

For a moment, there was quiet.

Wind rushed out of the trees, across the congregation. The badger tried not to listen to its words. Not to imagine the voice.

A deep breath.

Bodarn held out the necklace, up to the moonlight. It reflected that light down upon the jar below.

The crowd stirred in understanding, and Zohan spoke an incantation to bless the piece. When the fox lowered their voice, Bodarn eased the necklace around the neck of the jar, then stood back up.

"Why did it have to end like this?" the badger whispered. And it was for this, not for the loss, that the badger began to weep.

Those to each side of him, an otter and wolf, took gentle hold of the badger in an effort to comfort him, as Zohan began the ceremony.

"Calhaan is in the arms of the Gods now," they began. "When they saw Calhaan, they saw a man who wanted the best for his family and did what he could to see out that vision. When times became tough, he remained steadfast and strong as best he could. In the end, the Gods saw that making this sacrifice endure was unfair, and relieved Calhaan of his pain. We must imagine Calhaan happy and free of pain at last. In a place of peace."

The winds blew again, the fox pausing to let them flutter through. Pausing to allow the wind to speak.

Hedges rustled.

Trees rustled.

Bodarn screwed his eyes shut.

Tried to close his ears too.

Whatever the wind had to say, he knew he didn't want to hear it.

Please, just make it stop, was his silent prayer.

When the wind was quiet, Zohan continued.

"Calhaan is survived by his son, Bodarn," the fox said, looking at the badger for a moment, then back to the sky. "His son shares the sharp eye, the astute curiosity, and the cunning determination that is embodied in his father's spirit. His destiny will be unique, different to his father, but no less holy than that of Calhaan. Although the destiny of Bodarn, as decided by the Gods, will not match that which Calhaan had requested, we know that with hindsight and divine foresight, we shall see Calhaan proud of Bodarn for his accomplishments, both past and in future."

With the Dreamweaver's speech concluded, Zohan stood back, and the crowd turned towards Bodarn, inviting him to speak.

It was tradition to speak. For someone from the family to make a departing speech at the funeral. Sometimes, the surviving family is so over-encumbered with grief that this is, understandably, not possible.

Bodarn had no idea what to say.

It wasn't so much that he hadn't prepared.

More that nothing could prepare him.

On Calhaan, he had nothing to say.

On the resultant shards of broken feelings, he could speak for years.

As he stood, with those around waiting for him to speak, he spoke not a word.

For he did not dare speak the truth.

Not here.

Not now.

The silence hung for a while.

People shuffled and looked at him expectantly.

But there was nothing.

Not even the wind dared to interrupt him.

At last, Bodarn sighed and uttered, ever so simply, "I'm sorry."

It was said without direction.

To the Gods.

To Zohan.

To the attending masses.

To Calhaan.

To all of them.

To none of them.

Bodarn stepped back into the throng of people, now confused and uneasy. As Zohan stepped forward once more, they were the only person, other than the Gods, Bodarn, and Calhaan to properly understand what was going on. People now seemed to understand that something wasn't right, but they were all far too polite to ask. Certainly not right now.

To conclude the proceedings, the Dreamweaver began to sing a slow, mournful piece of throat music. People joined in as the piece rose in pitch to suit their own vocal registers. But even this was a little disjointed and uneasy.

The badger joined in with the song, and, as Zohan stopped singing to let the crowd carry it onwards, stepped forth again to aid the fox in laying the dirt over the jar. The act of adding the dirt was done communally, led by the family, but all assembled would participate, for as a community they were all burying one of their people.

With all hands, paws, and wings contributing, as the moon set down to touch the horizon, the last handful of dirt was cast over the jar.

Calhaan was gone.

Bodarn knelt by the grave, breathless, while the rest of the congregation paid their respects in near silence and, one by one, departed for home.

Many would look upon Bodarn and seem keen, so, *so* keen to say something. To broach the enormous silence, only to stop themselves short.

When Bodarn and Zohan were alone, the badger spoke at last.

"It is done," he said.

"It is," Zohan replied.

The badger sighed and got to his feet. "I think I'm going to have to answer a lot of questions in the coming months."

"Tell them the truth, if you feel you want to," the fox replied, putting an arm over the badger's shoulder. "The truth can only set people free."

"People won't want to hear it, that's for sure."

"Perhaps." Zohan nodded. "But that's true of all great truths, isn't it?"

Mark of the Stranger

Casimir Laski

The wanderer's torch cut a blazing red swath through the sea of stars as he trod the beaten path. Golden waves trickled and lapped over the coarse brown fur of his outstretched arm, and he raised his other paw, shielding his eyes from the glare, wondering what company an open flame might summon at this hour. Out there, somewhere, the crows who had haunted his steps since crossing into the foothills of Illyria still lingered beyond the sharp shadows, waiting. But he wasn't carrion yet.

A distant jackal-dog bayed its ghostly song to the slender moon, and even farther off, an invisible companion gave answer. Sikarios paused, careful to keep his tail from drooping to the muck of the road, and pulled his cloak tighter with his free hand. To the weary marten, the night's chill had teeth as sharp as any prowling beast. Months of winter rain had left mountain streams pregnant with bubbling snowmelt, and the feet of a thousand passersby had churned the once-sturdy highways to muck and mire, leaving his pads raw and aching. He had traded his finer clothes for thick traveling garb in a small village a few leagues outside of Aigos, now regretting that he had not bartered for a bristle-boar pelt or a hat of lynx fur.

Trudging on, the marten strained his ears for the telltale trickle of a brook, then hunted the free-flowing water down to slake his thirst and wash his muddied feet. Afterwards he let his canteen drink its fill. The moon was a bronzed sickle in the sky, like a shield battered and sundered. Sikarios settled down against a cold granite outcrop, studying it. In his heart, the marten knew he should press on, should claw as much distance as possible between himself and the battlefield that had rent his heart and damned his soul. But where was he to go that his sins would not follow him? Even if he were to slog his way up the coastline of the Adriatik, to seek employment in Istria or try for the wilderness beyond it, the shade of Alexios would still find him every time he lay down to sleep.

At the thought of his brother, Sikarios raised a trembling paw to the wound over his left eye, running his claws over the still-tender trio of gouges carved from his flesh. They were far from the only marks marring his body, but the rest had been cloaked by fur, a hidden map charting the course of these last four years. His mother had once compared the tinge of his pelt to cherry wood, but when he looked at it now he could not help but see dried blood. At least time had erased those wounds from the reach of wandering eyes.

The scars over his eye had never healed so; the fur there had grown back in a frail grey where it had done so at all, leaving him marked before gods and kounavi. As if he even deserved to be counted among his own people anymore. He could be named many things—Degenerate, Oathbreaker, Kinslayer—but not one of *them.* His father had lost two sons that day.

A scattering of pebbles clattered over his resting form, and Sikarios stumbled to his feet. He didn't even recall drawing his kopis; the short, curved blade burned softly in the moonlight, eager for blood. As the marten scoured the darkness with his good eye, the prior four years washed over him in a tide of burning, vivid clarity: he heard the tread of a thousand boots over the charred and torn Morrean soil, and felt the blood of a dear friend quench the fire in his own heart as the nearby Aegean churned and spat in indifference. When the ash cleared to reveal a sprawling starscape, and the tortured face of his companion bled into the shadows of the torchlit crags before him, each breath was its own fresh battle. Sikarios staggered back, slipping to the grass, the blades still glistening with the leavings of the evening's rainstorm.

The rugged hill country lay silent around him. The gods, too, were silent, as they had always been. Sikarios drew breaths deep and steady as the ocean waves, like his mother had taught him a lifetime ago, and her words whispered through the years on the nightly breeze. *You are stronger than you know.*

The trebled yap of a jackal-dog shook him back to the present. The creature was close, and their kind seldom traveled alone. The crafty mongrels who roamed the wilds of Epirus stood more than half the height of the average kounavi; even a marten would be hard-pressed to fight one off alone. Trusting that the burning light of his torch would prove more help than hindrance, he stumbled upright and wound his way among the rocks, seeking shelter. The cries continued to sound, and the thrill of being hunted washed the festering guilt from his mind like vinegar pressed to a fresh wound—a welcome sting, a reminder that he was still alive. He soon found a cave set into the side of a small hill, his fire throwing sharp shadows into the earthen recesses. Before he could investigate further, the marten's ears caught the telltale scuff of paws padding over dirt.

He whirled, thrusting the torch forward and drawing his kopis once more, this time with the practiced whisk of a warrior. Beyond the gaping mouth of the cave, a pair of golden eyes lurked within a shifting shadow. Savage teeth caught the firelight as the beast drew nearer, shedding the black of night for a patchwork of tawny fur with hints of russet and silver. A predatory spark gleamed in its eyes, that of one vagabond beast to another. Sikarios had seen jackal-dogs before, but never this close; from here the creature reminded him of the foxes his father's shepherds had fielded to guard their flocks, only twice as large and with a slender tail sharpened to a dagger's tip. He tried to picture his smaller kin standing before one of the canids: a mink or a weasel, perhaps a stoat from the northern forests or a polecat of the wandering clans. Herders were wise to fear them so, but the lone beast's efforts would be wasted here. With a final parting glance, and a strangely sly wrinkle of the face, the jackal-dog turned and slunk off into the night.

Sikarios watched for another few moments, just to be certain, before trudging deeper into the cave and laying down his traveling sack. He added his torch to a pile of dry wood, kindling a little flame in the earthen chamber and trying not to picture it as a tomb. As he huddled close to the low-burning tongues, doing his best to enjoy a meal of stale bread and an overripe apple he had salvaged from a flock of greedy magpies, his eyes returned to the far wall of the cave.

The shadows that had first drawn his attention were not shadows at all, but paintings: figures and beasts in black and carmine and ochre, a story stained into the very rock. Gritting through the final bite of bread, Sikarios forced his aching body upright and approached. The renderings were crude but easy to decipher; following the tale from left to right, he saw flames descend in strokes of white and orange, and from the ashes of the World Before, the familiar forms of his own people rising to inherit the earth. As he gazed at depictions of hunts and battles, seeing great beasts fall and heroes triumph, he wondered how long ago this must have been painted, if the marten or weasel who had dragged his claws over the rockface had seen the mighty cities of the Ancient Ones with his own eyes. And at the end of the tale, he found a hundred pawprints pressed into the stone, all a deep crimson, radiating outward from a central mark, like stars around the moon. He raised his own to the ghostly trace of his anonymous ancestor.

But when he pressed his pad to the mark, his paws were still slick with the blood of his brother, enough to paint every one of his sins upon the cold stone. The scars over his eye burned once more, and Sikarios turned from the mural, feeling suddenly unworthy to stand in its presence, to feel even a drop of kinship with this long-dead clan. He returned to the fire, and his worn cloth sack, rummaging through his few remaining possessions. Beneath a smaller pouch, heavy with three drachma and a pawful of obols, the marten found what he was looking for: a slender knife and a block of wood.

When he strained his eyes, Sikarios could see the lion lurking within the silver birch, waiting to be unleashed. Briefly he tried to recall the one Elias had carved, but seeking the memory was like probing an aching tooth with his tongue. Wincing, he set his mind to the present task, and began to steadily whittle away at the mane. He took little note of the fire's dwindling. By the time a majestic leonine face had emerged from the wood, drawn forth by fingers now trembling in the dark, the flames huddled close to the embers, like a mother eagle shielding her fledglings. Fearing what sleep would bring, and yet knowing that his body needed rest, Sikarios tenderly tucked the carving away before drawing his cloak tighter and laying his head upon the sack.

Sleep came quickly, and when it did, as always, he dreamt of his brothers: the one he had buried, and the one he knew was coming to bury him.

In his dreams he was young once more, loping through fields gilded with wild wheat as the first hints of autumn stirred on the breeze. His brothers were with him, and his family was still whole; Kyrios, the stalwart firstborn, led the way with a stick raised high, charging ranks of invisible foes as Sikarios and Alexios raced behind. The low walls of Nalanthis stood just beyond the tree line, calm and quiet in the shadow of the acropolis, from which their noble father ruled and their mother bore all the world's love in her breast. When their younger brother stumbled, Kyrios was there to help him up, and when Sikarios scraped his arm after falling from an oak, Kyrios found a patch of aloi to temper the wound's sting. He relived their expedition to the summit of Mount Nikthis: poor Alexi, legs still hobbled by youth, staggering the final league of the journey as their older brother sought out a cool-flowing mountain stream. Elias had come along that day, as he often did, and Sikarios and his friend had lingered near a ledge, choosing stones to hurl into a sky as vivid as the tourmaline necklace his mother was so fond of, listening and laughing as the rocks clattered their way down the slopes.

The memory of Elias' fur catching the evening light, the kine's amber coat bronzed with the lifeblood of summer, was like a knife through his heart. Slowly, the sorrow dredged Sikarios from the depths of the dream, and the marten awoke to find himself back in the cave. When he turned, a pair of vulpine eyes were peering into his own down a pointed snout.

Sikarios straightened, but at the first shift of his paw the fox snarled, then yapped sharply. The warning bark brought back a brief yet vivid memory of trespassing through a pasture with a pack of other young kines, the angry shouts of the shepherd following at their heels. It took the marten a moment to realize that he *was* hearing voices—only those of kits, whispering from somewhere beyond the snarling fox. A kine and a doe, he was fairly certain. Straining his ears, Sikarios began to catch words from the murmuring.

"... told you he wasn't dead." That was the doe.

"Maybe he's a dhampir," the kine shot back.

"Quiet! I think he's waking up."

The fox sniffed tentatively, then scampered back to the mouth of the cave when the marten heaved himself upright. "I'm not dead," he called to the silhouettes peering in from the wall of light. It had been several days since he had heard his own voice; the sound was harsher than he remembered, raspier. Sikarios shaded his eyes, then gathered his belongings and staggered forward. He heard the pair scurry out of his way.

The late-morning light, trapped and mirrored beneath a covering of thick, pale grey clouds, left him momentarily blinded. Rubbing his eyes, the marten took in the landscape, and found two young weasels standing a few paces away, watching him with bated breath and wary gazes. Each wore a loose-fitting cloth tunic, their feet clad in sandals. The kine, glaring from beneath a broad-brimmed hat, dangled a sling loosely from one paw, while the doe, standing a full head taller, had her claws wrapped tightly around a hooked staff. The vixen, nearly coming to the doe's waist, stood attentively between them, russet fur bristling, joined by a larger fox with a patchy black-and-white coat. Both bared their fangs in silence.

"Stay back!" the kine shouted, sling hand twitching. The doe hunched slightly, as if she were ready to crack Sikarios over the head. The marten raised his hands slowly, fingers splayed, pads out-ward. At least they still spoke Elladian here.

"I mean no harm to either of you, or your flock. I was merely passing through, and sought shelter for the night. If I have tres-passed upon your land, I—"

A bestial shriek cut his words short, and all three kounavi shifted their attention east, to the shade of the tree line. The larger fox took off at once, leaving the two weasels and the vixen to glance back to him before a second shrill cry drew them as well.

Burying his curiosity, Sikarios made for the road, only for a shout to stop him. Even from a distance, he recognized the fear in the kit's voice. He turned, letting his eyes follow the path the weasels had taken. *Nothing to concern yourself over*, the marten told himself. After all the world had burdened him with, all it had taken from him, what could he possibly owe it? Nothing he did could ever change the past, and if the gods could not be bothered to set things right, why should he?

But when Sikarios turned back to the road, a sense of dereliction churned in his gut with every step. He halted again, let out a weary breath, and trotted after the kits. Following their tracks through a ridge thick with trees, the marten clawed his way out onto open range. A dozen sheep heavy and bloated with wool clustered nearby. He caught sight of the weasels at the far end of the pasture, and a moment later noticed the black shapes circling overhead like shades loosed from the underworld.

By the time he reached the kits, the kine had already launched several stones at the razor-hawks, while the doe stood swinging her crook, attempting to keep the flock from the wounded ewe. The foxes snarled and barked, snapping whenever one of the raptors drew too near, the scent of their fear sizzling on the air. Some of the birds had lighted on the nearby trees, while others continued to slice through the air, veering in only to sweep away.

Sikarios knew all too well what a pack of razor-hawks could do even to a grown kounavi. Racing to the stricken sheep, he drew his kopis and shouted. Dagger-sharp talons strangled branches in anticipation of the kill, and eyes rich with murderous desire shifted to focus on his ragged form. The scars over his eye burned with the memory of violence.

"Keep close to me!" he shouted at the weasels. The pair shared a glance before hurrying to his side. Sikarios had hoped that the pack would flee, but the raptors were aflame with the blood they had already drawn. He lowered his voice. "Good kits. Now, when they rush in, do not break—that's what they want. Stand your ground, and never falter." *His brother's words*, a distant part of him remembered. From the corner of his eye, he saw the kine cock his head, eyes narrowing. The doe—his sister, Sikarios figured—nudged him roughly.

Two of the razor-hawks launched from their perches, catching the wind with feathers splayed. Sikarios steadied himself. But as they swept down, one of the birds tumbled from the sky, thudding to the earth with white plumage spouting from its breast. The other raptors veered sharply for the cover of the trees, and the trio turned to see a figure striding toward them across the meadow, a slender bow grasped firmly and another arrow already nocked. The marten finally let himself draw a normal breath, shuddering as he slunk to the welcoming coolness of the grass.

"Have you fought razor-hawks before?" the doe asked, still clutching her crook so tightly it looked about to snap.

Sikarios drew several more breaths, then looked to her. "I've seen my share of bloodshed."

"Father!" the kine cried, waving his paws wildly. The approaching figure quickened his pace, and Sikarios turned his attention to the prize that had drawn the ravening pack. The young ewe lay on her side, chest rising and falling with labored breaths, her white neck stained with carmine. Sikarios ran his fingers over her flesh, searching out the wound, feeling the beast shudder as his claws traced the gash. He looked up to find the doe staring at him.

"What's your name?" he asked.

"... Uh... Aeda." Her voice was shaking almost as much as his own paws.

"And him?" Sikarios inclined his head.

"That's Mylo, my—my brother." As she answered, their father arrived, and the marten rose to meet him. The new kine was a weasel like them, much older than Sikarios himself, sharing the golden-brown pelts of his offspring, only speckled with stony grey. The cream-colored fur of his chin and neck made the marten think of the one time he had seen snowfall. The grown weasel, slender in the manner of his kind, barely came up to Sikarios' neck, and he found himself suddenly conscious of how he must look to these poor shepherds, scarred and disheveled, with the wild eyes of a fugitive, armed with a blade likely worth more than their entire flock. The older weasel whistled sharply, and the two foxes bounded off toward the rest of the sheep. The marten whirled back to the wounded animal and stooped to his knees.

"We need yarrow," he said, trying his best to sound like his father, as if calm command were his birthright. He turned to the kits. "You know what that is?" The doe nodded, though her eyes were uncertain. "You may know it as woundwort, or staunchweed," he explained, shifting his gaze back to the ewe. "Green stem and serrated leaves, with clumps of small white-petaled flowers around golden seeds. Grows in high, dry places with ample sunlight." He retrieved his canteen, then tore a strip of cloth from the rags in his sack. When he looked back up, the kits were still staring at him. "You should be able to find some nearby."

The two scampered off, leaving their father to watch this strange marten tend to his livestock. Sikarios saw the kine's shadow fall across him, and scooted over for the smaller kounavi to join him.

"I am Tamyris," the stranger said. Sikarios merely nodded, and the weasel cleared his throat. "Thank you for your aid. I have never known a razor-hawk pack to be so brazen, especially not this close to town."

Sikarios nearly mentioned that the raptors who haunted battle-fields often grew quite bold after gorging themselves on corpses. That there was a small gap between the dead and the dying, and only a slightly larger leap from that to preying on the able-bodied. Instead, he simply asked, "And what town might that be?"

"Dalma," the kine said, pointing to the northwest. "It lies about half a league that way." He spoke Elladian without flaw, though his rugged Illyrian accent churned his words like a plow turning rich soil. "You... have some knowledge of medicine, marten?" Sikarios caught the slightest hesitation before the final word, a cautious probing.

"Enough to help here, at least." The patter of sandals echoed from the tree line, and a moment later Mylo and Aeda reappeared, each clutching a pawful of yarrow as if it were jewelry. "This will be plenty," he said, spitting into his own paws before gently kneading the flowers into a pulpy paste. The ewe winced when he daubed it on her wound, but did not cry out. "She should be fine," he said, running his claws delicately through her clumpy winter coat, "so long as you continue to apply that daily, until the wound seals. Let's help her up."

Together the four kounavi guided the ewe upright, grunting as her cloven hooves fought for footing. From there it was a short walk back to their cottage, where the foxes stood vigilant as the rest of the flock crowded into a cobblestone pen. The kits hurried forward to meet their faithful companions.

"Oh, *Pyrra*," Aeda crooned, kneeling to ruffle the fur of the russet vixen. "And Kokkin, good Kokkin," she added, turning to pat the dog fox before he whirled to lick Mylo's muzzle. Sikarios could not help but smile at the sight. After the injured ewe had been reunited with her flock, and the gate securely set over the thatch-roofed pen, the four kounavi retired to the cottage for a lunch of dried fish, legumes, bread, and cheese. To the marten's surprise, the family washed their meal down with milk rather than water or wine, a barbarian custom he had heard rumors of from youth. Above the doorway hung a crude wooden rendition of a weasel with a bow, poised to strike down some unseen wild beast: Iluvex, goddess of the wilds, an import from Sikarios' homeland. Here, on the fringes of the Elladene, he suspected they would know her by another name.

The four ate in silence, and Sikarios felt his presence as a weight around their necks, growing heavier with each passing moment, with each question left unasked. The young kine, Mylo, was the first to speak.

"So... where'd you get that scar?" he asked, the innocence in his voice underscored by a touch of awe. The marten froze as if a knife had been pressed to his throat. He heard his brother's voice, *I won't let you*, felt the dagger clatter from his blood-slicked paw. Saw the eyes he had known all his life staring back at him in shock and horror as the light trickled from them into the shadows of the tent. His nostrils filled with the scents of iron and fear and betrayal.

He jumped as a paw clutched at his tunic, finding himself back in the cottage, the doe watching him as if he were a wild jackal-dog. He swallowed, blinking rapidly, and cleared his throat.

"I..." Words trickled through his grasp like water. Tamyris cut in.

"There's no need to pry, son." He set a firm paw on the kine's shoulder, turning his gaze slowly to their guest. "By the look of things, you've been on the road for quite some time, stranger." As before, he stressed the final word, curving it up slightly, almost making it a question.

"Meletos," the marten said, hoping to keep the quaver from his voice. "And yes, I've—it's been quite some time. I... I have a long journey ahead of me."

The weasel met his gaze coolly from across the table, then drew in a deep breath and exhaled slowly, folding his hands over his stomach. "Kits, could you check on the animals?" He turned to his daughter. "Just to make sure they're all settled in nicely."

"But we just—" Mylo's protest was cut short by his sister.

"Of course, father." She ushered her brother out the door, shooting a lingering glance at Sikarios before closing it firmly behind her.

Tamyris held his gaze, then straightened in his chair. "We truly are indebted to you for your help today," he began, before storm clouds of worry drifted behind his eyes. "But I know when a kine is running from something." Sikarios opened his mouth to speak, but the weasel forestalled him with the wave of a paw. "Don't worry—I don't mean to ask any questions you aren't prepared to answer...*Meleos*, was it?"

The marten nodded absently. His host lifted a paw, running his claws through the cream-colored tufts beneath his jaw.

"Well, we are gods-fearing folk, and by rights we will offer you what hospitality we can reasonably spare. And I can tell you are no common brigand." He nodded to the sheath propped against the wall, beneath Sikarios' cloak. "You could've already accosted us and been on your way, were you so inclined. What I mean to say is... I just want your assurance that whatever trouble it is you're running from, you won't pass it on to anyone here. Not the townsfolk, not myself..." He trailed off briefly, and for a moment his eyes smoldered like the noonday sun. "And most importantly, not my kits."

Sikarios had stared death in the face, had looked into the eyes of a kine prepared to kill enough times to recognize that same readiness here. His mind wandered over questions he knew needed asking: *How long could he afford to linger here? Was it truly wise to stay for even a single night? Should he merely push on to Istria?* But he was tired, so tired. Brushing his doubts aside, the marten nodded again, more sharply. "I was just hoping for a place to rest for a few days, that's all. Whatever needs doing, I can earn my keep, and then I'll be moving on." He raised his paws. "Like I wasn't even here. You have my word."

Tamyris' eyes slid down to the table. He was quiet a long time. "I could pay, if you'd prefer," Sikarios added hesitantly, trusting the weasel's rugged rural pride to decline for him. "I don't have much, but—"

"A bit of labor will suffice. Nothing too strenuous, I assure you." The older kine's gentle smile thrust him back to the days of his youth; it was strange how the slender weasel could in that moment look so much like the father he had once known.

"Thank you," the marten whispered, feeling a millstone lift from his chest. He offered a silent prayer of thanksgiving to Pallas Milosha, Lady of Wisdom, his former patron. It was the first in months, and despite the fear festering deep within his heart—that the gods had forsaken him, that the best he could hope for was to avoid their notice altogether—Sikarios could not deny he felt a flicker of solace.

The rest of the day passed quickly, a flurry of mundane tasks that drained the hours until dusk crept up from the eastern depths as an indigo haze. The razor-hawks did not dare show themselves again within range of Tamyris' deadly bow, and under the shepherds' watchful eyes the flock returned to the meadow to graze contentedly. When nightfall came and the sheep had been safely ushered back to their pen, the four retired to the cottage once more for supper.

After a meal of salted fish, grapes, and olives, Tamyris turned to his children. "Meletos here will be staying with us for a few days." Mylo sat straighter at once, the kine's bright blues eyes tinged with reverent curiosity. Aeda simply said, "Should I make room for him in here?" She looked to the doorway, to the only other room in the cottage.

Sikarios cleared his throat. "I can sleep in this room—I wouldn't want to impose any more than I already have."

Tamyris nodded. "If you have need of anything, do not hesitate to ask."

Later, when the three weasels had retired to their sleeping quarters, Sikarios spread his cloak in the corner and stretched out, enjoying the simple luxury of secure walls and a sturdy roof. The gentle rhythmic breathing of the kits soon drifted to his ears from the other room, a comfort the marten had not realized he had so dearly missed. Somewhere beyond the mud-brick exterior of the cottage, the ghostly cry of an owl danced through the night. He let the strangely familiar environment draw him back, back to the days of his youth, when the world had made sense. And once more, he thought of Elias.

After years of youthful friendship, their shared fondness had given way to something more, something deeper. Sikarios had been frightened at first—they both had, fumbling for each other in the darkness as the autumn winds wound through the halls of his father's palace—but beneath the anxiety and peculiar, nameless shame he had found joy, and warmth beyond measure to brace himself against the cold of night. Familiarity soon smoothed the edges of their fear; the halcyon days had melted into one another, a time without true endings, where every parting was brief and every dusk promised a brighter dawn. Their bond had been like a secret fire, always in danger of being doused by an interloper or clumsy passerby, and yet all the more cherished for that vulnerability. But like all secrets, it could not hope to endure forever.

With a shudder, Sikarios recalled the night he had left the warmth of their bed to find his younger brother frozen in the hallway, eyes wide with shock and revulsion. Alexios had stared at his outstretched paw as if it were a burning brand.

"Alexi, please, wait." His desperate pleas washed over the young kine like sea spray against granite. "Listen to me, *please*," he said, lowering his voice, crouching down, wishing that the darkness could swallow him. "Please, don't tell anyone. Not father, not mother, not Kyrios or anyone. Can you promise me?" he asked, holding out his own paw once more, palm up, like a supplicant begging his liege lord. Tenderly, he clasped his brother's paw, hating the way the kine winced. "Promise me you won't tell anyone else?"

Alexi had closed his eyes slowly and nodded, his voice fragile as a shaft of moonlight. "I promise." On the other side of the wall, Elias had shifted in his sleep, still blissfully oblivious. The thought had made his heart ache. It still did, all these years later.

At the time, Sikarios had believed their secret to be safe. He recognized the truth only with hindsight: that it was a splinter from an arrowhead lodged deep within the beating heart of his family, cloaked from the eye and yet slowly festering, year by year. If only he had known then what he did now, lying beneath a stranger's roof, having donned a stranger's name. If only.

Tamyris and his family slept soundly only paces away, and the marten found a part of himself wishing that the life of a prince could be traded for something as simple and honest as theirs. By reflex his paw sought another, and found only empty air.

Sikarios awoke well before daybreak, the memories that had shepherded him into sleep still swirling behind his eyes. The cottage lay in the peaceful almost-silence of pre-dawn darkness. As his body livened, preparing to face another day, the marten dug through his sack and once more retrieved the block of silver birch, a lion's face now showing clearly. With the aid of the knife, his fingers freed more of the beast, wood melting away to reveal the back and chest. The work was strangely calming; his mind emptied of everything else as shaving after shaving drifted into his lap. By the time his ears caught the first stirrings of his host family, he had begun to shape the lion's mighty legs.

Scooping the wood shavings into a paw, he stepped into the twilight and let them drift away on the chill breeze before returning to help with breakfast. The children prepared a meal of tagenites, a kind of pancake consisting of wheat flour, olive oil, and curdled milk, topped with goat's cheese and drizzled in honey. As they worked, Tamyris showed Sikarios to the nearest well, located on the borders of their farm and shared by their neighbors, a family of goatherds. The sheep pen lay quiet as they trotted past, the occasion muffled bleat echoing from beneath the thatch roof. Aside from that, the farm contained a small shed and a chicken coop surrounded by a low fence.

After drawing two buckets of water from the well, the pair returned to the cottage, where the scent of crackling pastries sizzled on the air, a smell of spring mornings and easy laughter. Watching the steady, measured bites of his hosts, Sikarios had to stay the temptation to devour his own meal like a starving jackal-dog. This time, however, they did not eat in silence; Tamyris, chewing around a mouthful of the cake, walked his guest through the routine he would be learning.

In addition to sixteen head of sheep, and two foxes to aid in watching over them, the family possessed a good two dozen chickens. Several of his ewes were pregnant, though none would give birth until later in the winter, leaving the family dependent on barter for milk, and on the eggs of his other livestock for the material with which to do so. "We've considered acquiring a goat or two," he told Sikarios, "but with only three of us to watch over everything, we've got our paws full as it is, eh?" The marten chewed and nodded silently, watching the kits' faces for the telltale flashes of grief; every death leaves its mark in the world of the living, a gap in the light of the sun, a hole through the heart of a family, and that of a mother most of all. He knew that as well as anyone. But Mylo and Aeda simply carried on with their meal, as if their sorrow had long-since clotted and scabbed over, leaving a deadened callus to greet any mention of her absence.

The marten's eyes wandered to the shrine in the corner, a regular feature of any household—only upon this one, beside the icons of other gods and clusters of candles and prayer-beads, stood a little figurine of a raven, messenger of Mirod, the god of death. When his gaze focused on the little clay corvid, he noticed the flower resting in its shadow, a blue chrysanthemum, like a piece of the night sky carved out by the family's loss. *I'm sorry to hear about her*, he wanted to say, *I know what it's like*, and *She knows how much you loved her* floating behind the words. But Tamyris had fallen quiet, a pensive expression on the weasel's face, and Sikarios could not bring himself to pry open old wounds, of another or himself. The meal concluded in silence.

From there it was on to the daily tasks of farm life: Mylo distributed chicken feed and collected eggs as the others, Sikarios included, led the sheep out to pasture, while Pyrra and Kokkin ran yapping and yikkering around their hooves. The hours passed languidly as the sheep milled about beneath a clear sky, rich with clouds as white and fluffed as their overgrown coats.

Aeda returned to the cottage to prepare lunch, and Sikarios helped her bring the food to the others. They ate atop a cloth spread over grass still speckled with dew. A yellowhammer swooped by like a flash of sunlight, vanishing into the trees; the bark of a distant fox roused the ears of Pyrra and Kokkin, then was quickly forgotten. The pair loped across the meadow, ushering two bolder rams back to the safety of the flock.

"Would you care to see our humble town?" Tamyris asked, turning to his guest. He had donned a wide-brimmed straw hat much like the one his son wore, while Aeda had her own head wrapped in loose white cloth. "Mylo is going to be heading into the market later."

The marten found himself strangely curious. He nodded. "I'd be happy to." Their meal concluded, he helped the young kine bring their wooden bowls and plates back to the cottage, where his kopis rested by the doorway beneath his cloak, secure in its sheath. Sikarios reached for the weapon, then hesitated, fearful of being caught unarmed, yet knowing it was bound to draw attention. His paw hovered before the hilt, then reached up to swipe the cloak off its hook, leaving the iron in the cool darkness of his host's home.

Dalma, as the marten discovered that afternoon, was a rather unremarkable settlement, barely more than a village clustered around a central square, in turn surrounded by farmsteads, all nestled within hill country well suited to raising sheep and goats. The sea lay slightly under a league from the town; on calm nights, a keen-eared kounavi could hear the heave of the Adriatik as it hurled wave after wave against the rocky shoreline. Rather than a river, the inhabitants of Dalma had access to a shallow brook that snaked its way down from the rugged eastern wilderness, bearing pure, life-giving water as it raced northwest in search of the sea. The town itself wasn't significant enough to warrant a proper lord, Mylo explained, but one wealthy farmer, a mink by the name of Berychis, loomed large in civic functions. It was one of his many daughters who had assumed the role of sofianthe, tending to the local shrine and overseeing public rituals on holidays.

"Her name's Mira," the young kine said, letting the syllables drip from his tongue like honey, "and she's the most beautiful doe I ever seen." He swayed on his feet, staring up into the pale blue sky as the two trotted down the main road. " 'Course she can't marry, being a sofianthe and all," he added with a sigh, "but still…"

Sikarios smiled at the thought of young love, or what a young mind might think passed for it. The gods only knew how hard they could be to distinguish. He thought again of those long nights with Elias: their clumsy, fumbling forays into romance, after the initial hesitancy and uncertainty had been washed away in blessed reciprocation, but before his brother's discovery threatened to sever the ties that bound them.

"Come on," he said, nudging the young kine affably, "there's got to be a doe you fancy around your age."

Mylo shrugged, pausing to kick at a rock, scuffing his sandals in the dirt. "Well, there's Lylla—she lives in the farm beyond our neighbors'." His shoulders sagged. "But I heard from the other kines in town that Andris and Egnat have both been visiting her."

"Is she fond of you, do you think?"

Mylo's face brightened, and he nodded eagerly, tail swinging through the dust his feet kicked up. "Last time I saw her, she told me—" An embarrassed grin crept over his face. "Well, I think she likes me enough."

The marten tried his best to echo his own mother's memory, the advice he recalled her giving his lovesick brother when Kyrios had been pining after the daughter of an officer. "Then go and speak to her, and tell her how you feel. Let her know where your heart lies, without seeming overeager."

Mylo's face grew thoughtful. It was advice he should have been able to hear from his own mother, Sikarios considered; the thought drew black clouds over his own heart, and yet an untroubled joy still sparkled in the little kine's gaze at every turn. The marten found himself torn between relief and envy.

After a moment, the young weasel looked up at him. "You must know a lot about the world, mister, being so old and all." Sikarios furrowed his brow, but the kine's eyes were clear and innocent, and the sting of offense melted into amusement.

The marten forced himself to chuckle. "How old do you think I am?"

"I dunno, maybe..." Mylo squinted, cocking his head. He turned to walk backwards, paws clasped behind him. "Maybe 35?"

This brought genuine laughter. "How old are you?"

"I'll be thirteen this spring."

"Then I am not even twice your age." The kine gaped, and Sikarios nodded. "I am just shy of twenty-three." *Though the gods know I look older*, he thought, gently fingering the contours of his scars, feeling the weight of his past bearing down upon him.

Mylo seemed to sense his unease. "Don't worry mister, Aeda says you're still handsome in a way, like the soldiers who come through last summer." He halted, grimacing. "Please, don't tell her I told you." Sikarios chuckled softly. "Besides, she's got eyes for Gallas, not that she'd admit it," the weasel added, sticking his tongue out. "His father's a leatherworker in town. She's 14, so she'll be pairing off soon enough."

By then the conversation had brought them into town, a collection of wooden-framed mud-brick houses, the fraying straw of their thatch rooves bristling like pelts in the sea breeze. As they neared the central square, heading for the market, he spotted a trio of polecats haggling with a local over some bauble; the strange kounavi, with their spiked, sable fur showing patches of sickly ochre, chittered amongst themselves in their alien tongue, distinctive crimson coifs clinging to their heads. The wary mink they bartered with waited in silence. Mylo stiffened as they passed the group, putting the marten between himself and the members of the wandering clans. Despite his own misgivings about polecats, bred from generations of mutual mistrust and hardened through his princely upbringing, Sikarios could not help but feel a stab of guilt at how the townsfolk shot them glances laden with disdain and suspicion while he could stroll freely, even marked as he was.

Farther in, where kounavi of all types bartered and haggled amidst the bustle of the market, his ears caught the familiar ring of a blacksmith's hammer. Trusting Mylo to seek out what was needed and find him later, Sikarios followed the sound. In the shade of a wooden overhang, surrounded by scraps of metal and half-assembled tools, stood a peculiar creature: short and grey-furred, with a vulpine face and a bushy tail ringed in black. *A prokyon.*

Of all the kisenos, his people's term for members of the non-kouvani races, prokyons were the most common in Epirus—behind otters, of course. But where the latter were tall and sleek, traveling the continent's waterways and plying the currents of the Great Sea, and otherwise sticking to their own riverine fishing settlements, the former were stocky, ring-tailed forest-dwellers, known for their dexterous fingers. Among their people, it was customary for skilled families to seek employment in the cities of the Elladene, passing on the secrets of their trade from generation to generation. Sikarios' father had retained one in Nalanthis—Brennix, his name was, a taciturn creature, his thoughts always concealed behind those small, black, ever-watchful eyes. Growing up in Nalanthis, he had encountered far more than just kouvani: sandy-haired mankous from the jungles of Afrika, speckle-coated mardun of the northern taiga, even black-furred, thick-limbed viverrid traders from far east of the Indus. But while the sight of kisenos in larger towns and cities throughout the Elladene was common, to find one here was surprising.

The smith hammered delicately at something laid atop his forge, then wiped a dark paw across his ashen fur before glancing up and flashing a smile. Sikarios stepped nearer, watching as the prokyon set down the iron blade and fetched a bronze hilt. He held them up to his beady eyes, testing the fit before setting the blade aside.

"Do you require something?" he asked, his Elladian gently flavored with the earthy tones of the northern forests.

"I just... I am surprised to find one of your people here," Sikarios replied, "in such a small town." The marten raised a paw. "I do not mean to cause offense—"

The prokyon chuckled softly, retrieving a chisel-like tool and shaping the hilt. "We can't all find employ in great cities, or the estates of mighty lords. And after all, even small towns need black-smiths." He met the marten's gaze with a wink.

"Catharix," a voice called from across the street. Sikarios craned his neck to see a marten and two weasels approaching. The prokyon waved to them, brushing shavings from the bronze hilt.

"Still working on Berychis' sword?" the other marten asked. His companions smirked, and Catharix nodded.

"He figures one of his sons may soon enlist."

"The gods know the old bastard has enough to spare," one of the weasels snickered. His laughter spread through the crowd, and Sikarios felt a stranger among them. The other weasel's eyes flitted to him, his slender face hardening when they met the greyed fur and naked flesh of his scars.

Sikarios forced himself not to shy from the other's gaze. The weasel balked first, turning to Catharix. "Did you hear ol' Thestor is looking to our own lands for recruits now, for the campaign in the Morrea? They're saying he'll try for Haikoth again this coming spring."

Sikarios blanched at the familiar names: Thestor, King of Makketon, the mightiest kounavi in the Elladene, to whom his own father owed fealty. The Morrea, the land he had spent the last four years ravaging and bleeding over. Haikoth, the city that had broken him as it had broken so many armies against its walls. The city that had torn Elias from his breast. The city he had fled from, leaving the brother who had tried to stop him cold upon the blackened soil.

The others had continued without noticing, and he drifted back to the present to find them debating the foreign king's plans. Thestor's Makketonian League had warred with a coalition of rival cities for four long years, rending the Elladene and drenching its soil with the blood of countless fathers and sons, brothers and husbands. Tyrene, the coastal Anatolian republic, had led the resistance; with the fall of Haikoth they would stand nearly alone.

Of course, much of this was lost on a group of Illyrian farmers dwelling dozens of leagues from the nearest battlefield. Some of the rulers of the region's petty kingdoms might swear fealty to one side or another, but the war had, so far, left the hilly country untouched. As the three kounavi argued good-naturedly, and the prokyon's nimble fingers worked over the bronze hilt and a pair of gems meant for inlaying, Mylo skipped over to Sikarios' side.

"Hullo Gento," the young kine said cheerfully.

"Hullo Mylo," the other marten replied, then lowered his voice. "So you're responsible for bringing this vagabond into town?" He flashed a toothy smirk.

"This is Meletos, he's visiting with us. He saved an ewe from a pack of razor-hawks yesterday! And he has a sword!"

Four pairs of eyes centered on Sikarios, narrowing slightly.

"A sword, eh?" One of the weasels said.

"I, um—I'm travelling..." the marten muttered, "to see family in Istria. And with the war, the roads have been dangerous." As an uneasy silence settled over the crowd, Sikarios noticed the trio of polecats trotting past, and like foxes abandoning a scrap of bread for a slab of veal, the locals' shared suspicion leapt at the new target. Suddenly the marten was one of them.

One of the weasels spat and jutted his chin. "Best you keep an eye on that lot."

"There's too many strange folk passing through here of late," Gento said, as if he had forgotten Sikarios were standing right next to him. "Remember those Saarenians, come through last week, or the week before? Heading for the Morrea, I figure, same as all the other vultures." Through all of the talk of outsiders, Catharix had kept silent. Sikarios could see the faintest flicker of fear in his small black eyes, knowing that the flame of mistrust could just as easily catch on him.

It was Mylo's innocence that broke the unease. "Is there any news about the war?"

"Why," Gento asked back, "thinking about joining up?" He let out a deep, paternal laugh. "I don't think they take 'em so young, lad. Give it a few years, you'll get your chance at glory."

Sikarios did not share their laughter. He knew that the army would take kines as young as Mylo as runners and aides; he also knew how easy it was for those very same kits to find themselves with a sling in hand, or pressed shoulder to shoulder in a phalanx when a desperate commander had need of all the bodies he could muster. The marten studied Mylo's face, watching as the young weasel followed news of the war with innocent eyes, dreaming of bloodless prestige. The thought of his body lying cold and broken in some far-off field made Sikarios want to dig his claws into his own flesh.

But they could not know who he was, who he *truly* was. No one could. And so he held his tongue and bore his anguish in silence.

That evening, as the sheep grazed contentedly in the meadow under a sky stained with the fires of sunset, Sikarios once more returned to the carving. It was easy to lose himself in the pattern of the grain, the steady strokes of the knife keeping time with the beating of his heart. The lion had taken firm shape; all that remained was to free its legs from the remnants of the block the silver birch had once been. He drifted off, letting his fingers continue their work as his mind wandered back, to the summer of his sixteenth year. The storm clouds of war rumbling in every audience chamber, rumors abounding of the coming conflict. And he and Elias, both on the cusp of adulthood, eager to prove their worth, to win renown before gods and mortals, to carve for themselves a place in the storied halls of Elladian legend. Kyrios, the stalwart firstborn, had already been fitted for a suit of gleaming bronze armor, crested with a tuft of white bristle-boar hairs, and young Alexi, still wary around Sikarios, bounded through the halls of their home lancing invisible foes from atop an equally invisible mount.

They had lost their mother the year prior, and in his grief their father had taken closer counsel with King Thestor, whose firstborn had fallen to the Plague out of Parthus. Their plans of grand conquest had been birthed amidst tragedy; together they would make the world weep with them. As he sat on the hillside, his mind barely registering the grazing sheep, Sikarios remembered Elias racing across the field, eyes bright as the sun.

"You'll never believe it! I saw a *lion!*" The beasts were nigh-unheard of west of the Bospor, and yet the conviction in his friend's gaze was unshakeable. He had begun carving its likeness at once. "For strength," he had said, clasping a paw in Sikarios'. "If it does come to war. A charm to see us safely through." The marten's eyes watered at the memory.

"Meleos," a voice called, dragging him back to the sun-drenched knoll. Tamyris strode over, stabbing a crook into the soil. "You are skilled with that," the weasel added when he did not answer, lifting a clawed finger at the carving knife.

"Thank you. I... learned it from a close friend." Sikarios glanced up at the shepherd watching him with an arched brow.

"You know, it might be best to settle on one name." A smirk crept across the weasel's face. "Meleos, Meletos—you've answered to both." He raised a paw. "No, no, it's all right. Like I promised, I won't pry. There are plenty of reasons these days to guard something as precious as a name." He sat down, resting his back against the boulder. "I'm just a shepherd, so I don't expect to have seen as much of the world as you, despite my age. But I am also a father," he said, laying a steady hand on the marten's shoulder, "and my heart knows the sight of a young kine struggling."

Sikarios couldn't bring himself to meet the weasel's eyes.

"The gods and fates weave tangled webs of our lives, but you don't have to face it alone. We have a sofianthe here, a rather beautiful mink, if the gods will pardon my saying it." He chuckled, but the laugh felt hollow, trickling away as he waited in vain for his companion to join in. "Her name is Mira, and she lives in the hills to the northeast of town, in a little hovel by the shrine of Ilovek." His voice trembled, the faintest rumble of distant thunder. "When we lost Bero to sickness, several years back, she helped me through my grief. She... may be able to help you, too."

Tamyris stood, groaning as his bony limbs stretched. He cleared his throat. "It's almost time to bring the sheep in." The weasel started for the flock, but the marten's voice stopped him, turned him back.

"Sikarios." He let out a deep breath. "My name is Sikarios." He tensed, waiting for the flash of recognition, the shock that would quickly sour into fear or revulsion. Instead, the weasel just smiled, mouthing the name silently with a nod.

A day passed, and then another, and Sikarios allowed himself to ease into the lull of the rugged hill country, so welcome after months of flight and years of blood and fire. Deep within his mind, a voice whispered warnings of his brother; he pictured Kyrios striding into town clad in bronze, burning like the sun. *They would hate you if they knew,* the voice snarled. *You do not deserve to share their peace. Leave, while you still can.*

And yet a part of him pined for the comfort of a home filled with laughter, wishing dearly that he could shed his past like an old skin, could bleed his lifeblood into the brook night by night until nothing remained of Sikarios the kinslayer, Sikarios the oathbreaker, until a new creature had taken his place: someone worthy of the shepherd family who had taken him in. There was an honor to this life, he reflected, equal to that of any warrior. His father would have laughed at the sight of him casting feed to chickens, or mending the gate to the flock's pen alongside Tamyris, but soldiers needed food and clothing as much as anyone else. And the paws of a farmer, of a shepherd or carpenter provided, where for years his own had done nothing but take. Perhaps a life of humble labor would be enough to earn forgiveness from the gods.

Perhaps a life like this would be worth fighting for. Worth dying for, even.

One crisp, clear morning, when the hearts of the townsfolk lightened with the first hints of spring, Sikarios joined the two young weasels on a venture into Dalma. The marten's kopis jostled against his leg from within its sheath; he had taken to wearing the blade on his forays into town, as if imitating the kine he was before might wash the guilt and dread of the prior months from his soul. A flock of starlings speckled the sky with their northward flight, and he glanced at the two kits trotting happily beside him: Aeda cradled a basket of eggs, while Mylo shaded his eyes and looked south.

"Kyto said he and his brother might join up, when the recruiters come." The kine's voice sizzled with excitement. "A southerner passed through yesterday, said they were offering thirty drachma to anyone who fought, plus ten per month." Sikarios saw the weasel's eyes hungering at the thought of such a sum: a single drachma might feed a peasant for a week; a full thirty could purchase a plot of land and a few head of sheep or goats, perhaps even a pair of roe deer.

Your life is worth more than that, the marten wanted to say. Instead, he asked, "Do you know anyone who's fought before?"

Mylo nodded. "Kyto's father fought before I was born, when the Kimmerians came down from the north. They say he slew five of them at the gates of Istria, before their chief turned tail." He lunged forward, thrusting an imaginary spear, growling and grunting. "I'd love a chance to fight like him."

"And I'd like to marry a soldier," Aeda said. "That way I know he'd be brave and strong."

"The only thing Gallas fights is deer hides," her brother said with a snicker. She swatted at him, then raised her muzzle.

"He may join up as well," she sniffed. "The army has need of tanners, and he knows how to use a sling."

"So do I," Mylo added with a huff. He plucked a rock from the road and launched it into the grass. Sikarios' heart sunk to hear them speaking like this, echoing the words he and his brothers had shared, happily dousing themselves in oil as the fires of war crept ever nearer. He had seen that same eager gleam in Elias' eyes, and had lived long enough to watch them darken.

"There's more to warfare than glory and victory," he said softly, trying not to growl the words. The weasels' eyes darted to his face; Mylo nearly tripped over his own feet. Sikarios' claws found their way to the marks scoring his face. He halted to let the two stare, their innocent eyes taking in the jagged ridge of bare skin and patchy, grey fur.

He let the silence stretch. "Trust me, I saw much worse. I *dealt* much worse." Stifling a shudder, he breathed out deeply. The day suddenly seemed much colder. "When I was young, we spoke of war the same way you did, in my home. It was only later that I learned the truth." He set one paw on Mylo's shoulder, the other on Aeda's. "I will not deny that fighting may be necessary at times, but it is not something to rush into eagerly." He longed to explain further, to stomp out whatever embers might be lingering within their hearts, but feared to reveal too much. "I... I wish someone had told me that, before I marched off to war."

Without waiting for an answer, Sikarios started walking, hearing the slap of their sandals on the road a moment later. The trio remained silent the rest of the way into town. Dalma itself, however, bustled with activity. As soon as they neared the market, the marten noticed a number of strangers milling about, clad in tunics lined with dull bronze scales and draped in thick furs; smooth white or tawny coats showed beneath their armor, behind which dragged lithe, black-tipped tails. All were armed: some rested spears on their shoulders as they haggled with uneasy townsfolk, while others wore long knives or curved shortswords, or carried unstrung bows of yew that curled like the wicked horns of a steppe-beast. Sikarios found himself suddenly conscious of his own blade.

A local he didn't recognize waved the three over. "Stoats," the weasel muttered, "mercenaries from Kirkassios." Sikarios thought back to his father's maps: the Kirkassians were a long way from their rugged, mountainous homeland. But for the moment they seemed to be causing no trouble, and so the kits went about their business as he watched from a distance, the sight of so many warriors stirring up unwanted memories like silt in a shallow stream.

A raised voice drew his gaze to one of the townsfolk, standing in front of a stall, waving his hands at one of the stoats as another watched from nearby. Sikarios took a few steps closer. The mink held up three fingers, then pointed to the bowls of dried figs sitting on his stall. "*Three obols,*" he explained, dragging out each syllable, "for *one* cluster." Beside the fruits sat wedges of goat's cheese wrapped in arum leaves. The mink swept his arm. "*Two* for *one* wedge." The stoat said something in his guttural, singsong tongue, then turned to confer with his comrade before handing the mink a pawful of coins. Without waiting, he snatched up two wedges of cheese and a few clusters of figs, and began stuffing them into a sack.

"No," the mink said, "*three* for *each* of those!" When the stoat ignored him, his voice sharpened to a snarl. "Stop!" His claws swiped for the sack. The mercenary caught his wrist and shoved him back against the wooden stall, and the cloth went with him, spilling figs and cheese to the dirt. As the mink scrabbled to collect his goods, a knife appeared in the stoat's paw.

Sikarios stepped in between the pair before he could think, his left paw finding the worn bronze hilt of his kopis. The mink looked up before scrambling back behind the stall with a whimper. The stoat glared, but as his attention fixed on Sikarios' face, as his gaze traced the grooves in his flesh, something between respect and challenge flickered behind his deep-brown eyes. He muttered something, waving his left paw languidly at the mink, his right still clutching the dagger. The bone hilt of the blade was white as its owner's fur. Behind him, his comrade stood straighter, resting his slender spear on an armored shoulder.

Sikarios cleared his throat. "Give him what is owed." The stoat grinned, exposing a row of needle-like teeth. A pink tongue flicked over them. The mink cowered behind his stall, as if his fruits and cheese were battlements. Around them, the other locals had forgotten their mundane tasks.

Panic threatened to clot in Sikarios' throat like rancid blood. He seized the hilt in his right paw and bared a finger's length of the blade. His brother's words echoed in his mind: *Stand your ground. Make them come to you. Make them pay for it.* The stoat tensed, head lowering, white fur bristling. The marten's heart pounded in his chest like a war drum.

Then a shout ripped their focus from each other, and Sikarios turned to see another Kirkassian stalking over, taller than either of the pair, a plume of crimson feathers fluttering from atop his helmet. He clouted his dagger-bearing subordinate over the head, barked something in his own tongue, and then turned to the mink, exchanging a few sentences in Elladian. The first stoat hefted over another pawful of obols.

As the captain of the mercenaries made to leave, his eyes settled on Sikarios, and he nodded sharply. "Apologies. You will have no more trouble from us." His accent was crisp, words rustling like pines in a winter breeze. He strode away without waiting for a response, and just as soon, the marten felt claws clutching at his arm.

"Thank you," the mink started to say, but the rest of his words were lost in a rush of blood and fear as the world reeled. Sikarios staggered away from the market, away from the crowd of strangers to find himself plunging into the past, drowning in the wake of blood and fire that had eventually washed him onto these distant shores alone. He stumbled behind a mud-brick wall to cradle Elias' body, the lithe limbs that had once held him now broken and rent, the beautiful silken fur he had stroked in the moonlight now stained and clotted with crimson. He cringed as his brother's claws grappled for his own flesh, choking out a breath to find himself back in Dalma, huddled in the overlapping shadows of Aeda and Mylo.

Sikarios hated the way their eyes studied his wretched form, as if he were a crippled lamb, or a rabid jackal-dog. He gasped for air, wiping the tears from his bleary vision, wincing at the rapid stutter of his heart against his ribcage. The world slowly came back into focus, and the two kits gathered close once more, kneeling to help him stand.

"We saw what you did," Mylo said, the whisper laced with awe. "You really are a soldier, then—not that I doubted you, of course, but—"

"I'm not." The marten waved a still-trembling paw. "Not anymore." He sighed. "I left that behind."

"What happened?" Aeda asked quietly, eyes softened with pity. Closing his own, Sikarios swallowed the knot of bitter longing welling up within his throat.

"I… lost someone. And I hurt someone." He turned away, hating the way his voice broke, hating the ache in his chest, the flashes of terror and rage and bitter, biting pain. *I won't let you.*

"Please," he muttered, "don't make the same mistakes I did." His gaze flitted to the skies above, where the gods lurked, watching in silence. "There is hardship enough in the world without rushing off to find it." Without waiting for an answer, Sikarios rose. The kits followed him back in silence.

By the time dusk had drained most of the sun's light, the marten's nerves had calmed enough to allow him to enjoy their supper, and the modest dessert of chestnuts served alongside a glass of watery wine. But a part of Sikarios still craved fresh air and solitude, and so he offered to clean the dishes and utensils, lugging the basket out to the nearby stream as the moon rippled over its trickling surface. The marten worked his claws slowly over the crude wooden cutlery and flatware, letting the cold, pure water rinse the day's tension from his mind, settling his own heartbeat into the tranquil rhythm of the quiet countryside. Once he had finished, he sat beneath the endless depths of the starscape, bathed in its pale fire.

Again, the thought of remaining here flitted into his mind; he let himself wander back through the years, to the day he and his brothers had made the decision to leave home. Kyrios, ever ready to honor their family name, was to be given his own command, while Alexi, barely thirteen, would serve as an officer's aide, away from the frontlines and yet still near enough to share in the glory of battle.

Sikarios himself had been hesitant. He remembered Alexi's pointed taunts as their family had taken dinner with King Thestor's envoys: "Are you not strong enough, brother? Perhaps you would like to remain behind, weaving with the does?" And when the others had laughed, their minds ringing with visions of the honor and renown they would doubtless win, Alexi had leaned in and whispered, "Father will wonder, if you do not come. I am trying to *help* you, Sikarios. Make you *stronger*. For the honor of our family."

In the end, Sikarios had knelt and pledged himself alongside his brothers. Elias, naturally, had been quick to follow.

He recalled the pride gleaming in his father's eyes, still tinged with sorrow even as they dreamt of greater conquest. And when he had confessed his fears to his older brother, Kyrios had devoted many of their dwindling hours to sparring with him, always besting the younger kine with a grace and dignity befitting a firstborn son. His words still rang clearly, even all these years later: "Your problem, Sikarios, is that you hesitate at the crucial moment. Most individual fights last less than three heartbeats—in that time you will either have won, or be dead. But most people are not ready to face their death, and so by hesitating, or rushing in headlong, they meet it. You must stand your ground, and never falter."

And to assuage the last vein of his fear, Elias had shown him the wooden lion, barely larger than his paw. "For strength," he had said, lacing Sikarios' fingers through his own. They had each marked it with a drop of their own blood, drawn from the dagger his father had bestowed upon him.

An owl crooned into the night, dragging him back to the Illyrian hillside. The darkness quickly settled into silence. And in that silence, Sikarios remembered the shepherd's words: that there was someone here who could help him.

The following morning he rose well before the sun, leaving his kopis resting beside the door as a promise that he would return. All he knew of the town's sofianthe was that she dwelt in the hills, away from the coast, and so he trusted to the road and the first hints of daybreak smoldering in the east to guide him. One of the priestesses had served his father's court, though he could not remember her name; the short, ash-furred weasel had tended to a small shrine in the courtyard of the acropolis, but as a kine Sikarios had paid little mind to the workings of gods. It was not until the night of his enlistment that he had chosen Milosha as his patron, her warrior's wisdom a stark contrast to the passionate bloodshed of Voyokan, whom most of the other recruits had favored. And as far as the marten could tell, she had answered few of his prayers.

The path took Sikarios through brush greyed and withered by the wet chill of the Illyrian winter. About halfway up the hillside it passed a clearing containing a lump of stone, a small wooden structure nestled quietly in the shadows of the undergrowth nearby. As he drew closer, the marten recognized the worn, moss-covered figure of Iluvex adorning the shrine, various woodland creatures frozen midstride about her feet. The stone beneath her was charred and cracked.

"Hello?" Sikarios called. "I was hoping to speak with the sofianthe." At first the only answer was the high trill of a distant waxwing, but then a voice echoed from the hovel, smooth and gentle, younger than he had expected.

"Ah, you've come at last." A moment later a slender form strode out into the clearing, wrapped in a light grey cloak. She lowered her hood and bowed slightly before the shrine. "I am Mira, and I have the pleasure to serve the gods and Dalma as sofianthe."

The mink's eyes sparkled with calming warmth, and her coat of rich sable fur was dappled in glistening patches of bronze where shafts of sunlight pierced the canopy. Sikarios stared, and stared; it had been so long since he had known the warmth of another body against his own, and now before him stood one of the fairest does he had ever seen. A part of him knew how his longing smoldered in his eyes, fearing that the priestess would recoil at the sight, would see the beast lurking within his haggard face. *Murderer. Oathbreaker. Kinslayer.* But she did not so much as flinch, meeting his gaze as if he were but an injured kit, and she was a mother who could mend any wound.

"You... you've been expecting me?" he finally stammered.

Her smile took on a hint of playful amusement. "Well, word gets around, and I am not chained to this shrine. A scarred southern wanderer with a kopis at his side, here in humble Dalma?" She led him to the altar, staring up at the goddess of the wilderness. "And so, what is it that brings you here today?"

"I... I was hoping for advice, after a fashion." He drew his paw back, curled it into a fist, fighting the urge to dredge every last detail of his past, knowing it would only make things worse. "I... am sorry," he sighed. "It is difficult to speak about. But I feel as if the gods have forsaken me, and that every path forward has closed."

A shadow passed over Mira's face. "We are like children before the splendor of the divine, and discerning the proper path can often prove painful. I understand you are... hesitant to speak freely, and I will not presume to know what a soldier such as yourself has endured—" she paused as his mouth fell, giving him a look of somber understanding—"but we could try a divination."

Sikarios grimaced, remembering the few he had been present for in his youth: a hare dragged screaming to the altar, or a crow bound and squawking, where a silver knife would reveal the secrets of the world in their steaming entrails, leaving a crimson stain upon the cold stone. But Mira simply kindled a tiny flame upon the altar before producing a clump of white flower petals from a pocket. She smiled, her eyes filled with sly understanding.

"None of that mess, I assure you. The gods eat well enough without me sending them a squealing rabbit. Now let us see what your own fate holds." She sprinkled the petals atop the altar, letting them dance down on the currents birthed by the fire, already dying. One landed directly upon the flames and sizzled, its edges glowing red, the white flesh curling into char. The marten thought that did not bode well, but the mink's face remained dispassionate.

Her voice, when it came, seemed to echo in the glade. "I see a fire spreading northward, and withered trees embracing its flames. I see a kine bearing a torch in bleeding claws, coming to claim something that was stolen, and to take something more." The mink's paws hovered just above the scattered petals, as if afraid they might singe her rich brown fur. The last of the embers' light sizzled in the sheen of her coat. "And... I see a shadow racing ahead of the flames."

Sikarios tried to swallow the unease that welled up within his throat. Mira clasped her paws and peered up at him, as if the answers might lay behind his own eyes.

"Thank you," Sikarios said, failing to keep the quaver from his voice. He dug out a pawful of obols from the pocket of his cloak and set them on the altar.

"Go with the peace of the gods," the mink replied. He nodded, and left without another word.

The forest lay silent around Sikarios as he followed the same narrow, muddy path back. *A shadow, racing ahead of the flames.* A layer of thick, grey clouds settled in beyond the canopy, muffling the daylight and threatening rain. The pines rustled and creaked in the wintry breeze. For what must have been the thousandth time, the marten thought of home, only for the image of Dalma to seep into the memory.

When he neared the familiar cottage, Tamyris was waiting for him outside, with his crook gripped tightly and one of the foxes standing rigid in his shadow. Kokkin started towards Sikarios, but a hiss from his master stayed the fox. As the marten neared, fear bubbled up beneath his confusion.

"A messenger came through," the weasel said. "King Thestor has dispatched emissaries to our lands in search of recruits for the spring campaign. One will be here tomorrow: Kyrios, Prince of Nalanthis."

The mention of his brother's name tightened a claw around Sikarios' throat. The weasel went on, as if he were choosing every word with care. "The kine said... he said that this prince is seeking a deserter, an oathbreaker and kinslayer. His brother. A brown-furred marten, with a mark over his left eye." Tamyris' own eyes smoldered with betrayal, and the marten's words turned to ash on his tongue.

The shepherd lowered his voice. "I know that I did not press you for the details of your past, Sikarios..." His claws tightened, scoring marks into the yew. "But *this?*" He grimaced, shying from the marten's gaze, then waved a paw. "May the gods themselves bear witness to the hospitality we provided a stranger. But there is no place for you here anymore."

Sikarios let the silence stretch. "I understand," he finally said, desperate to keep his voice from breaking. "May I fetch my things?"

The shepherd nodded, stepping aside, giving him a wide berth. Kokkin shot a perplexed glance between the two. The marten retrieved his few belongings, buckling on his sheath before digging through his sack. Drawing out a drachma, he set it gently on the table.

"Thank you. You've shown me more kindness than I deserve."

Tamyris simply stared from beyond the doorway. As Sikarios stepped out into the first gentle patter of rainfall, he turned one final time to his former host. "Do the kits know?"

The shepherd's eyes softened ever so slightly. He looked away. "Not yet."

"Please, don't tell them."

Tamyris' gaze rose to meet his. "They're bound to hear it all sooner or later."

Dusk found him huddled beneath a lip of rock in the hills north of Dalma, paws stretched to draw the warmth of a paltry fire struggling for life. Sikarios still dwelt on the stares of the townsfolk as he had passed through; eyes that had welcomed him in days prior, or passed him over with no more than a moment's consideration, now burned with contempt or widened in fear. Fishers and fruitsellers who had greeted him eagerly now drew their wares back at his approach, muttering curses under their breaths. A part of him whispered that things were now as they always should have been.

Rain continued to thud down beyond the slim stone overhang. The fire hissed and sizzled like an angry serpent. With his tongue, Sikarios loosened bits of stale bread from his teeth, all that remained of his meager supper. Then, retrieving the carving, he began the final strokes that would leave the lion free of its wooden womb. His mind wandered back, back to the night before he and his brothers had departed. Kyrios, clad in armor that fit him so naturally he might as well have been born in it. Himself, anxious and yet eager to serve, to fulfill the oath he had sworn to their father. And Alexios, convinced he had salvaged his brother's honor, had saved him and their family from shame.

Kyrios had approached Sikarios that night with his own worries. "Alexi will be away from the frontlines, but... I still worry for him. He is young, and...*impulsive.*" He still remembered how his brother had grinned. "I have sworn to father that I will watch after you both, but my duties may lead me elsewhere. And if something should happen to me..." He had knelt, taking his brother's paw. "Promise me that you will look after him as well."

"I will," Sikarios had told him. "I swear it." He had made a similar promise to Elias.

Gently, he blew the wood shavings from the lion, examining it in the flickering firelight. As far as he could remember, it was near enough a match for the one his friend had given him the evening before their final day together. After four years of fighting, Sikarios had told him how the clang of iron on an anvil, the flash of the butcher's blade, even a sudden shout might cast him back to the carnage of some nameless battlefield. How he wasn't sure how much more he could endure. Elias had clasped the lion in his paws, had held until Sikarios' breathing steadied. And even full of concern and pity and fear, his golden eyes had still held the fire of the sun.

"For strength," his friend had said. Gazing into the flames, Sikarios could still see him. He went to sleep with the whisper of broken promises echoing in his ears, and awoke well beyond daybreak to find that the rain had ceased.

As the clouds thinned into wisps and the sun baked the stones of the highland, the marten caught a pair of slender, ghostly pale trout in the stream. As he ate, his eyes were drawn to the distant spread of Dalma; he wondered if his brother had already arrived. If he was a fool to have lingered so late, or to have fled for so long. The lion in his cloak pocket dragged like a stone. He was so tired of running, always running—and what solace was there to be found in Istria, or the northern wilds beyond it, if he never tried to make things right?

Sikarios ran his claws over the ridges of his scar, then rose from the rock and glanced south. From here the settlement lay quiet, and his heart ached to know the tranquility was a lie. Staggering down to where the rugged trail met the road, the marten glanced right—to the north, where the well-worn pathway would carry him ever farther from his past, into the fog of anonymity and exile—and then left, to the lives he had come to know these last few weeks. To a town full of fresh kindling, eager to welcome the coming fire. His sigh carried all the weight of the prior four years. Turning left, he began his descent.

By the time he reached the edge of Dalma, Sikarios could see that most of the townsfolk had gathered in the market square, where a few mounted figures loomed above the crowd. A voice addressed them, rich and confident, strong as stone. A voice he knew, that had offered him counsel and reprimand and reassurance. A speech he had heard many times before, in one form or another; he let the words wash over him like mist. Some of the locals shot him casual glances that shifted quickly into lingering stares. Faces melted into scowls or twisted in fear; eyes full of reverence narrowed in contempt. He walked on, feeling for the lion in his cloak pocket. *For strength.*

Sat atop roe deer, a few ministers in regal chitons turned to watch him, while their guards came more rigidly to attention. The crowd slowly parted, and the speaker's voice trailed off. And before him, across the dusty plaza, clad in a suit of gleaming bronze, stood his brother, Kyrios. Their eyes met for a moment, the warrior's mouth gaping, before Sikarios shied away. He turned to the townspeople.

"What you have here is more precious than you know. Do not be so eager to throw your lives away."

Ever agile, Kyrios overcame his shock quickly. "Death comes for all of us in time," he replied triumphantly, "so why not meet it with bravery, why not live a life of adventure? Win honor and renown, and know that if you die, it is for a cause worthy of remembrance!"

"He speaks to you of a warrior's honor," Sikarios shouted, letting his eyes sweep the crowd, before settling them back on Kyrios. "Well, brother, tell them of the honor to be found in an early grave, of the honor in a mother and father weeping over the memory of their son, buried in some far-off field. Tell them of the honor of striking down some other kine barely beyond adolescence, so that you might live in his place; of watching the earth drink the blood of your friends, one after another, while the kings who send you off to die grow richer and fatter. Tell them of the honor you will *truly* give them."

Kyrios strode forward, eyes blazing. "*Honor*? What do *you* know of *honor*?" He thrust a clawed finger at Sikarios, voice crackling with rage. "You, who broke your oath and deserted the service of the king you were sworn to serve. You, who slew your own brother when he tried to stop you." His roar trickled to a rumble. "And now, you come slinking back. Have you finally grown tired of living in the hills like a polecat? Are you ready to return and face justice?"

Sikarios glared. "I have not come to plead for mercy, Kyrios, from you or from Father." His kopis leapt from its sheath, the bronze cool against the pads of his trembling paws. He raised his free hand. "With gods and kounavi as witness, I challenge you to single combat."

His brother stepped nearer, until only a few paces remained to separate them, and lowered his voice. "I accept, though I take no pleasure in this," Kyrios growled. "But before I kill you, I want to know why. *Why*, Sikarios?"

"I never meant to," Sikarios muttered, blinking away tears, his scars burning at their sting. "But I... I just couldn't bear it—battle after battle, week after week, seeing comrade after comrade fall. And then, Elias..." He choked down a sob, tightening his grip.

His brother's face was hard as granite. "You think I haven't suffered these last four years? You think I haven't shed blood, haven't lost friends? But I let it strengthen me, shape me into something better!"

"Then I suppose you were forged from purer iron than I."

Kyrios' face softened, tenderness creeping into his voice. "Do you think I did not know what he meant to you?" A glimmer of pity diluted the hatred in his eyes.

Sikarios winced. Tears matted the fur of his cheeks, and he wiped them away with his free paw. "Alexi... Alexi knew as well. He confronted me that night, as I was leaving our tent." *I won't let you.* "I tried to explain, to make him see, but he—he drew a knife. And when I tried to take it from him, we fell." His voice grew panicked. "I don't even remember drawing my own knife..."

"There is still time," Kyrios replied, sounding so much like their father had, before. "Throw down your sword, come back with me willingly. Plead for mercy in Father's court. Even a dungeon, or a life of service in a temple would be better than this."

"No..." Sikarios breathed out with a shudder. Fear coiled around his heart like a snake. His pulse thundered in his ears, blood burning in his veins. *You are stronger than you know.* He took a deep breath, then another, forcing everything else from his mind. *Stand your ground, and never falter.* "No. I cannot go back. I *will* not."

His brother's eyes furrowed, fur bristling like a thousand dagger-points. "So be it." Snarling, he ripped his blade from its sheath and launched forward. *Three heartbeats.*

Sikarios brought his own kopis to bear, meeting his brother's slash. Iron screamed against iron. He buckled under the weight of the blow, and Kyrios swung again. Sikarios barely managed to meet it with a parry, then followed with a riposte that scored a crimson line across his brother's arm. As the older marten recoiled with a hiss, he brought his kopis down against the hilt of his foe's upraised sword, then gripped the flat of the other blade in his free paw and twisted. Kyrios stumbled back into a plume of dirt, his kopis sailing through the air to clatter to the ground with a clang.

Three heartbeats. When the dust settled, Sikarios' blade hovered only a hair's breadth from his brother's throat. Kyrios stared up at him with eyes that had faced death a thousand times. Neither dared to breathe: by the most sacred customs of their people, he held his brother's life in his paws. Slowly, Sikarios drew the blade back. "I never meant to kill him, Kyrios. And I will not take our father's final son from him."

He looked at his kopis. "If I could trade my life for his, I would do so in a heartbeat. But it is done. He is gone, and I remain. Now, if you truly believe that killing me will make things right," Sikarios went on, thrusting his sword into the soft earth, "this blade will work as well as any other." He unbuckled his scabbard and cast it to the dirt, waiting for the strike that would send him reeling into darkness.

But Kyrios merely stared. Finally, he bowed his head, eyes fixed on the kopis. "I will return this to Father, and tell him the truth: that both of my brothers are lost."

Sikarios turned away to find the people of Dalma watching in silence. When he advanced, they parted like water before him, muttering and whispering, clutching their kits close. But he paid them no mind until three familiar faces surfaced in the crowd. His throat tightened at seeing the shepherd's family watching him with the same revulsion shared by their neighbors. The marten stepped nearer, thankful at least that the trio did not flee from him.

While Tamyris glared and Aeda tensed with a shudder, Mylo simply stood there, gaze fixed on the dirt. Sikarios retrieved the carved lion from his pocket, and held it out. "You will hear many things about honor, and duty, and strength," the marten said, fighting to keep his voice level. He let out a slow breath. "But strength is not only measured by the force of a blade, or a spear thrust, or a sling-stone. It is not only found in palaces or war camps, and it is not only proven on the battlefield." At that, the young weasel finally met his gaze. "May you have the strength to know what is right, and to choose it, no matter what may follow. No matter what the world may say." As if handling a fledgling bird, Sikarios pushed the lion into the kine's paws. "And may you not make the same mistakes I did."

He rose without another word and started walking. Behind him, Kyrios' soldiers had helped their captain up, while the ministers who had accompanied them brandished tablets and bags of silver. Several of the locals had lined up, kines as young as Mylo among them. At the edge of town, Sikarios paused, and turned a final time to see Tamyris and his kits still standing off to the side. While his father and sister watched the proceedings, Mylo was running his claws delicately over the carving, tracing the wood's grain as if it held the answer to some powerful question.

Trusting that he had done all he could, and clinging to the hope that some worthwhile future waited for him beyond the horizon, Sikarios turned north and did not look back.

SakaraFox

SakaraFox would tell you he's from the mist-shrouded past some 12,000 years ago, but in truth he's a railway worker and prose-fiction writer who hails from the West Country of the United Kingdom. With a keen interest in history, enough railway photos to fill a hard drive, and an insatiable appetite for Mesolithic prehistory, it's recommended not to get him onto these subjects unless you're happy to have your ears talked-off. It's no surprise then that these make up the bulk of his writing, which mostly explores an ancient past which we often neglect. His work can best be found on FurAffinity, or followed on Twitter @Metro_Fox for updates on the latest works and happenings. FurAffinity: furaffinity.net/user/metrofox2/

Utunu

Utunu has been a video game developer since the mythical early '90s, and is fond of worldbuilding, linguistics, ancient history, fantasy, and Oxford commas. He's written a few short stories, and has received both a Cóyotl and Leo Award.

Huskyteer

Alice "Huskyteer" Dryden's short stories have been published in and out of the furry fandom, and have won two Cóyotl Awards, two Ursa Major Awards and one Leo Award. She edited the *Furry Megapack* for Wildside Press, and in 2019 she was Guest of Honor at Fur the 'More 007: Furry Never Dies.

J.F.R. Coates

J.F.R. Coates is a speculative fiction author living in Australia, though originally from the picturesque West Country of England. His stories tend to focus away from human characters, instead giving life to the creatures that dwell alongside the familiar. He has been the Furry Writers' Guild president since 2021.

NightEyes DaySpring

NightEyes DaySpring is a known troublemaker who is rumored to have a penchant for coffee and an interest in dead, ancient civilizations. He has been writing furry fiction for over twenty years, and recently published his first novel, *Scars of the Golden Dancer*. His short stories have also appeared in various anthologies, including *Werewolves vs. Fascism*, *Heat*, and *FANG*. Currently, he resides in Florida with his boyfriend where in his spare time he masquerades as an IT professional, plays board games, and doodles. Visit his website, nighteyes-dayspring.com, for more about his writing. For day-to-day nonsense, follow @wolfwithcoffee on Twitter.

Rose LaCroix

What Rose LaCroix lacks in recognition, she makes up for in versatility and staying power. Her first published novel, *Basecraft Cirrostratus*, has been in print since 2010. She writes both fiction and non-fiction, speculative and historical. Some of her medieval history research has been published on Britannica.com and her short stories and poetry can be read on Spillwords.com. She lives in the Portland area with her husband Kobi and their cat Venus.

Madison Scott-Clary

Madison Scott-Clary is an author and technical writer living in the Pacific Northwest with her two dogs and her husband, who is also a dog. She's the author of the Post-Self cycle, a series of gender-weird, meta-furry sci-fi thrillers, and the Sawtooth books, collections of short stories from a small town in a flyover state. Her work can be found at makyo.ink

Kayodé Lycaon

Kayodé Lycaon is a gregarious painted wolf living in the questionable habitat of southwestern Ohio. By day, he pretends to be a human, writing software. At night, his paws weave character-driven stories inspired from his own life. When not writing, he can be found dabbling in the dark arts of Linux, D&D, and home automation. You can find out more on his website, kayode.co.

Rob MacWolf

Rob MacWolf lives somewhere in North America waiting for the world to end. In the meantime he practices neo-paganism, writes poetry, and co-hosts the audiofiction podcast The Voice of Dog, at thevoice.dog.

Thomas "Faux" Steele

Thomas "Faux" Steele is an author and attorney who has been creating short stories since 2015. He enjoys writing in many genres, including horror, science-fiction, fantasy, and adult contemporary. He specializes in descriptive stories with rich world-building whose written words render a painting in the reader's mind. His work has been printed in many anthologies, including *FANG Vol. 7*, *Exploring New Places*, and *Beast Vol. 1* as well as many 'zines including #OhMurr. In his free time, he's an avid coin collector and fancier of antiquities and fine art, almost all thrifted or picked from estate sales.

Haya Baru

Born 3000 years too late to devote their life to the proud and noble art of extispicy under the tutelage of a state temple, Haya spends their free time reading history books, depressive 19th century philosophy, and gay romance novels instead. They have neither children nor pets, instead filling the resulting emotional void with an ever-growing conlang that was torn from the pages of an Akkadian language textbook. Although they work as a software developer, they plan to become a priest should the temple of Ištar ever return. If they ever undertake this momentous career change, they hope to revive the long-lost personality archetype of a smugly pious polytheist.

J.S. Hawthorne

J.S. Hawthorne was raised in New England, but now lives in exile on Long Island, where she pretends to be a lawyer by day and might actually be three magpies in a trenchcoat. When she isn't writing either fiction or law, she mostly enjoys running more Dungeons and Dragons games than is strictly necessary and collecting books written by her friends. She promises she'll get around to reading them eventually, honest.

Pascal Farful

Pascal Farful is an author, musician, fursuiter, railway enthusiast and photographer. At one point almost all of these occurred at once. He lives in a hollowed-out volcano on the outskirts of the UK where Angels Pizza Company fear to tread.

Casimir Laski

Casimir Laski is a writer, YouTuber, and literary critic from Virginia. He is the author of *Winter Without End*, a post-apocalyptic survival story told from the perspective of a dog, inspired by the animal stories he grew up reading. Additionally, he writes for Furry Book Review, and operates the YouTube channel Cardinal West, primarily devoted to discussion of literary xenofiction and western animation.